*For Bob —
Best wishes!
Brent*

ILLUSIONS

BRENT MONAHAN

ILLUSIONS
Copyright © 2014 by Brent Monahan

Words Take Flight Books printing: 2014

ISBN 13: 978-0692359303
ISBN 10: 0692359303

Printed in the United States of America

Dedicated to Rodney Miller,
who knows a thing or two
about Texas and travel

ONE

"I CAN'T HEAR you!" the drunken heckler called out from the back of the audience.

Beneath his faint stage smile, Frank Spiegel clenched his teeth. He continued executing Robert-Houdin's Ball Trick, a series of hyper-fast appearances and disappearances of small red balls that not fifty magicians in the world had the dexterity to perform. The trick used no distracting patter; the verbal silence challenged audiences to concentrate wholly on the magician's flashing fingers.

"Hey, two more little red balls just fell out of your pants legs!" the heckler shouted over the soft accompanying music. Several of the forty or so audience members around him laughed. Others turned with annoyance and made shushing noises. The open-backed lounge of the Desert Inn held only twenty-four tables. It was designed to provide a place to hold the Las Vegas patrons captive. They could take a break from gambling, be entertained at the same time and take some refreshment without needing to exit the casino. The stage was relatively small and intended for less-than-famous acts, not at all the large room for the headliners, with its three horseshoe tiers of tables and chairs, its snapping white linen cloths, its glitter and huge spotlights. Although his star was in decline, Tom Jones was the one pulling the entertainment crowd into the Desert Inn. The main room was as far away to Spiegel, Master of Illusions as the moon from the earth.

Only a handful of people close to the stage seemed enrapt by the magic act. Others conducted conversations in normal voices, glancing up at the stage when words failed them. Glasses clinked, smoke filled the air, waitresses walked without apology through the sightlines. Several couples had wandered in and out since the performance began. Laughter from private jokes exploded in inappropriate places. An old woman at the back noisily dumped a bucket of quarters onto her table and busied herself arranging them in stacks of ten. More than half the seats were empty.

"This is the worst ventriloquist act I ever saw. The dummy's got no jokes!" The heckler was a big man with a pronounced beer gut. He wore a narrow black tie, a sharkskin suit shot through with silver threads, 'fence climber' shoes and three garish gold rings. He had two younger male cronies seated at his flanks, braying like jackasses at his attempted humor.

In the wings, Alexander Voloshin rose from his chair, deserting the lighting and sound control equipment. "Enough already!"

Dexter Brown, who was preoccupied readying the paraphernalia for the next trick, reached out to grab the other member of the magic show's backstage crew. He missed and Voloshin rushed by, vanishing through a curtained archway out into the audience.

On the stage, Frank Spiegel's latest sleight of hand took a hitch as he caught sight of his technical man moving with haste toward the heckler. He opened his mouth to say something, but his beautiful assistant touched his arm. When he glanced in her direction, she smiled and gave him the nod he had come to know meant for him to plunge on.

Alex Voloshin came up to the table and interposed himself between the act and the heckler. "Listen, buddy, people are trying to enjoy the show."

"I'm tryin', too," the heckler slurred loudly. He pointed to the stage. "But that Bozo won't let me."

Alex set his hand on the man's shoulder. "Why don't you go back to –"

The heckler swung around and shoved Alex with enough force to send him flying backward into an unoccupied table, where he lost his balance and fell. A collective gasp of dismay rose from the audience in the immediate area.

Alex rose to his knees. Already up on their feet were the heckler's companions. Both balled their fists. They had hung their suit jackets over the backs of their chairs and their strong physiques were obvious beneath their shirts. They moved toward the rising tech man, but they momentarily paused as a very large, black man with muscles bigger than theirs closed on them at high speed.

Not another word came from any of the combatants' mouths as the five men threw themselves into the fight. The audience rose as a body and refocused its attention toward the rear of the lounge. Their reactions swiftly built into the high-pitched drone of a downed wasps' nest. One small man on the edge of the lounge began to throw chairs, both toward the brawl and at a nearby wall.

The casino guards arrived about thirty seconds into the fight, quickly followed by the floor boss. By that time, the magician had hopped down from the stage and inserted himself into the middle of the fray, imploring for cooler heads. For his peacemaking efforts, Frank received a hard punch in the shoulder and a scratch on his neck. The long seconds of extreme exertions had nearly exhausted all of the participants, so that they were either tied up in lung-heaving clutches with each other, or else had retreated to gather strength for a second attack.

"Get back, everyone!" the casino floor boss yelled, as his two guards pried Dexter Brown off one of the heckler's sidekicks. He turned to the large patron, whose face was radish red.

"What happened here, Mr. DeNunzio?" he asked.

"I was just tryin' ta relax, havin' a little fun bustin' on this poor excuse for 'n entertainer, when his goons jumped us."

"Bullshit!" Alexander Voloshin cried out. Frank Spiegel raised a warning forefinger in front of his tech man's face.

"You think you've had enough fun for a while, Mr. DeNunzio?" the floor boss asked.

"Yeah," he sullenly replied. "I wish Elvis was in town. C'mon, boys." He straightened himself up to his full height, shrugged his jacket into place and sauntered like a cock-of-the-walk out of the lounge, followed by his henchmen.

The floor boss lowered his head toward the guards and gave a terse order in a soft voice. They nodded and followed the trio onto the casino floor. Then the boss crooked his forefinger at Spiegel and his employees and led the way through the curtained archway to the backstage.

"Are y'all stupid, or what?" the boss spat.

"I politely asked the guy to leave and he knocked me down," Alex returned, not without his own added attitude.

"Then you should have got up and called a couple of guards from the floor – like I did. We can't have our acts beating up our clientele!"

"Don't tell me that drunk hasn't caused trouble before," Dexter Brown challenged the boss.

"That 'drunk' is Sal DeNunzio," the boss replied. "He drops at least a hundred thousand in this casino every year. So we put up with his trouble. What we *won't* put up with is trouble from a second-rate magic act."

"You have no concept of the difference between first- and second-rate. Your clothes and manners prove it." The insult came from the calm, measured voice of Elizabeth Coleman, Frank's stage assistant.

The boss focused on the stunning blond, opened his mouth to reply, thought better of it, turned on his heels and returned to the gaming area.

Frank Spiegel stepped out onto the small stage to address those gamblers who remained in the lounge. He brushed off his tails with a theatrical flourish, straightened his white dress bowtie and smiled broadly.

"Wait until you see our finale!"

Frank opened the door to his Desert Inn room and stepped back to allow Dexter to enter. The room was a modest one on the third floor. The hotel had allowed the magic troupe two rooms without charge for the length of their two-performances-a-day run. They had paid extra for Elizabeth to have her own privacy, and Dexter and Alexander, as they often did, shared a room with double beds. Dexter held two suitcases, the second belonging to his fellow crew man.

"Where's Sonder?" Frank asked.

Dex smirked. "Down at the bar in front of that stupid Pong game. He used to be addicted to pinball, but he's traded his allegiance to this new electronic stuff. He's killing time until that bimbo Dolores gets off work. He said to stop by on the way out and tell him where we're moving to."

Spiegel's group had been contracted to play the side stage at the Desert Inn for two weeks. Frank had known that the lounge gig would be humiliating, but Las Vegas sat directly on the return route east after their West Coast schedule. Gambling profits allowed casinos to pay even the lounge performers well. Spiegel, Master of Illusions, and his troupe had fulfilled thirteen days of the contract before their termination.

"We're not moving anywhere," Frank answered.

Dexter's head reared back slightly. "What do you mean? Did they or did they not fire us because of that drunken asshole? Hey, Bess."

"'Hey!' yourself," Elizabeth Coleman returned. She sat on the far double bed, with her closed suitcase and train makeup case next to her, looking her always beautiful, but less than usually effervescent, self.

Frank returned to packing his suitcase. "They did not fire us; they let us go."

"Same difference, man. Are we blowing Vegas tonight?" Dexter wanted to know.

"Nope."

"Then what?"

Frank smiled and straightened up. Dexter noticed then that both beds had been stripped of their linens and that they and the bathroom towels sat neatly on the beds, next to the pillows. Bess also had her linens and pillow beside her. "You have everything out of your room?"

"Are we stealing the sheets and towels?"

"Just borrowing," Frank replied. "We'll deliver everything to the front desk when we leave tomorrow morning. Give me your key so I can check you and Sonder out tonight. You do have all your stuff and Sonder's from the room, right?"

Dex nodded. He handed over the room key with confusion wrinkling his face.

"Great," said Frank. "Now follow us."

Elizabeth led the way out the door into the hallway, burdened with suitcases and bedclothes.

"What do you know about Howard Hughes?" Frank asked the group's mechanic/stagehand/driver.

"Lots. He owned the Desert Inn. It was his first purchase in Vegas after he left Los Angeles and sold RKO Studios. Then he bought the Sands, let me think, and the private airport, a TV station, the Frontier Hotel, Castaways Hotel and Casino, and…the Silver Slipper Casino." Beyond his many duties to the group, Dexter was a private man of business, obsessed with getting ahead and with learning how successful Americans had risen from poverty to riches.

The three came to the elevator. Frank pushed a button.

"You pressed 'up'," Dexter informed him.

"Right you are. And where is Mr. Hughes now?"

"Dead," Dex replied. "Died about six months ago. Not long

before J. Paul Getty. The first two men Forbes reported as American billionaires and they died one right after the other."

"And what happens when the obscenely rich die, even if they have iron-clad wills?" Frank asked.

Dexter's eyebrows furrowed. "The wills are contested?"

"Right again."

Dex sighed. But what does Howard Hughes have to do with us taking the elevator up?"

The elevator car arrived. Frank gestured for Bess and Dex to walk inside. After he set down his suitcase, he pressed the top button, which read '9'. "Mr. Hughes lived on the top floor of this building. The penthouse suites floor. Had it all to himself, even though he only used a corner of it."

"Do tell," Dex said, beginning to understand.

As the elevator ascended, Frank dug into his trouser pocket and produced a sophisticated lock-picking tool.

"You must have noticed what shabby shape this hotel is in," Bess said. "Until Howard Hughes' empire is settled, no work can be done. The top floor has been closed off, awaiting renovation."

"The penthouse floor has no guests," Dexter understood.

The elevator stopped on 9. Frank expertly twisted his tool in the lock. The elevator door slid open. Frank stepped into the line of the detecting beam, keeping the door open. "Tonight it does. I'll go down later and fetch Sonder. What time is he expecting his most recent conquest?"

"One minute past midnight," said Dex.

"Tonight, he and she get an entire suite, compliments of Howard Hughes and the Desert Inn."

"They owe us," Dex affirmed, "after that moron floor boss called our act second-rate. This low-class town is prejudiced against magic shows." He followed Bess into the hallway.

Frank stepped out and let the elevator close. "In general, yes. But they did give Siegfried and Roy the Las Vegas Entertainment Award for Best Show Act of the Year back in '72 and '73."

"That's not a magic show; it's a circus," Dexter declared. He would have continued his criticism, except that his attention was captured by the sight in front of him.

Directly beyond the elevator stood a desk and a set of filing cabinets that effectively blocked the hallway and allowed only a small passage between them. Past this was an alcove with a wire grill in the wall, like a guard station at a maximum-security prison. The hallway smelled musty. A layer of dust covered the desk and cabinets.

"Not what I envisioned for the penthouse level," Dexter commented.

"What do they say about beggars?" Bess riposted. She stepped forward. "I want to sleep in the same bed Howard Hughes slept in." She blew the dust from the desk, set down the bedclothes and looked at Dexter and Frank. "Do you realize what a ladies' man he was?" She started counting on her fingers. "He bedded Jean Harlow, Jane Russell, Gloria Vanderbilt, Ava Gardner, Jean Peters, Ginger Rogers, Terry Moore, Bette Davis, Lana Turner, Katharine Hepburn and a couple dozen more starlets and hopeful young things."

"How can you remember all those names?" Dexter asked.

"Because I was a typical teenage girl in the '50s and ate up the fan magazines. Why do you bother memorizing facts about the rich?"

"You dreamed of having your photos in those magazines," Dex commented, ignoring her question.

Bess's face took on a whimsical look. "Once upon a time. Anyway, tonight I sleep in Howard Hughes's bed without sacrificing my virtue." She opened the door to the suite with the grill and walked inside.

"We're never coming back to this town, are we?" Dex asked Frank hopefully.

"Not unless we come back as headliners."

"Then we better get some animals or half a dozen show girls with tits so big they have to crawl onto the stage."

Bess returned to the hallway. Her face was somber. "It's his suite, all right. Come in here."

She led the way through the central living room, to the bedroom on the left. It was about fifteen by seventeen feet, devoid of glamour. Next to the double bed, which was pushed close to one wall, was a nightstand with a lamp. A reading light had been secured above the bed. On the single dresser perched a 19" color television set. Centered in the room sat a stained white Barcalounger with an ottoman in front of it. Two telephones sat on the nightstand. A film projector and screen were stored in a corner. The room had no mirrors and the windows had been painted black and sealed around all corners with duct tape.

"Bizarre," Dex judged.

"He got more and more eccentric at the end," Frank said. He turned to Bess. "You sure you want to sleep here?"

Bess shrugged. Why not? It'll be a great story at dull dinners."

Elizabeth Coleman's scream was loud enough to penetrate every suite on the penthouse floor. She had left her front door unlocked, so that Frank and Dexter were inside within twenty seconds. Bess had abandoned the bedroom and stood at the far side of the living room. All three room lights blazed. Her eyes were huge with alarm.

"What is it?" Frank asked, expecting to hear about a rat having taken up residence in the unoccupied suite.

"Howard Hughes," she said in a small voice. "He was in the bedroom."

Dexter and Frank exchanged glances.

"You must have been dreaming about him," Frank offered, advancing slowly toward the shaking woman.

"The hell I was!" she shot back. "He was there!"

"What did he look like?" Dexter asked.

Sonder appeared at the suite's main doorway, still tugging on his bathrobe. "What happened?"

Frank raised his hand to silence the last member of the troupe.

"I was sleeping," Bess admitted. But then I felt someone in the room and I opened my eyes. He was standing at the foot of the bed, staring down at me."

"Was he solid or like a ghost?" Dexter prompted.

"Hard to tell," Bess replied. "I had left on that light." She pointed to a small fixture that could not have thrown much illumination into the bedroom. "He had a long, white beard that came down to his chest. His hair touched his shoulders. His fingernails were really long, like claws, and he had sores on his body." She blinked. "And he was completely naked."

"That wasn't a dream; it was a nightmare," Sonder Voloshin said softly.

Bess swallowed back a sound of fear that rose from her chest. "I was frozen to the bed. I didn't know what to do. He turned and walked into the bathroom. I jumped up and ran out here, screaming."

Without a word, Dexter strode into Hughes's bedroom and turned on the two lights. The rest of the troupe moved to the doorway as Dex entered the bathroom.

"All clear," he called. "Come on in."

Bess stepped first into the bedroom. She went up to the doorway of the bathroom and peeked in. Dexter shrugged at her. "Just a bad dream, Lady."

"A bad, very real dream," Bess said.

"He's dead," Frank assured his stage assistant.

She nodded and then shot embarrassed, apologetic looks at Dexter and Alexander.

"Unless you gotta take a piss or something," Sonder called in to Dex, "let's go. I got somebody waiting for me."

"Lucky bastard," Dexter remarked as he left the bedroom.

"Lucky is once or twice," Sonder replied. "The fiftieth time is charm, my man."

When they were alone, Frank said to Bess, "Why don't you sleep in the other bed in my suite?"

Bess nodded and began pulling the linens from the mattress.

"You've been unusually quiet the past couple of weeks," Frank noted. Is it this rotten Vegas gig?"

"No. I just become…a little sad this time of year," Bess responded.

"What? Shorter days? Dying leaves?"

"Something like that." She looked up suddenly. "You know, Howard Hughes hated having his picture taken. The last one was about twenty years ago. The man I saw standing at the foot of the bed was definitely him, but he was twenty years older. Why wouldn't I have dreamed of the image of the guy from the old photos?"

"Because your subconscious is smart enough to realize he aged?"

"Is it smart enough to have included burned hands and wrists?"

"I don't understand."

"I didn't mention that while Dex and Sonder were in the room. I didn't want a four-way debate. But only now am I realizing why I saw healed scars on Mr. Hughes. He was badly burned while testing a plane that crashed."

"But you knew that as well," Frank argued. "In your subconscious. Otherwise you couldn't be remembering it now. He was a dream, Bess. He had to be."

"Why not a ghost?"

"Because ghosts don't exist."

"How do you know?"

"Because since the dawn of history there's never been any hard, indisputable proof."

"But you can never prove they don't exist, Frank; only that they do. Why should every culture on earth, from as far back as the dawn of history, have ghosts?"

"Because people are the same around the world. They want there to be a life after death – and they want to have those who died before them prove it."

"That wouldn't prompt several groups of people to see a double line of dead monks walking in their abbey on a floor lower than the present one."

"I take it that ostensibly happened."

"They have photos and motion pictures of it."

"I'd have to see the monks myself to comment," Frank said. "People desperately want us not to be the only intelligent life in the universe – and they see aliens, too. Hard proof, Bess. Give me hard proof."

Frank's stomach had begun to knot. This was not the first time Bess had brought up her thoughts on the possibility of the existence of actual ghosts. It was more than playing devil's advocate with her, Frank was sure. And yet, when pressed, she said that she did not believe in them any more than he did. Never before, however, had she claimed to have seen one.

Bess persisted, "Maybe this was a ghost. It was where he felt most comfortable on earth, after all. He never came out of these rooms, twenty-four hours a day, 365 days a year. If you allowed the slightest sliver of doubt, Frank, you might one day see one. You know: the 'there are none so blind as those who will not see' theory."

"When you're dead, you're dead," he affirmed, allowing some of the exasperation he felt to creep into his voice.

"But where are you dead?" Bess countered, undeterred.

"If the spirit separates from the body, then not in this world." Frank picked up Bess's pillow. He slipped his free hand under her arm and guided her gently toward the living room. Let's get some sleep, eh? We have to find a cheap place to stay and kill a day tomorrow – and then it's back on the road."

Bess nodded and offered an anemic smile. She glanced over her shoulder at the foot of the bed and then into the bathroom. Then she walked out.

Frank Spiegel glanced at his wristwatch. The time was a bit past four in the morning. After he had arisen to relieve himself, he had checked to be sure Bess slept soundly and then had eased his way out of the suite. The still-burning outdoor lights of Las Vegas lit the hallway faintly from side windows. He walked warily down to the suite with the grille and entered it. The three living room lights still burned.

Frank crossed the living room and entered the bedroom. He stood next to the Barcalounger for a long minute, watching and listening. He wondered how and why one of the richest men on earth had elected to sentence himself to such a humble, dark prison, sealed alive in a tomb without sunlight. Howard Hughes had clearly been haunted long before he died. If any disembodied soul might still walk the earth, Frank supposed it would be that man.

"I wish I had seen it," he said to himself. He waited another half minute, then backed out and closed the bedroom door.

TWO

OCTOBER 17, 1976

"WAKE UP, GRUNT! Join the nightmare."

Alexander Voloshin jerked up from his sleeping huddle in time to see the lieutenant's crouched shape retreat into the darkness along the mud-caked boards. He fought through the liquid lead in his veins, from ten uninterrupted days of sleep deprivation. When he closed his eyes, he had said a prayer that the NVC would honor the Vietnamese New Year with a ceasefire, as they had in every other year since the conflict began. The first barrage of incoming ordinance told him otherwise. The earth shook all around him from the explosive onslaught. Blue Sector was the target for the current attack.

Voloshin peered through the pre-dawn gloom, along the trench to his left and right. Fellow Marines, both those he recognized and those he did not, readied their rifles for the next assault. He wondered for the hundredth time how someone so smart could allow himself to be trapped in this hell hole. He glanced longingly over his shoulder in the direction of the entertainment tent that he had been in charge of, before it had disappeared in smoke and flame on the first day of the siege, along with Khe Sahn garrison's main ammunition dump.

A canteen rattled and sloshed nearby, reminding Voloshin that his own was empty. His throat was beyond parched, but nothing as trivial as dehydration would move him from the trench that ran along the edge of the camp.

A mortar shell landed within ten meters of where he lay. He unwrapped the plastic that protected his M16 and snapped in a fresh magazine. A few Marines tumbled into the trench to fortify the position. One he knew slightly, named Johnson, ended up beside him.

"Hell of a way to celebrate my birthday," Johnson said, in way of greeting.

"Happy birthday," Voloshin wished.

A pair of "Made in U. S. A." flares zig-zagged into the sky ahead of the trench and came to brilliant life. In spite of his fears, Voloshin pushed up from his squat and peered past the barbed wire down the ravine.

"Jesus!" a voice cried out a moment before the firing began.

Like maggots writhing out of the skin of a dead beast, more than 200 VC regulars crawled up the impossibly steep incline toward them. Voloshin marveled at how cheaply life was valued on the other side, where thousands would be gladly sacrificed if the remotely placed division camp and airfield could be overrun.

Mortars, rockets and artillery shells continued to rain down around Voloshin's position. He alternated huddling in a tight ball with uncurling and emptying thirty-round magazines each time a flare lit the property in front of him.

"They're getting close!" Johnson shouted to him. "Use your grenades!" As if in demonstration, he pulled a pin and stood up.

Several bullets struck the Marine at the same time. The live grenade tumbled from his grasp. Voloshin snatched it up and tossed it over the barbed wire. It exploded in midair. He crawled to Johnson, who was still breathing but unable to speak.

From both sides of the trench, a Marine war whoop erupted. Battle-hardened men swung in a long line over the earthen lip, advanced to the edge of the perimeter fence, hurled clutches of grenades and laid down withering crossfires. Against his better judgment, Voloshin followed his comrades and emptied another magazine into grass and brush that seemed suddenly devoid of enemy life.

When he retreated to the trench, Voloshin found that a Roman Catholic priest named Murphy had miraculously appeared. The man was known to be fearless beyond all reason.

"Do you know if this man is Catholic?" he asked Voloshin.

Alexander shrugged. "His name is Johnson."

The priest stood over the dying man. He snapped open his field kit.

"In nomine Patri, et –"

A dark hole appeared in the priest's forehead. For an instant, his eyes went wide. Then he tumbled backward.

Alexander Voloshin dropped his rifle and cupped his hands over his face, hiding the sight from his vision. He moaned at the thought that there were no atheists in foxholes…and that there was also no God.

"Hey, Sonder, wake up! Come on, buddy!" Frank shook his friend's shoulder one more time.

Alexander 'Sonder' 'Sonic' Voloshin sat bolt upright in his seat. "Yeah, okay. I'm awake."

"You weren't a second ago," Dexter volunteered.

"Same dream?" Frank asked, as Sonder made sure of his surroundings.

"Just a little nightmare, okay? I'm in competition with Bess." He affected an easy smile.

"All right," Frank relented. He knew Sonder had no intention of letting them into his private world. He settled back in his seat.

The single-lane highway ran unbroken to the horizon, bracketed by sear landscape for as far as the eye could see. Franklin Jefferson Spiegel and his retinue were out on the highways yet again. As if Las Vegas had not been degrading enough, the months ahead to the new year looked as bleak to Frank as their present surroundings.

The troupe had departed Vegas just as Saturday turned to Sunday because they had a one-night gig in Lubbock. Not many quality acts stopped in the oil belt cities of West Texas, and the evening performance had been sold out for two weeks. Already a dozen hours on the road, Dexter Brown was pushing beyond the speed limit to get them to the theater with at least the three hours necessary to set up their many complex elements and test the lighting and sound systems. The bus rattled and creaked from the exertion. Welds had separated, shocks were shot and bushings bushed, and it never failed to remind its occupants.

"The Reds beat the Yankees 5-1 in Cincinnati," Sonder reported, having grabbed the newspaper to hide his embarrassment.

"We read it while you were sleeping," Frank told him.

"Did you read that Jimmy Carter's poll ratings have climbed since he admitted having 'lust in his heart' for many women?"

"The illusions we have aren't enough," Frank decided aloud, abruptly.

"So you've said," replied Dexter from the driver's seat.

"In Seattle, Shaky Town and in Vegas," Sonder echoed.

"And even if you're right, you just spent every spare cent on new ones already," Dexter reminded his young boss.

The three men and Elizabeth Coleman traveled together in a converted early Sixties school bus. The seats in the back half had been removed to make room for their luggage and the show's considerable paraphernalia. In the middle, a metal cot had been bolted to the floor on the driver's side, across from a small table and a pair of the old bench seats. Up front, four salvaged Camaro bucket seats provided the vehicle's only luxury. The exterior yellow had been over-painted. Across a black field floated playing cards, glittering rings and flowers. On each side was stenciled in white 'Spiegel' and, directly below, 'Master of Illusions.'

"It's a new age," Frank lectured. "Parlor illusions like rings and cards were fine when people gathered in living rooms around upright pianos and sang popular tunes together. Now the whole world of entertainment is magic, from King Kong and Ray Harryhausen in the movies to Jeannie the Genie crossing her arms, wriggling her nose and disappearing. We're thinking too small and too traditional."

Dexter shook his head with misgiving. "The Henning show in L.A. and Siegfried and Roy in Vegas are spectacle, not art."

"The audience doesn't care," Frank replied.

"They require eight, maybe ten people behind the scenes. And they stay weeks or months in the same theater, so they can get the lighting, the trap doors perfect. Is that what you want? If it is, you've got to abandon what you do best and learn how they scraped together the really big dough to afford all that."

Frank folded his arms across his chest, regretting that he had opened the raw wound once more. "They must have been lucky. You know, uncovered private financiers. No bank wants –"

Dex snapped his fingers. "Right. And it doesn't even matter that you're great at what you do, because the bankers know that any magic show is a dated art form."

Frank knew that the situation was even worse than the truth his driver delivered. The traditional magic show was indeed outmoded, and yet almost 3,000 competitors were practicing members of the American Academy of Magical Arts. In the current year and in the United States, magic could support fewer than a dozen stars. After those came a precipitous plummet in salary for the next tier of 100 or so, of which Franklin Spiegel was one. The remainder of the 3,000 had to be content with earning "second-job" money, like wedding and bar mitzvah disk jockeys.

"How do you know it was just luck with Henning and Siegfried and Roy?" Sonder weighed in.

Franklin let the question hang. He knew that Siegfried and Roy had met doing cruise ship entertainment, but who had fronted them was a mystery to him. Frank's mouth screwed up in frustration as he reviewed the royalty at the top of his profession. Carl Ballantine had cornered the comedy angle and had further built his name as a regular on *McHale's Navy*. Mark Wilson and his wife, Nani, had the kid market via their television show, with an attendant big budget for amazing illusions supplied by Kellogg's. The Dutch magician Richard Ross had height, good looks and an amazing wealth of blond hair to cement his popularity. Frank was of only medium height, with what his mother called a "pie face." Moreover, his brown hair had always been thin, and now before each performance the thinning spot on his crown, as large as a monk's tonsure, had to be sprayed over. The elegant beanpole with great hair, David Copperfield, had been coming on like gangbusters, spurred on by his affiliation with the Broadway hit *Pippin* and then his own musical comedy, *The Magic Man*. Razor-thin Doug Henning, with his own crop of curly, shaggy, Hippie hair, had a veritable circus of psychedelic helpers around him while he did his tricks. His money had come first from the Canadian government and then Canadian backers, to fund an extravaganza that eventually became *The Magic Show* on Broadway. The incredible Shimada had Oriental illusions sewn up. These were the dukes, earls, and lords of the profession. Currently, Siegfried and Roy were the king and queen. They had had just been voted Magicians of the Year by their peers and feted at the Beverly Wilshire Hotel in Los Angeles. Nothing galled Frank more than slaving at his Desert Inn lounge act while the handsome German couple made thousands a week down the street in the main room at the MGM Grand. He thought of the tired old standards they had revitalized by the simple addition of beautiful and dangerous great cats.

"Opera is a dated art form and it does great in selected places," Frank argued. "If I get myself into the top half dozen, it doesn't matter that magic is an old art. Think of that guy who kept the ten plates spinning on the tops of the poles. Every year, he came back on the Ed Sullivan Show doing the same incredible act. Just one fantastic, never-seen illusion can make a reputation."

"Our problem is that we don't have animals," Sonic decided, as if

Frank's mind was an open hat and the image of Siegfried and Roy a white rabbit to be plucked out. "People love animals. Especially baby rabbits and doves."

Dexter said, "I told Frank that the other day. Personally, I favor a couple six-foot Amazons in feathers with really big knockers. 'Cause who's gonna clean animal cages? Who'll catch birds when they escape inside a theater? Buying and keeping the goldfish alive is bad enough."

"Hey Choir,' either get a new hymn or shut up," Elizabeth complained from her fetal position on the bed. "I'm trying to sleep."

It was all rehashed material, every line of it as overplayed as a top ten tune. Frank knew he should not have (re-)resurrected the topic, but after the humiliation in Vegas and less-than-full houses in Anaheim and San Diego it was difficult to keep his mouth shut. He let his cheek press against a windowpane, staring at the monotonous landscape without seeing. He reflected on the long journey that had brought him, now twenty eight years old and ten years into his professional career, to the middle of nowhere.

It had begun innocently enough with a magic set that his cousin had given him for their annual Christmas gift exchange back in 1960. It was nothing more than two packs of cards, a cheap trio of plastic cups with foam balls, four Chinese linking rings, a box that made a penny disappear and a thin book of instructions. But it was like flint, steel and tinder to Frank Spiegel's imagination. Able to amuse himself, Frank found hours of happy diversion in the simple set. He quickly mastered every trick and pestered any and all who might serve as his audience. By the time he was fourteen, he had purchased every trick and magic gimmick offered in the backs of comic books and had inveigled upon his father into driving him from their home in Edison, New Jersey, into Manhattan, where Martinka & Co., the mecca of magicians, was located. Every penny from his birthday money and his paper route went into the props of illusion. By age sixteen, he had worn down his parents enough that they allowed him to take Saturday lessons with the old veteran Slydini.

Frank became convinced that the creation of astonishing illusions was his life's calling. He performed at church functions, local fairs, cabarets and the like to earn money throughout his four years at Rutgers University. Even though he attained a political science bachelor's degree and had taken the LSATs and filled out applications for law schools, he was unable to leave his long-time obsession behind. He felt deep within him something akin to mystical compulsion. Hope burned undimmed years later, despite the low points. After ten years of honing his skills and building a minor name, he owned a bus and a repertoire of six major illusions. He was about to unveil a largely revamped act for the new year. For a purveyor of a dying art form, he calculated that he had done relatively well. His mantra was, "It's a matter of paying your dues." He knew that history was filled with painters, writers and inventors who slaved for decades before becoming immortal. He expected the same to be true of Franklin J. Spiegel.

And then there were his assistants, what Frank called "my troupe" and what he considered his adopted family. He was the father of the group and gave them drive and direction. They supported him and made possible both the geographical increase in the audiences he reached and the complexity of his show. Like any family; they each displayed negative traits; but he knew that he would not be where he was, unspectacular as that might be, if it were not for the three of them. He could tell from their lack of eagerness to part when break weeks approached that all three had little life beyond the act. He was sure that, in a way, he had rescued each and given purpose to their lives; but he made it a point of honor never to probe into their backgrounds. Each, in turn, spoke seldom of home or relationships. In contrast, the group was perpetually plotting and planning together to reach their common professional dream. When Frank at last attained fame and fortune, he fully intended that would they share with him.

The first to join Frank's team, back in '72, had been Alexander Voloshin. He had answered an ad in Variety when Frank had scraped together enough cash to afford better lighting and sound. The man nicknamed 'Sonder' and 'Sonic' was accomplished at both. He was a Marine veteran of Vietnam, where he had learned his stagecraft supporting the constant flow of USO shows. He had an easy-going, charming personality – and he was also a ferret when it came to finding any required item, no matter how difficult. If a fishbowl needed to be no smaller than ten inches across but no larger than twelve, he scrounged it up from somewhere. In his spare time he haunted flea markets, second-hand shops, and electric and electronic stores. He dog-eared parts catalogues to provide improvements and innovations for the act. He prided himself on being able to correctly disassemble and reassemble anything. He made sure that every ounce of his extra labors was known and appreciated by his peers.

Most of what entered Sonder's eyes and ears went out his mouth. What was more, he had a sharp sense of humor so that his life was an open comic book. He spent way too much free time in front of motel and hotel televisions. His favorites were *The Carol Burnett Show*, *The Flip Wilson Show* and *Monty Python's Flying Circus*. Frank also knew him to be a prodigious drinker. Sonder had a double curse when it came to alcohol. His background was not simply Russian. After World War II, his father had managed to escape from Siberia across the Bering Sea to Alaska, where relatives had long since settled. There, he met and married a woman of half-Russian, half-Native American blood. Frank knew of the latter half's genetic predisposition to low alcohol tolerance. Moreover, the Russian preference for absenteeism due to fermented potato over sober labor for the common good of the Workers' Collective was renowned.

Frank's tours generally ran in eight-week cycles, with two weeks off in between for R and R. However long each tour lasted, Voloshin would resist temptation, furiously chewing gum as a substitute. Everyone else in the troupe referred to their tours as being "on the bus"; Sonic called it being "on the wagon." He also called each "a tour of duty." Then, for fourteen days, the charming thirty-two-year-old with the Cossack high cheekbones, beguiling dark eyes and straight black hair would crawl into a bottle of Smirnoff's with some willing and equally besotted female. Frank considered the man's spare time his own business and suggested to the others that they also turn a blind eye.

Dexter Brown had signed on when Frank began to accept gigs farther and farther from his New York area base. He came recommended by Sonder and was a large, powerful man, out of Harlem and tough in every sense of the word. He credited his salvation from the dangerous streets to an early friendship with the man who owned Washington's Garage on 127th Street. Dexter had hung there every spare moment of his early teens, assimilating the skills of the mechanic. From "General" Washington, he learned to harness his physical strength.

Dexter's mother had anticipated that he would be drafted for the Vietnam conflict and made sure that he went into the Marines for career training, as well as a stint. It was while serving and working for a number of motor pools that he completed his mastery of auto mechanics; but he had also decided that being cooped up inside a repair garage was not his idea of a life goal. Dexter was now twenty seven, with a love of driving big vehicles great distances. Frank figured that he had given the man a means of escape from a world that, in its own way, was just as deadly a jungle as any in Southeast Asia.

The big man was a reader and an aficionado of word games. When not working, a book, a magazine or a crossword puzzle was in his hands. A rainy, non-performance day was certain to have Dex pestering his mates to play a game of Scrabble. Far more vexing to Frank was the bus man/prop man's drive to amass money. He applied constant pressure on Frank to take on more performances, even if they paid less. His attitude was that no one in the major cities would know if Spiegel, Master of Illusions, took a five-hundred-dollar job in Kankakee and that every day not performing was a day of nothing but expenses, lost forever to the credit column. Dex vowed that he simply could not sit still at his age. If they hung idle two days in a town, he would haunt trucking firms, furniture and appliance stores, produce markets and the like to see if he could pick up a few hours of delivery work. Never, however, did he allow the extra hours to adversely impact the quality of the performances or his long-haul driving duties.

The last member of the current troupe was Elizabeth Coleman, who expected her friends to call her Bess. Frank had previously employed beautiful women as assistants, but they were either not mentally equipped for the split-second timing demanded by the craft or else they ran off to marriages or better-paying jobs. Elizabeth also came to Frank via an ad in *Variety*. The five-foot-eight beauty had started her career as a model and quickly gravitated into television shows, where stunning women were used to escort a guest on and offstage or to glamorize a product merely by holding it. Then she happened into the world of magic, where her brains as well as her body were required. As an assistant to Mrs. Richard Cardini, who went by the name of Swan, she had filled in for the woman toward the end of the couple's brilliant career. Her notoriety peaked with appearances on several episodes of Mark Wilson's *The Magic Land of Alakazam*, between 1966 and 1970. Then, for four years, she dropped out of the magic business.

Bess auditioned for Frank in the summer of 1974. He hired her full time after one performance. In spite of the fact that she was nearing forty, people frequently guessed her age to be several years younger. The main reason was that she kept herself thin and trim. Frank came to count on the fact that the combination of her natural blond hair, large blue eyes, flawless complexion, hourglass figure and shapely legs was invariably distracting. If Bess sashayed her spiked-heeled, sequin-suited self offstage, both male and female eyes looked away long enough for him to prepare the most complex trick. She had what the entertainment business called "it": that inexplicable inner radiance that commanded attention. As if this was not enough, she possessed a vitality that shone through even in her most depressed moments. Dexter pegged her as "the most alive woman I ever met." As soon as Frank's infatuation became clear, Bess informed him in no uncertain terms that she might supply the aura of sex to performances, but she would not supply the real thing to anyone in the troupe. Frank understood the soundness of her resolution. Almost immediately after this acceptance, he realized that she needed him more than he did her. She was a woman in search of people to shower with maternal affection. Bess willingly did the troupe's day-to-day shopping; she was their de facto doctor, nutritionist and arbitrator; she professed to enjoy doing wash, even in the most dingy, neon-glaring laundromat. She knitted during the road travel and waiting in her dressing room to go on, and everyone in the troupe had at least two of Bess's handmade scarves. Her unofficial nickname was "Good Queen Bess."

Bess had no caveats about enduring long stretches on the road. Whether solicited or not, she dispensed sage advice on virtually every subject. But about the subject of her own past Elizabeth Coleman was a sphinx. Sonic and Dexter had speculated to Frank that Bess might be one of those rare people who had no sex drive. While they and Frank occasionally brought females to their rooms for companionship, stimulation and recreation, Bess had never been known to succumb to male or female. Once, when Sonic passed a remark about her pure life, Elizabeth had smiled and said, "Yes. I'm the real-life version of Sister Benedict from *The Bells of St. Mary's.*" Most of her comparisons came from movies, which were her free-time passion. Dexter had countered, "Except that the woman who played her was a tramp." Bess had refused to acknowledge the riposte. Whatever the truth about her might be, it made no difference to Frank.

There was one other, invisible member of the team; and his part in the group had no glamour, no dysfunction and no mystery. His name was Allan Salkin and he had been Frank's agent for eight years. Although no Swifty Lazar, the canny sexagenarian claimed to have a file system that contained twelve thousand contacts, from high schools and colleges to convention centers and industrial shows; from county fairs to Elks and Rotary clubs, to every Knights of Columbus chapter and every nightclub that ever boasted a name performer during its heyday. He sided with Dexter, claiming that if Frank's troupe was willing to work for five hundred dollars a performance, he could book him at least forty more nights a year. Frank's pride and future aspirations prevented him from working for less than seven hundred in anyplace other than Vegas or Reno. So they performed about one hundred and fifty nights each year, and they traveled the length and breadth of the United States and Canada for forty weeks to do it.

We may be in the middle of nowhere for the moment, Frank thought, but we're not stopped. We're passing through on the way to the Big Time. If the new show doesn't do it all, it will still be a springboard. Like diving. Jumping off the edge of the pool is behind me. The backyard diving board is also. Next year will be the three-meter board. Which is the last stop before the ten-meter board. And the big splash. In spite of his personal pep talk, Frank did not look confident.

The bouncing of the bus brought Frank back from reverie.

"Jesus! stay on the road, Dex!" Bess exclaimed, sitting up in the bed.

"I am on the road, woman. I'm taking a shortcut."

"Ah, Christ. Not another of your infamous shortcuts," Sonic lamented.

"It'll lop at least half an hour off the trip," Dexter declared, "but only if I maintain speed. I wasn't the one who booked towns nine hundred miles apart! Lady and gentlemen, please put your seats and tray tables in a fully upright position and fasten your seatbelts. We're experiencing a bit of turbulence."

"You mean 'it's going to be a bumpy ride,'" Bess corrected.

"Where are we?" Frank asked.

"About twenty miles from Las Vegas."

"Las Vegas?"

Dexter grinned. "Las Vegas, New Mexico. We just left Interstate 40. We're now on Highway 84. We'll take it all the way into Lubbock. Trust me or take the wheel yourself."

"What happened to lunch?" Bess asked, pulling the ice chest toward her.

"It was your turn to fix it," Sonic answered, "but you were sleeping."

"So you couldn't feed yourself? Honest to Pete, I've become the title player in *Snow White and the Adolescent Dwarfs*!"

The banter flew back and forth as Bess fixed sandwiches. The sun had reached its zenith over the burnt land of the Llano Estacado. Sonder stopped talking and held up his hand for silence.

"Listen to that! Next time stay on the good roads, Dex, will ya? Things are shifting in the back," he declared. "We better stop and secure them before we hear glass tinkling."

"Okay. Next watering hole."

The watering hole turned out to be a gauntlet of wooden buildings bracketing the road. A series of stubby side streets connected to the main drag like the legs of a caterpillar. None of the streets dared too far into the flat and barren countryside that stretched to the horizon in every direction. Frank calculated that the town could not have held more than two hundred souls.

"Did you see?" Sonic asked in his clown tone of voice. "It had 'You Are Entering Puerta de Siempre' and 'You Are Leaving Puerta de Siempre' on the same sign. They probably sell maps of the town in the exact scale: one inch equals one inch."

"Wrong," Dexter shot back. "One inch represents one inch. I

hate it when people get that wrong."

"Pardon me, Professor," Sonic said in drawn-out syllables.

Dexter slowed the bus and prepared to steer into a spacious gas station lot. His head swung suddenly to the left. "Be damned!"

"What?" Bess asked.

"Look at that!"

Across the street from the gas station stood a small, one-story building with a tall false front. Whatever paint it had once sported had long since been blasted off by sandstorms, so that the wood faced the elements in dry, hardened silver gray. The display window, however, looked clean and ice smooth. Spaced among the middle two rows of its twenty panes were two words: 'GAMES' and 'MAGIC'.

"How's a place like that stay open in the middle of nowhere?" Sonder wondered aloud. "I can see a general store or a bar out here, but a toy store?"

"I'll find out," Frank said. "You and Dexter rearrange the back."

"Fine. Explore away, Dr. Livingstone"

The main road of the town was completely deserted. Bess accompanied Frank across the street, where a dust devil met them whirling with light menace from the opposite direction. They walked through the screened door coughing and wiping grit from their lips. A bell tinkled above them.

"Welcome," bade a male voice from amid the store's clutter. The place seemed considerably bigger than it had looked from the outside, and yet it was crammed full with merchandise. Even in the center of the store the shelves were so high that Frank could not find the voice's owner.

"Thanks," Frank said. "You must attract customers from miles around to afford to stock this much stuff."

"Those who find us must make great journeys," the voice returned, with a lilting accent.

The front twenty feet held nothing but games, from Chinese checkers to backgammon, Parcheesi, Go, mancala, hounds and jackals, cribbage and dominoes, to row after row of chess sets. Boxed classics such as Monopoly, Clue, Life, Stratego and Go to the Head of the Class filled one wall and the wall opposite was crammed to the ceiling with word games like Scrabble, Got a Minute, and Spill and Spell. No electric lighting hung overhead, so that only the penetration of natural light through the front window illuminated the merchandise.

Before Bess or Frank could advance deeper into the shop, the owner of the voice emerged from behind the shelving. The deep webbing of his wrinkles suggested great age. His skin was beetle-nut brown. A narrow and straight nose perched above curving lips and a fierce white moustache that extended from cheek to cheek. The turbaned head and out-of-place outfit conjured up images of the days of British India and the Khyber Rifles. His smiled as he approached. Then his eyes focused beyond his prospective customers, out through the display window. One of his hawkish eyebrows cocked.

"What possessed the owner to put this shop way out here?" Bess asked.

"Possessed?" the man replied. "It is where it must be. I am the owner."

His reply and the intense stare of his brilliant green eyes caused a stilted silence. Frank felt the need to nod. He noted an unusual dash of copper color in each eye, each dash close to the bridge of the man's nose. Frank tilted his head around the owner and gestured for permission to explore more deeply. The man stepped aside.

The area devoted to magic was smaller than that for the games, but it was large nonetheless. More surprising to Frank, it was not filled with the normal junk meant for the idle curious and the amateur. He saw no children's sets such as the one his aunt and uncle had purchased for his cousin to give him. The space was divided into three areas. The first displayed about four hundred books. Many were how-to manuals, but just as many were reprints of ancient tomes of spells and incantations. Mixed in were several books that Frank judged had to be from the earliest age of moveable type printing. Oddly, books on flower gardening butted up beside those on herb gardens. Gorgeous photography books, cookbooks and volumes on travel existed alongside magic manuals. Even though the new greatly outnumbered the old, a musty odor permeated the place.

In the second area sat a myriad of bottles, flasks, urns and jars. Each was clearly labeled: Love, Forgetting, Visions, Tranquility, Friendship, etc. Tabletops displayed paraphernalia, both those traditionally associated with magic and garden-variety household items. An ornately engraved, silver-clad spade sat beside a crystal ball held aloft by brass dragons. A painted and glazed flowerpot was positioned behind a rowan wand. Wind chimes dangled above amulets.

At the very back of the shop were large performance items. A human-sized guillotine, an ornate lacquered Mandarin cabinet with sword slits already cut in at various angles, false-bottomed bird cages, hollow prop stands, a temple screen, a zig-zag cabinet, stood packed in, shoulder to shoulder.

Frank's gaze wandered over the familiar props of his profession. His eyes stopped at a large, dark box, tilted slightly back against the farthest corner, nearly invisible in the gloom. He realized that if it had been set upright it would have stood half a dozen inches higher than his five-nine frame. Its lines were sinuous, widening at the shoulders and with the head area curving in, like a sarcophagus from the time of the pharaohs. Moreover, it appeared to be made from the Egyptian black stone that had been used for so many statues and hieroglyphic tablets during the dynasties of the great kings. What riveted Frank's attention was the ornate lid below the crossed crook and flail. In bas relief across the entire surface writhed and contorted the figures of men and women, while devils and fire tortured some of them. The space looked like a sculpted version of a medieval vision of the Apocalypse, not at all like the formal patterns of an Egyptian mummy box. High on the cover, just under the abbreviated chin beard, was a disk like the oversized gem of a necklace. It appeared to represent either the sun or a ball of fire from the wavy flames emanating in rays all around. The burning circle, however, was apparently made of glass and shone blackly, as would polished obsidian. He ran his hand over the images and was surprised by their coldness. The box felt too cold to be made of stone. He guessed it was a dull, brushed metal alloy. Halfway up its front, at his right side, was an ornate keyhole. He turned to comment to Bess and found instead the owner standing just behind him.

"What does this do?" he inquired.

"Magic."

Frank simultaneously felt like laughing and violently twisting the man's nose. "I mean what kind of illusion is this?"

"It is not an illusion," the man stated. "I see from the wording on your vehicle that you deal in illusions. I do not. This is magic."

The man's words touched a raw nerve in Frank. This was more than mere semantics to him; it was a subject about which Franklin Spiegel felt passionately. He could not let the moment pass unchallenged.

"I have the word 'Illusions' painted on my bus because I am an honest man," he declared, widening his eyes offensively. "The age of attempting to trick other men into believing I control the supernatural is long past. I perform the seemingly impossible because I have practiced long and hard. There is no such thing as magic."

The man smiled. "Strange that someone like you should say that. Magic lies all around us. It is inside the mystery of life and the greater mystery of death. It manifests itself in the sunrise and the stars. It is –"

"Spare me the mystical blather," Frank interrupted. "You're lumping the unseen and the unknowable under a word that no longer has meaning."

In answer, the man dug his left hand under the folds of his baggy outfit and produced a pair of large, brass-colored keys on a golden ring. They looked as if they had been fashioned during the Crusades, with valleys and protuberances on all sides. The man stepped forward, inserted and turned one of the keys and pulled back on it to open the box. Its hinges creaked slightly – it was empty inside except for a small hourglass. The hourglass was suspended just above where the occupant's left shoulder would be, held up by levered rods and clearly engaged by the opening of the lid.

"The box can do magic," the man gently insisted.

"Whatever it does or doesn't do, it's impressive as hell," Bess judged.

Frank's sharp eyes narrowed. "The rest might not be worth much, but the cover would really make an impact on television. Close up, y'know?"

Bess nodded. She knew that Frank was determined to use television appearances to propel him to the top of the ever-shrinking ranks of successful illusionists.

"Hello, hello!" Dexter sang out from the front of the shop. "I have died and crossed the Jordan! Look at all of these games!"

"Dex, come back here," Frank called out, "and bring Sonder with you." He turned to the shop owner. "How much do you want for it?"

"It's not for sale."

"Then why is it in your store?"

"It's waiting to be picked up by its owner."

Frank ran his forefinger over the ornate surface work and pulled off considerable dust. "It's evidently been waiting a long time."

"Since the first day of last February."

"So, he stiffed you. Why not sell it?"

"I can tell from your accent that you come from somewhere around New York City," the owner said. "The one who ordered it also came from there."

"I know most of the illusionists in that part of the world. Who is he?"

"Simon Magus."

Behind Frank, Dexter whistled. In their world, Simon Magus was like Bobby Fisher was to chess masters. He was the undisputed master of magic, but an inveterate recluse. Virtually unknown to the public, he performed only to private, intimate groups, and his fee was reputedly five thousand dollars for the evening. Those who had seen him work swore that what he did was indeed magic and not illusion.

The turban-headed man said, "He refused to give me his address or telephone number. Do you know him?"

Every gear in Frank's brain engaged. "I know how to find him. Are you looking for someone to deliver this trick?"

"It is doing no good sitting here," the shop owner answered.

"I agree."

"Are you returning to New York soon?

"Within a few weeks. I promise you, we would take very good care of it along the way."

"Do you intend to be in this part of the country within the next year?"

Bess looked at Frank. Frank said, "Yes, we do. We make a circuit of the United States every year. Why?"

"I could not let you take the box without your leaving behind significant collateral, to insure that you would either see that it is delivered or returned to me."

"I see. What kind of collateral would you need?"

"Take out your wallet," the man said.

Frank pulled the wallet from his back pocket.

"A photograph of someone you love. If a photograph is precious enough to be carried all the time, it will do."

Although the request seemed ludicrously liberal, Frank winced. His wallet's plastic sleeves for treasured photographs were all empty. "It was too bulky, so I took the pictures out," he lied.

"I see. Then you will have to give up your most prized illusion."

Bess tugged at Frank's elbow. "C'mon. This guy's jerking you around."

"I am in earnest," the man affirmed.

Frank looked at Bess, Dexter and Alexander. "We work as one."

"That is laudable," said the owner. "Then you must all give up your most prized illusion."

Frank smiled. "I need to confer with my troupe. Excuse us."

The quartet walked single-file out of the store onto the sidewalk.

"Are you doing this as an excuse to meet Magus?" Dexter asked.

"No, dolt!" Sonder broke in. "If we can borrow the trick, I can figure out how to copy it."

"That would be unethical," Bess judged.

"Not copy precisely," Frank said. "But to study it and perhaps create our own version. Magus only performs privately; his original and our version could exist simultaneously."

"But this man is asking for our most prized illusion," Bess reminded the group.

"Who's to say what that is?" Sonder argued. "That's subjective. We haven't used the levitation illusion for months. It doesn't produce the results we had hoped for. Half the time stage limitations prevent us from using it anyway."

"You're the boss," Bess said to Frank.

"Why not? We get our trick back after a year anyway."

"Yeah. He's providing free storage space," Dexter said, laughing.

"But we should try for more," Sonder said. "Let me handle this."

The four returned to the back of the store, where the owner waited patiently.

Sonder reached out and slid his hand down the surface of the sarcophagus. "Did you build this thing to specifications?"

"It already existed," the owner answered.

"That's a good thing, because I would have been disappointed in Simon Magus if he had specified black. This would be far more impressive if parts of it were sprayed with gold gilt, candy-apple red and lapis-lazuli blue."

"That would be a most inadvisable act," said the shop owner.

"We're not going to spray somebody else's property, believe me,"

Frank reassured, regretting giving Sonder the lead.

"You know," Sonder jumped in, "gas and bus space don't come cheap. What if we were to use it in our act until we delivered it?"

The owner looked at Frank. "Your leader says you deal in illusions. This is magic."

"How does the magic work?" Frank asked, hoping against hope for an answer.

"It would be unethical for me to divulge that. The one who should pay for your troubles is Simon Magus. Negotiate with him before turning over the sarcophagus."

"Has he paid you already?"

"Indeed. One hundred percent, up front."

The group exchanged glances for several moments.

Frank turned to the shop owner. "You have a deal. I'll offer my most precious illusion."

"You said you worked as a group," the man pressed.

"That's right," Sonder jumped in again. "One for all; all for one."

"I am happy to hear that," said the dark-skinned man. He took Bess's hand and pressed the two keys into her palm. "The keys are identical. If you lose both, the box cannot be worked by anyone... even the keeper of its secrets. What is more, no locksmith will be able to fashion duplicates for you."

Frank knew of lost wax and other methods for copying the keys, but he merely said, "We'll take good care of them."

"You must do all the lifting," the old man replied. Never once since the travelers had stepped into the magic section of his store had he shown the slightest trace of emotion.

"Holy crap!" Dexter exhaled as he attempted to lift the metal box. "This thing must be made of lead. Sonder, give me a hand here!"

Frank had insinuated his way behind and under the coffin to take the top end when Dexter lifted the bottom. He braced himself when Sonder bent down to help. As the box tilted backward against him, he winced at its weight. It was all he could do to keep his knees from buckling as the bulk of it came onto his hands. Once it was horizontal and Sonic took the middle third from underneath, it became manageable. Mincing forward among the tables and shelving, they worked the box toward daylight.

"Simon Magus must be nuts," Dexter decided. "This monster is way too unwieldy for a stage."

"I can see the headlines now," Sonic grunted. 'Magic trick flattens audience member.'"

"Maybe it becomes light as a feather when the key is turned," Bess said sarcastically. "Remember, it is real magic."

"That's what the Indian said," Frank added.

"Wrong kind of 'Indian' for these parts, isn't he?" quipped Sonder.

"Yeah, I thought the rule was that the white man traded the Indians things they didn't need and not the other way 'round," Dexter contributed. "You'd better be able to pull this thing apart, Sonic."

"Piece of cake," the soundman bragged, "I'll have it figured out before we leave Lubbock."

They maneuvered the box across the deserted street to the back door of the bus. While Frank and Bess delivered the levitation illusion to the owner of the store, Dexter and Sonic worked to stow the over-large cabinet.

"Jeez, this thing is long," Dexter said.

"Less finesse and more muscle, big guy," Sonic advised. "Like so." He put his shoulder to the bottom of the cabinet and shoved with all his might.

From the opposite end came the sound of glass crunching.

"Great, just great," said Dexter. "You smashed Frank's practice mirror. Now, who gets the seven years' bad luck: him or you?"

Sonic shook his head ruefully. "I get the bad luck; I pay to replace it."

Lubbock's Gaiety Theatre was a gal from bygone ages, when live acts and later the silver screen ruled the entertainment world. She sported a vaulting fly above the stage and a wooden floor with trap doors. It meant that the most elaborate of the troupe's tricks could be executed. Sonic loved the shows where all the stops could be pulled out. Unfortunately, the house was so old that lighting and sound were run from offstage right rather than a booth at the back, obliging him to listen more carefully and crane his neck to see around the masking black curtain legs.

The first act had gone as well as it ever had. Sonic had rarely watched Spiegel, Master of Illusion, perform with such energy and élan. The packed audience, sensing something special, had responded with encouraging rolls of applause. The sound and light man was certain they would adore the second act, where members of the audience were constantly pulled up to the stage to act as Frank's foils and to witness the impossible at point-blank range.

Frank began with Gold Fishing. He cast what appeared to be an ordinary fishing line out over the audience, and before their eyes a goldfish appeared at the end of the hook. Frank reeled one after another in and deposited them in a glass bowl. After he had caught four, he invited a boy from the front row up to confirm that they were indeed live fish. As his prize, the boy was allowed to take the fish and the bowl home.

Disappearing for a moment, Frank returned wearing a derby hat. When he doffed it to take a bow, a clear glass ball rolled from his head and shattered on the apron of the stage. Dexter rushed out to clean up the mess, receiving his own share of applause and bowing deeply. Then, Frank called for another glass ball, which cued Sonic to fill the auditorium with undulating Levantine music, rich in oboe nasality and the clinking of hand cymbals. Bess glided from stage left, dressed in an abbreviated, gossamer harem outfit that swirled and danced around her arresting figure. She held what appeared to be an identical glass ball in her uplifted right hand. She stopped beside Frank. When he turned to capture the orb, it suddenly rose directly up into the air, just out of reach. He stood on his tiptoes and the ball went a bit higher. He turned to the audience and informed them that the Lady Thin-tima (who used to be called Fatima when she was much heavier) was the magician of the troupe. He was only an illusionist. With that, the ball settled back into Bess's hand. Frank took it and lifted his derby. Before retreating from the stage, Bess thrust her left hand out and a clap of thunder, a flash of light and a puff of smoke filled the center stage. After a little more banter on Frank's part, he replaced the derby on his head with the ball underneath. Carefully, he set about juggling one, two, three and then four Indian pins. As he was engaged, Bess reappeared, moving silently upstage of Frank. When she pulled a comically large mallet from behind her back, the audience began to titter. The more she signaled for quiet, the louder they became. Frank, apparently oblivious, inquired what was so funny. At the height of the levity, Bess struck the derby from above, crushing its curving top. No liquid appeared. Frank lifted the hat. The glass ball had disappeared.

Before Bess could escape, Frank took her arm and told the audience that Bess the Magician had the power to change her weight at will, even though her shape would remain the same. He invited five men up to the stage. After comically interviewing the men about their lives, then giving instruction in a witty manner, Frank had two of them place forefingers under Bess's insteps, as well as two under her armpits and one under her nose. With apparent ease, the five were able to lift her about eighteen inches off the ground. When they tried it again, they could not budge her. They repeated the trick in the orchestra center aisle, just to be sure there were no stage magnets holding her down. The audience erupted with delight. In spite of having seen the trick of tensing and relaxing hundreds of times, Sonder could not help smiling with satisfaction as he listened to their reaction.

Yet another member of the audience, a frail grandmother, was invited to the stage to be sure that a square of plate glass was not only solid, but heavy and shatterproof. Nevertheless, when Frank placed a cylinder under it, then a vase and another cylinder atop it, a moment later the vase had disappeared from inside the top cylinder and was found by the grandmother to have moved down to the lower one. Her mild oath at the end helped immensely in capping the illusion. For her assistance, Frank presented her with a miniature version of the vase.

The tiny, aged lady had shuffled to the steps at the edge of the stage apron when Frank said, "I wonder if you could help me get rid of this table? Oh, never mind."

The table had four legs appearing under a long tablecloth. Frank grasped the top of the table with both hands and for a moment seemed to push the piece of furniture into the floor. An instant later, he whisked the cloth high into the air and clapped his hands together, rolling the cloth into a large ball. The table had disappeared.

Before the applause died, Sonic changed the lighting and potted up an eerie compilation of sounds and music. Bess came onstage with a café table, its top supported only by a thin column, which widened gracefully to a round base. She carefully placed it where the other table had been.

"My lovely assistant is not the only one with supernatural powers," Frank announced. "I have in my employ a spirit. He's a bit mischievous, but often he can be coaxed to cooperate. He loves it when audiences call his name. It's..." With that, Frank made the rude, wind breaking sound of a Bronx raspberry. The audience laughed. Soon enough, they were all invoking the ghost spraying each other with spit-flinging verve.

"Now Pffft loves to smoke," Frank told them with a twinkle in his eye. "He tells me where he now lives he smokes all the time. But he also enjoys an occasional cigarette. He thinks the rule of not smoking in theaters is absurd and he'd like to invite a member of the audience up here to help him break the rule. Who among you after ninety minutes in this place is dying for a deep drag?"

A son of the plains, dressed in jeans and a plaid shirt, and wearing a string tie and cowboy boots, thrust up his hand from the center aisle, third row. Frank assessed the volunteer with a practiced eye and assured himself that the man's easy smile signaled an affable nature that could be counted on to cooperate. "How about you, cowboy?"

"Yeee-hah!" the man crowed as he pushed himself out of his seat. He strode to polite applause slightly bow-legged toward the apron steps.

"Can you assure the rest of the audience that you are not a shill?" Frank asked as the man loped onto the stage

"Ah ain't no shill," the volunteer announced. "Ahm Billie Bob, from Earth."

"An' he is, too!" someone in the third row shouted.

"From earth, eh?" Frank said, as Bess appeared with a large red fire extinguisher. "That's good. I believe everyone here except for Pffft is from earth."

"Not that 'earth'," the cowpoke said. "Earth is a town jes' west o' Plainview."

"I hesitate to ask what's south of Plainview. Are you a farmer or a cattleman?"

"Farmer. I own so much land it takes mah tractor half a day ta git from one side ta th' other."

"I once owned a tractor like that," Frank quipped, drawing considerable laughter. "Then you must be rich."

"Ahm not rich; ahm Billie Bob."

"Let me do the jokes, fella. If you're rich, then why do you need to bum cigarettes?"

"How do ya think I got rich?"

"One more smart remark and I turn you into a pile of cow chips. Judging from the way you're dressed, you look like a Marlboro Man," Frank said.

"Ahm any kind that's free, man," Billie Bob affirmed.

"Well, we met Pffft…sorry." Frank pretended to wipe his spit from the man's shirt. "We found Pffft in a cemetery. He's a Marble Row man."

The audience groaned good-naturedly.

When offered a cigarette from a pack of Marlboros, Billie Bob elected to put one in his mouth and park another one over his ear, saying with a wink, "Savin' 'im fer later." He selected one matchstick from a metal cup on the table, and when he drew the match against the side-striking surface all the other matches sprang two feet in the air. In his surprise, Billie Bob dropped his match fall onto the stage, where it went out.

"I think Pffft feels you overstepped his generosity in taking more than one of his cigarettes," Frank advised.

Billie Bob shrugged. "Sorry, Pffft."

A moment later, as Billie Bob was bending to retrieve another match, the cigarettes in his mouth and over his ear burst into flame. The one in the cowboy's mouth fell among the matches as he slapped his hands repeatedly against his temple to put out the flames that had ignited wisps of his curly hair. Bess finished the job with a few squirts of water from her extinguisher.

The audience convulsed with mirth.

Frank shook his head and stared slightly upward. "Shame on you, Pffft! You owe Mr. Billie Bob a favor for pulling such dirty tricks." He turned to the farmer, who stood scowling with his arms folded across his chest. Bess reemerged holding a large sundae glass.

"Ah'd rather git mah favor from this heifer," Billie Bob leered.

"Keep your shooter holstered, Big Boy," Bess said, handing him the glass and retreating smartly to appreciative applause and jeers from the females.

"That is a regular drugstore sundae glass, is it not?" Frank asked.

"Fur as ah kin see," the volunteer obliged.

Frank reclaimed it and set it down on the center of the table, first knocking on the wood to show that it was solid. "Now may I trouble you for a coin? A quarter if you have one."

"Ah want that back," Billie Bob said, handing over the coin.

Frank dropped the quarter into the glass – it struck the bottom and rang with a predictably bright sound. "Ask Pffft any three questions that can be answered with a yes or no. Two jumps of the quarter means yes; one means no." He stepped back from the trick.

"Alraht." The cowboy moved closer and peered down into the glass. "Will ah live ta be nanty?"

The quarter jumped twice, ringing the glass. The audience gasped in wonderment.

"Shee-it!" Billie Bob exclaimed. Then he remembered himself and apologized to the audience. "This here is slicker'n cat snot on a fencepost," he assured them. He cleared his throat and bent low over the glass.

"Will ah git a date tonight with Miss Thin-tima?"

The quarter jumped up and struck Billie Bob in the nose, causing him to jerk back. It landed and lay still. The audience laughed and cheered.

"Are ya really a ghost?" Billie Bob asked.

The quarter jumped once. The audience was silent.

Frank looked out across the sea of faces. "Pffft indeed tells the truth. He and everything you see tonight are illusions. But that doesn't make them any less fun now, does it?"

The audience agreed.

Frank reached into the glass. "You asked for your quarter back. I believe Pffft has changed it into a silver dollar." Frank held up the visibly larger coin. "Are you sure you wouldn't rather trade?"

For measure, Billie Bob bit the coin to be sure it was real before taking several immodest bows and quitting the stage.

Next, Sonic and Dexter worked lighting and trap door with practiced perfection as Bess rolled out of the rear of the glass-lined Cabinet of the Vanishing Lady and down onto a raised mattress in the basement. The audience gave the split-second illusion its due appreciation.

"So, you like it when things disappear?" Frank asked. They whistled, stomped on the floor and applauded in unison until the old theater's walls vibrated.

"Very well," Frank relented. "For our final illusion of the night, we offer Don Quixote de la Mancha, the last of a dying breed of knights!"

The stage was cleared so that nothing stood on it. After a moment of near-total darkness, bravura Spanish music accompanied brilliant white lighting and the appearance of a full-sized white mechanical stallion, which Frank pushed to the center of the stage.

"We are very careful that no animals are ever harmed in the performance of our illusions," Frank called out. "The crew, however, are expendable. Tonight, as Don Quixote, we have the redoubtable Señor Dexter Brown, from the windmill-dotted plains of Harlem, New York. Mr. Brown has indicated his desire to return to New York City with all speed, and so he is the perfect candidate for this illusion. Tonight, we will send Dexter and Trigger…or whatever his name is…halfway across this great nation of ours. What is more, we will send him in the blink of an eye. I present now, for one night only, our Goodbye, Good Knight!"

The mechanical horse's head moved slowly up and down. Its tail swished gracefully back and forth, and its back and flanks were caparisoned with ornate trappings, blanket and saddle. Frank stepped to downstage left, and Dexter appeared wearing the battered armor of Cervantes' benignly insane knight, complete with a shaving basin for a helmet. In his right hand he held a jousting lance. He bowed to the applause and made his way with dignity to the horse and thence by stirrup up to the saddle.

The music swelled. A black, weighted curtain descended toward the floor directly in front of horse and rider, with less than two extra feet of width beyond either extreme. More than ten feet of the stage to the back cyclorama could be clearly seen on either side. When it had descended to within four inches of the stage the curtain stopped, so that the dolly on which horse and rider sat was clearly visible.

The time for banter had passed. The music became louder. Trumpets blared. Drums rolled. Bess appeared from the downstage right wing. She held up her hands, showing the audience a bunched-up golden cordon rope. She traveled upstage. Frank mirrored her path on the stage left side. Bess crossed behind the curtain and handed Frank one end of the cordon. They stretched it between them as they reappeared far left and right. Their clear purpose was to show that horse and rider could not escape upstage.

"Help me send Don Quixote home!" Frank cried out. "When I say 'Three,' you all shout 'Home!' One!" Frank waited a beat. "Two! Three!"

"Home!" everyone in the house shouted.

Just behind the curtain, a burst of light and a clap like thunder exploded. A cloud of smoke billowed out and rose, but not as quickly as did the curtain. It climbed and climbed, exposing the stage behind. The smoke was drawn transparent by the sudden movement. Horse and rider had disappeared. The dolly stood where it had been. Frank held the golden cordon on one side and Bess held the other.

The audience leapt to its feet, throwing admiration at the stage in rhythmic waves of applause.

Frank led Bess forward with a graceful tread. He retreated to allow her moment of solo adulation. Then, from his swallowtail coat, he produced a dozen red roses for her. She, in turn, threw them one by one into the audience. The audience's reaction grew louder. Bess curtsied once again and rushed from the stage, leaving Frank alone. He wiped his forehead with a handkerchief drawn from his outside coat pocket. He found with dramatic surprise that it was tied to no fewer than twenty other colored handkerchiefs. The audience dissolved in laughter. Frank stepped back three paces. He blew kiss after kiss into the dark house, winked down at those close by as if he knew and adored them, and finally bowed low, pressing his hands together as if in prayer.

The stage went black for two seconds. The lights flashed back up full. Spiegel the Illusionist had disappeared.

Bess finished packing away the small compressed oxygen tank she used to create the column of air that supported the balloon "ball" in the Derby Hat trick. Dexter loosened the ropes from their belaying pins and held on so that the mechanical horse would not descend from the fly too quickly when the counterweights rose. Sonder swept up and reclaimed all the non-broken matches and made sure that the spring attached to the striker surface still worked.

"That went fairly well, m'lady," Frank said, indicating with a tiny smile his delight at the evening's performance.

"Fairly well indeed," Bess echoed.

"Next performance is not until Friday in Dallas," Sonic remembered. "What do we do with all this time on our hands?"

"I hate it when I get time on my hands," Dexter quipped, securing the horse to its dolly. "It's so hard to get it off."

"We could just kill time," Sonic snorted. "But then where would we bury the body?"

"We could put it in our new coffin," Bess said.

Frank winced. "I've infected all of you with my bad puns. Listen, I was just approached by the manager of the theater. He'd like us to stick around. He thinks he can put an ad in the local paper below the review and use some radio spots for an added performance on Wednesday. He'll pay for two nights of lodging whether it happens or not. Maybe his efforts and word of mouth will put some extra coal in everybody's holiday stocking. What do y'all say?"

Sonder wagged his head back and forth. "I don't object to free lodging. But what do red-blooded city boys do in Lubbock for three days? I mean, we're the only entertainment for miles around."

"You always have your television," Dexter shot back. "My televisions are warmer than your books, but they don't have the kind of warmth I'm thinking about." Sonder's eyes narrowed mischievously at Dex. "Problem down here is they keep the white women and the black women segregated."

"So? Who needs your company to tomcat?"

"Excuse me. Unless we do another performance, nothing's happening in this house the rest of the week," Frank interjected. "We can work on the new act and take a quick look at Simon Magus's coffin."

Dexter looked at Bess, who looked at Sonic. The three shrugged their acceptance, as casually as if Frank had said, "Let's take a quick look at what's playing on T.V. tonight." He was not fooled by any of them.

"Okay then!" Frank said brightly. "We all crash and then work on breaking into the Big Time tomorrow morning at ten."

THREE

OCTOBER 18, 1976

BY FIVE MINUTES to ten, the entire troupe had assembled on the Gaiety Theatre stage. The theater was not to be used until the coming weekend, so the heating had been turned off. Night chill lingered in the big space. Everyone except Frank wore a sweatshirt; he had put on one of his formal swallowtail coats.

Frank cleared night phlegm from his throat. "Okay, let's examine this so-called real magic."

Frank felt the pent-up tension in his troupe become electric. Until he had vocally acknowledged its existence, everyone had studiously avoided looking at the black coffin standing on end between the black leg curtains that defined the border between the wing and the stage proper. Dex crooked his fingers for Sonder's help. By using an industrial dolly, they brought the large metal box to the center of the stage. Frank assisted them in standing it on its narrow bottom end.

"Put some counterweights or sandbags around the back and sides before we do anything else," Frank directed his crew.

Full stage lighting was expensive to run, so only two small spots shone down from just behind the proscenium curtain. The steep downward angle of the light accentuated the shallow carvings on the box's door. Beyond the pool of center stage light, the rest of the house was inky black. The air in the theater was still, as if even the building was expectant.

The box looked dangerously top heavy, but a dozen rigging counterweights shoved up against it proved stable when Frank attempted to rock it.

"Maybe we should put it down on its back again." Dexter slapped his hands together to wipe off the stage dust.

"No. Let's keep it upright," Frank returned. "Like it would be when used."

"It has no breathing holes." Dexter ran his fingers along the back edges. "That means you're not supposed to be inside for very long."

"Find the escape hatch," Frank directed. "This is obviously an escape trick."

"I looked at the bottom while it was in the bus," Dexter reported. "It was solid as Gibraltar."

"Then where is it?" Frank demanded.

After Dexter made a complete circuit, Sonder took his turn.

"You think that old guy tricked us?" Sonder asked the rest of the troupe.

"What do you mean?" Bess said.

"He was about to move to someplace where he could actually make a living, and he used us to get rid of this black 'white elephant' and steal a perfectly good trick?"

Frank admitted silently that Sonder's supposition was the most probable scenario. To the group he said, "We need to study it from inside out. Bess, you have the keys."

"After what the old man said I don't want responsibility for both." Bess removed one key from its golden circlet and handed it to Frank. "Here. Take good care of it."

Frank nodded. He removed the gold chain from around his neck, opened the clasp and attached the key so that it dangled next to his ornate Roman Catholic cross. He then inserted the key carefully into the box's lock and turned it clockwise. It refused to budge. "Great. Dex, get some silicon spray."

"Wait! The old man was left-handed," Bess remembered. "I think he turned the key counterclockwise. Try that."

The lock released and the door swung open. A pair of metal arms pushed forward as if spring loaded. Attached to them were cam-like mechanisms that flipped horizontal a small, neck-high hourglass. Some of the sand slipped through its transparent bottleneck.

"Okay, so it unlocks counterclockwise," Frank noted, as casually as he could manage. He pushed the door back to the limit of its swing, until the inside surface came into the light from one of the overhead spots. "The rod goes into this hole." He turned his attention to the center of the upper part of the surface "Hey, the thing that looks like a sun from the outside is a viewing port. This is a clear glass lens." He put his eye up to it. "It's a fish-eye lens. I can see maybe a hundred and twenty degrees."

"Why would an illusionist need that?" Dexter wondered.

"Not an illusionist; a magician, remember?" Frank said wryly. "It remains to be seen."

"You know, this metal circle around the lock plate is actually a swivel ring," Bess observed from the outside of the door. "Yeah. I can lift it up. So you don't have to pull on the key to open the lid."

"There's one on the inside as well," Frank added. "Hell, this is an exact duplicate of the outside of the lock. Exactly the same keyhole shape. This lock can be worked from both sides."

"That's ridiculous," Dexter decided. "What lock does that?"

"Old locks," Frank answered.

Sonic knelt in front of the outside keyhole. "But if that's true, shouldn't I be able to see a little light through here?"

"Maybe not." Frank inserted his key into the inner keyhole. It went in with no trouble and turned clockwise. Bess repeated the process on both sides of the door.

"Whoa! What is this?" Frank squatted on his haunches.

Three heads craned around the door to see what Frank had found.

Frank ran his fingers lightly in a circle. "The magic shop was too dark for us to find this, I guess. Even in this weak light it's hard to spot. There are twelve circles, each about the size of a penny, arranged like the numbers on a clock face." He got down on his knees and put his face closer to the inner door. "Jesus!"

"What?" Bess asked, her near-whispered single word nonetheless charged with tension.

"Every one of them is glowing. Just the faintest green."

"Let me see!" Sonic said, coming down on his knees.

As Frank backed out to give the technical member of the team room, he reported, "Outside of each circle is etched a faint symbol."

"Like signs of the zodiac?" Dexter hazarded.

"Not our zodiac," said Frank. "Maybe for ancient Egyptians."

"All twelve circles are lit up," Sonder affirmed. He tapped on several of the circles. "Feels really hard. Like quartz, or ballistic glass." He sprang to his feet. "Let me get my electrician's tool box."

In a twinkling, Sonder was again at the back of the coffin's door. He placed a meter near and then on it and watched the needle. He twisted the main dial on the meter and repeated his testing. When he looked up at the group, his brows were furrowed with confusion.

"I can't detect any electrical pulse. I tell you, this thing can find a current through dry wall and studs. I've dialed down to a hundredth of an amp. Nothing."

While Dexter and Frank tilted the coffin backward, Sonic searched in vain for an outlet for recharging or small plug for changing batteries, both in the back and along the underside of the door.

"Current could be passed through the hinges, if they're insulated," he said, his entire demeanor showing his sense of defeat. "But who the hell would go through that much trouble?"

"I think it's time I climbed inside the thing," Frank said.

"Maybe we should just stick it in the bus and forget about it," Bess suggested.

"Like hell!" Dexter and Sonder said as one.

Frank clucked his tongue several times. His head canted on his neck as he stared at the coffin. "If I was somebody as mysterious and weird as Simon Magus, I don't think I'd trust the entire trick to one supplier. This is probably only part of the illusion. Remember: The Indian man said it was a ready-made piece and not manufactured to Magus's specs. It needs to be converted from whatever purpose it used to serve."

"Then you want to forget about going inside, like Bess said?" Dexter said, his face pleading against such a decision.

Frank shook his head. "No, I'll go in. We just shouldn't expect much, given the little we've found."

"Well, you're not going into it until I get my power drill, a crowbar and some other tools," Dexter told Frank. "Not with inside hinges. I don't want this coffin look-alike turning into your real coffin."

While Dexter assembled his tools, Frank hunted up a flashlight and a spare set of batteries. For the sake of safety he also carried a ball peen hammer and a nail countersink so that he could knock out the hinge pins if necessary. Dexter silicon-sprayed the hinges and tapped them up a hair to be sure they could be popped out. Watching the precaution, Frank debated slipping off his swallowtail coat to give himself more room inside the tightly confining box. He decided he would like to see how big a challenge it would be to operate if he removed nothing of his formal clothes rigged with bulky gimmicks.

Frank slipped the necklace with the key over his head. He searched his mind for a snappy sentence that would cut the group's tension, but everything that came to him sounded like gallows humor. He faced the dark auditorium, drew in a deep breath and backed into the box. As he grabbed the pivot ring, he noted that his faithful crew stood in ascending order of height, Bess, Sonic and Dexter, with the back two angled so that they could watch him over her shoulders. "Here goes nothing," he said. He pulled the door closed.

In spite of many experiences inside trick cabinets, a wavelike sensation of claustrophobia overwhelmed Frank. He shuddered from the darkness and the confines of the coffin. He turned on his flashlight and angled it upward. He felt the cool metal of the rods against his neck but could not turn enough to see the hourglass. He leaned forward slowly and put his eye to the porthole. Something blinked at him. His head reared back. A half-second later, he realized that one of his troupe was trying to see him. He put his finger up to the glass and wiggled it back and forth in his flashlight beam. The eye moved away, giving him the barest beam of light. He saw that the curious one had been Sonder. His face was still rather close to the outside of the door and it was too wide, distorted by the fisheye lens.

Frank's fingers spidered blindly up and down the coffin sides, searching for a newly appearing release latch or spring. He felt behind him as well and found nothing. He realized that his fear and rapid breathing had already raised the temperature inside the box a couple of degrees. Muttering his frustration, he felt for the pivot ring, found and turned it, and opened the door.

Bess, Sonder and Dexter looked like a still life, frozen in expectation some six feet from the coffin's door.

"Nothing," Frank said.

"What did you do?" Bess prompted. He told them. "Did you try turning the key in the lock? Remember, it works from the inside as well," she said.

"Yeah! Maybe that initiates something," Sonder added. "If not some entire trick, then maybe something we can extrapolate from."

Frank turned and looked at the inside of the box. It now seemed infinitely more forbidding. He sighed. "What the hell. We've come this far." He drew in a slow breath, pivoted and backed once more into the sarcophagus. "Take two. Here's goes nothing." He pulled the chain over his head and took hold of the golden key. Again, he pulled the door closed.

"Who wants to look through the porthole this time?" Sonic prompted Bess, a moment after the door shut.

"Did he or did he not give you a no-no sign the last time?" she inquired.

"Probably because I scared him. Come on; take a look!"

Bess moved forward quickly, went up on tiptoe and put her eye close to the black curving glass. "Nothing. I guess he hasn't turned on his flashlight." She waited several more seconds, her eyes wide in vain expectation.

"Man!" Dexter said. "Not even a little thumping this time. When's he gonna put the key in the lock?"

"He's okay," Bess wished aloud. "I'm sure. If we opened the door on him, he'd be pissed. Wouldn't he?"

"I know how we can do it so he won't be," Sonder said. "You both know Señor What's-his-name on *The Ed Sullivan Show*, the guy with the head inside the box?"

Dexter's eyebrows knit. "Yeah?"

"Well, Frank's in a box. We pretend he's the dummy. We throw open the door and say, 'Zallright?' just like the Spaniard does."

Bess stared at the box with pursed lips. After several seconds she nodded. "Let's do it."

Dexter hooked his fore- and middle fingers inside the pivot ring and yanked back. The door swung out.

"Zallright?" the three cried out.

Then Bess screamed.

Frank shone the flashlight on the keyhole, inserted the key and tried to turn it to the left. It refused to move. Then he remembered to twist clockwise. He heard what sounded like tumblers engaging. He paused. The box was so silent that he heard the blood pounding through his ears. He believed that he could even hear the sand sliding through the narrow neck of the hourglass. He was surprised that he had not heard these the first time, but the sounds he had heard on his first excursion inside the box, from his team on the other side of the door, were gone. He leaned forward to see what had become of the three witnesses.

Bess, Sonder and Dexter had vanished. Vanished also was the spill of the twin overhead spotlights. The blackness beyond the porthole was so profound that Frank could gain no bearings at all. He worked his free hand up with slow effort and replaced the keychain around his neck, methodically tucking the key down inside his shirt. Now holding nothing, his left hand moved down to the lock's pivot ring. He swung his face left to peer to the limit of the glass's vision. His entire body tensed.

At what seemed to be a distance of about one hundred and fifty feet he could just discern the outline of a crude oil pumping machine, its enormous metal arm working slowly up and down. He became aware that he could feel the rhythmic thumping of its movement through the floor of the box.

Without warning, the well erupted in a column of flame, geysers of yellow-orange gas shooting upward to the limit of his sight. He blinked several times in shock and then narrowed his eyelids to slits against the undiminished intensity of the light.

"God Almighty! It can't be real!" he told himself. He realized that the brilliant flames were illuminating the terrain all around the well. He saw lines of iron piping leading from the fire. He also noted a red Chevy pickup truck in good condition, but from the early '50s, just at the limit of the flames. As he stared in horror, the truck's gas tank ignited. The truck catapulted tail first into the air from the force of the explosion. When it landed, it tipped over onto the passenger side. Within a few more seconds, the driver's door came up and the figure of a man clambered out through the licking tongues of flame. He was on fire. Frank gasped as the man rolled back and forth on the ground, gradually extinguishing the flames. He continued to roll down a slight decline, toward Frank and away from the intense well blowout.

Frank found himself unable to move, unable to take his eye from the porthole. "I'm having an hallucination," he counseled himself.

"I'm inside a theater. Maybe I'm running out of air and my brain is oxygen starved."

Frank cracked the door open the slightest bit. He pushed his nose toward the thin opening and inhaled deeply. The air came into his nostrils surprisingly cold, but at the same time he felt a wash of strong heat against his forehead and lips. He dared one more fortifying breath and yanked the door shut.

The intense, pulsing light invaded the porthole. Squinting, Frank look out once more. Nothing of the horrifying image had changed, except that the burned man lay still. Frank fully expected that the figure, real or not, would never move itself again. But he was mistaken. The charred body was immobile for about ten seconds. Then with excruciating slowness the burn victim moved his hands and knees under him and came up into a catlike position. His head swung from side to side. Even from the considerable distance, Frank could see that he struggled for air. The twisting of his head became more pronounced until, with one exaggerated motion to the right, it stopped. The man appeared to be staring directly at Frank.

The man stood and began to stagger on blackened limbs only partly covered with cloth. He kept his face fixed in Frank's direction. Slowly at first, and then with greater and greater speed, he lurched forward, never looking away. One hundred feet. Seventy. Fifty. On he came, his smoking work boots barely keeping him upright.

Frank saw that all but stubs of the man's hair had been singed away. He witnessed the third degree burns and worse, the charred pieces of skin hanging from the man's cheeks and hands. He registered the missing left eye.

"Oh, Jesus Christ!" Frank cried out. Beads of sweat that had sprung from his forehead spilled over the dams of his eyebrows into his eyes. As he swiped them away he realized that, in spite of the holocaust beyond the coffin, the air inside the box was cool.

Frank registered that the fingers of his left hand maintained a death grip around pivot ring. Frank reached up with his right hand to retrieve the door key from around his neck. He realized it had become buried beneath his formal shirt and tie. He would never be able to take it out, fit it into the lock and turn it before the man reached the door.

"Shit, shit, shit!" Frank wailed. His right hand fingernails clawed desperately against the skin of his neck to find the chain.

The burned man loomed in front of the porthole. He lurched on. Ten feet. Five. Then he hit the box with the full force of his body.

The box rocked backward.

Frank braced himself for the fall. Somehow, the cabinet weathered the impact.

Fists pounded upon the door.

Frank forced himself to look through the porthole.

The burned man's baleful good eye was almost against the glass.

Frank retreated one step, colliding with the back of the box.

The burned man screamed. His noise pierced the cabinet. It echoed and reverberated – agony such as Frank had never heard, more than normal lungs – much less those scarred by flame – could ever produce.

The man pounded against the door a few more times.

Frank winced and squeezed his eyes shut.

Then there was silence, except for the distant sound of a roaring, out-of-control oil well fire and its reverberation through the box's bottom.

Frank looked out the window.

The burned man had disappeared.

Frank strained his ears to listen for movement. He heard nothing. He counted to twenty, just to hear his own voice. It quaked so that he could almost not recognize it. His bladder ached to expel the urine inside. He realized that he was quivering like a can in a paint store shaker. At first, he credited it solely to abject terror. Then he realized it was also due to the intense cold that surrounded him. The air beyond the box was not the coolness of the theater but a profound lack of heat that knifed like icicles through flesh to the very marrow of his bones.

The flames from the well abruptly died back to a low roar. Frank's panoramic view of the largely barren terrain shrank. He heard no movement close by, felt no jarring of the box. He wondered if he should dare to peek outside. He put his eye once again to the door.

The burned man appeared from the corner of the glass. Now Frank could see that his eyebrows and eye lashes had been totally singed away, that his nose was all but melted and that so much of the left side of his face had been destroyed that he could see the man's molars, which were clenched in rage. Frank marveled that the burn victim was still alive. He was certain that shock and human system failures would kill him within minutes.

The man pounded again on the door. Then he looked down with his surviving eye and fixed it on the door lock.

Frank braced himself.

The burned man had found the outside ring. He yanked on it.

The door came open several inches.

Frank yanked it closed again.

"Go away, goddamnit!" Frank screamed at the glass.

The burned man's head snapped back, as if only now realizing that another soul stood on the opposite side of the door.

Frank thought he heard the man grunt. It was a sound of surprise. In fact, for a moment the man did not seem in any pain. Then he moaned. He staggered back from the box. Burned nearly beyond recognition as it was, Frank thought he saw the emotion of confusion on what remained of the figure's destroyed face.

"Go away!" Frank shouted again. He pressed his face against the porthole.

The man turned slowly and lurched off, moving to Frank's right but not so sharply that he disappeared from Frank's line of vision until he was more than one hundred feet distant. A pool of light seemed to follow the man, as if someone was working a weak follow spot from somewhere far above him.

Frank realized that the well fire had all but burned out. It was now no higher than a football rally bonfire. Several moments later, when he could no longer see the burned man, the fire eased back to that of a campfire. And then it flickered out. With its dying, the lines of pipe and the charred pick-up truck also became invisible.

Frank sighed. "It can't be real," he lectured himself through chattering teeth. "Blowouts don't cap themselves." He found the chain, fished the coffin key out of his shirt, and fitted it into the lock. He was not about to be surprised without a means to relock the door if another creature appeared out of the blackness, hallucination or not. When he was sure it was tightly lodged, he reached to a jacket pocket where he had stuck the business end of the ball peen hammer. He hefted it in his right hand. Gingerly, he turned the pivot ring and pushed the door open with his left.

The terrain had disappeared. It was as if the box were floating in space but without stars. The lack of orienting objects disturbed Frank profoundly. The air seemed completely devoid of heat. He could feel his heart pummeling his rib cage. His breaths came in short, ragged gasps, not helped by the crystal-cold air. Quaking, he backed away from the edge of the door. When he had regained a shred of courage, he leaned out slightly and peered around the left side of the box. He looked straight up and then straight down. He could see absolutely nothing. The hammer slipped from his grasp and struck something with a metallic ring. A whining filled his ears. He collapsed backward. The door closed. He reached out for the key and twisted it to the left. His eyeballs rolled up into his skull. His eyelids fluttered and then lowered. He crumpled limply against the front of the box.

"He's gone!" Bess gasped, directly after her knees buckled and Sonder caught her.

The two men peered into the box. Franklin Jefferson Spiegel had indeed vanished. Sonder laughed.

"What's so damned funny?" Bess asked.

"You," Sonder replied. "We thought we'd play a trick on him? He beat us to it. He must have snuck back here last night or early this morning and figured out how the coffin works. Were all of us here in front when he closed the lid?"

"You know we were," Dexter said.

"So? He went out a trap door in the back. What's with the looks of doubt? We of all people should not be fooled by cabinets that seem solid."

"It is solid," Dexter declared. "And there are counterweights around the bottom of the back."

Sonic turned a tight circle. "Bullshit! What's the alternative? He really disappeared?" He looked left and right. "Okay, Frank, you got us. Frank? Joke's over."

Dexter, whose hand had not let go of the pivot ring, pulled the door back as far as it would swing and stared inside. His expression was grim. He gestured into the empty box and then gestured to Sonder.

"Look for yourself. Find the release mechanism."

"Hey, I'm no magician." The light and soundman caught his verbal faux pas. "I mean illusionist. For all I know you're in on this scam and ready to lock me inside."

Bess reached out and swung her hand hard against the box's lid. Dexter's fingers lost their grip. The door slammed shut with a metallic clang.

Dexter stared at Frank's stage assistant with surprise.

"I'm sorry," Bess said. She reached for the pivot ring to open the door. Before she could grasp it, they all heard the sound of the lock mechanism turning.

Frank tumbled out of the box.

"Frank!" Bess cried out, going down on her knees and pulling him toward her, so that his legs and feet came clear of the dark cabinet.

Frank's entire body quivered. His teeth chattered like dice in a cup. His eyelids blinked furiously.

"Holy crap!" Sonic stepped back from the box.

Bess's hand went to Frank's forehead and then his right hand. "He's like a block of ice," she reported. Her fingers curled lightly around his wrist. "And his pulse is slow."

"What the hell happened?" Dexter asked no one in particular. He moved to the box and waved his arm inside it to test the temperature. "How could he get so cold in less than a minute?" No one replied. "Hey, look at this!" He swung back the door, showing the others the key stuck in the inner keyhole, the chain and cross dangling below it.

Frank moaned and tried to move.

Bess hugged him close, offering her body heat. "Frank, where were you?"

Frank struggled to control the shaking of his jaw.

"No...no...nowhere."

FOUR

OCTOBER 19, 1976

OCTOBER 19, 1976

NOT LONG AFTER they left Lubbock, Frank realized that Dexter had refrained from his usual lead-foot driving. The troupe's driver eased all the way off the bus accelerator as he steered through a right turn at the little town of Fort Sumner, New Mexico, following the sign for Highway 84 West. Everyone in the group had been extremely solicitous of Frank, in spite of his apparent complete recovery within an hour of entering the sarcophagus. Every few minutes, Dexter glanced at Frank in the rearview mirror.

"I'm fine. Fine! How many times do I have to tell you guys?"

"I believe you," Sonic affirmed. "If I look funny, it's just because the whole thing is still creeping me out."

Frank was not "creeped out" in the slightest. Their discovery of real magic had galvanized him. Everyone agreed that they could not admit having used the coffin within a day of picking it up to deliver to someone else. They also all agreed, for varying reasons, that they needed to revisit the magic shop. Frank determined to engage the owner and draw from him all he could of the nature of the magic box and where it brought the user. More importantly, he would try to negotiate for a similar "trick" for his troupe. Dexter and Alexander had agreed to pool every penny of their free money with Frank and even borrow from friends to get the act something as spectacular as the black metal cabinet. Surely, they told each other, within a few

62

months of unveiling it, they would be at the very top of their profession and making a collective fortune. Bess would have no part in the pact.

Frank watched Dexter pull the bus to the shoulder of the road. While the right turn signal clicked noisily, Dex consulted his road atlas.

"Trouble?" Frank worried.

Dexter swung in the seat and looked over his shoulder. "Not really. I remember a few landmarks from the trip down to Lubbock, but since I'm driving the route from the opposite direction I want to be sure."

"Good thinking," Sonder chimed in. "These tiny plains towns look so much alike."

Frank agreed. Indistinguishable, dusty huddle-ups of humanity clung to an equally universal asphalt ribbon that tied them tenuously to civilization. Buildings were more often formed of wood rather than stone or brick, sometimes false-fronted, not very different from the pioneering structures in Westerns. The pickup trucks that dominated this region of the States were apparently regulation, as was parking them facing the sidewalk at an angle

Frank looked doubtfully out the bus's front windows. "You're sure the town was named Puerta de Siempre?"

"Sure it was," said Sonic. "Remember? 'You are entering Puerta de Siempre and you are leaving Puerta de Siempre on the same sign'?"

"Maybe we've forgotten the exact name," Frank suggested.

"There's nothing even close to that on the map," Dexter replied, setting down the atlas. He put the bus into gear and steered back onto the shimmering asphalt.

Frank swung his bucket seat around toward the back of the bus. Bess lay on the narrow bunk bed with her eyes closed. Her supine position and pursed lips had exempted her from the discussion. The ability of the box to make Frank disappear had shocked her Catholic sensibilities and led her to pronounce that they were "playing with a tool of the Devil." Beyond her, beyond the woven wire wall, the sarcophagus-shaped box remained quiet in the back of the bus, like a nuclear bomb in the hold of a bomber. Dexter and Sonic had made certain it was well lashed down.

"That swarthy son of a bitch," Sonic murmured, speaking of the magic shop owner. "He's gonna explain what happened, or I'll know why. How could three of us agree that Frank was only inside the box for less than a minute, and he's just as sure it was at least fifteen? He 'fesses up, or I'll shake the dot off his head."

Frank had said nothing to anyone, but he had determined to approach the shop and its owner by himself. Nothing could be gained by Bess's voicing of her religious fears or by Sonder's demands and threats.

"Puerto de Luna?" Dex doubted, as the bus approached the prominently displayed metal town limit sign with five bullet holes piercing it. "I was sure this was where Puerta de Siempre was."

Bess sat up. Sonder rose from his seat and moved to the front of the bus. "I didn't really pay much attention to anything but that magic shop," he admitted.

Dexter eased his foot off the gas pedal. "I know one thing for sure: it had a gas station on the west side, about two-thirds of the way through. There's a gas station on the opposite side of the road, and it looks pretty much like I remember."

"Pull over, Dex!" Sonder ordered, pulling out a fresh stick of chewing gum.

"Hey, what I tell you about back-seat driving?"

"This isn't back-seat driving. I'm standing right next to you."

Dexter steered the bus into the large parking area beyond the gas island. He pumped the brakes to a slow halt and turned off the engine.

Every member of the group stared across the street, where they expected the shop to be. Instead of 'GAMES' and 'MAGIC', the lettering on the display window of the building directly opposite read 'GUNS' and 'ROD & REEL.'

"What the f –?" Sonic glanced guiltily at Bess as he cut himself off mid-expletive. "What the hell? Where's the towel-head's place? He did get out of town fast!"

"Vanishing that fast would be impossible," Frank said.

"Or black magic," Bess remarked softly.

"Or knowing we'd be back," Sonder added.

Without contributing another comment, Dexter yanked open the bus doors, pushed Sonder aside and climbed out. He moved with long strides toward a man sitting on an aluminum lawn chair in the shade under the gas station's eave, reading a newspaper. The man was in his forties and sat so quietly he might have been a statue. He didn't look up from his paper as he spoke, with Dex standing over him staring down. In a heavily Spanish accented voice he said, "We don't have diesel."

"I don't need diesel," Dexter replied. "Is there a town close by here named Puerta de Siempre?"

Still not looking at Dex, the man scrunched up his face at the name, as if it offended him. "No."

Bess, Sonder and Frank came up behind Dexter, content to let their driver carry the conversation.

Dexter said, "This here town is Puerto de Luna."

"Always has been."

"The names are kind of alike."

"I don't think so. Our town is Port of the Moon. 'Puerto' means 'port'. 'Puerta' means 'door'. 'Puerta de Siempre' is 'Door to Forever'."

"Shit," Frank said slowly, like air escaping from a tire.

Dexter dug into his pocket for his wallet and grinned grimly at the attendant. "I got twenty dollars inside here that says you can direct us to an Indian gentleman. Not an American Indian. The kind who wears a turban. An Indian gentleman who runs a shop with games and magic stuff."

The placid attendant's reaction to Dex's statement was unexpectedly animated and instantaneous. "Not around here. Not within fifty miles of here!" he exclaimed, putting down his paper and staring at Dex.

"You are from these parts?" Dexter confirmed.

"Forty-three years."

Dexter turned to the group. "It was this road. I'm positive I took Route 84."

"I believe you," Frank said.

Sonder kicked an empty oilcan out into the street. It bounced and then rolled noisily. Immediately, he marched after it. He bent to pick it up but did not stop walking when he had it. Instead, he crossed the road and walked up to the sporting goods store. He peered inside, cupping his hands to the glass to improve his view.

"Now what?" Dexter asked Frank.

"Now we turn around and continue our tour," Bess broke in. "We keep that scary thing in the back of the bus and deliver it to Simon Magus for a hefty haulage fee."

"What about the expensive illusion we left as collateral?" Dexter wanted to know.

"What, what, what," Frank said in a sarcastic tone. "We are dealing with major masses of magic here. We move very carefully, one step at a time. One thing is certain: we were entrusted with the box. I say we are its keepers until I am convinced otherwise."

"And I say it's Pandora's Box," Bess said quickly.

Frank watched Sonder yank open the door to the Guns and Ammo store and move inside without hesitation. "I'm not at all sure you're right, Bess. I have always heard that there is just as much white magic in the world as the black kind. I believe that shop was here because I wanted it to be here. I've been obsessed with finding the one unique trick that will set us apart."

"I, not you, decided to turn off the interstate," Dexter declared.

"Really? Was it your decision?"

"The box belongs to Simon Magus, not you," said Bess.

"A man none of us has ever seen. Who nobody we know has ever seen. Who never came for the box. Who left it like unclaimed freight. Which we have effectively paid for with our levitation illusion."

Dexter cupped his hand to his ear. "What do I hear knocking? Could it be opportunity?"

Frank only half listened to the two debating. His attention was riveted on the store across the street. Shaking his head, he broke into a trot and headed for its front door.

When Frank entered the store, he found Sonder confronting the man behind the counter, both hands pressed against the display glass, leaning aggressively forward.

"...I don't know. 'Indian' – like Ghandi," Sonder said in sharp tones. Ironically, the man he addressed was white, but quite brown-skinned from many years in the intense Southwest sun. He wore a cowboy shirt and denim jeans on his heavy-set frame, and his mouth turned downward in an unfriendly manner.

"I understood you the first time," the man replied. "No Indian ever worked in this town, much less this store."

Sonder thumped the counter with his fist. "This whole thing is a shell game!"

Frank took a step forward; but before he could take a second, the man produced a Colt six-shooter from behind the counter. He cocked it as he swung it up toward the ceiling. "Brother, this is my kind of shell game – and if you don't vacate my store in ten seconds, I'll consider that you mean to do me harm."

Frank grabbed his soundman's arm. "Alexander! Look around! See how much brighter this place is." He pointed up at the double row of florescent lights. "Look at the dust."

"I'll thank you both to take your carcasses out of here," the man said in a low, edgy tone.

"We're going," Frank told him.

As they exited onto the sidewalk, Sonder twisted to face Frank. "Different guy, different merchandise – even different lightning; but the store was exactly the same size. The counter was in the same place."

"Whatever's happened here," Frank countered, "we're never going to get the truth, no matter whose face you get into."

"Fine," Sonder said, as they neared the bus, which Frank knew meant anything but agreement.

There was no need for Bess or Dexter to inquire about Sonder's foray; they read his unresolved anger clearly on his face.

Frank gave Sonder a consoling pat on the shoulder, took one more look at the dusty town, and asked, "Who here thinks we'll find Puerta de Siempre by driving around the rest of the day?"

No one raised a hand.

"Me neither. So we get in the bus, drive back to Lubbock, and earn ourselves some extra money. I call Allan and have him use his thousands of contacts to find Simon Magus."

"And if the man can't – or won't – be found?" Bess asked.

"Then we embrace opportunity with eight collective hands," said Frank. "Does the box or does it not make a person disappear?"

Dexter and Sonic nodded emphatically.

Bess scowled. "Perhaps…" she stopped herself. Turning away she muttered, "Forget it…"

"I think know what you wanted to say," Frank interjected. "'Perhaps forever'. But I returned. I wasn't prepared. I panicked – and still I returned. Think of what we have in the back of our decrepit rattletrap, people!"

Everyone looked at the bus.

Frank continued professorially. "Let's suppose the box was meant for our talented troupe. I say the biggest challenge we face is not controlling it but rather letting it do its thing. Displaying it so there is

absolutely no possible way I could disappear other than pure magic."
Frank leaned toward the others in his excitement. "Don't you see?
Three hundred years ago, everyone in the audience would have
believed a disappearance was magic no matter how poorly a trick was
pulled off. Nowadays, everybody knows it's an illusion, no matter
how impossible it seems. We can make that work for us in the biggest
way possible. Next year at this time, we win the Las Vegas Award for
Best Act of the Year. Next year, I win the Magician of the Year, with
you three standing beside me. This is not a nightmare, friends; it's a
gift horse. Let's ride it, not run from it."

Bess was the first among Frank's team to begin the silent march
back to the bus.

FIVE

OCTOBER 25, 1976

LUBBOCK JOINED A seemingly endless string of performance venue memories. Austin was the troupe's next stop, and the first weekend of performances had gone fairly well. The houses were almost filled and were guaranteed to be packed the next weekend as well. The nearer that shows like Spiegel, Master of Illusions, played to Halloween, the more sold out the houses tended to be and the more in a mood for magic the patrons became. Following a draining three performances, the team took their time reassembling at the Zachary Scott Kleberg Theater on Monday.

The sound of nearby church bells sounded out the noon hour as Frank stood in front of his team to speak. "Okay. I just got the word from Agent Salkin. Allan has exhausted his resources in finding Simon Magus. The man is indeed a recluse and bachelor. He owns an expensive brownstone on Gramercy Park. He has no known help in maintaining the huge place. The few who have been invited inside believe the upper floors are shut off. The last day he was definitively seen was January 16th."

Frank watched Alexander begin counting the months on his fingers. "That's more than seven months. His booking agent admits that Magus missed three performances. He had no word concerning his client's disappearance. The agent has been using bank accounts he manages to keep up payments on the brownstone and other expenses. He said that once, a few years earlier, his client vanished for three months and then reappeared and refused to give any explanation."

"But this is more than twice as long," Dexter commented. "That's a long time without claiming the box."

Frank dipped his head in agreement. "Here's my take on it: If he's hiding from the world, nothing will get him to show himself faster than if we begin using his magic box."

"Whoa!" Sonic ejaculated. "And what if he sues us?"

"Who is going to vouch that it's his?" Frank answered. "The guy in the turban? And then what happens when the box is dragged into court, and we show what it can do? Who answers for its power?"

"Great," said Bess. "Frank can write a non-fiction bestseller about it from jail. We'll be rich by the time we all get out."

"We'll be rich long before that," Frank countered. "We've sat on this wrapped-up treasure for long enough. Dex, Sonder: I want you two to go on a scavenger hunt." He dug into his pocket and produced a wad of bills with a slip of paper and a rubber band around it. "Here's my extra performance pay from Lubbock, along with a shopping list. See if you can get it all by four o'clock, and let's all rendezvous here then."

Frank glanced at Bess for what he expected to be a patently negative reaction. He saw that she had taken out her knitting and begun to work. He figured that her strategy was to allow him to get into enough trouble that he would quit exploring the box on his own. He hoped fervently that she was not the smart one of the quartet.

By four o'clock, Dexter and Sonder had scrounged up all the items on Frank's list. The mountaineering anorak was guaranteed by North Face to protect the wearer to thirty degrees below zero Fahrenheit. The outfit Frank wore to investigate the dimension outside the coffin's door also included fur-lined gloves, fleece-lined boots, corduroy pants, battery-operated socks and a wristwatch supposedly watertight to a depth of sixty feet. Dexter had scared up a Boy Scout compass and a scout knife that looked like a minor version of the one carried by Jim Bowie, while Sonder had purchased two flashlights advertised to throw their beams a quarter mile, plus a dozen pairs of white dice with black spots.

During the afternoon, Frank had cajoled the owner of the theater into allowing the use of an entire strip of overhead lights for the team's development of a new, large-scale illusion. Sitting on the floor in front of the cabinet were cymbals sometimes used in the act and a pair of trashcan lids Frank had liberated from the back of the theater.

"I think that's everything," Frank said. "Let's synchronize watches, Dex. My second hand will reach the twelve in six, five, four, three, two, one."

Dexter started the special second hand on his expensive chronometer. "I feel like we're NASA headquarters preparing for a launch," he commented. No one cared to respond.

The box stood waiting, upended, in the center of the barren stage. Piled about ten feet to its right were the four quilted movers' blankets Dex and Sonder had wrapped the forbidding sarcophagus in directly after Frank's frightening experience. Once again, massive, iron counterweights had been stacked against the coffin's sides and back.

"I'll be fine," Frank reassured Bess, who nevertheless felt the need to hug him and then brush his cheek with a motherly kiss.

Frank tightly gripped his golden key. As Bess used her key to open the coffin's cover, he tugged on his right glove.

"One small step for man," Frank said as he backed into the dark, confining space, winking at Dexter. "One giant leap for magic." He saw that all of his crew were holding their breaths. Frank grabbed the inner pivot ring and closed the cabinet door.

Frank turned the key clockwise in the inner lock and listened for the movement of the gears. Absolute silence swept in. The sand slid down into the bottom of the hourglass. Frank leaned forward and peered out the porthole. Ambiguous emotions collided within him. What he viewed was the auditorium of the Zachary Scott Kleberg Theater and the seats he had played to for the past three nights, albeit now empty. Plenty of light shone onto the theater from above.

"Nothing happened," he said aloud. "Dammit!"

Then he realized that Bess, Dexter and Sonder had again vanished. So had the set of cymbals and the trashcan lids they were supposed to be banging. Frank became aware that the box had grown palpably colder. He placed the key and chain over his neck and yanked his left glove on.

"Maybe it takes time," he said. He switched on his flashlight and consulted his wristwatch. Only thirty seconds had elapsed. He waited another thirty seconds and peered around the limits of the porthole. The theater was devoid of humanity.

"Nothing ventured," Frank told himself. He reached for the pivot ring and turned it. The door opened. He stepped out onto the stage.

The box remained behind him. He looked left and right, into the deserted wings. The rest of the house was just as vacant.

"Hello?" he called out, not too loudly. He noted that his exhalation turned to an opaque fog in the frigid air.

Frank dared three more steps, up close to the stage apron. He pivoted in a clockwise direction and flinched.

A man stood between the right wing upstage curtain legs. He was engrossed in some activity back near the wall, oblivious of Frank's presence.

"Hey!" Frank called out.

The man turned with surprise. He was an old coot, with at least seventy years etched into his chassis. He toted a huge belly that concealed his belt. He was mostly bald on top, and what hair he had stood out on the sides in white shocks. His complexion was profoundly pale. Under his dark, unbuttoned vest he wore a white shirt. The cuffs of his size forty-four trousers drooped over canvas espadrilles.

Frank did not recognize him as one of the theater's regular employees.

"What's your name?" Frank asked with force. He realized that his voice sounded strangely weak.

The man came forward several steps. He opened his mouth to speak. His lips moved. But no sound came out. He tried again, to no avail.

The old man began to walk toward Frank with purpose. The look in his eyes was wild. He raised his arms straight forward and his fingers curved into talons.

Frank retreated a step and then realized he was at the edge of the stage.

"Hold it right there!" Frank dug into one of the anorak's outer pockets and brandished his knife. "Stay back! I'll stab you if you come closer!" he threatened.

The man did not seem deterred in the slightest. He continued without success to try to speak. His hands remained thrust out in a predatory manner.

Frank swung the flashlight up and thumbed it on. Its beam struck the old man full in the face.

Finally, a noise issued from the apparition. It sounded more like the creaking of ancient door hinges than a human voice. He drew his hands back, covering his eyes. Then he turned his back on the harsh beam.

The stage became black. The old man vanished as if he had dropped through a trap door. Frank peered into the stage right wing space and could see nothing. He pivoted counterclockwise. The proscenium had vanished. The orchestra seats and the walls of the house were gone. The ceiling ceased to be. Under his feet, the boards of the stage had been replaced by absolutely blackness.

Frank reeled. His right foot went backward for balance. He expected to fall into the theater pit. He found solid ground beneath him, in spite of the fact that he could not see it. He scudded his left foot forward. Again, he found unyielding footing. About seven paces away, the coffin stood atop apparent nothingness.

Frank turned a full circle. No sun, no moon, no stars he thought. And then the words total eclipse came unbidden into his head. He wondered the reason as he took baby steps back to the box over the invisible, flat surface. Then it came to him. They were the words of an aria he had heard at Rutgers University. The Douglass College chapel, actually. The sister school of Rutgers, back when he was in one of the last all-male classes at the University. His girlfriend, Sandy, had dragged him to the recital, and he had actually enjoyed it. He had managed by force of will not to think about Sandy for several weeks, but free association had pulled her image along behind the song. He felt as if a gauze bandage had been yanked off a bad wound not scabbed over.

In spite of the daunting cold, Frank dug into his jacket for the compass. He shone the flashlight on it and walked in a tight circle. The compass was not following a magnetic pole. The needle swung and swayed as if it had a mind of its own. Frank concentrated on the red arrow and willed it to find north. He discovered he had no power over it.

Frank tucked the compass away and zipped his coat up tight under his chin. He glanced at his watch. Almost five minutes had elapsed.

"Hello!" he called out, as loudly as he could. He had hoped to hear an echo but realized that the sound was swallowed up by the nothingness.

Frank reached into a pocket for the clear plastic candy cane tube that Sonder had filled with white dice. The dice were intended to provide the same kind of trail that the breadcrumbs had for Hansel and Gretel. The tube's end resisted the efforts of his gloved fingers. When it popped open, he lost his grip. The twenty-four dice tumbled out and down. They landed on the invisible black surface, spreading as they would on a street. He shone the flashlight beam back and forth among them.

"I'll be damned!" he exclaimed, and then instantly realized the possible irony of his words. Every die lay with one dot facing up.

Frank knelt to pick up the nearer of the dice. His glove brushed the blackness beneath them, and he could feel the incredible cold of the invisible surface. He bent again and again, until all the dice had been retrieved. He fitted them back into the container.

With emboldened steps, Frank paced off the short distance back to the dark box. He walked around it once in a tight circle. When he had completed a full circuit he spiraled outward, turning the beam back to the dark cabinet every few paces. Standing where he judged to be about fifty feet from the metal coffin it began to blend into its inky surroundings in spite of his powerful flashlight beam. He retreated to it, took out his second flashlight, laid it on the lip of the open coffin floor with the beam facing out and stepped back. In spite of being low, the flashlight cast a long, powerful beam. Frank turned once again and scanned the void. He thought he saw the gray shape of a large house at about four hundred feet, reflected in the farthest reach of the flashlight's illumination.

Frank consulted his watch. According to its hands, he had now been in the box's thrall for nine minutes. He skated over the smooth, invisible ground to the front of the box. He opened its cover and shone the light on the hourglass. He judged that about a sixth of the sand had poured into the bottom chamber. It was, he realized, a true hourglass. His mind filled with the image of the Grim Reaper holding a field scythe in one boney hand and an hourglass in the other. He became convinced that when the last grain of sand fell through the glass neck, he would have overstayed his welcome, and something he did not want to discover would happen to him.

With fifty minutes of sand remaining in the glass, Frank determined to walk up to the mansion and touch it. It now seemed to be closer, standing three hundred feet from the box.

Frank kept his flashlight trained on the large house as he walked with increasing confidence over the uniformly flat, but invisible, ground. His vigorous exercise warmed him somewhat. When he was yet some two hundred feet distant from the large house, he realized that a stretch of railroad track and a crossing banjo signal had materialized at the right corner of his vision. He swung his head left, so as not to be surprised by a sudden appearance from that flank. He saw, as if emerging from a fog, a shoeless and ragged man, with a beard down to his belt loops and wild, uncut hair standing out all around his head. The man was chasing a goat. The closer the goat came, the more the space beneath it materialized into dirt road.

Frank heard the sound of a steam locomotive approaching, from the direction of the railroad track. The banjo signal came to life, causing Frank to jump.

The goat was almost to him. It was a male but rather young, so that its horns did not look too dangerous. Frank tried to reach out and touch the animal's fur, but it dodged aside at the last instant. The hairy man abandoned his pursuit of the goat and riveted his attention on Frank. His mouth opened as if he wished to speak. From it issued a low, creaking moan, like a wooden yacht rolling atop a wave. His hands came up, in the same talon shape he had seen with the burned man and the stage worker.

Frank swung the flashlight beam directly into the hairy man's eyes. At the same moment, Frank blinked. When he opened his eyes a fraction of a second later, the hairy man had turned his back and folded into a tucked position. The train was now clearly visible when Frank spun around. Moreover, somehow the track had slipped directly under him without his feeling any movement. His feet rested atop ballast, in between crossties. The headlamp of the locomotive was at least as powerful as his torchlight. The banjo signal clanged louder and louder. Frank jumped backward.

The track had once again moved under his feet. The train was now no more than the length of a football field from him. He decided to jump this time in the direction of the mansion. When he landed, the track was farther behind him than the length of his jump. He exhaled a thick, white cloud of relief. Then he saw another man staggering toward the crossing signal. The creature was a caricature of a drunk, dressed in a dirty raincoat, with a two-day growth of whiskers, and clutching a liquor bottle protruding from a badly crumpled brown bag. He was clearly on a collision course with the locomotive. Frank heard the engine's whistle shrieking out a warning to the man, and yet the drunk stumbled forward.

"Hey!" Frank cried out. "You!"

The drunk looked up at Frank. His eyes went wide in surprise.

Frank pointed down the track. The drunk turned his head. He flinched at the sight of the barreling locomotive. One of his feet retreated too far. He fell down onto his side and lay staring at the enormous driving wheels of the outdated articulated steam engine as it roared by. The coal tender came next, followed by eleven freight cars and a caboose. All the while, the drunk's head pivoted back and forth as he tried to focus on each car. Frank felt the rumble of the ground beneath him, the rush of disturbed air. When the train had passed, the drunk came to his feet with great effort.

The banjo signal stopped. The track vanished. The drunk stood looking where they had been. He studied Frank for a long time. Frank braced himself for another attack. He lifted his torchlight and swung it wildly in the drunk's direction, afraid he would be fallen upon while helpless. He blinked rapidly, as if hoping tears could restore his sight. When he at last registered the flashlight in his grasp, he also saw that the drunken man had disappeared. The hairy man and the goat had vanished as well.

"Curiouser and curiouser," Frank mumbled as he sucked in a large breath – and then regretted it for the flame-like frosting it gave his lungs. He took a quick physical inventory. His feet were almost comfortable, indicating that the battery-operated socks worked and his flashlight shone with indefatigable power. The Vaseline he had applied to his cheeks and chin seemed to give some protection. Nevertheless, he had begun to shiver. In spite of the heavyweight weave of his trousers, his thighs were beginning to tingle as they had when he was a kid and had played out in the snow too long.

No more humans, animals or vehicles approached. He checked his watch and saw with surprise that twenty-two minutes had elapsed. While he could detect no motion due to the absence of location markers, he could swear that the buildings were coming to him as rapidly as he was moving toward them. The mansion had drifted off to his left, but was perhaps fifty feet closer than the last time he had looked at it. He made a snap decision to hurry to the other building behind it. When he reached it, trying not to gasp in the frigid air, he read the words carved into the stone set in the old brick:

Metz Elementary School.

It was clearly a cookie-cutter standard of the thousands of public school structures erected soon after education was guaranteed for every American child up to the age of sixteen. Frank cautiously approached the front doors and reached out his hand. The doors had some substance. He involuntarily laughed at the discovery and pressed his hand hard against the wood. It collapsed inward as if made of sponge. When he jerked his hand back, it restored its shape. Even up close and with the flashlight fixed on it, the doors and jamb looked like perfect duplicates of painted and slightly weathered wood.

Frank pulled the door open. Although it occupied as much space as a real door, it had little weight. He put his gloves on either side and attempted to compress the door as hard as he could, ultimately getting it to no thinner than half its volume. He gingerly stepped into the hallway, hearing only the sounds of his own footsteps. Frank wrinkled his nose at what believed to be the smell of chalk. He shone the light through every windowed classroom doorway as he worked his way deeper into the ghostly structure.

At the fourth door, Frank thought his light caught movement. He peered in and could see nothing. He opened the door, which squeaked authentically. In front of him were four rows of six children's desks, each with a chair behind it. The chalkboards had simple mathematical calculations scribbled upon them. Above were the familiar placards showing the alphabet in block printing and in cursive. The American flag drooped from its skinny pole. It had a pattern of forty-eight stars.

At the front of the room stood the large teacher's desk, with a globe upon it. Frank studied the countries and realized that the globe dated from before the Second World War. He heard a noise and started. It had come from the cloakroom at the back of the class. He listened for a long moment and heard nothing more. He gathered his courage and advanced, light held high, knife unsheathed and ready. He peeked into the cloakroom.

Two little girls huddled on the floor, buried under a pile of coats, scarves and hats, their wide eyes peering out from spy holes. First one, then the other shrieked when Frank's light fell upon them. The stridency of each voice was as it would have been in the real world, but the intensities were halved. Frank retreated into the classroom. He heard the door open. A young woman wearing a plain dress down to her mid-calf, with her hair in a bun, darted into the room.

Frank lifted his light. The woman closed her eyes and backed out of the door into the hall. Frank followed a moment later. When he passed through the doorway, he swung his light left and right. The woman could not possibly have run out of the hallway in such little time, but she was not to be seen.

"Whoever you are," Frank called out, "please come back!" Even in the confines of the hallway, his voice had no echo. "I won't hurt you. I want to know who you are. If you can't talk, you can write on the blackboard. Hello?"

Frank suddenly felt extremely cold and enervated. He walked out of the schoolhouse with long strides. The mansion was now uncomfortably close to the coffin. From a different side of the cabinet loomed another building, the design of which was bureaucratic in nature. The two large structures seemed to be drifting toward the cabinet like great icebergs drawn to a doomed steamship. Frank feared what might happen and lengthened his stride as much as possible. He thought about running, but did not believe his muscles or lungs could endure more exertion.

Huffing and puffing, Frank lifted his wristwatch in front of his flashlight. He realized in a panic that the light beam had turned from a blue-white to yellow. He saw that forty-nine minutes had elapsed. He tried to redouble his pace, but found that he was instead slowing. He had only fifty feet left to traverse, and yet it was like climbing the final fifty feet to the summit of a Himalayan peak. His body felt drained. Finally, he stood before the cabinet. He snatched up the second flashlight, which had also begun to fail. Just before he turned it off, he caught sight of two more separate figures, that of a man and a woman, converging on the box from opposite directions. The man was fully clothed, but dripping wet. The woman's clothing dated from the turn of the century. They both regarded him with forlorn expressions. Their hands came up, in pleading gestures.

Frank backed into the box, closed the door and turned the key counterclockwise.

Sonder approached the apron of the stage with two folding chairs. Bess paced back and forth in front of the cabinet, still holding the cymbals. Dexter had his right hand pressed firmly against the cabinet, feeling for telltale vibrations.

The three froze at the sound of the locking mechanism turning inside the box's cover. The door opened. Frank stepped out.

"Did you miss me?" he asked.

The group stared at him as if he were insane.

"What?" he asked, shivering slightly.

"You look like Nanook of the North," Dexter managed. "You're covered with frost."

Frank opened his mouth to respond. Before he could, his legs buckled. He crumpled to the floor. Bess cried out. Sonder and Dex rushed in to lift their leader. Bess recovered and quickly fetched a folding chair.

"You lunatic!" Bess scolded.

"I had five minutes to spare," Frank defended. "The hourglass and my watch said fifty-five minutes."

Dexter held his watch in front of Frank's eyes. "According to our minds and this watch, you were only in there for fifty-five seconds."

Frank tried to raise his arm to show his watch. He felt as if it had been anesthetized.

Dexter helped him. "Damn, he's right! The two watches are off by fifty-four minutes and a few seconds. Time goes by sixty times faster where you just went."

"What are you feeling?" Bess worried.

"Very cold and a little light-headed," Frank admitted. While his team rubbed his arms and legs to stimulate circulation, he related what happened in such minute detail and answered so many questions that the retelling required nearly half an hour.

"Einstein would love this. It's another dimension, with its own time," Sonder decided.

"It's another plane," Dexter corrected.

"It's something much more specific," Bess declared. Shortly before Frank had stepped into the box, the manager of the theater had entered the auditorium, satisfied himself that Spiegel, Master Illusionist and Company, were at work, and had ducked back out. "Nobody move; nobody take any more wild guesses until I return!" She hopped off the apron of the stage, jogged up the aisle, and disappeared into the foyer. Two minutes later, she reappeared with the manager in tow.

"Mr. Hutchinson, tell my friends what you just told me."

The middle-aged man in the cheap suit shrugged good-naturedly. "When I was just a kid and first working here, we had a stage manager by the name of Tom. Old Tom we all called him. He had been around since way before the big war."

"What did he look like?" Bess prompted.

"Heavy. Had real jowls. You know…double chin, maybe triple. Big belly. Bald on top with white hair on the side that he hardly ever had cut."

"Did he wear a vest sometimes?" Frank asked.

"Sometimes?" Mr. Hutchinson smiled. "All the time. I'll bet you're asking because somebody here saw him," he said matter-of-factly.

Three heads rocked back as one.

"Actually, I did," Frank admitted.

The theater manager nodded several times. "You're not the first. Although it's been maybe ten years. He died back in 1961. Had a fatal heart attack right back there." He pointed to the right wing stage door. "Only a couple days after that, doors began opening and closing. Props vanished from the prop tables and then mysteriously came back. Lighting levels went up and down by themselves. Some actors said he stole their belongings, but I think that was other actors." Mr. Hutchinson waggled a finger at Frank. "Very few people have ever seen Old Tom. You're the third, I believe. You really must have some magic power."

"I've acquired it recently," Frank said.

"Well, don't be afraid of Tom. He's never hurt anyone. What's with the Eskimo clothing?" the manager asked.

"Oh. Part of the new illusion."

"I hope it's a good one," he said, as he sauntered away, looking over his shoulder to where Old Tom had died.

"Everybody's a critic," Sonder shot back, not bothering to keep his voice down. "As if you've seen better than Spiegel."

"I have, Sonny," the man parried, without turning around. "I have indeed."

Sonder opened his mouth to hurl a few choice words, but Dexter clamped his large hand over the soundman's lips. "Let it go, man."

"He'll be whistling a different tune in a few weeks," Frank said from his slumped position on the chair, his chin resting on his chest. "He'll be bragging he had us in his theater."

Bess crossed to Frank and poked him hard in the shoulder. "What does that mean? Are you actually thinking of using this regularly in the act?"

"Hell, yes!" Frank replied.

"Not Hell, Frank," Bess said softly. "Limbo. Or maybe purgatory. You heard that guy: You met a ghost."

For a moment, everyone stared at each other.

Sonder snapped his fingers. His eyes lit up. "I bet that others you saw were ghosts as well! I'll bet the first guy died in an oil well explosion."

"I know you've read books on this sort of thing even though you didn't used to believe, Frank," said Bess, kneeling in front of him. Her voice went from conversational to concerned. "Are you sure you're okay?"

Frank straightened up. "I'm fine."

"What's the most popular opinion about the existence of ghosts?" Bess asked him.

"They're people who weren't ready to leave Earth."

"Generally people who refuse to believe they're dead, right?" Bess delved.

Frank nodded. "The unwilling dead. Frequently victims of accidents. Like they're crossing the street and are hit by a car."

"Or a train," Sonder added.

"Not just accidents," Dexter joined in. "I read that the Gettysburg battlefield is thick with ghosts. Guys who were sure they'd survive the battle who were hit in the head or heart by a bullet and just dropped down."

Bess sat on another folding chair she had set across from Frank. "They can't stay on Earth, because they lost their bodies. So they're

84

trapped in nowhere."

"But there were three dimensions," Frank said. "There was the oil well, the piping, the truck. And today there was the theater, a mansion, railroad tracks, a school."

"As long as the dead people were there," Dexter noted. "When they left, so did the objects around them. They must drag the place they died around with them like a crab does a shell. It's a big, empty astral plane with them wandering around in it, disconnected."

"Somebody or something guides it," Frank said. "Otherwise, why did the dice all land the same way?"

"Dead people to the left and right," said Sonder. "Shit. Did you love haunted house rides when you were a kid?"

Bess pushed herself up so fast from her chair that it folded backward and landed on the wooden stage with a resounding crash. "We have no right to be fooling with this."

Frank wagged his forefinger at her. "If you could, you'd love us to set this coffin up in the Desert Inn on the ninth floor. You'd love to know if Howard Hughes was your dream or a ghost. Tell the truth!"

"The truth is that children who play with fire get burned," she said, slightly annoyed, lightly kicking the bottom of Frank's shoe.

"Children who never learn to harness fire go cold and hungry," Frank replied. He nodded over his stage assistant's shoulder at the upright coffin. "That will soon be in the show."

SIX

OCTOBER 28, 1976

WORD HAD GOTTEN out that Spiegel, Master of Illusions, was creating a new trick on the stage of the Zachary Scott Kleberg Theater. Curious heads kept popping through the rear auditorium doors, until Frank finally lowered the main curtain.

Alexander Voloshin returned from a pay phone outside the building. The look on his face was one of annoyance.

"They don't want to sell us the coffin handles," he reported. "They say people have built coffins in their garages and basements and buried their dead themselves. They don't want to be involved in lawsuits."

Frank sighed. "I give up. We'll have to wait until we get to New York and talk to a casket company with balls. Pardon my French, Bess."

Bess rolled her eyes, long since inured to the men's language.

"I can't get the right hoisting gear out here in the hinterlands either," Sonic said. "So why not wait until we get back to New York to work on it?"

"Because we're losing precious time," Frank answered. "If we have to wait to hoist it, so be it. But I want my part in this illusion perfected by then."

Bess laid her delicate hand lightly on Frank's shoulder. "I've been thinking a lot about this, Frank. This is a really big thing. Bigger than

us. We should turn it over to religious men or scientists...
somewhere."

Sonder threw up his hands. "If we're gonna do that, we better do
it right away. Let's forget about Simon Magus and the sahib in the
turban for the moment. If the box is now truly ours, we can't use it
to create the perfect impossible illusion for a time, build up our
reputation, and later let the world know the magic is real and we did
nothing. People would be so pissed at us that we'd be washed up
forever."

Frank shook his head vigorously. "Would they? And who's to say
the box will work for anyone else? That magic shop appeared for us.
I believe if a priest or scientist stepped inside, even with one of the
keys, nothing would happen."

"You want to bet your future on it?" Sonder asked.

"Maybe. The future remains to be seen," Frank replied. It was
one of his favorite responses, particularly in its ability to stop debates
in their tracks. "And besides, who in this world is pre-qualified to
walk among the unwilling dead? As far as I know, nobody has more
experience than I do."

"As far as you know," Bess said.

"This is kismet, friends," Frank barreled over her comment. "It's
our destiny. I'll understand if you don't want to work with me, but —"

Bess cut in, "Do you know that when you went into that coffin
the last time, I was looking through the peephole? For an instant, I
could see right through you! Do you think that's a good thing to do
to your body?"

Frank was spared from replying by Dexter's return from running
errands. Among his tasks was the scaring up of two Mars lights, the
variety of rotating, intense beams used on police and emergency
vehicles.

"Get everything we needed?" Sonder asked.

"And more." The team's driver had visited an Austin bookstore
and picked up a thin volume titled *Ghosts of Austin*. He began by

reading the chapter on the ghost of Zachary Scott Kleberg Theater. While Old Tom's activities were detailed, the book did not name the specific man.

"Because nobody ever saw him clear, see? Mostly just what he was doing," Dexter said. "Okay, just a second. You'll love the stuff about your hairy man."

It seemed that dozens of witnesses had seen the semi-transparent figure of the hirsute man and the goat he perpetually chased. So prevalent was the telling of these sightings that the local government had changed the name of the rural road from Hairy Man to Harry Mann, at the demand of property owners who could not unload their homes.

"What about a guy hit by a steam locomotive?" Frank asked.

Dexter shook his head, even as he held the book up in front of Frank. "No railroad crossing ghost. Is this the mansion you saw?"

"That's the one."

"We can walk over to it later. It's the Governor's Mansion. A small bedroom on the second floor is haunted by a boy, nineteen. The nephew of Governor Pendleton Murrah. He shot himself in the head right there in 1864."

"Why?" Bess asked.

"It says, 'A niece of the governor's wife refused to give him her hand in marriage.' The haunting began almost immediately. The servants refused to enter the room because of the moaning. No matter how hot the weather, it was always ice cold. It says, 'Following the Civil War, then-Governor A. J. Hamilton had the room sealed. It was not reopened until 1925. The room has since maintained normal temperature. However, from time to time and particularly on Sundays...the day the boy committed suicide...sobbing noises can still be heard.'"

"Well, he's evidently still in there," said Frank, "and he doesn't move. The mansion came toward me...or I suppose toward the light on the box, actually...but I saw nothing of him. He's an old ghost. Maybe he's running out of energy and can't leave the mansion. What about the Metz Elementary School?"

Dexter consulted the index. "Nothing. It could have been the little girls or the teacher. Or both."

The members of the team looked from one to another.

"So, the geography in this other plane is roughly the same as the place where our box is," Frank posited, "but it's somewhat skewed."

"Skewed to the ghosts of the area," Dexter supplied.

"And their power, apparently. Some can only produce rough terrain; another can reproduce a schoolhouse so I could barely tell it wasn't real."

"You know, most haunted places around the world are described as being cold," Bess interjected, latching onto the subject with a speed that surprised Frank. He noted with relief that instead of the stormy, knit-browed scowl she had been wearing for days, her eyes were now bright and excited. Something said had suddenly engaged her. "Where the disturbed spirits live is definitely cold," she went on. "Either the cold invades our dimension along with the ghosts when they cross back, or else the spirits are sucking heat from our side to use for energy. Fascinating."

"Here's another photo," said Dexter. He held it up in front of Frank. "Is this the other building that moved toward you?"

"Exactly," Frank replied.

"It's the Old Music Building at the University of Texas. Up the hill behind the government complex. Actually, what's haunted is the Jessen Auditorium inside the building. Some guy named Dallis Franz is the spirit. He was a pianist and professor."

"How long ago did he die?"

"Not that far back. A few years. There are about twenty more stories in this book. Did you see a phantom wagon driven by a cowboy?" Dexter looked up at Frank, who shook his head. "Another theater ghost haunts the Capitol City Playhouse. There's one in the Driskell Hotel. Another in the Littlefield House." Dexter held up the photograph of the place.

Frank shrugged. "The man and woman walking toward me might have come from those places or have never been seen or detected in this world. Anybody have a pen or pencil?"

Sonder raised his hand.

"Pass it to Dexter. Bess had a fascinating theory about the cold," he praised, to seal her participation. "Let's write it down along with some other things we've learned. Write it on the inside cover so we don't lose it, Dex."

In the ensuing minutes, the group came up with numerous conjectures, based on Frank's trips inside the cabinet and the reports from the book on local ghosts. The first was that not every former human being who was caught in the dimension had manifested itself in the normal world. More than a few were unable or unwilling to break through from their current plane into their old one. The second was that not every so-called haunting reported was necessarily a true one. And yet, productive as humanity was at inventing ghosts and hauntings, the combined Lubbock and Dallas encounters proved that there had to be thousands of disturbed dead trapped in the plane all around the world. The third was that time and space operated differently in what they all, for the sake of convenience and a common terminology, began to call "limbo." The energy of the place seemed to be generated almost solely by the spirits themselves. The world had little heat. It also had no light except that around the dead. Light beyond what they created was so rare that it attracted them like moths to a flame. Then, when they got too close, its unaccustomed intensity drove them back and frightened them.

Limbo's physicality was evidently created by those residing in it, most likely as resurrected by their memories. Wood could look as solid as wood did in the world of the living, but it was clearly not wood to Frank's touch. Because they were constructs of the mind rather than things of mass, train tracks, locomotives and buildings could all move as easily as the creatures who conjured them. All of it converged on him or the box for a reason. Many of the dead wished something of Frank, if only to understand what he was.

"Do you think they know they're dead?" Bess asked the group.

"If they did, wouldn't they move on, to Heaven, Hell or Oblivion?" Frank countered.

"Not if they're stuck there," Bess argued. "Let's say for awhile they don't realize they're dead. Their will to live is so strong that they constantly create what looks like the real world around them. But then, over time, they do realize, and they want out. They might be hoping you're some kind of angel, sent to lead them to paradise through the box." She looked at the troupe's other two assistants. "They think Frank and his light might be the key."

"I like it!" Sonder enthused. "'Head toward the light'!"

"You said 'over time'," Frank pointed out. "That's the catch. I'm not sure they have any time as we know it. They're stuck in a constantly cycling loop where they never stop to wonder why the world isn't bigger, or brighter, or peopled with strangers they've never met. I don't know if any of them ever move on to another plane, but it's clear that some of them have been there a long time."

"Except not too long," Bess added. "Maybe two hundred years. You saw no Native Americans in traditional costume or conquistador Spaniards. The fallen Spartans who were reported in ancient scrolls to have haunted Thermopylae are no longer seen. Ghosts in Roman tunics are never spoken of today. Maybe the energy they take with them from this world only lasts so long. They eventually wink out, like flashlights."

"And then where do they go?" Dexter asked.

"Maybe nowhere," Bess replied. "Maybe there's nothing left to go anywhere. I don't know. The whole thing makes my head ache."

"If only they could talk," Dexter said.

"Perhaps they can," said Frank. "But not to me."

"All this speculation is just parenthetical," Bess said.

Sonder rocked back in his seat. "Wow. What's that mean?"

Bess stood and stretched. "A waste of time and an idle diversion from our main purpose. Creating an impossible illusion is all you want us to think about, right, Frank?"

Frank had known Elizabeth Coleman too long to fall easily into her verbal traps. He paused and considered the ramifications of various replies.

"Isn't it, Frank?" Bess demanded.

"We live in this world," Frank answered. "Our success in this world is extremely important to all of us." He pointed to the stolid, black box. "I'd like to make so much money with that thing as the centerpiece of a great show that, within a couple years, none of us will ever have to work again."

Bess nodded somberly. "And become famous in the bargain. Pragmatic answer. Then since that's our goal, why don't you bring a crossword puzzle into the box next time? Turn the key after five seconds and stay inside for twenty minutes. Open the door and venture outside only for as long as you need to change. Maybe three minutes. We keep our side of the door open no longer than twenty-five seconds. Once we close it, you can return to this world safe and sound and sit in the box for the last twenty seconds of mumbo-jumbo. Limit your risks with the unknown, Frank."

Frank rocked back on his chair. "I do have to open the door to have enough room to change and to refresh the air. We know the box is airtight. Your suggestion sounds reasonable."

"Are we absolutely sure it's airtight?" Sonder asked. He left his chair before anyone could debate him and went over to the upended sarcophagus.

"Does that mean you'll listen to me?" Bess asked Frank.

"I'll listen," he promised.

Bess approached the coffin slowly, her hands firmly on her hips. A pair of high-powered Klieg lamps shone down with full intensity on the front of the box from a ceiling opening above the audience. "Good. Because it's one thing to enter this thing dressed like Nanook of the North; it's another to step inside in formal clothing, like you're about to take a stroll on the Easter Pa–." She bent slightly, cocking her head to one side, staring hard at the surface of the sarcophagus door.

"What?" Frank asked her.

"These carvings. I think they've changed."

"How can that be?" Dexter asked.

"Magic," Bess reminded him. She touched one section. "I think this looks like me."

Frank came up by her side. "In a dress right down to your toes. And you're holding hands with a man in a suit."

"You and the guy look like the figures we made by folding paper many times and cutting out shapes with a scissors," Sonder added. "I don't see me."

"Are you kidding?" scoffed Dexter. "You're the guy holding up a bottle in each hand. Booze bottles."

"No way," Sonder replied. "But that is definitely you with the book in your hand. So this one must be Frank, standing next to this miniature of the sarcophagus. What's this all about?" He looked from one member of the troupe to the next, but no one offered an explanation. He shrugged. "Creepy. At least it knows who its owners are."

"Maybe it's saying it now owns us," Frank said softly.

Sonder opened the door and went down on one knee. "I wonder if it's changed on the inside, too. Guys. Something important."

The trio crowded close to Sonder's kneeling figure.

"The first time we opened this monster, Frank found twelve glowing circles. Green circles."

Three heads bent closer.

"And now...?" Frank said.

"Now only ten of them are glowing. Frank used the box twice to enter Limbo. Twelve minus two is ten."

Dexter looked at Frank. "Did you ever hear the story of the magic pencil that its user wore down to a nub? Then the magic ran out."

SEVEN

OCTOBER 30, 1976

THE MANAGEMENT OF the Kleberg Theater had decided to award two ten-dollar prizes at each of the Halloween weekend performances for the best and scariest costumes. The Friday crowd had proven something of a disappointment, but Frank had been in the business long enough to know the psychology of audiences. Unless they were purely kids, teenagers or college students, Friday night audiences were inevitably more staid and low key. They were formed of adults who went out more frequently than Saturday night, but who were nevertheless exhausted by the week's labors. The group had been appreciative, but neither big applauders nor laughers – and certainly not big-time costume wearers.

The Saturday night crowd was different. More than half the audience wore costumes. At times, Frank had difficulty concentrating on his patter as he looked down on a pair of unblinking eyes behind a Richard Nixon mask or a serious expression under clown makeup and above an enormous polka-dot bowtie. Every so often, he burst into laughter and asked the employee working the spotlight to shine it on one whimsical outfit or another. During the second act he flirted for a moment with the idea of inviting both the front and back ends of a horse up to the stage but decided against it.

Frank arrived at the point in the act with the spirit Pffft and the smoking tricks.

Sonic changed the lighting and potted up his eerie compilation of sounds and music. Bess walked onstage with the café table and carefully placed it where the other table had been.

"My lovely assistant is not the only one with supernatural powers," Frank recited. "I have in my employ a spirit. He's a bit mischievous, but often he can be coaxed to cooperate. He loves it when an audience calls his name. It's..." Frank made the Bronx raspberry cheer sound. The audience laughed and wholeheartedly launched into a collective tongue-vibrating ghost summoning.

"Pffft loves to smoke," Frank said. "He tells me where he lives now he smokes all the time. But he also enjoys an occasional cigarette. He thinks the rule of not smoking in theaters is absurd, and he'd like to invite a member of the audience up here to help him break the rule. Who among you after ninety minutes in this place is dying for a deep drag?"

An impressive gray-haired-and-bearded figure sat in the shadows of the far stage-left first row. He was dressed in an expensive butternut-grey general's outfit that looked more like Civil War re-enactor gear than Halloween costume. His immediate neighbor was a huge, shaven-headed man dressed in leotards and a leopard skin who had a dumbbell resting at his feet. The soldier jumped up without raising his hand and being invited and was to the first of the side-stage steps before Frank noticed him. Frank registered that he stood a couple of inches over six feet tall.

"Charge!" the man cried out.

"Whoa! Is this General Pickett?" Frank asked.

The man marched into the stage light with his sword scabbard clanking at his side. "No, sir. I am Robert E. Lee. And, as you can see, the South has risen!"

The audience reacted appreciatively.

Frank's eyes narrowed. He could not see through the wig, fake whiskers, or make-up to perceive if the man looked like trouble or not. He hesitated for a moment and almost immediately regretted his inaction.

"I didn't know you smoked, General."

"That's because you're a Yankee."

The audience guffawed and cheered.

"Smoking and beards don't mix too well," Frank counseled, heeding the alarm bells clanging inside his head. "Perhaps you might serve as an eagle-eyed observer, and I will call another –"

The volunteer smoothed down his beard. "I'll be fine, sir."

His reply drew applause. Frank knew the show's inertia would be damaged and the audience energy level would be sapped if he insisted on another participant. He had been swiftly blindsided.

"I understand that this theater also harbors a spirit," the uninvited guest declared loudly. "Perhaps you could recruit it for your act as well."

"No, thanks," Frank replied. "I've already got one Pffft in the grave."

The audience howled with laughter. Frank's quick wit had momentarily regained him the upper hand.

Bess, who was ever alert to the dangers of using audience members, had rushed onstage and offered a cigarette from the pack of Marlboros before the house's reaction died down. She gave the man a toothy smile and, through barely moving lips, said, "Please cooperate."

The general bowed gallantly toward Bess. Rather than put the cigarette between his lips, he held it by the pointer and middle fingers of his left hand.

Frank offered him the matchstick holder. "Take a match, and strike it on the rough side of the cup, please."

"No need for that," the man said. He plucked a matchstick from the metal cup, lifted his boot, and attempted to ignite the match head on his rough heel. He failed.

Frank held the cup high on an outstretched hand. With apparently no movement on his part, the remaining matches sprang two feet in the air.

"I think Pffft is offering you a new match," he said.

Before the audience could react, the cigarette in the volunteer's fingers ignited by itself.

"Never mind," Frank hastened to say. "He's lit the cigarette for you."

The audience applauded almost as enthusiastically as when the trick went perfectly.

Bess had been standing nearby holding the water extinguisher. She took two quick steps forward and put out the cigarette with a stream of water. "Our heroes shouldn't smoke," she said loudly. "It's a bad image for our children." Her aim lifted, and she caught the unruly volunteer momentarily in the face. "Oops. Sorry."

The audience clearly appreciated the business.

Frank shook his head, both as he usually did at this point and because of Bess's impromptu punishment of the general. "Shame on you, Miss Thin-tima! Now we owe General Lee a favor for wetting him. Please fetch Pffft's ice cream glass." Bess had reached the edge of the curtain by the time he finished his last words and immediately returned holding the large sundae glass.

"Even though a Southern president's wife introduced it in our country, I don't eat ice cream," the figure of General Lee declared.

"Do you spend hard coin?" Frank rejoined. He held up the prop. "This is a regular drugstore sundae glass, is it not?"

"What's a drugstore?" Jessup returned, drawing a few laughs.

"Does it appear solid?" Frank drove on, even as he calculated how to get the man off the stage with a minimum of disruption to the act.

"It does indeed," the general said, looking suddenly serious.

Frank set the glass down upon the center of the table, first knocking on the wood to show that it was solid. "Now might you have on your person a coin?"

"Let's see." He dug into his trouser pocket and emerged with several coins. He held up a penny. "This one's no good. It has a profile of Abe Lincoln on it. What about this one with George Washington of Virginia?"

"Perfect. A twenty-five cent piece." Frank dropped the quarter into the glass. It struck the bottom and rang brightly. "Ask Pffft any three questions that can be answered with a simple yes or no. Two jumps of the quarter means yes; one means no."

"Very well. Will I and my brave troops prevail in the War against Northern Aggression?"

The quarter jumped once. The audience moaned in sympathy.

"Will Mr. Lincoln reach old age?"

The quarter sounded only once again. The theater was still.

"Will he at least have an automobile named after him?"

The coin jumped twice. The audience laughed in relief.

Frank reached into the glass. "Thank you, General Lee. You don't favor coins with Mr. Lincoln's portrait. But what about a coin featuring Miss Liberty? I believe Pffft has changed your quarter into a silver dollar." Frank held up the visibly larger coin.

As the audience applauded roundly, Frank turned his back on them to offer the man the coin. "Thanks, dumb ass," he said softly. The epithet was his father's favorite, although in the German version: Dumm Esel."

The man smiled as if he had been complimented, accepted the coin, took a deep bow for his efforts, and began his walk back to his seat.

Frank swept out his hand to usher the man away. "Ladies and gentlemen, since he was General Lee on good behavior, please show this volunteer our appreciation."

The audience patted out merely polite applause as the man took his seat, clearly sympathizing with the trouble he had given the illusionist.

The second act resumed smoothly. By the time Dexter and the white mechanical horse had disappeared, the audience was well satisfied.

Frank led Bess forward with graceful steps. He retreated to allow her solo moment. Before he could produce his usual dozen red roses for her, the man dressed as General Lee had reached under his seat, stood, and thrown his own dozen yellow blooms of hybrid teas at her feet. Frank elected to leave his flowers hidden. Bess curtsied low and scooped up the roses, nodding at the man. One by one she threw them into the audience, pointedly declining to toss any in the giver's direction. Bess rushed from the stage, leaving Frank alone. He wiped his forehead with a handkerchief drawn from his outside jacket pocket. He found with dramatic surprise that it was tied to no fewer than twenty other colored handkerchiefs. The audience applauded more vociferously. Frank stepped back three paces. He blew many kisses into the dark house, winked down at those close by as if he knew and adored them, and finally bowed low, pressing his hands together as if in prayer.

The stage went black for two seconds. The lights flashed back up full. Spiegel, Master of Illusion disappeared.

Frank and Bess had been assigned what once had served as a chorus dressing room in the theater, its halves separated only by a well-worn Japanese screen. Both had changed into their street clothes and were cleaning off the last of their make-up in front of bulb-circled mirrors.

"Seven hundred eighty-three in the bag," Frank intoned. He had a tradition of proclaiming the number that his professional appearances had climbed to after each performance was completed.

"Seven hundred eighty three. That's about how old I feel tonight," Bess remarked.

"Nonsense. You're like *She* from that H. Rider Haggard novel," Frank said. "Eternally youthful."

Bess tossed a wad of soiled paper towels into the wastebasket next to the screen. "Would that it were true, you smooth talker. By the way, you handled that wise ass in the general's outfit quite well."

"Quite well, indeed." The answering voice came from the opening main door of the dressing room.

Frank turned in his seat and found himself looking at the very man of whom Bess spoke. He had doffed his wig and beard and wore a wool topcoat over his costume. His braid-decorated hat was in his hands. He was a good-looking man, with wavy black hair going to gray.

"I was indeed a dumb ass and a wise ass," he continued, using an upbeat tone. "Isn't it interesting how opposite terms can be used to express the same meaning?"

"You know, it's customary to knock before entering a dressing room. What can we do for you?" Frank asked in a cold voice. He noted the massive figure of the circus strong man standing just behind the general.

"Actually, you should ask me what I can do for you. My name is Harlan Jessup." He paused as if he expected recognition. Not receiving any, he continued. "I apologize profusely for my bad behavior tonight. However, I believe that actions speak louder than words. I'd like to make amends by inviting you and your assistants out for dinner and some fun. I'd also like a chance to explain why I went out of my way to act like a wise dumb ass. What do you say?"

Interestingly, would-be rebel general Harlan Jessup's car was a stretch Lincoln Continental. Jessup and Frank had worked out a complex itinerary, whereby Frank and Bess would accompany the intriguing man back to his home while he changed. The strong man strongman, who Jessup introduced only as 'the Colonel,' had street clothing in the car's trunk and would change inside the theater and then guide Dexter and Sonder in the bus to their rendezvous point.

"You work well with a live audience, Mr. Spiegel," Jessup judged from the wheel of the limousine. "So well that I had to throw a couple of wrenches into your act, to learn just how good you are.

You have a quick wit. That reply about 'one foot in the grave' was masterly."

"Is ruining shows a hobby of yours, Mr. Jessup?" Bess bristled, coming to her boss's defense.

The man laughed lightly. "Harlan, please. No, I'm usually well behaved. But if you were buying a sports car, Miss Coleman, wouldn't you feel the need to take it out on a superhighway and stress the engine a bit?"

"Our show is not for sale," Frank said, as he shot Elizabeth a nonplused look.

"Is your show open to the notion of capital investment?" Jessup asked.

Bess leaned forward. "You invest in show business acts?"

"This would be my first."

"What do you do for a living, Mr. Jessup?"

"Many things. Real estate, banking, leveraged buyouts, mergers and acquisitions, restructures, futures. I invest medium piles of cash in anything that promises large piles."

"And you think we have that promise?"

"Indeed. You're only a few stops from the crest of Money Mountain. You just need somebody to spot you to a few tanks of gas and the right roadmap."

The metaphor was close enough to the self-hyping repertoire Frank used that it effectively captured his attention. Bess looked at Frank with raised eyebrows and an outthrust lower lip.

"I don't hear you saying no," Jessup noted. "We're almost to my little place. We'll talk there."

The "little place" was not little but less grand than Frank had imagined. It was a brick townhouse not far from the state capitol complex. Out front, it had a double set of windows on either side of a stately Palladian door. The center-staircase structure rose three stories and ran back forty feet, so that there were four large rooms on each floor. The first story had a formal parlor and dining room toward the street, with a modern and spacious kitchen and pantry in the rear on one side and a library office on the other. The first story ceiling was ten feet high, and in the library the maple bookcases ran right up to it. A wall of glass in the back of the library exposed a beautifully designed and manicured formal garden. Off to one side, two stories high, were built servant rooms in the Charleston townhouse manner. Every bit of the home was impeccably decorated in the Georgian period.

Jessup left the pair of performers in the parlor while he changed upstairs. Bess commented appreciatively about the furnishings to Frank. She pointed out a collection of photographic portraits on the Steinway parlor grand piano. Several were of Jessup standing with businessmen and politicians of national stature. Two young men posing alone they guessed to be sons. Photographs of a wife were conspicuously absent.

The library beckoned through opened French doors. The two decided that the man's collection of books was the most impressive aspect of the home. They lingered in front of the bookcases, staring at titles.

"You can learn a great deal about a person from the books he reads," Jessup said, making his reappearance in slacks, a broadcloth shirt, and a cable-knit sweater, catching Bess and Frank perusing shelves of novels and textbooks.

"Then business and the law are definite passions with you," Bess observed.

Jessup walked over to one of the six bookcases that filled the south wall and squatted.

"But travel and cooking are passions as well." When Jessup stood, he held half a dozen books cradled in his arms. "And here's why I have such interest in your show." He fanned out the books he had selected along the red maple conference table in the center of the room.

Frank and Bess approached the table. They saw that every book was about the creation and performance of magic.

"It's one of my fascinations," Jessup revealed, "although I personally have never performed. I'm someone who can't see a trick without learning how it's done. I knew your show would be in town, but I was away last weekend. You must explain why you have the word 'Illusion' on the side of your bus instead of 'Magic.'"

"Magic does itself," Frank said. "People create illusions. I want the credit for what I do."

"But you don't create illusions, do you?" Jessup asked, with a soft, almost apologetic tone. "My books tell me you perform tricks created by others."

"Variations of standard illusions, but always with my own contributions," Frank defended.

"Nothing completely new?" the older man probed.

"The rainbow illusion you saw is all mine."

"Congratulations. But that's a minor trick in your repertoire, isn't it?"

Frank set down the book he had riffled through. "You're suggesting that our repertoire is not first-class and that you could advance us the money to create the best."

"That's right. Take advantage of all the improvements in technology. Perhaps holograms. Your ability to work a crowd and to deal with them face to face is better than fine. It's your gimmicks that need improving."

"Actually, we're about to add two spectacular new illusions to the act, Mr. Jessup," Frank said.

"Call me Harlan, Frank."

"So thank you but no thank you, Harlan. At least for the moment."

Jessup offered a perfect, toothy smile. He reached into his wallet, pulled out a business card, and handed it to Frank. "Moments have a way of slipping by until they collect into a heap of regrets. Your refusal in no way affects my dinner invitation. If you should happen to change your mind about using backing, call the top phone number. They'll know where to reach me at any time. Spectacular new illusions, you say?"

"Nothing less."

"I would very much like to see them."

Bess shifted her stance so that her hip thrust provocatively to the side. Frank had long ago registered it as one of her power moves. "Then you'd have to come to the New York area, because we're unveiling them there in a few weeks."

Jessup laughed. "No problem. I have a penthouse apartment overlooking the southwest corner of Central Park. I spend about a third of my time in The Big Apple. Well, I'm glad for you and your spectacular new illusions. It's not often people can afford to decline my generosity. Let's go celebrate your future success."

The Broken Spoke, a roadside honky-tonk, is a landmark of Texas's capital city. It resembles a shack on steroids, low but big. The eating area is built around a long dance floor on ground level, with railings fencing much of it. Beyond that and slightly elevated are groups of tables and café chairs and the stations where the BBQ ribs, corn on the cob, baked beans and coleslaw are generously dished out, to be washed down with schooners of unsweetened tea or something harder from the bar.

Bess sat between Frank and Harlan. The Colonel sat at his boss's side. He had changed into black trousers, a black turtleneck sweater, and a loose-fitting, dark charcoal jacket. Alexander and Dexter had chosen seats to the Colonel's left, but at the moment they were up bird-dogging women.

"You're not married, Harlan?" Bess asked.

"Not anymore. Was for thirteen years."

"Divorced or widowed?"

"Divorced."

"Divorce is a national plague and disgrace," Bess declared.

Jessup did not seem embarrassed by her harsh words. "You can look at it like that. Hundreds of years ago, when marriages were arranged, you could easily understand unhappiness. Now the problem seems to be impetuousness. I've come to believe that human beings' brains aren't mature until about twenty-five. Ego prevents them from realizing this. So they rush into marriage. Women have the church wedding and gown images thrown at them left and right, by friends, relatives, celebrity magazines, soap operas, and the marriage industry. The men think they're chasing the women, until the women catch them. It's called the 'Tender Trap', but it's a trap on both sides. The women get so caught up in being queen for a day that they don't stop to consider the kids and their thousand needs, the mortgage, sicknesses, accommodations, the in-laws, their interference and their needs, the familiarity that breeds not only kids but contempt. And then there are the many other interesting members of the opposite sex they'll meet along the way."

Bess recognized a well-rehearsed speech when she heard one. "Is that what happened to you?"

"Actually, Alberta was the one who sued for divorce," Jessup revealed.

Bess nodded slightly in apology.

"Might I call you Elizabeth?" Jessup asked, setting his empty beer bottle down touching hers.

"You may."

The rich man turned to Frank. "Do you mind if I take Elizabeth out on the floor, Frank?"

Frank waved his hand. "That's up to the lady."

"I don't know Texas dancing," Bess said, even as she allowed herself to be guided from her chair.

"The two-step is easy," Harland insisted. "I'll show you how."

Within a minute, Bess was falling gracefully into the gaudy parade. Predictably, she turned male heads. When Frank grew tired of watching them, he looked over to the massive man seated across from him. He had noted that the Colonel was the same height as his employer. However, he weighed perhaps thirty pounds more, and not five of those pounds were fat. He looked to be in his early fifties. His eyes were rather close-set, which added to his dangerous look. He had a square jaw which seemed perpetually set. Frank saw that although the man kept his head shaved almost to the skin he was far from bald. He had two male-pattern darts of pink above his forehead, but the rest of his scalp was dotted with thousands of healthy, dark nubs of hair. At the moment, he had his large arms folded across his chest. His eyes were focused on the establishment's front door.

"Just how rich is Mr. Jessup?" Frank asked.

"Rich enough," came back the answer. Just when Frank thought that would be the extent of the reply, the Colonel added, "He says he's worth twenty million."

"And how long have you known him?"

"Two years, two months, twenty-one days."

"Interesting that you should know so precisely."

The man merely nodded.

"Have you gone to many magic shows with him?"

The Colonel shook his head.

"You protect him?"

"I work for him."

"I see."

The man had yet to lock eyes with Frank. "No, you don't. You couldn't possibly see."

At that moment Dexter and Sonder returned, carrying three bottles of Dos Equis and an ice tea for the sound man.

"So, tell us a little about the Green Berets," Dexter invited the Colonel. "It wasn't like the movie, was it?"

The Colonel accepted the bottle of beer and half downed it in one long, Adam's-apple-bobbing draw. He wiped the back of his hand across his lips. "The Duke is a pussy and the sun don't set in the East." He stood. "I gotta tap a kidney." Having excused himself, the large man walked off to the restroom.

"He looks like the monolith in *2001: A Space Odyssey*," Sonder observed of the black-clothed figure.

"Among scary sons-of-bitches, that one ranks as a colonel," Dexter agreed in a low voice. He bent close to Frank. "Did you notice the shoulder holster under the jacket? He's packing a piece."

Frank nodded. "Jessup's worth twenty million. I guess that merits a bodyguard."

"Jessup's scary in his own way," Sonder decided. "I'm glad we don't need his money."

"But isn't it amazing how things are turning around for us?" Dexter asked his companions. "First the box comes into our hands, literally out of the blue. Then this millionaire shows up, offering to shower us with money."

To Frank it was more than amazing. Cocky as he acted in front of his troupe, he was badly frightened by not only what the box could do but also the unknown reason why it had been offered to them. Not running from the coffin had proven to Frank exactly how desperate he was to climb to the top of his profession. And now, for no apparent reason, a multi-millionaire was offering him money to assure his ascendance. Scary was the word for the turn of events. One complication is enough for now Frank thought.

"Let's keep it as simple as we can; we walk away from Jessup and his beefy bodyguard," Frank told his companions. He looked out to the dance floor. The music had changed to a waltz. Harlan Jessup had his hand lightly on the small of Bess's back. Although he stood about six-foot-two, he danced like he was made of thistle down. Bess's long and lithe figure looked good following him. Frank felt a pang of jealousy.

"Well, at least we got a free meal out of it," Dexter philosophized after a barely concealed belch. "And Bess is getting the kind of attention she deserves, poor thing. Week after week with the three of us. You're her buddy. Sonder and me are like the juvenile delinquent teenagers who came with you. She needs to be treated more like a woman and not like she calls herself: Wendy and the Lost Boys."

"She deserves the best," Frank agreed. "I tell her that almost every day. You two should, too." He loved his parents with a son's unconditional love, despite the problems between them and him. His feelings for Bess had initially been largely lust but had grown over the years to something far deeper and more selfless. Only one other woman owned more of his soul. Her name was Sandra Greenfield. Ever since thinking of her in the coffin's void, she had been drifting in and out of his mind. He decided that his love for her would never die; it could only be tucked with effort into the recesses of his mind. He looked at the couples gliding gracefully over the rough wood dance floor, and he felt the emptiness of his hands. Two roads had definitely diverged, and Sandy's choice had not been his.

Sonder excused himself to engage an apparently unattached young woman.

Not done with the subject of Bess, Dexter shared, "She got a bit nostalgic the other night. She was talking about working on one of the game shows out of New York and how every so often they let her keep some of the stuff the manufacturers were pitching. She said that was how she got the best hair dryer she ever owned. Then this big smile lit up her face and she said, 'That was also the day I met...' And then she caught herself." He quaffed the last of his beer. "That's the most she's ever opened up with me. She plays her cards close to the chest, at least as far as I'm concerned."

"Don't take it personally," Frank said, watching her expertly following Jessup's lead. "She volunteers next to nothing whenever I broach the general topic of relationships." He declined to point out that Dexter was the same way, that all of them in fact 'played it close to the chest.' The subjects of serious love affairs, commitments in the eyes of the law and God, or their breaking were tacitly considered taboo. None of them had ever opened closet doors more than a crack, and no skeletons had ever been exposed.

"It's unnatural," Dexter complained. "I wonder why."

"That's her business."

"Sure it is. But that doesn't mean we can't be curious as hell. She takes the Woman of Mystery stuff to the limit."

"I'm not about to do anything that would make her uncomfortable and rock our tight boat," Frank said, verbalizing his credo concerning all members of the troupe.

"So? She doesn't have to know we're looking. We check up on her private life like the fuzz would: on the QT."

"Don't, Dex," Frank warned.

Dexter trained his annoyed look on another table. "Don't tell me you wouldn't love to hear whatever I found. Do you even know where she grew up?"

"In the Bronx. Near Tremont Avenue. Haskin Street."

Dexter gave out a small guffaw. "I thought you had no interest in her private life."

"That isn't why I know that. She and I are both Catholic, and we've traded war stories about our educations. She went to St. Benedict's up to eighth grade. Then Preston in the Bronx and later to Assisium High in Manhattan. She did some modeling in high school and never bothered with college or trade school."

"And then? What about men…or women for that matter?"

"I have no idea. She talks enough about her father, her sister, and her two nieces."

"That's not the kind of relationships we're talking about." Dexter made a purring sound in his throat.

"Confine your detective interests to novels," Frank advised.

The Colonel returned and eased his considerable mass onto the café chair. He made no attempt to communicate with the other men. Frank and Dexter contented themselves with watching the dancers in silence. After returning with Bess from the waltz, Jessup regaled the group with tales of his travels to Hong Kong, Japan, India and Nepal. It was clear to Frank that he was doing his subtle best to impress Bess while not appearing vulgar. There was no name dropping of famous international personages, no talk of private planes or even top deck staterooms. His obviously well-honed tales were definitely diverting and even, at times, self-effacing. Nevertheless, at 12:50 Bess yawned theatrically and asked her comrades if they were ready to turn in.

"Already?" Jessup moaned. "I thought we'd dance until dawn."

"Not this girl. I work for a living, Harlan."

"And that's a pure shame. A woman like you should have nothing but free time."

Bess stood, and Frank, Dex and Sonder came up around her. "'Idle hands are the Devil's workshop,'" she quoted, grabbing her clutch purse. "I look down my nose at kept women; I wouldn't be one if I could."

Out in the parking lot, Jessup kissed Bess's hand in the continental manner before slipping into the back of the Lincoln limousine. The Colonel drove it away without haste.

"He's got his eyes on you," Dexter said to Bess.

"What would a millionaire want with a washed-up old gal like me?"

"You're a lot better than you think," Sonder said.

Bess curtsied. "Why thank you, you old smoothie!"

"Don't trust him an inch," Sonder lectured, as the dust settled over the parking lot. "That kind thinks he can dazzle with his money, pay for what he wants with a diamond bracelet, and then move on to the next conquest. He wasn't kidding about visiting us in New York. He's not done with you yet."

"And how can you be so sure?" Bess inquired.

Sonic spit his gum into the bushes. "For one thing, because he came to the theater with a dozen roses. He must have seen that picture of Frank and you in the newspaper and decided that a magician's assistant on the road is an easy target. For another, this is the kind of stuff I'd pull if I had piles of money. All men are pigs or dogs, if you haven't already found out. The poor ones are pigs; the rich ones are dogs."

Bess looked at Frank.

Frank shrugged. "The man speaks truth."

Bess cleared her throat. "Well, I'll be on my guard. But a girl must look out for her future. Where will I be left when you kill yourself inside that damned coffin?"

"It's not going to happen," Frank assured. "That 'damned coffin' is going to make us all rich. Three mutts and a blond bitch."

"We'll see," Bess said. "We'll see."

EIGHT

SEVENTY MILES OUT of Austin, just south of Waco, the bus dropped dead. It was nothing simple like an alternator or even mildly disastrous like a blown transmission. All the oil had leaked out of the pan, and the engine block had melted into a solid hunk of metal. Steam had been pouring from under the hood for several minutes across Interstate 35.

"This is effing impossible!" Dexter's strident voice sounded from under the front of the vehicle.

"What happened?" Sonic dared to ask.

"It's a small, triangular hole. Not big, but big enough. It must have been a piece of metal thrown up at the pan, but I don't see how the wheels could have done it. And I sure don't remember seeing or feeling anything large on the highway."

"Why didn't a gauge tell you the engine was overheating?" Frank asked.

"Because the low oil pressure warning on this old piece of shit is just an idiot light. By the time it comes on, it's too late. I never thought to replace it because there's a gauge for the water temperature and that never went above normal."

"Why?"

Dexter pulled himself out into the hard sunlight by laboriously digging the heels of his boots into the asphalt on the highway's shoulder. "Hell if I know. If it goes from the bottom when it's cold to the middle when warm, I assume it will climb when the engine is hot."

"Could you have been concentrating on the road and missed it?" Bess asked.

Dexter's withering glare provided his answer. His professional expertise was not a thing to question.

Frank looked at the long road ahead. "What will it take to fix it, Dex?"

"A whole new engine. You know how long it would take to hunt down this old model's engine, not to mention installing it? I don't have the garage and we don't have the time. The bus ain't worth putting that kind of money into anyway."

Frank kicked the rusty front bumper. "I knew our luck was too good lately. Well, I can't say I didn't get my money's worth out of the old bucket. I got it for a song, and we must have put eighty thousand miles on it."

"Now what?" Sonder asked.

Dexter reached for a rag that the sound and light man held out for him. "We rent a truck, and you and I drive it and our stuff to Memphis. Frank and Bess can take a Greyhound from Waco."

"And then what?" Frank asked. "We'd still need a replacement for Nelly Belle here. There must be used buses for sale in Texas."

An eighteen wheeler roared by at high speed, causing a brief windstorm. When it had passed, Bess said to Frank, "We're back to the discussion we had the other day, when you three wanted to buy your own magic box. We've spent pretty much every free dollar for the new act. For something this big, we need to tap into our mutual savings and start begging friends and relatives."

In response, Frank reached into his back trouser pocket and took out his wallet. He produced Harlan Jessup's business card and held it up for the group to see.

"Oh, man!" Dexter moaned. "Is there any other way?"

"He's not that bad, Dex," Sonder said.

"How do you know? He's got a bodyguard that carries a gun."

Sonder was unruffled. "So does the president, and you can't say Gerald Ford's a bad guy. We've met a few other rich people in our travels. What about tapping one of them?"

"We could ask the Hearst family," Bess said through a smirk, "but they just posted a million and a quarter bail for Patty."

"Thanks, Bess," Sonder said. "You're really helping." He looked past Dex and saw that Frank was climbing over the low wire fence that defined the edge of the Interstate. "Where you goin'?"

Frank pointed to a lone concrete building at the bottom of a decline several hundred feet from the interstate, on a feeder road. The high fence around the property, the large equipment on the grounds, and the repair trucks indicated that it was a power utility sub-station.

"Maybe we should pray for help," Sonder suggested.

"Say what?" Dex rejoined. "You suddenly get religion?"

Sonder knelt and peered under the bus. "Why shouldn't I? Whenever we go somewhere I can walk to church on a Sunday, I'm goin' from now on."

"What church?" Dex asked.

"Any one. Don't matter. They all pray to the same God."

"Has that cabinet given you religion, Sonic?" Bess asked.

Sonder stood and brushed off his hands. "It's given it back to me." He marched past her into the bus.

Bess faced Dexter, who gave her a bemused look. Bess indicated that he should follow her inside the ruined vehicle. They found Sonder sitting in one of the Camaro seats with his hands in his lap, his head down, and his eyes closed.

"Are you praying now?" Bess asked in mild astonishment.

"And what if I am?" he countered, not opening his eyes.

"You told me Vietnam shook any belief in God right out of your head," Dex challenged.

"Wars have been going on since before man could write, and still good men have managed to hold their faith," Alexander answered.

"What kind of god allows the misery in this world?" Dex persisted.

Sonder cocked his head and glared at his friend. "Look, I'm working on faith first. Enlightenment may come later. Maybe your question will always be beyond an answer. But that box proves that there is a creator. One plane of existence might have been a fluke, but two cannot be." He retrained his focus on Bess. "You and Frank are both Catholics, right?"

"Yes."

"But you never go to church."

Bess sat across from Sonder. "I go Christmas and Easter and a couple other times a year."

"How come never while we're on the road?"

"Because we perform every Saturday night and then eat. Unless we're on the road, I'm sleeping Sunday morning."

"What about the weeks we're off?"

"That's vacation."

"God doesn't take vacations," Sonder said.

"How the hell do you know?" Dexter asked in an annoyed voice. "For all you know, he could be in Acapulco right now, working on his tan. Man, there is nothing worse than a convert. Why don't you get this serious about quittin' drink?"

In reply, Alexander tossed his balled-up chewing gum foil at Dexter's face. "I don't have to. I can stop and start that whenever I want. What about you, oh Permanently Tanned One? You have a religious background?"

Dexter flung himself into the driver's seat. He banged on the water temperature gauge repeatedly. "Piece o' shit. My momma's AME."

"What's that?"

"African Methodist Episcopal."

"What about you?"

"She used to drag me to services until I was about thirteen. Didn't your momma drag you?"

Sonder opened his eyes and regarded his companions. "My mother and father worshipped together at the Church of St. Smirnoff. Their idea of religion was taking me around to see the Christmas lights." He smiled ruefully at his own jokes. "Did either of you doubt God exists before last week?"

"I don't see why last week has anything to do with God," Dexter asserted.

Sonder rocked back in his seat. "Come on! That coffin is the front gate to Limbo. You both call it that. There are thousands, maybe millions of dead people on the other side of its lid. How can that not prove God's existence?"

Dexter rolled his eyes. "How can it? Frank didn't see God, Zeus or Buddha. He didn't see angels. He didn't see signs that pointed toward 'Heaven' or 'Hell.' Maybe those folk he saw are the only ones who live on for a time after death. They're just too stubborn or confused to die completely. And when they finally accept the fact or run out of energy, they vanish forever, like everybody else."

Sonder looked at Bess. "Is that what you think?"

"I understand what Dexter's saying, but I just don't know. I used to buy all the dogma along with the ritual when I was a kid. I was very comforted by the incense, the ringing of the bells, the chanting in Latin. God seemed near. But now I don't know, Sonder. When I stopped letting the nuns read to me out of the Bible and picked it up for myself, I saw that Jesus said he had come for the End Times. He believed he would be back soon. But either his timetable isn't ours, or else he was mistaken, too. Maybe he was just a very good man whose mother convinced him he was God because that was the only way to make her illegitimate child legitimate."

"Whoa!" Dexter exclaimed. "That's some theory."

"I guess I'm on a spiritual journey of discovery that's not

116

finished," Bess said.

"But you believe Frank has been telling us the truth about his experiences in the box?" Sonder persisted.

"I do."

"Then why can't there be a heaven and hell as well?"

Bess crossed to the bus windows to look out for Frank. "Why not indeed? But if I lead a good life, according to my conscience, why should I worry until I die?"

Sonder swung around and pointed to the back of the bus. "Because of that damned box, that's why!"

Dexter shook himself, like a dog just in from a heavy rain. "Brrrrr! All I know is we keep telling each other how much better our lives are gonna be soon because of that box, and ever since it came into our lives we've all been jumpy as hell. Now, because of those little green lights, we all agree we can't afford to explore it any more until we actually use it. It's like each of us gets three wishes from the genie and no more, and Frank already used up two of his."

"That's probably a good thing," Sonder said. "I'm scared the thing will swallow up whoever uses it the next time. Between the cold, the darkness, the desperate ghosts and the sand running through that hourglass..."

Bess and Dexter nodded their agreement.

"Frank's back," Bess reported.

Frank loped up the slight hill, hurtled the fence, and came into the bus with a light step.

"All fixed," he announced, although he did not look especially elated. He explained that Harlan Jessup had returned a call to the utility station one minute after Frank dialed the number on the business card and related their situation to an unnamed woman. Jessup had said that, luckily, he was doing little that day and that he would come out to pick them up. He was also happy to lend the money to buy a replacement bus.

"So now we just sit here," Dexter grumbled.

"Unless you want to take a side trip inside the box," Sonder said. No one laughed.

Harlan Jessup's limousine held no more than five persons. It arrived with a black Ford pick-up truck behind it. The Colonel drove the limo; Jessup, dressed in jeans, a Western shirt, Frye boots, and wearing a Stetson, piloted the truck. Following the greetings and thanks, the millionaire invited Frank to drive with him. Jessup got right to business, as he steered back onto the interstate and tromped on the accelerator.

"I've arranged for your bus to be towed to a nearby junkyard. Your man is sure it's beyond repair?"

"He's an auto mechanic by profession," Frank replied.

Jessup pushed the cowboy hat back from his forehead. "Then that's that. I took the liberty of making a call on your behalf before I left the house. I know the agent for the Eagles. You know..." He sang the first line of Desperado in a not-unpleasant voice.

"I like that group," Frank volunteered.

"Me, too. Next time you're in Texas, I'll see that you meet them. Anyway, you know that they're doing very well and touring a lot. I had heard that Don Henley had been shopping for a new bus. Sure enough, the old one is for sale. It sounds like it's perfect for your needs. Has two pair of bunk beds toward the back. Now, three of you can sleep at a time."

"That's an improvement," Frank agreed.

"This is no school bus. It's a for-real touring machine. It has a slew of other amenities as well," Harlan added. "The agent says it has a huge eagle airbrushed on each side, but that's easily fixed."

"And the price?" Frank asked.

"I think reasonable." Jessup quoted a figure. "But I'm sure I can talk him down a little for a guaranteed quick sale. We can probably have you on the road by Thursday. How many dates do you miss?"

Frank folded his arms and listened to the growl of the big truck engine. "Maybe none if we can start early Thursday morning. We're scheduled for Little Rock that night, Memphis that weekend and Nashville and Knoxville the week after. Then we have off until right after Thanksgiving."

"What a grind," Jessup judged. "Better you than me."

"It comes with the job," Frank replied.

"Not if you hit it big. Then you can stay in big cities and run for a solid week. The public will drive distances to you." Jessup leaned on the horn. "Come on, asshole!"

Jessup had long since moved into the fast lane and showed no sign of relinquishing it. He had already overtaken three vehicles. The first moved out of his way on its own. The second responded to Jessup's flashing lights and tailgating. The driver of the third, another pick-up truck, had ignored the signals. Jessup laid on the horn again. The other driver tossed him the finger in his rearview mirror. Although the lead pick-up was doing seventy-five, Jessup mashed his foot to the floor and passed on the right as if the owner was Sunday driving. To make his displeasure manifest, he swerved back into the fast lane less than a truck-length from the passed vehicle, whose driver now laid on his horn.

"Y'all like speed in Texas," Frank remarked, approximating a Texas accent.

"We're the biggest state in the Union, including Alaska, which is Rhode Island under all that ice. I've got too much to do, even on my day off, to be loping along at sixty," the driver declared, glancing into his rearview mirror. "There goes his finger again. Someday somebody's gonna blow that nasty digit off. So, you go to your parents' for Thanksgiving?"

Frank tried to calculate the last time he had shared Thanksgiving dinner with his parents. It was in the late Sixties. "Probably not."

Jessup raised an eyebrow. "Don't tell me the four of you spend your time off together as well."

"Sometimes. Sonic's heading alone for Miami Beach. His folks are a pair of alchies."

"Too bad. Why do you call him 'Sonic'?"

"He got the nickname in Vietnam. He pronounces his first name the Russian way: Alek-zondr and calls himself 'Sonder.' Some guy in the USO thought he said 'Sonic.' Since he's a sound man, it stuck."

"Weird," Jessup said. "And what about the colored guy's family?"

"It's just his mother, sister and nephew. The mother used to hold down several jobs, but she's retired now. The sister is a beautician. Dexter usually picks up more work short haul driving."

"Your group sounds more like a three-ring circus than a magic act."

Frank felt his stomach tighten. "I told you: I do illusions, not magic."

"You told me two times. The first time from the stage. That's a mistake," Jessup pronounced. "Because the public wants magic. What you do isn't much different from musical theater. The audience knows that people don't suddenly stop in real life and begin singing their feelings in neatly rhymed sentences. But they willingly suspend their disbelief. They want to do that with you. In my opinion, you steal their fun by insisting that they understand what you do isn't magic."

"Why should I give magic the credit for something I've worked so hard to perfect?" Frank defended.

"Because your public doesn't give a damn about that. Think less about your point of view and more about theirs. They don't care that a violinist has practiced two thousand hours so he can play the *Flight of the Bumblebee*. They just want to enjoy it." Jessup reached out and jabbed Frank's thigh with his forefinger. It was more than a tap, a physically uncomfortable punctuation that could not be ignored. "Now, just because I'm willing to lend you money doesn't mean I want to make sweeping changes to what you do. In fact, I have no intention of it. If most of your act wasn't real good already, you wouldn't be sitting there. But I have to protect my investment, so I will insist on a few changes. The first is that you give up the word 'illusions.' From now on, it's magic."

Frank thought of the sarcophagus sitting in the back of the ruined bus and what it did. He reflected that every famous person or pair in his profession either used the word "magic" or else merely used their names. What the would-be benefactor asked was not that much.

"All right," Frank relented. "What else?"

"Lose the bad puns."

"People laugh at my puns," Frank defended.

"I didn't say all the puns. Just the bad ones. No more Thin-tima. That's the worst."

"What else?"

"Why don't I write them down? There's less than half a dozen. When I catch your new act in New York, maybe I'll have more."

"And what's the total damage for borrowing from you?" Frank asked.

"Twenty percent interest a year; everything paid off within three years."

Frank watched Jessup's profile to see if there was room to negotiate. The man stared straight ahead and gave him nothing. "That's really steep," he countered.

Jessup explained about the considerable risks of investing in something as intangible as a magic act, where almost no collateral existed if Frank were suddenly struck by a meteor. He offered a terse lesson in venture capitalism and finished with the words, "You can always get a more reasonable loan rate from a bank once you're on top. Then pay me off. No penalties for prepayment."

"If my show is such a credit risk, tell me again why you're investing in it," Frank invited.

"I believe in you."

"Dexter and Alexander think it's because you're chasing Elizabeth," Frank stated. He harbored the same suspicions, but decided it was more political to stay the good guy and let his assistants take all the blame.

Jessup's laughter seemed overloud to Frank. "I won't bother to deny that I like Elizabeth, but I don't really know her, do I? You tell Dexter and Alexander that I have far too many women throwing themselves at me to have to lay out thousands of dollars on the off chance your assistant might fall for me."

Frank had no response. He stared out at the Texas sky. It was a bright, warm blue, completely the opposite of the frightening blackness that dominated the world inside the sarcophagus. He shivered involuntarily. Jessup noticed.

"Are you catching a cold?"

"No. I don't know what it is."

The temperature outside was mild, but Jessup turned on the truck's heater without being asked.

"How long have Dexter and...what do you call him...Sonic... been with you?" he asked. Frank told him, and the financier nodded. "And what's with Sonic drinking only iced tea?"

"He's three-quarters Russian and a quarter American Indian," Frank revealed. "It doesn't mix well with alcohol."

"He ever get drunk during tours?"

Frank decided to tell the truth, since he was not sure Jessup would believe a lie. "Twice. But he sobered up enough to hit all his cues for the performances. And that was in his first year with me. Since then he's been totally dependable."

"How many performances do you give a year?" Jessup asked, as he looked into the rearview mirror.

Frank turned and looked back. Straight as the highway ran, the limousine could not be seen. The Colonel evidently did not share his employer's lead foot. "A hundred and ten. A hundred and fifteen at the outside."

"I know what you charge for a performance," the money man revealed. "Don't get upset. Checking is normal. We call it due

122

diligence." His eyes blinked as he did a quick calculation. "No wonder you haven't been able to afford the best equipment. That's a lot of days of downtime. Too much outlay in between performances. You can't be paying your people that well. I need to invest in a stable team."

"They're very loyal," Frank asserted. "They share my dream. They'll stick with me at least through next year, unless something really unexpected happens."

"Like what?"

Frank was beginning to chaff at the interrogation. "I can't think of anything."

"I can. But you're right about the loyalty. I read it at the Broken Spoke. How does Elizabeth fit into the team?"

"What do you mean?"

"Does she go home to somebody during breaks, or is she a full-time member of Spiegel's circus?"

"She has a family. Her mother died when she was a teenager, but her father's alive. She usually stays with her sister during down times. The sister is younger and has two kids. Ten and twelve. Bess baby sits so Eileen and her husband can do things. Take little vacations and so forth."

"Bess," Jessup said, as if savoring the sound of the word.

"She's Bess only to her close friends," Frank said, protectively.

"I'll remember that," said the man at the wheel. A few moments later, he began humming something familiar to Frank. It was a song that Sandy had had on a classical recording. Gershwin, he believed.

NINE

NOVEMBER 25, 1976

THE HOUSING DEVELOPMENT Franklin Spiegel had grown up in had looked so much bigger when he was a child. The Edison, New Jersey streets were more than wide enough for pick-up touch football games or six-player baseball then. Now they seemed like alleys. He credited some of the change to his perspective from the towering tour bus driver's seat. He realized that the trees between the curbs and sidewalk that had been saplings when he was eight were now fully mature. Their leaf-barren limbs stretched like cathedral fan vaulting over the road.

Frank took his foot off the big metal accelerator pedal and let the tour bus coast purely on momentum as he neared his house. He was glad that Dexter did most of the driving; the monster machine was intimidating. The neighborhood had filled up with second and third cars parked in the street, requiring him to maneuver carefully along the center. He saw with relief ample room directly in front of his parents' house. He pulled forward as much as he could, but the tail end still blocked the driveway.

"Good," he muttered softly. "They won't be able to escape."

Frank felt his heart pummeling his ribs as he opened the bus doors and stepped down. His father, Helmut, had been raking leaves in the backyard and had come around the house to see what had been rumbling and releasing compressed air out front. He stopped near the blue spruce, which had grown into a giant and needed three guy wires to keep it from falling over. Frank had inherited his father's male-pattern baldness, and the old man's gleaming dome with the wreath of silver hair beneath it made him look a decade older than Frank had remembered him. He leaned on the rake and allowed his son to come to him.

"Happy Thanksgiving," Frank said, walking as slowly as he could up the dead-leaf-dappled lawn. He held a boxed apple strudel in his left hand.

Helmut nodded his reply. His eyes fixed on the bus. "Vat is zis mit de eagle?" he asked. In spite of having lived in the country for twenty-five years, he still had a heavy accent. Articles, prepositions and other short, common words came out in German.

He's willing to talk at least Frank thought with relief. "Oh, I just bought the bus from a famous country rock group. The Eagles."

"I never heard of zem."

"That's okay. Is Mom inside?"

"Yah." Helmut had yet to move or release his hands from the rake. Frank noted that the split-level behind him had gotten aluminum siding but needed a new roof.

"Are you celebrating Thanksgiving at home?"

"Yah, zat's right."

Frank shifted his weight to his opposite foot. "You want some help raking?"

"No. Go inside and see your mother."

He's letting me inside. Frank felt a sudden warmth suffuse his chest.

"I will. Thanks."

Elsa Spiegel allowed herself a few tears and her son a brief hug before she accepted the strudel and asked, "What did your father say?"

"Not much. You married him, Mom; you know how he is."

"Yes, yes," she said hurriedly, setting down the present. "We have not even a turkey. Just a chicken, since it's only the two of us."

"If you don't have enough…"

"What? Are you crazy? We eat in ten minutes."

The lines in his mother's face had etched deeper in the several years since he had seen her. He noted for the first time the prominent veins and liver spots on the backs of her hands and the loss of color in her cheeks. Only her voice was untouched by time. She kept her arms at her sides, as if afraid they might spring up to hug him again. She labored a large smile.

"You don't bring a girlfriend?"

"No. I've been too busy working. I'm doing well."

"That's good, good!" his mother said with enthusiasm.

"No, very well, Mom. Come here!" He tugged her out of the kitchen, down the steps to the recreation room and the big bay window. He pointed proudly to the bus.

"You drive a bus now?"

Frank laughed. "No. I'm still a…a magician. I told you on the phone last year that I have three assistants."

"Yes. I remember"

"And now I have a new act, and it's going to make me rich and famous. I bought this big bus for touring."

Elsa studied her son's eyes. "Okay," she said. "Good. I must see to the carrots."

Frank followed her back into the kitchen. As she lifted the pot lid and peered through the steam, he asked, "Have you heard anything from Gretchen?"

Elsa's eyes stole toward the stairs. She shook her head.

"How long has it been?" he wanted to know.

"Almost a year. The last time she came asking for money, your father would give her none. She stole some of my jewelry."

Margaretha, called 'Greta' or 'Gretchen' by her parents, was the cross borne by the Spiegel family. Every time they called her by any of the three names, she corrected them and insisted that she was

'Maggie.' Frank had once struggled to think of one happy moment associated with her or one kind thing she had done for him. He was devastated and yet not surprised when he failed. She was three years older than he. When he was little, she had had no use for him and acted like he was invisible. When she was eleven and twelve and forced to baby sit him, she invented ingenious mental and physical tortures. As soon as she reached thirteen she latched onto the Beatnik movement. She elided seamlessly into a Flower Child and then a Hippie as the counterculture shifted its streambed. She worshipped Lenny Bruce, Timothy Leary, Silvia Plath, Janis Joplin, Jimi Hendrix and anyone else clearly on the path of self-destruction. Cigarettes were followed by alcohol. Within three months of her starting, the Spiegels' meager liquor cabinet with decade-old bottles of opened whiskey, rum, rye and schnapps had been emptied. Marijuana escalated into hashish and then cocaine and heroin. Frank suspected that she had experienced sex at fourteen. When he discovered her needle tracks, she told him she gave blood often. By age seventeen, she had run away from home three times. She never finished high school. When battling with her father, she would mock his accent and call him an "old Nazi." She loved to quote Robert Frost's line from *The Death of the Hired Man*: "Home is the place where, when you have to go there, they have to take you in."

The Spiegels had paid for several types of counseling and two stints at methodone clinics. They had sent her away to a wilderness retreat in Idaho. Nothing had worked.

She's probably dead Frank thought. But she's still here. A ghost of their minds. He pictured her in Limbo, searching for her next fix. The image chilled his spine.

When they at last sat down at the dining room table, Helmut invited his son to say a prayer of thanks.

"For what we are about to receive, let us be truly thankful. In Jesus's name, Amen," Frank recited.

"It's good to hear you haf not forgotten your religion," his father commented, as he took both legs and a generous helping of white meat from the meat platter before passing it to his wife.

"Frank is doing very well as a magician now," Elsa reported brightly. "What do you think of his bus?"

"Vat is 'doing very vell' anyway?" Helmut asked. "Is it thirty thousand dollars a year?"

"It will be much more than that next year," Frank said firmly, accepting the platter from his mother. "I could help you replace your roof next spring."

His father grunted.

Elsa stole her second sidelong glance at the dining table's empty fourth chair.

"Have you looked for her?" Frank asked his father.

The old man took his time chewing what was in his mouth. "Vy should I? I spent a fortune already. I could haf retired by now venn instead I had invested that money. Now ve are finally doing 'very vell' ourselves, Franklin. I haf four veeks of vacation. The union protects my job and gets me excellent raises. Next summer, your mother and I can finally visit de old country and see de relatives."

"That's good, Dad," Frank said, meaning it. He was glad to hear that his sister was not killing them.

"If you're becoming so rich, you should look for your sister," Helmut stated suddenly. "Zat vould be a good zing to do mit your money."

"I don't think so," Frank returned.

Helmut reached for the dish of steaming carrots. "Never mind a new roof. It vould be a good present to us after all your years of neglecting us," he said, without looking at his son. "A good present to make up for your share of our disappointments."

Frank lifted the napkin from his lap and set it on the table.

Elsa reached out to her son. "Please, Frank! He doesn't mean it."

Frank stood. "Yes, he does. I've stayed long enough."

His mother rose from her seat.

"Elsa, sit!" Helmut said, in a soft but hissing voice.

"Thanks for inviting me inside, Dad," Frank said. The split-level was not large. He needed but two steps to stand at the top of the steps. He turned. "I'll call you, Mom," he said, and then descended as briskly as his dignity allowed.

After Dexter stepped out of the rented car he leaned against it, watching the church's jazz band playing *When the Saints Go Marchin'* In in dirge time. His sister Sharlene had to retrace her steps from the cemetery roadway and take him by the hand.

"Nobody but you is blaming you, Dexter," she assured him.

Dexter's eyes were bloodshot from tears and then pent-up tears. His large chest heaved from choking back emotion. "She never lived to see it."

"See what?" Sharlene said, as she captured her little boy with her free hand.

Dexter self-consciously adjusted his silk regimental tie. "Real comfort. Real security."

"She had everything she needed," his sister insisted. "Come on."

Still, Dexter hung back. He turned toward a statue of a weeping cherub that sat on the corner of an ornate grave marker.

"At least I can show her how much I loved her one last time," he said. "I'm gonna get her a stone angel. A life-size stone angel to watch over her."

He looked to Sharlene for a reply, but her mouth was rigidly set. She pivoted toward the open hole with the coffin poised above it and dragged her brother and son resolutely toward it.

TEN

DECEMBER 1, 1976

PHILADELPHIA'S ACADEMY OF Music is both venerable and busy. Opened in 1857, it is most associated as the home of the world-famous Philadelphia Symphony Orchestra. Its parquet, balcony, family circle and amphitheater levels together hold more than 2,900 people. Like New York's Carnegie Hall, it hosts an eclectic variety of events, including orchestras, solo recitals, chamber groups, load-in opera companies and ballets, rock, folk, and pop stars. More than any other personal engagement of 1976, the booking signified to Frank that he was on the verge of "arriving." It was not that the venue had reached out to book him; the management accepted virtually any legitimate enterprise that could pay their hefty fee for hosting a performance. Rather, as a backyard city from his home, Philadelphia had been kind to Frank in the past few years. His growing reputation in the area finally allowed him to draw the numbers to at least break even on the evening.

Allan Salkin had not been happy to book such a large, expensive theater, but he understood the cachet associated with being able to include the house on the season promotional brochure. From Memphis, Frank had transmitted to his agent his excitement and confidence concerning the new act and, in particular, the "Egyptian coffin." He used every ounce of his verbal skills on the telephone to hype the professional hype artist and to compel him to flog the daylights out of the Philadelphia premier of Spiegel/Master of the Impossible. By the time the first day of December had arrived, no fewer than eight theater reviewers, from as far south as Wilmington, west to Harrisburg, and north to Princeton, had agreed to attend the event and witness what promised to prove the act's new name. Salkin had also worked with the Philadelphia Diocese and the public school system, as well as a local magic club and two give-away radio stations to 'paper the house.' Last-minute radio interviews had been arranged. Dexter spent several hours the two days prior to the performance driving the newly-repainted bus around the City of Brotherly Love. Nevertheless, the expected attendance was only 2,050. Frank knew well the psychology of theatrical auditoriums. Audience members picked up their clues from each other as to what degree they should be enjoying a performance. If a house was less than two-thirds filled, the first clue of empty seats already depressed the attendees. Then the lack of bodies in a large house prevented the kind of responsive noise that would fortify itself. At three-quarters filled, a house of attendees could experience total enjoyment. A totally filled house rarely exited unhappy. The simple answer at the Academy of Music was to close the two, "nose-bleed section" upper tiers and force the audience together.

As the hands crept up to eight o'clock on Frank's watch, he stole a peek from the corner of the house curtain and satisfied himself that the requisite number of people was indeed there. He was rewarded with not only the sight of them but also an energetic chatter that only came with feverish anticipation. Somewhere out in the house sat his agent. Salkin had called Frank that afternoon to say that he was so excited about developments that he could not bear to wait until the troupe's arrival in Newark to catch the new act. Frank was certain that his arrival by train was to protect his own reputation and to do damage control if necessary.

On the road, the group had settled on calling the act they had built around the sarcophagus "King Karnak's Coffin." The shape of the cabinet and the bas-relief figures on its lid naturally begged for such a name. The deciding factor, however, was Frank's need for protection against the cold. For a time they had dabbled with a background story using Alaska, Klondike gold and mukluks with a hood fur coat. Finally, Bess had hit on an Egyptologist's pith helmet, loose-fitting safari coat, jodhpurs and knee-length boots. As if providing a mystic signal that the solution was the right one, Sonic had happened in a second-hand shop upon a pith helmet with a small miner's headlamp. The sound and light man had also had no trouble wrangling from a casket-making company the handles and other fittings required to hoist the cabinet into the air. After one dry-run rehearsal on the Saturday afternoon following Thanksgiving, they were as ready as they could be to create a public sensation.

Act One ran flawlessly. Because it no longer needed to be the biggest sensation of the evening, 'Don Quixote de la Mancha' had been moved to the close of the first half. It produced its usual thunderous applause, but this time the audience was left wondering what could possibly top it. Frank allowed the intermission to run a full twenty minutes, to increase the anticipation and buzz.

They began Act Two with a classic illusion Frank had improved on, called 'Desdemona and the Orange Tree' Bess and Dexter took costumed roles, as the tragic wife and the jealous Moor made famous by Shakespeare. Since Sonder was at too great a distance working the expansive lighting and sound boards in league with a union professional, a temporary actor with magic show experience had been called in to play the bit part of Iago and to pull ropes. In spite of the long intermission, the showy trick brought the audience energy right back up. 'Gold Fishing' had a delightful new fillip suggested by Dexter, whereby Frank somehow caught a Piranha among the ornamental fish and managed to be bitten. The little ichthyic monster was placed in a separate bowl, and the larger one with three goldfish was presented to an adorable girl with pigtails. The Floating Glass Ball was too successful to abandon, as was Lifting Lady Lakshmi, the former Thin-tima. Capitalizing on Bess's popularity with the audience, the Vanishing Vase was dropped in favor of a large rotating disc to which she was strapped. Above her, but with her head and feet still in plain view, was affixed a circular wall of white paper. Frank was blindfolded, an audience member affirmed that Frank could not see, the disc was set spinning, and the magician proceeded to throw a dozen knives through the paper into the disc all around the revolving Bess. When Frank whisked away the paper cover, the Disc of Death was shown to be bristling with a dozen knives, some within inches of his assistant. The audience reaction was every bit as good as Frank had anticipated. He understood that if his show was to play to houses with more than a dozen rows, the use of real playing cards, coins, ropes, and the like became increasing counterproductive due to their small size. Big houses required big presentations. The new show was scrupulously faithful to this need. If a trick required small objects, Frank made sure to include one or more audience participants as surrogates for those seated in the back, so that everyone might be assured the trick was intimately mystifying.

Pffft was also too valuable an element of the show to drop. In order to extend the act, Frank incorporated a trick designed at least three-quarters of a century before. He had devised a variation on the Horn of Plenty. The horn provided half a dozen members of the audience with paper flowers, candy, and toys, but, halfway through, the volunteers were allowed to see that the cornucopia was being resupplied from behind Frank's back. At that point, he took off his swallowtail coat and managed to produce twice as many gifts from the apparently empty horn. As always, his interviewing of the volunteers and the badinage with the quick ones produced nearly as much delight to the audience in general as the tricks.

At last, the time for King Karnak's Coffin had arrived. Cloaked in evocative light and sound, dressed in diaphanous, form-fitting silk, and wearing a golden crown and black wig reminiscent of Anne Baxter's most seductive costume in *The Ten Commandments*, Bess took center stage. She weaved the exotic tale of the discovery of the king's coffin and the terrible curse that accompanied it: Whoever opened the sarcophagus would be drawn into the ancient king's world. Only the most intrepid of explorers would ever be able to escape.

Still dressed in his Moorish outfit, Dexter pushed the coffin on from stage right. It rested horizontally upon a rolling mechanism that many had seen being used to move coffins from funeral homes into hearses. A collective murmur rose from the audience. Bess invited four large males from the front rows onto the stage. With much business, she first instructed them in bringing the heavy cabinet upright. Using a microphone, she had each participant affirm the weight of the box. They explored the box with their hands and eyes and assured themselves there were no false walls. She guided each of them to play a part in threading the chains that descended from the stage fly space through the coffin handles. Large locks were provided to secure the chains. She instructed the four to take up places at the four corners of the box. Only then did Frank emerge from stage right wearing his explorer's outfit. While he spoke, Bess placed an open, specially-fashioned, three-step steel ladder in front of the coffin. The coffin was elevated two feet off the stage floor. Frank invited the volunteers to test if the floor was indeed solid beneath it. Frank then shoved the ladder's top step under the bottom of the sarcophagus until it was lodged securely. While Frank made final preparations, Bess climbed up and used her golden key to unlock the lid. She stepped down and away. Unobtrusively, she pushed back the gauze sleeve of her Egyptian costume so that she could study the sweep hand of her wristwatch.

"I now risk a journey into eternity," Frank called out. "Only the famous magic words 'Open Sesame' can possibly bring me back. Please...do not forget them!"

The volunteers were instructed by Bess to brace their corners to keep the coffin from twisting.

"To ancient Egypt!" Frank cried out as he backed into the coffin and closed the lid.

Frank twisted his key in the lock and heard the familiar meshing of tumblers. He listened for the telltale hiss of sand through the hourglass, inhaled deeply to test for the first hint of invading cold. He resisted the temptation to look out the glass porthole and concentrated instead on solving the riddle of devising yet one more illusion that would make his show the most difficult ticket to get for the next few years. If, as everyone in the troupe suspected, the coffin allowed only twelve trips in total, it would need to be replaced by something almost as spectacular in rapid order. He liked Harlan Jessup's notion of using holograms. He had heard that Disney was about to incorporate them into their Haunted Mansion attraction. But he could not envision how a three-dimensional image could be made effective to people who were confined to theater seats.

The box was like a sensory deprivation chamber to Frank. No sights or sounds, tastes or smells distracted him. He thought about holograms for as long as he could, but nothing novel came to him. He snapped on his miner's helmet light and consulted the time. He still had twenty minutes to kill. His increased breath rate told him that he needed to open the door soon and refresh the air. He peered through the porthole glass and saw only blackness.

As tropical and lightweight as his outfit looked, it had been well designed for cold. The widening of the jodhpurs was packed with fibrous material that trapped warmth. His boots, one size too large, had not only a layer of fleece inside but also room for his battery-operated thermal socks. Under the crown of the pith helmet was a pair of furry earflaps that folded down. The jacket had a thin, quilted under layer, but it also hid a gossamer caftan of many colors, gloves, a flexible gold-plated mask, and the crook and flail that symbolized the ancient kingship over the Upper and Lower Nile. The coffin was so confining that Frank could not possibly have made the change inside it, but the disparity in the passage of time between Limbo and the world of the living was so great that he had more than enough opportunity to accomplish his transformation outside.

Frank tugged on the gloves. He consulted his watch once more. He began to whistle the triumphant theme from a new movie called Rocky that Bess had dragged him to just before Thanksgiving. He had been pleasantly surprised to learn that it took place in Philadelphia, and that the city was the venue for an underdog to make his mark in the world. He thought that perhaps when this night was over and the reviews were in, he, too, would stand on the steps of the Museum of Art and dance around with his arms upraised.

The dark circle of glass at eyelevel beckoned to Frank. He leaned forward. Two men dressed in Revolutionary militia outfits and carrying muskets strolled by carrying a lighted lantern. They seemed unable to discern the near-black sarcophagus from the surrounding darkness. He registered the bayonet hanging from the belt of the one nearer him and shivered. He wondered if any of the spirits he had and would encounter could harm him and what, if anything, he could do to defend himself.

At last, twenty-five minutes passed. Frank opened the coffin door. He squatted and consulted the circle of lights. Nine remained lit. Next, he made sure the hourglass and his watch roughly agreed. Only then did he peer around the coffin, into the inky, featureless expanse. The cold attacked him like a ravenous wolf. He peeled off his gloves, unbuttoned his jacket, and unwound the caftan from his torso. Rather than trust the black surface he stood upon, he set his gloves, the mask, the crook and flail on the floor of the box. He buttoned his jacket and slipped the loose-fitting robe around it. Then he placed the helmet carefully in the back of the box, slipped the mask over his face, and took up the crook and flail.

Off at a distance too great for Frank to judge, a lightning storm lit a corner of the void. He wondered what spirit had conjured it and how many times the same storm had flashed around the poor soul.

At twenty-nine minutes after first shutting the lid, Frank stood inside the sealed coffin, changed and ready. He made a last-moment decision to wait until the thirty-seven minute mark, to give Bess an extra two seconds where she was. He realized that his heart was racing. He knew he was reacting to yet another visit into the unknown world, but he realized it was as much due to worry over the audience's reaction. He put himself in their place and frankly would not have known what to think about the empty coffin.

The cold was beginning to get to him. He had barely moved and yet felt weak-kneed. As he closed himself into a tight, shivering huddle, he wondered if his tolerance for Limbo was slipping.

Bess climbed the abbreviated ladder and turned the ring grip on the coffin lid. She backed down the two steps and moved to the side, so that the audience could view the confines of the now-empty box.

A collective gasp seemed to lower the air pressure in the enormous auditorium. A moment later, the two thousand viewers broke into thunderous applause. It rolled on for much longer than Bess had expected as she ducked into the empty space and waved her hands up and down its length. She was acutely aware of the racing seconds. Before the noise had stopped she instructed the four burly men to twist the coffin around so that each could also see the magic. They took their time. Smiling through her panic, she urged them to return the cabinet with lid facing front and to brace it swiftly on the ladder's top platform.

Bess closed the lid with both hands and faced the house.

"Gone!" She paused. A two seconds later, she heard the telltale click of the tumblers that signaled Frank's return from Limbo. Immensely relived, she continued with no hurry, "Gone like the Colossus of Rhodes, the Lighthouse of Egypt, and the Hanging Towers of Babylon." Finishing, she made a gesture that looked to the audience like emphasis but which put her tiny wristwatch in front of her eyes. "Only you can summon Spiegel back through time. Call out with me now, with all your might: Open Sesame!"

The audience's reply shook the walls of the great theater.

Bess grabbed the pivot ring and yanked the door open.

The unmoving figure of a royal Egyptian greeted the theater-goers, a mask of gold topped with the snake and jackal gods covering his face, a floor-length silken robe of many colors shot through with filaments of sparkling gold around his body, his hands folded across his chest with the crook and flail held high. In the high-tension silence, he stepped slowly and majestically out of the box, onto the little ladder, and thence to the stage.

Several dozen in the audience gasped at the unexpected sight.

Bess moved forward and whisked off the mask. Frank Spiegel beamed his best smile at an adoring audience. A roar of delight shook the huge auditorium. The applause went on and on. The men behind him crowded forward to offer their amazement and congratulations. Frank handed Bess his props. With his caftan flowing behind, he advanced to the footlights and took several bows. Then he led Bess forward, where he encouraged her solo bow. The applause grew louder and louder, so that he could not make himself understood to Bess even shouting in her ear. For the first time since he was thirteen and had only his friends and relatives in front of him, his entire audience had risen as one to its feet. He looked out at smiling faces, at couples who confirmed to each other just how much they had enjoyed the evening.

"Encore!" A deep male voice near the back of the parquet seats shouted when the human thunder had finally died back.

"Encore? Where would you like me to go next?" Frank called out good-naturedly.

"Go to hell!" the voice returned.

The audience laughed at the repartee. Inside his safari jacket, Frank shivered.

ELEVEN

December 3, 1976

BY MAGIC, FRANK Spiegel had instantly transformed into Allan Salkin's number one client. Salkin suddenly found time from his perpetually busy schedule to attend the next booking as well, at Trenton's War Memorial Auditorium. Frank had played the theater two years earlier and had attracted just short of 1,000 magic lovers in a fundraiser for the Brothers of Israel. The house seated 1,851 and this time was sold out.

"There are about three-dozen people at the outside box office clamoring for standing room," Salkin crowed. "Brother, what a couple rave reviews and word of mouth can do!"

Frank continued to apply his make-up, letting the old agent rant on and hype himself in the process. The reviews that had made the press so far were more than a couple. Two were indeed absolute raves. Another was an enthusiastic report of the evening, but the reviewer described the tricks as if they had done themselves. The last asserted that "the astonishing King Karnak's Coffin could only have been accomplished if all four men on the stage were accomplices, which is not playing fair with the audience." As far as Frank was concerned, even this negative publicity served to get his name into the public eye.

Salkin glanced at his watch. "Fifteen minutes to places," he announced. "Okay, time for the big news."

Frank set down the sponge and stared into the mirror at the agent. "How much bigger does it get?"

"The Academy of Music wants you back as soon as possible. That's not until right after Easter Sunday. Another one-nighter. But the biggest news is that some people in New York must actually read The Inquirer. Two venues have already inquired about hosting you."

"Which ones?"

"Small potatoes. We can do better. I'm working on it, trust me. How are you feeling?"

"Fine."

Salkin rubbed his hands together, like a greedy banker from a silent film. "Great! And Elizabeth?"

Frank stood. "I was just going to check on her."

"Good idea." Salkin grabbed his greatcoat. "I'm heading into the house before my seat is stolen." He winked at his star client.

Like a shark smelling blood, Frank thought. But it's good to have the shark working for me. He walked across the hallway to Bess's dressing room door and knocked.

"Are you decent?" he asked.

"When was I ever decent?" Bess replied. "But I have my costume on."

Frank entered. She was decent indeed. She had her wealth of golden hair trimmed above her shoulders and temporarily tied back with a black ribbon. The baubles, bangles, and beads of her opening costume scintillated in the bright dressing room light. Bess spun around on her stool. Frank glanced involuntarily upward at the lighting.

"Are you using different make-up?" he asked.

Bess spun back to face the mirror. "I haven't put it on yet. Has this old gal at last lost her English rosebud complexion?"

"You're looking a touch yellow. How are you feeling?"

"Tired."

"I thought so."

"Well, you've been tired lately, too," Bess riposted.

"I have an excuse: the cabinet."

"As in 'of Caligari.'" Bess reached for the Albolene Cream, which she spread into the pores of her cheeks, chin, and forehead. "My excuse is you. I'm still worried."

"But the act is a smash. Stop worrying. You've definitely lost weight," he noted. "I haven't been around you much the past three weeks, but I'll bet you've almost stopped eating. You didn't even have popcorn at the movies."

Bess did not bother to deny his accusation.

"How long has it been since you've had a complete physical?"

"A couple of years," She muttered.

"I want you to make an appointment tomorrow. If you don't have a physician —"

"I can take care of it," Bess said.

"But will you?" Frank persisted.

"Yes, yes." She looked up and smiled, and he saw the Bess he had hired. "Let me be absolutely clear about the change. We're locked in on forty seconds," she said, speaking of the revised timing for the coffin finale.

"I'll aim to turn my key in the inside lock at forty-one seconds on your watch. Plenty of time for you to have shown the box empty and closed the cover."

"So, if I need to drone on to sixty seconds it won't matter," Bess confirmed.

"Correct. Just as long as you call out loudly when you want me to appear. Anybody you know out in the house?" he inquired.

"Not that I'm aware of. What about you?"

Frank shook his head. "But they'll be coming out of the woodwork within a few weeks. People you forgot you knew will somehow find you to beg for tickets."

Bess beamed, stood, and gave Frank a warm embrace. "What a wonderful problem! You've arrived at last."

142

"We've arrived," he corrected. "Couldn't have done it without you, Lady."

Bess pushed back, lowered herself onto the stool, and swiftly returned to applying her make-up. "And you can't do it tonight without me either, so get out and let me finish this before the music starts!"

Amazingly, the first hundred and ten minutes into the evening went even more smoothly than the opening in Philadelphia two days earlier. Frank had long ago noted that athletes who were on a winning streak always seemed more relaxed. He credited the same mindset to himself and his team. When the time came to step into the box and close it, he resigned himself to thirty minutes of standing in the extremely claustrophobic space, seven minutes outside to effect his transformation, and another four to give Bess a cushion. Most of the time he kept his eyes closed and thought about developing new tricks. Twice in the first half-hour he peered out through the porthole but saw nothing. Only when he finally ventured out to change his costume did the world of Limbo become active. This time, instead of setting his helmet with the miner's lamp inside the box, he plopped it on the top, with the beam shining out past his shoulder. When he began rearranging his costume, nothing existed on any side. When he finished, he turned and was confronted with not merely a large building coming at him but an entire hill of structures. The buildings in Austin had approached the box so slowly that he had not been sure at first whether he alone was doing the moving. This apparition fairly rumbled forward. He saw that most of the area was made up of brick townhouses. At the forefront of the advance, however, was a corner building with signage that identified it as the Mill Hill Tavern. The bottom of the image faded into darkness, so that it seemed to float in space perhaps twenty feet above him.

Frank knew the place. He had dined and drunk there two years earlier, on his last professional visit to Trenton. He saw not one human being, spirit or otherwise, but he was sure that some tortured soul had spotted his light and was willing the entire blocks of his or her memory to go to it.

Quivering more with terror than cold, Frank first consulted his watch, then grabbed for the miner's helmet, fitted it to his head, and switched the light off. He still had five minutes to wait before turning the key on the inside lock. The tavern, which was tilting down in his direction, would long before have collided with the cabinet.

It's like I'm trapped in a valley he thought. And then the words he had had to memorize for Sunday school came back to him: Yea, though I walk through the valley of the shadow of death, I will fear no evil.

Cursing, Frank worked his way blindly around to the back of the box. He saw that the buildings had slowed slightly. He guessed that the spirit had been confused by the sudden disappearance of his light. And yet the blocks of houses and shops continued on their path toward him and the box. He thought about tilting the box back upon himself and dragging it away from the softly glowing structures. Then a fear came into his head that if he moved the coffin, when he turned the key in the lock it would not be precisely lined up with its parallel in the world of the living. His body would suddenly appear half inside and half outside the box, divided in two. He wondered if he would remain alive long enough to see the looks of horror on the faces of the audience. He sprinted from the box toward his right. When he was some two hundred feet distant, he switched on the helmet light. The buildings stopped moving for a moment. Then they warped into a left-turn pivot and shifted the direction of their advance. He realized that Limbo had sucked a tremendous amount of energy from him, but the adrenalin of panic had almost compensated. Forcing himself to breathe more slowly through his nostrils, he continued to use the lamp to lure the unseen spirit farther away. When he calculated that another half-minute had passed, he switched off the helmet light and backed around in a loop toward the coffin.

The Mill Hill Tavern had definitely changed direction, but structures farther along the block still lay within feet of the box. Frank opened the door and switched from pith helmet to mask. He realized that he stood upon the flail and crook, but there was no time to claim them. He grabbed the golden key from his pocket, fitted it to the inner lock. His watch told him that only thirty-nine minutes had elapsed, but he dared wait no longer. He closed the coffin lid and turned the key.

Frank listened for long seconds. Through the thick walls he heard at last Bess's voice, followed by the welcome noise of nearly two thousand voices shouting "Open Sesame!" He took a few moments to pocket his key, adjust his mask, kick the gloves and helmet to the back of the box, and open the door.

The audience, which had been murmuring with anticipation, erupted with appreciation.

Frank felt himself falling. With a supreme effort, he caught himself and willed his foot to step carefully onto the ladder.

Bess rushed forward and offered her arm to steady him. Frank drew in a fortifying breath.

"I'm okay," he reassured. "I can take it from here."

Frank whipped off his mask with a flourish and made a slow bow to the audience. The applause rose like a tidal wave. He approached the apron of the stage with the caftan flowing behind him. He bowed again, this time more deeply, feeling a grateful rush of blood to his head, and then gestured for Bess to take her solo bow. He threw a few kisses at his adoring fans as he moved with deliberation to the stage right wing. When he passed the house curtain, he allowed himself to collapse onto the floor.

Dexter was beside him in a moment.

"What happened?"

"Get me back up, Dex," Frank replied. "Quick, before Bess sees!"

A union house man had the main curtain almost lowered.

"Bounce it!" Frank commanded, and then said, "Dex, come out for a bow with me!"

The two men walked out as the curtain rose. Dexter had his right arm under Frank's right armpit as if in a brotherly show of affection but in fact to help support him. Bess had her attention riveted on the house full of people, where only a few raced up the aisles and the rest lingered to make sure that the performers who had given them such a show got their due measure of applause.

"Encore!" a deep, male voice called from the back of the house.

Frank was convinced it was the same person who had shouted the word at the Academy of Music.

"Where would you like me to go next?" Frank obliged.

"Go to hell!" the voice shouted back.

Some of the audience laughed, but more turned toward the voice and booed and hissed.

"You first!" Frank called out with bravado, eliciting a special burst of applause. He allowed the reaction to carry him into the masking wing, where he remained in spite of persistent clapping. A sudden suspicion of who the owner of the voice was sent an icy shock shooting through him. He was very glad he had not been moving when the thought came to him.

"What was it this time, Frank?" Bess demanded, as the pair walked toward their dressing rooms.

"A couple buildings came too close to the box," he replied. "I had lure them away at high speed. That really drained me."

"Good grief!"

Frank stopped. "It was a freak occurrence. Somebody must have died badly only a couple blocks from here."

"This is so dangerous," Bess fretted. "You can't control Limbo. Every time we move to another theater, the world outside the box changes."

"It's the price for fame and fortune," Frank said, in as calm a voice as he could muster. "You only have to worry eight more times."

"Eight big chances for it to swallow you whole," she warned.

Frank pushed his forefinger against her lips and then hugged her. "Just because you're right doesn't mean you should keep warning me. It's the price of glory, Bess, and it's still not too high. I say it's not too high, and I'm the one inside the box."

"I can't help worrying about you," Bess said in a small voice.

Frank set his forehead against hers. "I know. And I love you, too. All I can say is I'm being as careful as I can. Let's deep six this discussion once and for all, okay?"

"Okay. Do you have enough strength to eat?"

"I think I can lift a fork. Anyplace but the Mill Hill Tavern."

Bess put her arm around the crook of Frank's elbow and guided him out of the stage area. "Why not there?"

Frank did not answer. His gaze had suddenly locked on a figure standing outside his dressing room door.

"Hi, Frank," the young woman said.

She was dressed in an expensive lamb's wool coat and a matching cap. Underneath, she had on a sweater and a pleated skirt. She wore low heels, but she was still as tall as Frank. Even inside a heavy coat, it was apparent that she was built on the slight side. She had enormous dark-brown eyes and a petite nose. Her bottom lip was especially full. She was smiling, which fetched a pair of dimples from her cheeks.

"My God!" Frank exclaimed. He looked back at his companion and then again at the stage-door Jane. "Bess, this is Sandra Greenfield. Sandy, Elizabeth Coleman."

"Ah," Bess said, through a smile that grew larger and larger. "I have indeed heard your name before."

Color instantly came to Sandy's cheeks.

"What did I say?" Bess wondered.

Frank stepped closer and bussed Sandy lightly. "Don't worry. She blushes at the drop of a hat," he told Bess as he pulled back.

Sandy took Frank's hand and squeezed it. "You were wonderful! You both were wonderful. What a show! And that last illusion!"

"Don't ask how it's done," Frank warned. "A professional magician never –"

"Yes. I remember."

"So…I've got to get my make-up off," Bess said. "And then I'm going out with Dex and Sonic."

Sandy tilted her head. "Aren't you going out with your group?" she asked Frank.

Frank doffed the caftan. "That depends. Are you available for dinner?"

"Unfortunately not. I'm with –"

"Ah."

"I'm with my parents. They're waiting outside."

Bess backed toward her dressing room. "It was a pleasure finally meeting you. Frank, we'll leave in ten minutes. Let me know if you're coming with us."

Frank nodded and drew Sandy into his dressing room. "You came to Trenton just to see me?"

Sandra retreated to the far wall, pivoted, and faced Frank. "Well…not exactly. I sang here last night with the New Jersey Symphony. You know how they travel around the state delivering concerts?"

"I think so."

"Well, this was the last of three nights with them. I sang *Mia speranza adorata* and the *Exsultate, Jubilate*."

Frank had no idea what the pieces were. He assumed she was one of a group of soloists for some concerted piece such as an oratorio. From his three-year association with Sandra, he knew that directly after Thanksgiving began the sacred music season with such pieces as Handel's *Messiah* and Bach's *Christmas Oratorio*. Sandra was a high soprano, capable of singing in the coloratura range but with more weight than most women of that vocal category. She had come to

Douglass College, the sister school of all-male Rutgers, with five years of vocal studies already behind her. The music department at that time was more devoted to history and theory than performance, but mezzo-soprano Elizabeth Strauss taught there sporadically between performance engagements, and the state-supported school was all Sandy's parents could afford.

Having Sandy stand outside his dressing room door was a moment of déjà vu for Frank. In his sophomore and her freshman year, he had wangled a gig performing magic at a Douglass College freshman orientation event. Nine years earlier, his repertoire was decidedly more primitive and more dependent on sleight of hand and small gimmicks. Nevertheless, his dexterous skills and verbal patter had so impressed Sandra that she had summoned the courage to go backstage at the little Corwin Horseshoe theater and meet him. He, in turn, was deeply flattered to have garnered such a pretty fan and sufficiently emboldened to ask her on a date. He learned of her musical talents, her quick wit and facile mind, and of aspirations for a performing career no less determined than his. Only later did he learn that she had quirky interests in what she called "real magic," in the occult, Tarot and palm readings, Ouija boards, summonings and other psychic contact with the dead – anything that explored the possibility of a world or worlds beyond that of the living. Soon enough, he convinced her that he had no interest in the paranormal or supernatural and that his form of magic was not even historically linked to any such elements. By that time, she loved him and had put away her former dalliances.

When they were both students they never seriously addressed the day when their different career paths would pull them apart. For a time, it had not. Sandra finished her last year of school, while Frank slaved at making a living from illusions. He worked out of an apartment they shared in New Brunswick. She talked often in the last months of what she would do with her life. He either listened out of one ear, too absorbed in his own career, or assumed that she would inevitably defer to him and find work with her excellent voice around the Northeast. He reasoned that, after all, if she could not find enough singing work from Washington, D.C. to Boston, with its tens of millions in population and hundreds of venues, then she would not find it anywhere else in the world. It was a rude shock to have her inform him that most classical singers needed to establish themselves in Europe, where more cultured societies supported opera and concert singing than in the States. In May of her senior year, she accepted a contract at the opera house in Bonn, Germany.

Sandra was hardly less guilty of assumptions in their relationship. From her point of view, performing magic was an art form more appreciated by Europeans than Americans. She reasoned that, with his background in the German language gotten from home, Frank could perform throughout Germany and Austria. Moreover, all of the British Isles were accessible to him via short plane flights or by trains and ferries. When the time came for her to announce her intention of signing the German contract, she told him as much. What was more, she added, he had had almost a year of full-time efforts in elevating his standing in the American magic community, and he was hardly better off financially or by reputation than he had been in his senior year of college.

Her words had cut Frank deeply, all the more because they were true. Each had stood their ground until their separation was unavoidable. The break was made easier for Frank because he had a pretty part-time assistant then who was throwing herself at him. When the girl quit five months later for a job opportunity in California, Frank had flown to Germany to visit Sandra. He saw with displeasure that she was doing well in her milieu. He thought about a compromise but found no ready opportunities to establish himself as an illusionist there. After his visit they rapidly drifted apart. But he had never since found a woman of such quality as Sandra Greenfield.

"A three night gig, huh?" Frank echoed. "That's great."

"And since my parents live in Hamilton Square, I figured I'd crash with them for two nights. I saw that you were performing here and got three of the last tickets yesterday. They're a very hot item."

"Yeah. I'm doing well," Frank could not help saying. "Really well, in fact."

Sandra leaned back against the wall. "I'm glad for you. What a difference from the act you had in college."

"I was a kid then."

"We were both kids." She labored a smile.

"So, are you performing a bit during a vacation?" he asked.

Sandy's brows knit. "Vacation? Oh, from Germany?"

"Right."

"No. Actually, I'm home now. I'm through with long-term contracts in Europe. I was too homesick for the U. S. of A."

"I can imagine," he said, even as he thought, "That's a face-saving remark if ever I heard one."

"I'll be fairly busy singing in the next few months, though," she told him brightly. "The Indianapolis and Memphis Symphonies. An evening with the Reading Chorus. And a stint with the Delaware Valley Orchestra."

Frank willingly acknowledged that he knew less than he should about classical music. But he had not heard mention of the Philadelphia Symphony Orchestra, the New York Philharmonic, the Boston Symphony, the Metropolitan, Chicago, or San Francisco Operas. Not even City Center, the Cleveland Orchestra, or the Detroit or Pittsburgh Symphonies. She had once mentioned how American colleges were turning out singers in such quantity that European houses hired them for next to nothing, used them for four or five years, then tossed them away. It sounded to him as if this was the case with her, and she was doing her level best to salvage some kind of career with second- and third-level classical groups. Most of him felt badly for her, but one ignoble corner exulted at his triumph and her failure.

"Did you come home with anyone?" Frank could not help asking.

"What do you mean?"

"A significant other? A husband?"

Sandy blushed again. "No. I had a serious relationship in Germany for two years, but it didn't work out."

"Sorry," he lied. Having her within arm's length made him want her as much as he had on their first date.

"What about you?"

Frank laughed. "My act has been my mistress for years."

"What about that exquisite lady I just met?" Sandy fished.

"Bess is purely platonic. That's the only way to keep an act together."

Sandy nodded. "Well, you were wonderful. Good luck."

"And it's about to get much better," he boasted.

Sandy sidled toward the door. "I can hardly imagine how. Look, my parents are waiting…"

Frank moved to cut her off. "I'm going to be in the New York area for the next three months. I have quite a few nights off. Can I take you out to the opera or a Broadway show sometime?"

"I'd like that," Sandy said.

"How can I reach you?" Frank asked, stretching to the make-up table for a pen and a scrap of paper.

Sandy wrote down a New York address and telephone number. He marveled that she had enough economic wherewithal to afford to live in the very expensive city. He was not surprised when she told him she did not expect to be there too long.

"I will call you very soon," he promised, leaning in. He expected that she might turn her cheek to his lips at the last second, but she did not move. Her eyes softened, and her generous lower lip dropped a millimeter, inviting him to kiss her fully. She did not object when he gathered her into his arms and pressed her lightly against his length. Only when the moment had become long did she lift her hand and gently push him back.

"I really have to go."

"I understand," he replied. He opened the door and found Bess, Dexter and Sonder standing like suspects at a criminal line-up on the opposite side of the hall. He nodded goodbye to his one-time lover and watched her walk through the double doors that separated the house from the performing area. When he turned, his company was still waiting for him, wide-eyed and smirking.

"What?" he asked.

"That singer ain't no fat lady," Dexter said. "And it certainly ain't over."

TWELVE

DECEMBER 5, 1976

THE PENNSYLVANIA RAILROAD cuts New Jersey diagonally from southwest to northeast. Its path puts it through Metuchen, on the way to Newark. Although he had lived only a few miles from the cozy suburban town virtually all his life, Frank had spent little time there. The place was a bit rich for his family. It had four traffic arteries, which were laid out like a tic-tac-toe grid, with the railroad station off to the northeastern corner. Whenever Frank thought of the place, he pictured it at Christmas with festive lights and garlands hung over the main street and its clutch of stores outdoing each other with displays and holiday images sprayed from cans of fake snow. To his delight, it was no different this year.

Dexter had dropped him off in Metuchen very early on Saturday morning and continued up to Newark, where he proposed to drive the bus proudly around once again, even though the huge auditorium was sold out. The vehicle had made more than enough of an impact on Skytop Road as Dex downshifted to climb to the farmhouse that Frank had been using as their headquarters for the past eleven months. Lights in several houses winked on at quarter past two in the morning. The commuters to New Brunswick, Trenton, Philadelphia, Newark, and New York did not appreciate having their suburban weekend invaded by noise. The hilltop farm had supported a sizable orchard until the early fifties, when most of the land was sold off for ranch houses. Its main value to Frank was the surviving barn that stored his personal and business lives. The property was owned by a former professor who had taken a sabbatical to France with his wife for twelve months. They were due to return in the first week of 1977. Among other tasks, Frank was confronted with the onerous task of relocating himself. He had done the same five times in the past nine years. House sitting saved him money, since he was only off the road about two months total a year. But he was rapidly becoming too old to have no roots at all, nothing permanent to return to.

It took some priming of the carburetor to bring his professor's old Thunderbird to life. A nest of sparrows had taken up residence in the rafters and whitewashed everything below, including the tarp that had managed to slip off one fender. Frank resolved to get the car washed and detailed on his next day off. He drove slowly through the town, admiring the comfortable feel of the place. He stopped at the post office, to send off the twenty-odd holiday cards he had written and addressed the day before. After the performance in Trenton, it was about all he had found strength to accomplish. At that, he had not arisen until two-thirty in the afternoon.

The train station was virtually abandoned. He locked the car and hefted his suitcase, heading for the northbound tracks. Sunday trains did not stop often at Metuchen. Frank sat on a bench in the nippy air, feeling anxious. The day was beautiful. He was on his way to a sold-out performance at a major venue. He had his "one spectacular illusion" and it had transformed his life. Through innovation and sheer force of will he had kept his dreamboat afloat for more years than most men would have and had reached the far shore with his faithful crew. Allan Salkin was working like a dervish to make the name of Frank Spiegel a household name. He would be playing large auditoriums in New York City in a few more days. And then there were the Everest and K2 mountaintops of his profession to anticipate: The Las Vegas Performer of the Year and the Magician of the Year awards. And yet the specter of the missing Simon Magnus haunted his mind. Frank could not get it out of his head that the voice in the Philadelphia Academy of Music and the Trenton War Memorial belonged to the rightful owner of the coffin. Without revealing himself, he was trying to frighten Frank into abandoning King Karnak's Coffin.

I've had enough of clawing for a living, Frank decided. He thought about the piles of money he would make in less than six months' time, and he realized he could buy any house in Metuchen if he wanted. After this performance, he would take the Thunderbird out for a long spin after having it washed and see exactly what real estate was on the market in the area.

Frank sat up straight on the station bench, his jaw tensed with resolution. If he wants his coffin, he really will need to personally send me to Hell to get it.

Frank backed into the cabinet, closed the door, and turned his key in the lock.

For the first time, light poured instantly through the porthole. It was blue and bright but not unpleasantly intense. Nevertheless, Frank blinked several times at the unaccustomed sight. He paused to be sure the hourglass was operating.

Cautiously, Frank put his eye to the glass. He found himself looking at a tropical clearing with rocks in the immediate foreground and white sand just beyond, gently shelving into an ultramarine pool of water. Past the rippling pool, a waterfall, divided into several cascades, tumbled down over gargantuan boulders flocked with moss. Above the crest of the falls, the sky was a solid, cerulean blue. It was the sort of scene shown in shampoo commercials on television. But no one bathed.

There was no way Frank was about to maintain his promise to Bess to stay inside the coffin for the first thirty minutes. He turned the pivot ring and opened the door. He heard the steady churning of the water and smelled the verdant forest life. A large dragonfly buzzed by. A slight wind caressed his face. Unlike former visits, this time all of his senses were being supplied with stimuli.

"Now what?" he asked aloud, in spite of the beauty of the scene. He knew absolutely that no such landscape had existed in the Newark region for at least millions of years. Moreover, nothing was as high as the cliff in front of him east to the Palisades and west to the Watchung Mountains. Frightening as the black void had been in his past intrusions, at least it was consistent.

Frank stepped cautiously from the box. He realized almost immediately that he was not being attacked by cold. Rather, warm sunlight fell upon his back. He saw the shadow of his figure and of the box. He took two steps forward and felt the sand give slightly under him. He turned a slow circle.

The entire panorama enclosing the box was jungle. It was, however, an extremely manicured version of a jungle. Only a few pieces of detritus existed on the sand. He reached out to a leaf of what appeared to be a succulent plant. He bent the leaf, expecting it to break and yield its milky white liquid. It bent but refused to break. He was fairly certain that, detailed as it was an authentic to the touch, the leaf was nevertheless not real. He wondered if he had gone into yet another world. He wondered if the blue above him was a solid bowl, as the ancients had thought of the sky.

Frank walked out of the vegetation and onto the expanse of sand. He knelt and felt its welcome warmth. He tried to dig his fingers deeply into the grains and found that, despite their gentle undulations, a very hard and flat substance existed less than an inch below. Moreover, it was icy cold to the tips of his fingers. He brushed the sand away and found the usual absolute black base of Limbo.

"Who are you?" a feminine voice asked from behind him.

Frank yelped and started to his feet. He whirled around, arms defensively thrust out.

"Obviously an explorer," the young woman said, speaking of his outfit. Dressed in a bikini with a silken wrap knotted around her waist, she was possibly the most beautiful female he had ever beheld in person. She reminded him elusively of a movie starlet in some Christmas movie from the '40s that Bess had inveigled him into watching with her one night. Frank saw that her slender figure was altogether alluring, curvaceous with the promise of voluptuousness as she grew older. And then he realized that she would never grow older.

Because of her unnatural beauty and the exotic surroundings, Frank was instantly on guard. Instinctively, he understood that he must gain as much control as he could of the situation.

"I am the gatekeeper," he said in measured tones.

The woman, who looked to be just beyond her teenage years, stood next to the black cabinet. She reached out tentatively and touched it with her fingertips.

"The gatekeeper to heaven or hell?"

"Both."

The girl-woman laughed, with a sound like little glass bells. "I don't think so. There's no heaven or hell."

"Why do you think that?" Frank asked.

"Well, I never believed in them when I was alive, and I certainly didn't end up in either place, did I?"

The argument seemed illogical to Frank, but he saw no purpose in pursuing it. "What's your name?" he asked.

"What do you think it is?"

The starlet's name flashed into Franks' mind. "Loretta."

"Yes! Exactly! I am Loretta."

"I don't believe you," he said.

She pushed away from the box and undulated closer to him. "I'll be anyone you wish."

"Why do you want to please me?" he said.

She extended her arms to the unpopulated horizons. "Who else do I have to please?"

Frank walked to the edge of the water, purposely turning his back on her for a moment to show his confidence. "No one I see." He kicked the water, and it sprayed liquid diamonds into the pond.

"If you want to dig in the sand again, it's deep now."

Frank faced her. Now she was dressed in a bright yellow sundress. "I'm sure it is. Why don't you invite those who live in the dark parts of this world to this place?"

The young woman paused to reassess Frank. "Because most of them are people I don't want to know. Drunks. Drug addicts. Violent people. The insane The desperate."

Frank remembered that, other world or not, this part of Limbo was somehow rooted in Newark. The city had a reputation for being one of the toughest and most dangerous in the country. The types of persons she listed no doubt died traumatically more often than the average citizen.

"You pick a name for yourself," Frank invited.

"Emily," she said without hesitation. She ran past him, ankle-deep in the water. "Come, swim with me," she invited.

"Tell me more about the others here," he said, holding his ground.

"Most of them are very unhappy. If they've been here many years, they almost all lose their voices."

"I know. Why do you think that is?"

Emily grabbed her sundress by the hem and hauled it over her head. She was naked underneath, and her body was milky-white and without blemish. She faced him with no embarrassment. "You lose what you don't use. They don't want to communicate with others. They're trapped in their own past." She smiled, backed into the water until it was up to her waist.

Frank looked around at the lush tropical foliage. "Aren't you trapped in your past?"

"Why would I want to keep reliving a nightmare? Does this look like I'm caught?" she replied.

A split-second later, the landscape around her shimmered as if it had slipped into the Mojave Desert on a summer afternoon. The colors and shapes swirled and blended so wildly that Frank was forced to close his eyes to keep from falling. He smelled the tang of seaweed. When he opened them, Emily still stood waist-deep in water, but now they were at an ocean beach. The waves gently nudged her toward the raw-sugar-colored sand.

"Come on in; the water's fine," she said, laughing at her words.

Frank turned in a circle and saw that he stood on what looked like an Eastern seaboard barrier island. Sawgrass rustled in a gentle wind on the hillocks of sand just beyond the high tide mark. Seagulls wheeled and cried above. Down the beach to his left stood a whitewashed lifeguard's post. To his right were dune fences. A red, plastic child's bucket and a bright yellow shovel lay half-buried in the sand next to the shell of a dead horseshoe crab.

"You're very good at creating environments," Frank praised, trying to remain calm in spite of the shock of his surroundings.

"Thank you." Emily splashed out of the water and came up close. "I'm so glad you're here."

"I'm enjoying your company as well. Why don't the others do this?"

She shrugged. "I think it's because they don't have my imagination. Or maybe it's because they refuse to work out their old problems. I've moved on. They don't want to be here. They want to go back. I don't."

Slowly, Emily reached out and touched Frank's arm. He could feel the light pressure of her fingers as they closed around his wrist. She was a creature of some mass.

"You're earthborn," she decided. "And undead."

Frank managed a smile. "But not a vampire."

Emily laughed. "No. You've never died."

He thought of his past ruminations and ultimate rejection of the notion of reincarnation. "Not that I know of."

"Amazing." She looked past his shoulder. He turned and saw that she was staring at the cabinet.

"Sit, Emily," Frank invited.

She obliged him, putting her dripping posterior down on a striped beach towel that had somehow materialized. Frank sat beside her, trying not to focus on her beguiling beauty.

"When did you die?"

"November of 1972. When are you from?"

"It's 1976. December. You've been dead a little more than four years."

"That long? I should have been trying to keep track of time," she decided.

"You were young. How old?"

"Nineteen. I would have been twenty in two months."

"What happened?"

"I was going to college part-time and working as a waitress. There was a man in one of my classes who had been put in prison years before for murdering someone."

"How old was he?"

Emily shrugged. "Maybe thirty-five. He said he had only been defending himself. Anyway, he had served about ten years, and they were letting him out two days a week to take classes. He sat next to me and kept bothering me. Asking me out. I knew he couldn't go out and told him so. But he kept bothering me. One day after class he followed me home to my parents' house. As I was putting the key in the door, he ran up and began stabbing me." She winced. "Over and over. I screamed, but no one helped me." Her lips tightened, and she seemed to fight to maintain calm. "He stabbed me in the back." She twisted around. "I can never see there, even with a mirror."

She died because of her incredible beauty, Frank decided. How sad.

"Are there marks?" she asked.

"No marks," Frank assured. "You're perfect."

Emily leaned forward and bestowed a light kiss on Frank's lips.

Although the pressure felt like the kiss of a guardian angel, she had a degree of substance and warmth. If he had not already visited other regions of Limbo, he would have thought himself in paradise.

"Thank you," he said. He understood how any man, sane or insane, could become entranced and obsessed by her. Even her voice defined femininity. "And this happened in Newark?"

"Yes. What's your name?" she asked.

A warning bell jangled inside Frank's head. He recalled that most of black magic was predicated on learned the names of spirits, demons, and gods. Once a name was known, a certain power was gained over the being. Perhaps, after several relatively tame trips inside the box, it was finally trying to spring the trap on him by having him pronounce his name. He decided not to reveal it.

"I'm Holden," he said.

"Holden? Like the guy in *Catcher in the Rye?*"

"That's right."

"I read that in high school."

"So did I."

She shook her long, auburn hair. "Tell me everything that's happened on Earth since I died."

He obliged her as best he could. He longed to turn the tables and pump her for more information on her present world, but her delight at listening to him was too patent to disappoint. Moreover, he felt a profound sympathy for the life out of which Fate had cheated her.

"Are you from Newark?" Emily asked suddenly, when he paused to remember more world events.

"No."

She stole another glance at the coffin. "Then from where?"

"Edison."

"Edison! God! So close."

"Are you really happy here, Emily?"

She tilted her head. "Mostly. Like you said, I've only met two people who could talk normally. And they didn't want to be with me very long, even though I could make so many beautiful places. They kept fixating on their own wants, y'know? And the weird thing is they thought I was crazy for not wanting to go back. They wouldn't believe they were dead. Both of them kept arguing with me that they were caught inside a bad dream, and I was just one more part of it. Bobby thought he was lying in a coma somewhere. Once he was revived, he was sure he'd pop right back to Earth. All of them keep building the places they had left behind."

Frank gestured at their sunlit surroundings. "This is the Jersey shore, isn't it?"

"Island Beach."

"What about that place where I met you?"

"I was never there. It was a place I saw in a movie. And photos I'd seen of different plants and stuff. It wasn't easy making it at first, but with nothing else to do I got good."

"You know, this world is as big as the world you came from," he informed her. "I've visited it in Texas and Pennsylvania. You could travel. Look for others like yourself."

Emily shook her head. "Too far. Too cold. Too few signposts. You have to go by what the others make, y'know? And you can't rely on them."

"You mean what they create around themselves?"

"Yeah."

"Have you gone as far as New York City?"

"Yes. Once I put the George Washington Bridge over the Hudson and walked in. I think I made it, but I couldn't be sure. It looked like it from the buildings and things the others were making. It was still lonely. That's the bad part here."

Looking at Emily's torso, he realized that her chest did not rise and fall. She no longer needed to breathe, and she had neglected to duplicate an act that was automatic in life. "Why don't you make people as well as places and things?" he suggested.

"I've tried that. They only say what I'm thinking. I'm never surprised."

"Why do you stay here?"

"Where else can I go? There's no heaven or hell."

Her certain declaration disturbed Frank. "You can't be sure of that just because you ended up here. Wouldn't you choose heaven over this?"

"To sing at the foot of God's throne forever?" Emily rolled her eyes. "I don't like what they described in *The Bible*, Holden. Sounds boring and ridiculous."

"But —"

"I've been two places already. I'm afraid. Why don't you stay with me?"

"I can't," Frank told her.

"I can make you anything you want. Look!"

The landscape shimmered again, the colors and shapes bent and coalesced. When Frank opened his eyes, they sat together on the banks of the Nile, with the dark, unique shapes of the great pyramids off in the distance. The sun had set. Night had risen enough that a few of the brightest stars twinkled behind them. An evening breeze swept in, filling the sails of the dhows in the river. The breeze had a chilling effect. The cold suddenly reminded Frank of the coldness of Limbo. He glanced in a panic at his wristwatch. Forty-five minutes had elapsed.

Frank leapt up. Emily reached out and tugged at his legs.

"Don't go!"

"I must!"

She gripped him with demonic energy, pulling herself forward until her breasts mashed against the backs of his legs.

"Let go!" he cried out. He twisted violently and tore himself free. Without looking back, Frank began running up the beach toward the upright coffin. He judged it to be less than forty feet away.

In a single heartbeat, a high wall of coarse brown stones appeared around him on three sides, so that he could see nothing of his surroundings but the ocean lapping the beach. He tried to bull through it. It yielded like a huge expanse of plastic wrapping, but it would not break. He reversed his direction. Then he heard the familiar creaking of the coffin lid.

"Don't go in there!" he shouted. "You'll disappear!" He came around the wall and saw that Emily had obeyed him but was holding the door open and staring inside.

"Don't you understand?" he said to her sternly. "Your earthly body is gone. You would have nothing to return into. You can't go back."

Emily turned. Her exquisite face had contorted into a mask of agony.

"I'm lonely!" she wailed.

Terrified as he was, Frank willed himself to walk without haste toward her. "I understand. But now you have me. I'll use my box to hunt for others like you. I'll bring you together."

Emily's head jerked back with suspicion. "Will you?"

"Yes." Frank raised his hand. "I swear it."

The young woman stepped back. "All right. I'm sorry for the wall."

Frank glanced again at his watch. The second hand was coming up to forty-seven minutes.

"I must go now." He leaned toward her and placed a pristine kiss on her cheek. "I won't forget my promise."

"Go," she said softly.

Frank backed into the coffin and closed the door. He fished into his pocket and found the golden key, placed it into the lock and turned it.

Frank heard Bess's muffled voice calling out loudly, "Let's try again. Louder this time!"

The audience screamed in unison, "Open Sesame." He realized that he still wore his explorer's costume.

To buy another few moments, Frank knocked three times on the lid. Then he wormed one hand under the back of his jacket for the thin flail and crook and the mask that folded out into a three-dimensional shape. He shoved the pith helmet backward off his head and heard the lamp smash as it hit the bottom of the box. Frank pulled the mask over his head, pivoted the ring, and popped the door latch.

Bess pulled the coffin cover back. By the time it was fully open, Frank had the crook and flail folded across his chest. He stepped carefully down the short ladder. Bess whisked the mask from his face.

The audience went wild with applause.

Hobby's Deli had not changed since it first opened. Even after the fire that destroyed it, the owners managed somehow to scrounge up the same cheap linoleum to replace the floor and the same inexpensive paneling for the walls. But the food was wonderful. For the Newark after-concert crowd in the know, it was the place to go.

Frank sat beside Bess in one of the booths, with Dexter and Sonder seated across from them. They had all but finished their late-night dinners.

"I know you were in a hurry, but did you have to be so rough with the helmet?" Sonic complained to Frank. "You can't pick up those old bulbs in any electric shop, y'know."

"I'm sorry," the boss apologized.

"Hey, replace the socket assembly and use a newer bulb, lackey," Dexter suggested. "Accidents happen."

"So it was what? Forty-eight seconds?" Frank said.

"It felt like forty-eight minutes," Sonic responded. "Just thank your ass that Bess knows to listen for the sound of the tumblers clicking." He winked at her.

"But my point is that this time I didn't come out of it exhausted. Not only could Emily keep the cold at bay, but somehow she protected me from having my energy sucked away."

"Maybe the cold alone does it," Dexter posited.

"Nah!" Sonder said. "Do you feel totally fagged out after forty minutes in the cold?"

"In the freezing cold...when I'm shoveling snow," Dex countered.

Sonder gave him a shove with his shoulder. "Where the hell did you ever shovel snow in Harlem?"

"Not in Harlem, jackass."

"Frank isn't shoveling. You'll say anything to win an argument." Sonder pushed the end of a pickle spear into his mouth.

"And what is it with that guy who keeps shouting out 'Encore' from the back?" Dexter asked. "That's three times in three performances."

"A magic junkie," Frank surmised. "We've had them before."

"Maybe a male camp follower," Sonder said. He nudged Dexter again. "I been in the army, but not the Greek army. You can have him."

Frank refused to panic the troupe with his suspicion that it was Simon Magus.

Dexter finished his cup of coffee. "It ain't me he's after. Maybe Frank will have women and men from two worlds after him. Speaking of that..."

From the corner of his eye, Frank caught a teenage girl approaching. She held a napkin and a pen and offered it to him along with a sheepish smile.

"Hi! I saw your show tonight. It was the most amazing thing I've ever seen. Would you...?"

Frank took the pen. "Sure. What's your name?"

"Angelica."

"Pretty name. How's 'Thanks for sharing the magic' and my signature?"

"That would be super!"

Frank did the honors and handed back the napkin and pen. The girl rushed off to display the prize to her friends.

"Now, why don't the twenty five year olds do that?" Sonder asked.

"They will," Dexter said. "Just in a more subtle way. Except in Limbo."

"Not funny," Frank said. "I feel really bad for lying to her. The portal is open for only seven more trips if those lights mean what we think they do."

"That's enough trips to find someone else like her in this part of the world," Bess spoke up.

Frank turned to regard her. She had said only a couple of sentences since they sat down. She looked every bit as tired as she had in Trenton. She had eaten little of her egg salad sandwich and nothing of her fries. For the first time, in spite of Frank missing the timing by an onstage eternity, she had not scolded him or expressed her misgivings about using the coffin. From her look, however, he assumed that worry was gnawing at her.

"You think there are others like her?" Frank asked the group in a bright voice, to indicate how healthy he felt.

Dexter and Sonic nodded as one.

"Shit, yes!" Dexter said. "She can't be the only one of her kind on that side. I tell you what: Tomorrow or the next day I am going to the Newark public library and check the newspapers for November of 1972. We'll see just who this young lady was and the details of her death."

"For what reason?" Frank asked.

"Clues, man. Why she's different from the others. This is fascinating."

"And then what, bookworm?" Sonder asked, blithely liberating a handful of French fries from Bess's plate. "You can't exactly publish your findings, remember?"

"Why does everything have to become a book?" Dexter countered.

"There are so many things I should have asked her," Frank lamented.

"Are you kidding?" the prop man came back. "You did great. If I had stepped into that scene, I'd have first filled my pants and then tripped over my tongue."

"You should have asked her if she ever tried to cross over by herself," Bess said softly. "She said she lived with her parents. Did she ever try to at least contact them, let them know she was all right somewhere else?"

"You're right. That's exactly the kind of thing I should have asked," Frank said.

"You should have asked her if she ever talked with the others in Limbo about heaven and hell," Sonder said, in a suddenly somber tone. "That was the most important part of your conversation by far."

"Why?" Dexter asked.

Sonder looked at his friend with incredulous eyes. "Are you kidding? What's that quotation from Oscar Wilde you love to use?"

"'In this world there are only two tragedies,'" Dexter obliged. "'One is not getting what you want and the other is getting it.'"

Sonic nodded slowly several times before he spoke. "And what if everyone who decides in this life that heaven can't exist is doomed to Limbo instead?"

The statement cast a pall over the group. Dexter wiped his mouth with his napkin. "You've become the religious version of Nutsy Fagan, man. If aliens arrived from the Dog Star, you'd think heaven was up there. And if Frank had hung around to ask another twenty questions or so, he'd have died. That's what we've all agreed the hourglass is about."

"Getting faith is a good thing. You three should try it," Alexander said in his subdued voice.

"We could play here again, Frank," Bess suggested, causing all three men to stare at her. "Allan may find it's got a dark night in the next month or so, and there will be plenty who missed us with twenty dollars in their pocket. And it's the only place where you can visit back-to-back with another performance night." Frank had made it clear to the troupe that even thirty seconds inside the coffin, followed by another seven outside it and then four more for safety, robbed him of so much energy that he could not possibly perform on the next day.

"You can always tell her you're still looking for a companion for her in Limbo. And even if you just visit her, she'd probably be as pleased as if you hooked her up with some other brutalized soul."

"She has a point," Dexter granted.

"I'm really not in the market for a spirit girlfriend," Frank said. Dexter offered no rejoinder to his remark, but the hint of a smile curled the corner of his mouth. "Yeah, go ahead and fantasize, Dex. She'd mesmerize you so fast you'd be dead before you knew the hour was up."

Dexter rolled his eyes and flung himself back against the seat padding. "I'd rather she looked like Dorothy Dandridge, but Loretta Young ain't bad for a white girl! What a way to die!"

"What's most fascinating about tonight," Bess said at a measured pace that revealed she was assembling her thoughts even as she spoke, "is Emily's assessment of the others in Limbo. What does make their death experiences different? How did she learn to control the place when so many others didn't? I wonder just how unique she is."

"You may get your answers as I keeping backing into that coffin," Frank said.

THIRTEEN

DECEMBER 6, 1976

DEXTER BROWN GUIDED the enormous bus into Montclair and calculated just how close he could get it to his sister's house. The neighborhood was paradise in comparison to the 127th Street tenement they had grown up in, but it was almost as old. The street was too narrow for such a behemoth vehicle. Dexter remembered a church parking lot around the corner from where he had purchased the house, and he found the place without much trouble. He locked the bus up tight and took the sidewalk to the three-bedroom cottage. He was pleased to see that a few new shrubs had been planted and that a white, two-seat swing had been installed on the porch. He was not pleased that the two houses immediately across the street no longer had manicured gardens and lawns and that one of them was littered with children's toys. He took the steps in a single bound and pushed his thumb hard on the doorbell.

Attitude was written all over Sharlene Brown's face as she opened the door. "Well, it's about time!" she complained, stepping back.

"I'm sorry," Dex said. He had had the foresight to stop at a florist shop and buy his sister a dozen white chrysanthemums, which were her favorite. After kissing her on the cheek, he held the flowers up as an appeasement. "The show ran late."

Sharlene's fingers were spread out across her thighs, flattening out the apron she wore. It was their mother's apron. "I waited up on you 'til two."

"I said I was sorry. What's with the properties across the street?"

"What do you mean?"

"Why are they getting run down?"

"I don't know nothin' about lookin' run down. But I do know they now have black owners." Suddenly, Sharlene's accent shifted to Black Harlem. "You done a good job of bustin' this here neighborhood. Which I am sure is not what you intended."

"Damn," Dexter exhaled.

"You said you'd be here from Newark last night." Sharlene's accent reverted to a more neutral English as she steered back to her own agenda. She made an abrupt turn and headed into the kitchen. "Same crap you pulled with Momma," she muttered just loud enough so he could hear, "so why should I expect better?"

Dexter trailed behind, laid the bunch of flowers on the dining table, and took his usual seat. "I know what I said. But, you see, the garage that I had to park the bus in locked up at midnight. So I had to camp out with Sonic."

"Why don't you use that man's real name?" Sharlene asked, as she pulled down a vase from an open cabinet.

"He never goes by 'Alexander.' You want to see the new bus?"

"After lunch."

For a moment, the room was so silent that Dexter could hear the ticking of his mother's Kit-Kat Klock. He watched its large eyes roll back and forth, countered by its black tail.

"You gonna keep that old clock?" he asked.

"It tells time perfectly. Why shouldn't I?"

"That's not the point. One of those big Regulator clocks would look so much more tasteful there. The kind they put in train station waiting rooms."

"My skin color was not welcome in those waiting rooms. You hungry?" Sharlene asked.

Dexter had smelled the meatloaf the instant the front door

opened. It was Vera Brown's recipe. The stack of griddle cakes he had consumed with Sonder an hour earlier felt like lead in his gut. He suspected Sharlene had made his favorite childhood meal for a reason other than sisterly love. "I will be, in about an hour."

"You better. I'm cutting hair in ninety minutes."

"How's Darnell?"

"In kindergarten, where he should be."

"How's he taking his grandma's passing?"

"Not well. They were closer every month."

"Is it affecting his schoolwork?"

"I won't let that happen." Vera cut the bottom of each flower stem with a shears she took from a drawer. "And how you doing?"

"About Momma?"

"No. Your work."

Dexter's right hand flew up. "Unbelievable! We have a new show that's driving the audiences wild. I forgot the clippings out in the bus. I'll show them to you later. Frank has finally made it, and that means I'm gonna be rich, too."

Sharlene said nothing.

"Did you hear me?" Dexter asked.

"I heard."

"Who planted the shrubs?"

"Momma did. Just because she lived in Harlem most of her life –"

"Right."

Sharlene turned so quickly that her lacquered hair caught up a moment later. Her annoyance read plainly on her face.

"Did she also put up the swing?" Dexter asked facetiously.

"Johnny did."

Johnny was Dexter's cousin. He lived in Newark. Each time Dex came off the road, he slipped Johnny a twenty to look in on his mother and sister weekly.

"It's nice."

Sharlene proceeded to arrange the flowers. "It is. Momma

enjoyed it immensely the little while she had it."

"You weren't telling the truth at the cemetery," Dexter said. "You do blame me, at least partly, for Momma's death."

"Not at all. Not unless you gave her septicemia. What I blame you for is not being here for Thanksgiving."

"Because if I had been here I would have insisted she go straight to the hospital," Dexter said with vehemence. "But how was I to know this time she really was sick? I mean this is the third straight Thanksgiving you put out an all-points bulletin telling me our mother was sick. And was she the other two times?"

Sharlene took the flower-filled vase and hurled it as hard as she could against the only stretch of open wall in the little kitchen. It shattered with a raucous noise. She leaned on the table and glowered. "You feel put upon because the only way your mother could get you home was to fake illnesses? Other sons take off from work on holidays to be with their families!"

"And because so many do, companies pay time-and-a-half for drivers willing to work!" Dexter answered, matching her shrill voice. He dug into his pocket and plunked ten twenty-dollar bills down. "Like this two hundred dollars."

"Put it toward your mother's big, white angel," Sharlene said in a small but pointed voice. "Or, better yet, keep it yourself. This way you'll be rich faster."

Dexter thumped the table with his fist. "Damnit, Sharlene, I work hard for you and Darnell just as much as for me."

Sharlene whipped out the chair and sat opposite her brother. "Don't you understand what Momma wanted, what I and Darnell want is to have you home at least a couple months each year? We don't want extra money. We're doin' fine."

"Fine for here," Dexter said. "But you're not gonna be here forever."

"And why not?"

"Because I want better for you and your son. Someplace more…"

"More what?" Sharlene asked with catlike speed. "More White?"

"No. More..."

"Less black, then."

Dexter exhaled. "It has nothing to do with color. You need more room."

"How does that make sense? I need more room with Momma gone? I'm happy with this place," his sister affirmed. "I like the neighborhood. It's safe, it's clean. I like our church. The people are good folk. Like a second family. What more do I got to have?"

"But if I can afford more –"

"Why do you have to chase the almighty dollar, Dexter?"

"For the future." Dexter came off his chair and stared out the kitchen window, at the tiny back yard with the rotting sandbox and the almost-new swing set. "I feel like I'm throwing money down a hole contributing to the mortgage. You don't understand neighborhood dynamics and market appreciation on houses."

"I will not move anyplace else. I have a good job in this town. I've started dating a man who might get up the courage to ask me to marry him. Even if he don't, I'll be just fine here with Momma's insurance."

Dexter turned around, bent, and began picking up the pieces of the broken vase. "Halfway is not good enough if you can go farther. Momma never understood that. She was always talking about protecting me and you. Bragging how she linked me up with Mr. Washington, pushed me into the Marines. Do you have any idea what I protected her from?"

Sharlene shifted in her chair. "Why don't you tell me."

"First of all, I didn't hang around Washington's garage for the pure love of it. Other teenagers get allowances. She never had a cent for us. Where do you think our spending money came from? When you found an extra five-dollar bill in your purse, didn't you wonder where it came from? I paid for your prom dress! I was always doing that...protecting your pride and Momma's."

"Anything else?" Sharlene asked with a tranquil air.

Dexter laid the pieces in the sink. "I'm a learner. I always have been. I've had a respect for knowledge since I was in first grade. Do you know what a millstone that was to carry where our mother raised us?"

Sharlene elevated her eyebrows and lowered her lids but showed no inclination to anger. Dexter knew that when she wanted to, she could wield equanimity like Sergeant York used a Garand rifle. He determined to shake her.

Dexter continued, "But she dogged on in that fleabag tenement. I love books, love their power. The world is inside good books. I tried to borrow them from the school library when I was little. I got beat up. You know they called me Poindexter. They threw one book down the storm sewer grate."

"She did the best she could in the only place she knew how to cope in," Sharlene defended.

"She could have asked Johnny's folks to help us move to their neighborhood."

"They were in no position to give us help."

"Are you sure?" Dexter shook his head. "You can go right on blaming me for wanting to make it big in the land of opportunity. But you'll be thanking me when Darnell becomes a doctor or a teacher. Tell me you don't want him to go to the kind of schools that get three-quarters of their kids into colleges."

"He can get into a college from here if he applies himself."

"People's self image isn't good enough here," Dexter argued.

"What people?" Sharlene asked loudly. "I feel just fine about myself. Darnell does, too. But if you plunked him down in some high-class town like Livingston or, heaven forbid, Millburn he would surely die of shame. I can just imagine when he's twelve listenin' to other kids talk about their ski vacations to Colorado or their Christmases in the Bahamas."

"You're afraid to climb any higher," Dexter baited.

"You say. I say I'm already high enough for a good view on life." His sister turned on the full force of a warm smile. "Let me set you straight on a few things, Bubba. Momma knew how much books meant to you. Do you really think it was Duke Washington scrounging up those books he gave you? It broke her heart to put rips in some of them and to print 'This book belongs to Avery Smith' so you wouldn't catch on they were new. That's mostly where both our allowance money went. Now, as for the market value of houses, appreciation, and that stuff, I'm sure you know more than me. But houses are mostly for livin' in. You say you're gonna be rich. That's fine. But I believe that when you sit upon your first million dollars, you're gonna look down and say to yourself 'There's inflation, and there's depressions, and I'll be a lot safer when I make two million.'"

"I would be safer with two million," Dexter affirmed, "and if I can make it, why not?"

"Because of the price it takes. Because you can't be with your family for holidays. You want to do something to honor Momma? Forget the damned statue. Be happy in the skin God gave you. Look around and see what you got already."

"I'm getting more, and I'll be even happier," Dexter asserted.

"If you think that then you are living an allusion."

Dexter moved back to the table and sat. He noted that the cash was where he had left it. "The word is 'illusion,' Sharlene," he said. "Allusion means to make a passing reference."

Sharlene Brown rose from the chair and moved with deliberate dignity toward the oven. "Your grandparents brought their family up North when Adam Clayton Powell was promisin' a better life. They had no bathroom, no running water, one pair of shoes each. That's what you bust your ass to climb up from. This house and this town made your momma happy. They make me happy. If you must have better than this, Dexter, maybe you'll never be happy. Maybe what you need is a little disillusionment."

Alexander Voloshin had his parents' new address in his hand as he exited the elevator. He tucked the paper into his jacket pocket the moment he heard his mother's familiar strident voice. He was still two doors away from their apartment.

The hallway had not been painted in years; the grime in the carpeting was too embedded for even an industrial cleaning service to restore it. A light bulb had been out in the downstairs entryway. He knocked.

Mischa Voloshin answered the door. Alexander held his hands out wide. Mischa ignored them and gestured his brother inside. He looked manifestly unhappy. Behind him, their father was swearing at their mother in Russian.

"Are they drunk?" Sonder asked.

"Since when do they have to be drunk to curse each other?" Mischa returned.

"How close is the nearest liquor store?"

"About a mile. Too far for them to walk. They pulled their usual crap when they first moved in, stayed on their best behavior and conned a neighbor with a car into fetching a stock for them."

Sonder rolled his eyes and tsked in sympathy.

"They know the drill," his brother said. "If they don't cause too much trouble, it's one quart a week for each of them. Where were you the past month?"

"On the road."

Mischa closed the door. "Don't bullshit me. You had off at least two of those weeks."

"Sonder?" his father called out.

Sonder pushed past his brother. "I'll tell you later. Hey, Pop!"

Alexander Voloshin the Elder sat ensconced in his stuffed rocking chair, in front of the color television Sonder had provided two years before. Some of the main characters from *One Life to Live* were doing the usual ignoble deeds to each other.

"Kak Bbl Aenaete, Tovarich?" his father greeted.

Sonder bent down and gave his father a hug. Over his underwear the old man wore an unbelted robe Sonder had given him for the last Father's Day. He had not shaved in several days nor combed his hair. From the reek of his breath Sonder guessed that he hadn't brushed his teeth in a while. He reflected that it was a shame when the old man was out of work. When he had a job he kept himself presentable. In his youth, he had been a truly handsome Cossack. He still looked good when he was off the bottle for a week or so. His hair was thick and showed the vestiges of his usual crew cut, which, when he worked, he kept bristling with Butch Wax. Only his nose provided a perpetual giveaway to the man's drinking; it had become spongy and webbed with enlarged veins.

"How come you're not working, Pop?" Sonder asked.

"Ah, fucking bastards at UPS hate Russians. Screw 'em. Let Christmas packages sit in warehouse 'til January."

Sonder glanced over his shoulder at his brother, who had his head cocked to one side and stood silently watching the scene.

"And what's the yelling I heard?"

"Who else but your mother? She wants to know where I put her shoes. She probably put them in freezer again."

Sonder looked around. The place was claustrophobic, but relatively neat. He saw their canister vacuum cleaner. He assumed his brother had been cleaning while waiting for him to show. Except for the television and a new coffee table, all the furniture was the same from when Sonder had left for his military service.

"You know, you can tune in soap operas every three weeks and still you know what is going on, they move so slow," his father observed.

"We have a new magic show, Pop," Sonder said, moving into his father's line of vision.

"That's nice."

"It's doing real well."

"Good." The man shifted to his left to see around his son. His eyes were riveted on the screen.

Sonder gave up. "I'll go look in on Mom," he said.

"Yeah, good. See what she wants."

Sonder walked through the tiny living room into the back of the apartment. It had only one bedroom. Mischa tailed behind in no hurry. Sonder found his mother sitting on the bed, staring at the wallpaper. She was dressed in a housecoat and had furry slippers on her feet. She held a hairbrush in her hand, but her hair was wildly disheveled. He realized the brush belonged to the dog.

"Hey, Mom!" Sonder said with enthusiasm. He crossed the room and planted a loud kiss on his mother's forehead. He noted with relief that neither she nor his father smelled of alcohol.

Gallena Voloshin looked up at her older son. "Oh, Mischa! When did you get here?"

"I'm Sonder, Mom," he corrected, his heart sinking.

"Sonder. You've been gone a long time."

"Yeah, but I'm back. I've been working on that magic show. Traveling all over the country. You remember."

"Sure. The magic show." She smiled. "You want to do some magic? Find my shoes."

Sonder straightened up. He looked at his brother, who made a signal that he should carry on. Sonder went down on one knee and peeked under the bed. He saw several boxes and lots of dust but no shoes. "I don't see them. Are you going somewhere?"

"I wanted to walk the dog. She hasn't been walked today."

"We'll walk the dog," Mischa said.

Gallena turned her head slowly and registered her second son. "Would you do that, Mischa? I don't know why, but I'm tired." She looked well past her fifty-four years to Sonder. The ravages of heavy drinking were mapped across her body.

"Sure."

"The leash is next to the front door."

"I know."

Mischa crooked his forefinger for his brother to follow him. They walked past their father in silence. The dog, Milyinkie, sat in her cushioned bed just inside the kitchen, below the heating vent. She made no protest when Mischa snapped the leash onto her collar. Sonder opened the front door, and the dog trotted out into the hall. It was a mutt, mostly English spaniel, given to the Voloshins six years earlier.

"What's the matter with Mom?" Sonder asked, the instant the front door closed.

"Tell me first where you've been the last few weeks," Mischa replied. "I called your agent, and he said your group was off the road as of November 16th."

Sonder regretted having given his brother Salkin's number, but Mischa had insisted he be able to reach Sonder at any time.

"It was a really tough fall," Sonder began. "We had small crowds and had to add extra performances. We must have put seven thousand miles on the bus, running from town to town. And then the damned bus broke down, and we had to replace it."

"My heart bleeds," Mischa broke in. "And what does that have to do with the past few weeks?"

"I flew down to Miami for some much-needed R & R."

Mischa slammed the flat of his hand against the elevator door. "You know, I have needed some R & R for the past four years, but I never get it."

"I'm here now," Sonder said.

"Yeah, you're here." The elevator opened, and the dog led the two men inside it. Mischa whacked the ground floor button.

"What exactly is wrong with her?" Sonder asked, both to change the subject and to have his concern addressed. "Can you have dementia when you're not drinking?"

"I don't know if it's dementia. Whatever it is, she has it all the time," his brother answered. "Some days worse than others. And it's been getting worse. She calls me 'Sonder' and Pop 'Mischa.' She's constantly misplacing things."

The elevator door opened. The dog trotted out toward the sunlight.

"She had Milyinkie out this morning already," Mischa revealed. "She's tired because she walked him around the same block ten times. Last week she came in from a walk, unleashed the dog, walked into the living room, stared at the leash and took the dog right back out."

"Jeez!" Sonder exclaimed. The day was shaping up a lot worse than he had expected – and he had expected very little good.

"Other days, they both forget to walk her at all. She gets even by shitting on Mom's shoes. Mom's down to one pair now,and I wouldn't be surprised if the dog hid them."

"So, what do we do?" Sonder asked.

The mix-breed turned right and trotted east. The apartment building was on the heights of Fort Lee, although set on a block that benefited neither from the view across the Hudson to upper Manhattan nor out across the swamps of North Jersey to the hills beyond.

"What do we do?" his brother echoed. "What do you ever do?"

"Wait a minute, man," Sonder said. "If I'm not mistaken, I provide about a third of their income and you don't even come close to that."

Mischa stopped walking. "I'm the one who's here for them. If I was professional help, I'd be providing three times as much as you do."

Sonder thrust his hands into his coat pockets. "Hold it, hold it! Let's not go for each other's throat over them. Mom has the maternal instinct of a wolf spider. Dad was never there for us growing up, whether he was working or not. Let's face it: We're on this planet as the by-products of sex."

"So, you're saying that we should walk away from them?" Mischa asked.

Sonder groaned. Ever since he had witnessed Frank's disappearances inside the box and heard about Limbo, he had been reading motel room Gideon bibles. He had gotten to the Ten Commandments a month ago. He had paused for some time on the words that told him to "Honor your Father and your Mother/That your days may be long in the land that the Lord your God gives you." Just when he was feeling his worst about his care for his parents, Mischa had to ride him on the subject. And, naturally, his mother and father had never been so helpless.

"No, of course we don't walk away from them," Sonder retrenched. "But there's only so much –"

"Believe me, I'm not suggesting that you should ever have kids, Sonder," Mischa broke in, "but if you do, I bet you'll expect them to help you if you're down. I expect to be there for you, and I hope you'll be there for me when we're pushing sixty."

"Well, sure."

"It's what the Jews call being a 'mensch'."

"I know. A person doesn't have to be an accountant to have Jewish friends." Sonder nodded toward the Hudson River. They started walking again, with the dog straining at the leash to accomplish his habituated stroll. "It's just that we got such a shitty deal with those two as parents. You met Elizabeth Coleman once, right? The woman I work with?"

"Three times."

"Okay. Well, this summer she makes me sit up with her in a Las Vegas motel room and see the Nevada version of The Late, Late Show. It's running a movie called *The Days of Wine and Roses*. You ever see it?"

"No."

"It was not a fun night for me. This was the story of our parents. We could sue the writer for theft." Sonder spit out his gum.

"I don't want to hear the negative from you," Mischa said. "I live it three or four times a week."

"But you gotta cut me a little slack here," Sonder argued. "For the past six years I put nothing away. Everything went to tuition for you or things for them. By the way, why did they need a new coffee table?"

"Dad passed out and fell over backward. Flattened it." Mischa yanked back hard on the leash, unwilling to be dragged at the dog's pace. "I bought it. And forget negotiating here with the money you gave me for school. We had that discussion. I told you I didn't want it if it had strings."

"Okay, okay, but –"

"It would have taken me ten years on my own, but I would have had the degree anyway, Sonder. Do you know what today is?"

Sonder felt another trap being sprung.

Before he could respond, Mischa said, "My birthday."

"Oh, I thought you meant something other than that! Why do you think I'm here," Sonder danced. "I'm taking you and Rebecca out to dinner tonight."

Mischa gave his brother a baleful look. "I'm thirty years old. I've been engaged for three years. It's time I got married. I can't keep up this care of Mom and Pop, get married, hold down a job, and start a family, man! I just can't do it."

"All right!" Sonder exclaimed, feeling that nothing was all right.

"Especially in tax season," Mischa drove on. "I need to do people's tax returns at night from February 'til April to pay for the wedding, and I can't give those two any time then." They had crossed the street that ran along the edge of the Palisades. A tiny ribbon of a park ran parallel with the river. Where they stood were several benches with stone chessboards cut into them. Mischa sat. The dog lifted its leg against the iron fence next to the benches and peed. "Look, you've been footloose and fancy free since you came back from the Marines. You don't need to be on the road. With the sound and lighting skills you have, there's no reason you can't work in Manhattan or over here. There are literally dozens of theaters nearby that could use you. It's time for you to invest personal hours in the old folks and not just money and lip service."

Sonder looked around. Considering that they were in one of the most densely populated places in the world, he could see an enormous swath of open sky and a large expanse of water. And yet he had never felt so boxed in. His chest seemed to have invisible barrel stays tightening around it. He dropped to the cold bench seat.

"I've been doing the best I can. We'll work it out. I'll be in the area for the next few months, and I promise I'll visit them at least twice a week. But you have to understand, Mischa, the show I work for has finally turned the corner. We're about to become really big time. You won't have to trust me on this; you'll be reading it in the newspapers this week. I can't afford to leave it now."

"You don't know what other places might pay," Mischa said, unconvinced.

Sonder tapped the table. "There's another thing. When I'm on the road, I don't drink. If I have to see them too much, they'll drive me to drink full time. Without the people I work with hounding me, I'll become like Pop. I'm sure you don't want to ask that of me."

Lightning like, Mischa's open hand swung up and cuffed his older brother in the side of the head. "Who the fuck do you think you're talking to? You can tell that to yourself, but I know you're not like the rest of us. I knew at sixteen that if I drank I'd never be able to stop. So I just didn't do it. Because I saw first-hand what that life would be like. But you could always start and stop whenever you wanted. You drink because then you have an excuse to be a self-centered shit. You can forget important dates and obligations. Life is funnier; you think you're wittier; the women who drink are easier to bed. But nobody stops you from drinking but you. And nobody can drive you to drink. That's a fantasy of yours, big brother. You live life for nothing but your own benefit. And you never took care of me. What you did was throw guilt money at me. That was your second illusion."

Sonder stood and walked to the fence, pretending to stare at the skyline. "I'm not strong like you, Mischa," he said, shaking his head vigorously. "I swear that I do the best I can."

"And that's bullshit, too," he brother said softly. "You can do a whole lot better. You just never tried. You chose a life of running away. But now you're here, and I'm begging you to try. For you, for me, for the folks." He stood and spit over the fence, and then turned back toward his parents' apartment high rise. "I know what I can do. I know I've done all I could for fourteen years. I can't do as much anymore. I've said my piece. You do the rest of the talking to yourself. For once, really find out what your best is." He began walking. "I'll take a rain check on that birthday dinner. Heel, ya goddamned dog!"

Elizabeth Coleman parked the rented car two doors up the block from her father's Haskin Street address. She wondered if the Bronx block would ever get curbs. The tree in the grassless yard in front of the two-story apartment house had buckled the sidewalk with its roots. As she locked the car, she stared with dismay at the rusting wire fence that surrounded the forty-by-sixty-foot property. The gate creaked as she swung it open. She assumed that a new family had moved into the dreary half apartment in the basement, as a little girl with two missing front teeth smiled at her from the front stoop. She smiled back and climbed past her.

She used the key to her father's apartment so infrequently that she often thought about removing it from her ring. Now she fitted it into the door and turned it, thinking as she did of the sarcophagus and its pivot ring.

"Hey! You home?" Bess asked as she swung the door in.

"In the living room," her father called back.

Bess removed the key. "Where's your car?"

"In the shop. Getting a new alternator."

The apartment was strangely laid out. The two-story house had originally been built for a single family, but had been converted. To get to the living room, one had to enter the house through the kitchen, go left through the bedroom, and then through another door toward the front of the house. A downstairs bathroom had been appended to the first floor at the back of the kitchen. The bedroom she had shared with her sister, Eileen, was the only one she had ever known with its own door to a back yard.

Bess walked the circuitous route into the living room. Her father sat on the sofa reading a copy of the New York Post. The sofa was a convertible and had served as his bed for twenty-five years. Bess paused at the doorway. He set down his newspaper and looked up, smiling.

"If it isn't Good Queen Bess!" he said, a greeting that was more than thirty years old.

Bess crossed to him and gave him a firm kiss on the cheek. "What's with the white dress shirt? You're retired, remember?"

George Coleman waved the observation away. "I've got a closet full of them. Should I throw them away?"

"Yes!" Bess said. She sat at the opposite end of the couch and set her purse on the coffee table that had to be pushed out of the way every night.

"You look as beautiful as when you were twenty," her father admired.

"Thanks," Bess said gratefully. The lighting in the room was not bad, and the man who had known her all her life was sitting right beside her. She knew then that she had lost none of her makeup skills from her modeling days. Her usual English rosebud color had come that morning from several tubes and compacts. She suspected that she had a touch of anemia, either from heavy menstrual flows or else from a hemorrhoid that periodically bled. Something temporary that had lowered her red blood count and was also making her tired. Nothing serious. "We've been running all over creation with the show," she said, thinking of the other explanation for her lack of energy. In spite of her breezy tone, she was not taking chances. She had already made an appointment to see Dr. Franz, their longtime family physician.

"How's it going?" her father asked.

"Unbelievably well. It's half new. Incredible illusions."

"I'll have to catch it, then."

"I'll make sure you do."

Bess looked around the living room. It had barely changed since her mother died twenty years earlier at the age of forty-two. Bess was nineteen and Eileen sixteen. Gwyneth Coleman had always had a pathological fear of physicians. Her attitude was that if she didn't have an annual checkup, they couldn't tell her anything was wrong. By the time the symptoms had manifested themselves, the cancer had spread throughout her body. She had only lived another five months. But part of her legacy survived in the apartment. The upright piano she had brought to her marriage still sat against the hallway wall in the living room. No one else in the family had played. It took up an enormous amount of space, but George would not part with it. Gwyneth's collection of porcelain figurines still adorned the Irish-linen-covered piano top.

"It's good to see ya, Bessie," her father beamed, shaking her knee affectionately.

"You, too."

"Are you happy?" he wanted to know.

Bess replied with a little grunt. "Me? What about you? When you die, should we just shovel dirt around this old place?"

"If you do, I won't be in it."

Bess started. "What do you mean?"

"You know my old fishing buddy, Charlie, down in Florida?"

"The one with the boat?"

"The same. He called me last week to say the bungalow next to his is for sale. I made an offer for it. The closing is in two weeks."

"Get out!"

"No, really. I'm spending the rest of my life working on a tan. So now when you come north, you'll only have Eileen and her brood to look after."

"I'll visit you in Florida when the show swings by."

"You'd better. Free fish dinners for everyone." George stretched, grunted and pushed himself up from the sofa. "You want some coffee?"

"That would be swell." Bess rose as well and followed her father.

George paused in the bedroom, as if replaying scenes from the past.

"I want to ask you a favor, Dad," she said. "Can I sleep here tonight?"

Her father blinked in surprise. "You haven't slept here since… since shortly after the…"

"That's right."

"One last time before I vacate, for old time's sake then?" George guessed.

"Something like that."

"Well, of course."

"I have a suitcase out in the car."

George continued into the kitchen. "Plenty of time for that. Let's have our coffee first."

They continued around into the kitchen. While her father put up the pot, Bess washed her hands in the bathroom sink. The porcelain was permanently stained with rust from the dripping faucet. The fixtures had never been replaced. She dried her hands and once again stood in a doorway, watching her father. He seemed quite hale for a man who had spent most of his life at a desk. He had only a hint of a pot belly, and the wrinkles in his face were not too deep.

"You're still quite a dashing man for a guy in his sixties," Bess remarked.

"Thank you. But I shall always maintain that you and Eileen got most of your looks from your mother."

"We kept pushing ladies at you after she died, but you never seemed interested."

"Ah, I'm a one-woman man, I guess. Like you."

"I'm no one-woman man," Bess jested.

"You know what I mean."

"Yeah, I know."

"But it's not too late for you, Elizabeth."

"Why didn't you move into the bedroom when Eileen moved out?" Bess asked, unwilling to reply to his words.

George glanced over his shoulder momentarily. "Oh, habit I guess."

"I have a question to ask you, Dad. You're going to think it strange, I know."

"Ask me, and I'll tell you what I think."

Bess sat at the little kitchen table. "In the middle of the night, when you went through the bedroom to the bath, did you ever happen to look out the window and see anybody?"

"Someone in particular?"

"The figure of a man."

George reflected for a moment. Bess could not tell whether it was to address the question or to wonder what was wrong with his older child. "Can't say that I did. Why do you ask?"

"Nothing."

"You must have asked for a reason."

"I…used to think I saw someone."

"When you were little?"

"No. Just before I left."

"You think someone was looking for you? Someone who read about the accident in the papers?"

"Maybe."

"Well, you are a beautiful woman. I could see a man being curious. Especially after what happened. Did you get a good look?"

"Forget it," Bess said. "It was a stupid thing to ask."

George Coleman shrugged. "If that's the reason why you always stay with Eileen instead of me when you're in the area, that's crazy." He set two mugs on the table. "I tell you what: If you see someone tonight, holler out. I'll be there in a flash."

Bess looked at the bedroom doorway. She could see the door to the back yard but not the window. "Okay."

Her father hugged her lightly. "You may be big, but your daddy is still here to protect you, Queenie," he said.

"Thanks, Dad," Bess replied, doing her best not to cry.

FOURTEEN

DECEMBER 7, 1976

THE OFFICES OF Allan Salkin, the talent agent, were a front and back room on the eighth floor of 1663 Broadway. The receptionist cum secretary worked only in the morning, so Salkin made sure to schedule before noon any appointments where he wanted to impress someone. For the sake of privacy, Frank arrived shortly after one. He knocked on the door more than once and heard the agent's slightly gruff voice asking him to be patient.

"Hey, Magic Man! Nice coat," Salkin greeted as he unlocked the door and threw it back.

Frank unbuttoned the camel's hair topcoat he had just treated himself to at Abercrombie & Fitch. "Thanks."

"Why didn't you call first?" asked the agent. "Are you ready for tonight?"

Lincoln Center's Avery Fisher Hall had had just two dark nights in the month of December, and Salkin had leapt to secure them the morning after the Academy of Music unveiling of the new show. For what they charged to outside performers, Frank had not been surprised that the dates were open. The ticket holders for their scheduled YMCA theater performances had been informed of the change. Even paying for both houses, the much bigger size of Avery Fisher Hall and its cachet allowed the troupe to make a tidy profit.

"Am I ready? I am ready, willing, and able," Frank affirmed. He held sections from three separate newspapers. "I have here the *Brunswick Home News*, the *Newark Star Ledger*, and the *Asbury Park Press*. All raves." He passed them to Salkin and moved toward the back office.

"I got the – wait a minute!" Salkin said. He was not in time to prevent Frank from passing through the inner doorway and spotting Harlan Jessup, who had made himself comfortable in the chair Frank usually occupied.

"Hello, Frank," Jessup said, half-rising from the chair and offering his hand.

"You aren't the only one surprised," the agent informed his client. "I think you told me Mr. Jessup might be up in New York, but nobody said anything about this week."

"I wasn't specific with Frank," the Texan revealed. "Allan and I were just talking about your reviews. I have a clipping service, and I had your name and show added to the list of my interests. You've scored top marks in Philadelphia and Trenton as well. Here's a paper I managed to get my hands on." Jessup lifted a newspaper from the space between the chair's padded arm and its seat. He gave it to Frank. It was the previous day's Trenton Times.

"It's wonderful that Mr. Jessup has taken such an active interest in you, Frank," Salkin said, grabbing the straight-backed wooden chair positioned in the far corner of the office and pushing it up near the one the financier sat in. Frank put himself on it.

"I spotted real talent in him before this new version of his act," Jessup announced. "It's nice to have my opinions validated so quickly."

"And you came up here for what specific reason?" Frank asked him, feeling defensive and slightly annoyed.

Although Jessup wore a three-piece suit, he managed to look completely relaxed in it. He sat with one elbow cocked over the upholstered arm of his chair and the other with his wrist resting lightly on his crossed knee. The Rolex watch had a black alligator band. "I came up here to meet your agent and see if there's more I might be able to do. I don't have to tell you that you're fiercely independent. You'd be the last one to put a hand out to elevate your act even farther. If that bus hadn't broken down, I still wouldn't have helped."

"I have to see this bus," Salkin interjected, keeping his voice in the discussion.

"I also wanted your city address so I could contact you," Jessup continued smoothly. "I think I have a really good idea for an illusion, and I wanted to get it to you quickly."

"What's that?" Frank asked.

"You remember I thought that a hologram might be a wonderful inclusion?"

"Yes."

"You must know that your last name means 'mirror' in German."

"I do."

"Then a mirror trick fits right in. Picture this: You're best at the talking part. You know, selling the illusion. This time you work up a spiel that you've secured a mirror capable of showing a man's soul when magic words are pronounced." In some detail, Jessup described the use of a mirror fashioned overlarge, so that the farthest members of a good-sized audience could see it. The frame of the mirror would be wide, ornate, and on casters. The apparatus would be rolled onto the stage facing outward, so that the audience could see parts of the house reflected back to them. The surface of the mirror behind the glass, however, would be the relatively new material called Mylar, which was incredibly thin and flexible but nearly as reflective as silver-clad glass. As Frank stood in front of it, roller and cam mechanisms inside the frame would flex and bend the Mylar surface so that Frank appeared alternately thin and fat, as he would in fun-house mirrors. He would announce that he did not appreciate the mirror's sense of humor. He would call for a white bed sheet, which Bess would bring on. While Frank covered the mirror, a turntable underneath them would revolve in a full circle, showing the audience how thin the mirror was and how no one could possibly be hiding inside or behind it. When the mirror faced out to the audience again, he would pronounce his magic words and yank off the bed sheet. During the covering and removal process with the bed sheet, the Mylar would have been rolled up into the frame by a motor. Now, the image behind the thin non-reflective glass would be a hologram motion picture. The filmed images of Frank would be split-second timed to musical cues, so that Frank could play off the action exactly, even if his back was to the mirror.

"And the turntable continues to operate," Frank said, catching on.

"Not for about the first fifteen seconds," Jessup answered. "Whatever the exact time is that you duplicate the images in the hologram. However, once you and your supposed reflection begin to show separate personalities, the turntable starts to swing back and forth through thirty or forty degrees. Since the people can't move from their seats, they need to get the benefit of the hologram's three-dimensionality. It's not just the holograms that will be expensive but also the timing of all the elements. Here's the great part. You tell the audience that you have a complicated soul. Sometimes you're a devil and sometimes an angel. For each, even though you continue to duplicate your image's movements, the shape of your supposed reflection and its costume transform. Then you say that sometimes you wonder if you have a soul at all. Your reflection vanishes." Jessup's eyes went wide, pantomiming the audience's reaction. "You give them a second to register the disappearance. Then a flash of light, a clap of thunder, and a puff of smoke. The Mylar descends behind the cloud of smoke, and your real image is back. What do you think?"

What Frank thought was that Jessup and not he should be the magician. He, who had read virtually every magician's handbook on the market and who had studied the art of illusion for two-thirds of his life, had not been able to divine a holographic trick after a month of brain wracking. Jessup, who no doubt had most of his life preoccupied with matters of high finance, had been able to come up with something that not only sounded possible to achieve but was also extremely effective.

"I think it's not for our old road schedule," Frank answered, trying not to sound excited. "It would take far too long to rig."

Jessup refocused on Salkin.

"You're not going to be doing the one-night stands anymore," his agent piped up, glancing for a second at Jessup. "The rigging is certainly reasonable when you're a whole week in a city. Isn't that what you've always wanted?"

What Frank did not want was Jessup suddenly shouldering into the team. He knew the financier had stuck the words in the agent's head. "We should talk more about it."

"How about lunch on Friday? The Palm Court at the Plaza?" Jessup asked.

"All right."

Jessup stood. He reached to Salkin's desk for his hat and, with the other hand, reached out to the agent. "It's been a pleasure meeting you, Allan."

"Same here, but double, Harlan."

"Let's say half past one on Friday," Jessup said to Frank. "You'll want to sleep late – and the holiday ladies' clubs are in town with a vengeance this time of year. They've usually returned to shopping, the shows or the museums by then."

Frank could see that the man knew the pulse of the city. "I'll be there."

"Let me walk you out," said Salkin.

Frank half-listened to their parting words as he reviewed Jessup's description of the proposed trick. He tried to punch holes in it but failed. He was fairly convinced that the illusion would keep the act flying when they could no longer use the sarcophagus. He saw himself accepting the Magician of the Year award for 1977, but he did not feel elation commensurate with the image. Neither King Karnak's Coffin nor the mirror trick was his. He glanced at the rogue's gallery of head shots framed on the south wall. Virtually all Salkin's clients were there. Among the twenty-four faces, few Americans would recognize eighteen, including Franklin Spiegel. The other six had once been names, but had lost their high-powered agents along with their high demand. He felt like a fraud, an anomaly among all of them.

Frank switched chairs and sank into the padded one, sensing the heat of Jessup's body in the leather. He leaned out to be sure the millionaire had disappeared.

"Pushy bastard," Frank declared.

"He is aggressive," Salkin agreed, locking the outer door. "But he's clearly got your best interests at heart. More importantly, he has money in case you need it. He might be the one to get you the television show. Or at least he'll drive a lot of wealthy and influential friends your way."

"I suppose," Frank said grudgingly.

"Don't look a gift longhorn steer in the mouth, my friend. So just how dangerous is that King Karnak's Coffin trick?" Salkin asked, as he reached the inner office again.

"Why do you ask?" Frank evaded.

"Because of that review in the Star Ledger. Who the hell was the unnamed guy who caught the reporter's ear?"

As the name 'Simon Magus' echoed inside his head, Frank answered, "I have no idea. All I can guess is that he's the same one who had seats in the back of the orchestra section in Philadelphia and Trenton. You heard him. The one who shouted out 'Encore.'"

Salkin had shattered a vertebra early in life and suffered chronic back pain. He lowered himself carefully onto his chair. "Oh, him. I didn't catch the Newark show, but I did see what he saw in Philadelphia and Trenton. He was right: The timing wasn't the same for the trick. The four guys on the stage in Trenton told a reporter you collapsed offstage, but recovered quickly. And what happened in Newark that you not only obviously came out several seconds after you should have but didn't have all of your costume change on?"

"If I told you the reason I'd have to explain the trick," Frank said. "You know I won't do that."

"Swear to me it's not dangerous," Salkin said.

Frank welcomed the course of the conversation. "I can't, because it is dangerous. But look at the effect it produces!"

"It's a fucking impossible trick," Salkin granted. "If I didn't know you so long I'd think you were the Devil himself pulling it off. And one night I'm gonna get up on the stage and be one of those four guys. I have to see it point blank."

"You still won't understand it," Frank said.

"Don't challenge me. It sure has Jessup interested as hell. He actually asked me if you had shared the secret with me! He managed to wangle a scalped ticket for tonight. Paid a C note! If that doesn't say you're hot, nothing does." Salkin's eyes narrowed to slits. "You know when you want to get something out of somebody you often sneak into it?"

"What do you mean?"

"Say I want to learn something I think maybe I can't get. So I begin to talk to the person about other things. And then, after about five minutes I say "Oh, by the way…"'"

"Okay. And?"

"Well, Mr. Jessup is too clever to stick in the 'Oh, by the way,' but I think the main reason he came up here today was to learn all he could about Elizabeth."

Frank was not surprised. "What did you tell him?"

Salkin hunched up his shoulders. "What could I tell him? I dug out her head shot with her credentials on the back and handed it to him. But he wanted more. He asked how long I'd known her, what her outside interests are. That kind of thing. Then, to throw me off the track, he asked the same stuff of you. Claimed it was easier and less nosey-seeming to ask me. Says he wants to get to know both of you much better."

"Yeah, yeah, yeah. He's got a thing for Bess," Frank said. "It doesn't make sense for a guy with so much money and so many opportunities."

"But who can control the heart, eh?" Salkin asked, offering a sly smile and a wink. "She is a dish. And a good age for him. Anyway, I didn't think it would do any harm to tell him that the four of you have rooms at the Sheraton while you're in the city." To cut off any criticism or objection, Salkin snatched up a piece of paper on his desk, cleared his throat, and said, "I've got great news for you, kiddo. I've booked the Neil Simon Theater from the 14th right up to and including the 31st. At the rate your show's reputation is growing, you'll be the New York location for New Year's Eve."

"Where the heck is the Neil Simon Theater?" Frank asked.

"That's right. You've been away from the city most of the year. You know it as the Alvin. The Schubert organization bought it and renamed it in honor of 'Doc.'"

"That house is way north, isn't it?"

"52nd, between Broadway and 8th. Hey, this time of year beggars can't be choosers," Salkin lectured. "It was the only empty house available for a run."

"How big is it?" Frank worried.

"Just the size you like. Twenty rows in the orchestra. Shallow balcony and mezzanine. Nobody will be too far from you. But we'll still make bundles of money. I'm placing the radio and newspaper ads as soon as you get out of here."

"I'm glad you haven't done that yet," Frank said as he recrossed his legs. He wanted his body to seem relaxed when he delivered his news. "Don't advertise Karnak's Coffin as your lead. At least not directly."

Salkin's eyes went wide. "Why not?"

"It is still too dangerous to perform on a regular basis. Nobody wants to kill the goose that lays golden eggs."

"You've got to be joking."

"I am not."

The agent threw himself backward in his chair and glowered at his client. "Well, that's just plain unacceptable. People have read your reviews. They're buying tickets based on that one trick. They'll demand their money back."

"It can't be helped," Frank said.

"I don't want to hear that. You'd better think how to make it un-dangerous in a hurry, because this is unacceptable."

"Not at all," Frank assured. "I thought you said you were a creative agent. What's the biggest drawing card for Siegfried and Roy? It's not just the beauty of the big cats but the fact that they're lethal beasts. So is King Karnak's Coffin. I want you to make a big deal of how the trick has nearly killed me. It's already been in the press how I made a late reappearance onstage. Tell the press the Spiegel troupe is working hard to tame it, but they will only be testing it on select, unscheduled evenings. People must buy their tickets after the two Lincoln Center performances based on that proviso. It's PR gold, Allan!"

Salkin's face had turned red with irritation. "Well, you'd better perform it at least every other performance."

"What's more important," Frank asked, "our safety or your precious percentage? Hey, don't pause to answer!"

"Okay, okay. It is PR gold if correctly presented. I'm sure it will fly... if we lower the ticket prices by a few bucks."

"Which makes them only twice what we would have commanded a month ago."

Salkin grinned and rocked closer to Frank. "Meantime, see if you can make it totally safe, huh? This is the town that makes or breaks you."

"I know. Money and influence aside, what does your radar say about Jessup as a person, Allan?" Frank asked his long-time mentor and confidant, to end the coffin discussion.

Salkin weighed his answer. "He presents himself as a stand-up guy. But you know what they say about that kind of money: 'Behind every fortune is a crime.' Oh, before I forget." He bent to a lower drawer of his desk and took out a manila envelope. He handed it across to Frank. "Your fan mail. It's picking up."

Usually, Frank received about two dozen pieces a year. All the company's promotional material and posters listed Allan Salkin's address, which was clearly what die-hard fans used for contact. More than half were amateur magicians, writing about being inspired or begging to know how a certain trick was accomplished. This large envelope contained more than twice what Frank would normally have expected. He dumped it out on his lap and thumbed through it.

"There's one weird one without a return address on the envelope," the agent said.

Frank found a legal-sized envelope with a hand-stamped black skull where the return address should be. Allan handed him a letter opener, and he tore out the sheet of paper inside.

"What's it say?" Salkin wanted to know.

"It's typed. 'Dear Mr. Spiegel,'" Frank read, 'King Karnak's Coffin is the Devil's work. Unless you stop performing it, it will kill you before New Year's. Consider yourself warned.' It's signed 'Concerned'."

"It came in today's mail," Salkin informed him.

Frank looked at the date mark over the postage stamp. The envelope had been processed the day before."

Frank's agent laughed loudly and waved his arms. "What? It's some rival magician, afraid you'll steal his bookings with that trick. Are you gonna let a stupid thing like that scare you?"

"I'm scared enough already," Frank replied, as he tucked the letter into the pocket closest to his heart.

Frank decided to take a walk up to the Neil Simon Theater,

introduce himself, and see just what the stage was like. He remembered that he had seen a couple of musicals there. On the way, he made a detour. On performance days, he ate between the hours of two and three in the afternoon, because he would not eat again until after the show. Corned beef on rye was one of his great weaknesses, and because he loved a good, lean sandwich he would not indulge in anything less than the best. The best in Midtown was served with German mustard and snapping fresh kosher dill pickles at the Carnegie Deli. Even in mid-afternoon the holiday shopping crowds had the place jammed. He waited his turn for a table, re-reading the newspapers with his unaccustomed rave reviews.

When he folded the pages of the *Trenton Times* Jessup had given him, he spotted an interview. It was a dual article, with a critical review of the Friday performance of the New Jersey Symphony concert and a personal piece on the guest soprano of the evening, "Young diva Sandra Greenfield." To his chagrin, Frank learned that the *Mia speranza adorata* and *Exsultate, Jubilate* were Mozart arias. Evidently, the second was a terrifically difficult concert piece that only the best sopranos attempted. There were no other soloists that evening; Sandy was "the" guest. The critic's gushing appraisal was that he had only heard the piece sung better by two sopranos, and those performances were on recordings. The same critic had cornered Sandy after the performance and wheedled an in-depth interview. It seemed that she was returning in triumph from Europe, where she had spent the past two years singing at La Scala, Covent Garden and the Berlin Staatsoper. Two seasons hence, she would be jetting back and forth between the Metropolitan and Chicago Opera houses, singing three leading roles. She explained that the best opera houses had their stars committed as far as five years in advance. In the meantime, she was taking smaller opportunities as they arose, studying periodically at Indiana University and learning several new operatic parts.

Frank was stunned: not only by the news, but also by Sandy's modesty. She had let him brag on and on the night she came to see his act without ever blowing her own horn. But that was always her way, he remembered ruefully. She had always supported him as much as her own ambition allowed. He was ashamed that he had not been a good enough friend to stay in touch or even to try to follow her career via the press.

Frank pictured Sandy standing alone in front of a full symphony orchestra, with only her voice and her musicianship, using no borrowed magic or illusions. He finished the article and tucked the newspaper under his arm. He found himself staring at his own reflection in the delicatessen front window. He decided that, in spite of the expensive camel's hair overcoat, he did not look as good as he thought he should.

"Okay, are you ready?" Dexter asked. He had one book perched on his lap and another opened, with several pages dog-eared. He sat on a café chair behind Frank, as the show's star applied his make-up in an Avery Fisher Hall dressing room.

"If you must, you must," Frank replied.

"Hey, this could be valuable to you," Dexter insisted. "If you were a general, would you go into battle without reports from your spies?"

Frank grabbed his eyebrow pencil. "Just read, Dex."

"This won't take long. Since we're pretty far north on the West Side, I'll confine my citations to that area."

"Are you sure your intelligence is up to date, Mata Hari?" Frank asked wryly.

Ignoring the sarcasm, Dexter flipped to the book he held. "This one was printed in 1972. The other one's from '69. That's not too long ago...especially as far as ghosts are concerned."

"Fire when ready, Gridley!"

"Okay. We've got a couple teenage punks killed in a gangland rumble a block from here. Remember that this was where they filmed

West Side Story. They actually delayed tearing down a few blocks until –"

"No editorializing," Frank said, glancing at his watch. With twenty minutes until perhaps the most important curtain of his life, he wanted at least ten minutes alone to relax and focus.

"Suit yourself. There's a bag lady who walks Broadway from 72nd to 74th. Two sisters, Rosetta and Janet Van der Voort, skate on the Wollman Ice Rink in Central Park this time of year. One wears red; the other wears purple."

"Now that I would like to see," Frank admitted.

"There's a ten-year-old boy who haunts Apartment 77 in The Dakota."

"What's The Dakota?"

"A swanky apartment house on the corner of 72nd and Central Park West. It was the first one built in this area. It was so far from everything else that people said it had been built in the Dakota Territories."

"I'll never need an encyclopedia with you around, Dex."

Dex ignored him and continued. "Also, a sixteen-year-old girl with braided blond hair and wearing a Victorian blue dress. This one's on West 87th Street, in a five-story brownstone called the DeGeldern House. It was built in 1894, so she had to be an early resident. There's a noisy ghost who touches people in the Hotel des Artistes on West 67th."

"You can skip the indoor ghosts," Frank said. "I'm not making myself known, so I don't think they'll come out of their buildings or move them toward me."

"Then that's it. Oh! Except what I found out about that young dead woman you met in Newark."

The words brought Frank to a halt. He turned his chair around and gestured with his fingertips for Dexter to spill his story.

"I got this stuff from the *Star Ledger* morgue. Her name actually was Emily. Emily Lord. The newspaper published a photograph of her from her high school yearbook. She was absolutely gorgeous.

What a crime!"

"What a crime to happen to anyone, plain or beautiful," Frank said.

"You're right. And they had a picture of her in front of her parents' house on the lawn, with a blanket covering her. You could see the shape of the knife sticking out of her back. Gruesome. From what people said, she was really well liked and a very nice person." Dexter grimaced. "The crazy bastard who killed her was named Frank. It's a good thing you told her your name was Holden."

Frank nodded.

"There's more."

Frank lifted his hand. "I don't want to hear it."

"Nothing bad."

"It doesn't matter."

Dexter's face registered his understanding. "This other world is getting to you."

"It is," Frank admitted. "It's bad enough reading about people's tragedies in the newspaper. Watching them relive their sorrows in Limbo is a lot worse. And now there's one who talked to me. I got to know her. It rips at my guts. I've visited her in my dreams." What he did not say to his friend was how much he dreaded the possibility of seeing worse in his last seven trips to Limbo. "Why don't you make a last-minute inspection of all the illusions?" he suggested. "We can't allow a single hitch tonight."

"Right." Dexter closed his books, stood, patted Frank on the shoulder, and quit the dressing room.

Almost immediately after the prop man's exit, Frank heard him and Elizabeth exchanging low words in the hallway. Frank turned and tried to listen. He could not make out what they said. He was about to rise and cross to the door when Bess appeared. She held a filled, brown grocery bag in one hand.

"How are you?" she inquired, as Frank went back to applying his makeup.

"Great! You?"

"Equally great."

"What's in the bag?"

"A way to slow down your aging and maybe getting half a dozen more uses of Karnak's Coffin."

Frank set down his sponge and stared at Bess's image in the mirror.

"Don't tell me you haven't been noticing your hair coming out in handfuls since you first entered the cabinet."

Frank sighed and nodded.

"I've been with you long enough to know the advance of your male pattern baldness intimately," she went on, "but what was a crawl has turned into a forced march. Not to mention that your skin is abnormally dry in places. You've even got the beginning of two crow's feet at the corner of your eyes. Every time you turn the key in the inside lock, I figure it's stealing around six months of your life, Frank."

Frank had wondered when Bess would notice the obvious. "And you can stop that?"

"In a way. This aging phenomenon may be why the box's designer won't allow more than twelve trips. Tonight will be your sixth trip. I'm convinced that if you use the box tomorrow night as well, it will age you twice as fast. From now on, you and I alternate."

"Ah, no," Frank replied firmly.

Bess came around to his side, compelling Frank to turn. "Hear me out. You had no trouble putting me in the Vanishing Lady box and dumping me four feet through a trap door every night," she argued.

"That was a trick; this is real vanishing," Frank reminded her.

"And you've been telling me not to worry about you for weeks now. Reassuring me that there really isn't any great danger in Limbo. Yes or no?"

Frank realized he was caught by his own arguments. Moreover, the solution was reasonable. There was no firm reason why he had to be the one of the team to disappear.

Bess opened the bag, dug into it, and dragged out a khaki army ropical weight jacket and a pair of jodhpurs very like the ones Frank used. "And what if the twelve green lights reset when I use it? We could theoretically get twenty-four total uses, but I'd be happier just aging myself a little, thank you. I've already done the shopping. I can add the insulation tomorrow. All I need to do is find boots my size. I can use the same helmet you do. My hair will make up for the difference in our head sizes, Oh Great Receding One."

"You've thought of everything, have you?" Frank asked.

"I have. The caftan and the mask will fit me, too, since you and I are pretty much the same size."

"You want to experience Limbo, don't you?" he guessed.

Bess set down the bag. "I won't deny it." She leaned against the edge of the dressing counter. "You don't want me calling you a sexist pig, do you?"

"Okay," Frank relented. "You do the next performance."

Bess nodded smartly with satisfaction. "I deserve a favor for saving months of your life."

"What's that?"

"You said we don't start at the Neil Simon Theater until the 14th. True?"

"True," Frank replied.

"On the 13th, which is a Monday, I want us to do a show for charity." Bess spoke quickly. She had obviously rehearsed her speech. "I told you that my church when I was growing up was St. Benedict's in the Bronx."

"The Fortress."

"The same. My father is high up among the lay people. He told me about some of the charities they're supporting, and they sound very worthwhile. I'd like to do this for him as his parting gift to the parish before he heads down to Florida." She dipped her head. "We could test to see if the green lights reset for me. It's also a way to shut up any critic who says we're gouging the market with our inflated prices. We come off as good guys, you see?" She flashed her best smile. "And it's a way for the girl voted Most Likely to Succeed to finally show off in her old neighborhood. I'll go inside the box that night."

Frank reached out and squeezed Bess's hand. He inwardly winced at using one of the coffin's twelve trips to Limbo for such a mundane appearance. But more than two years of putting up with him, Dexter, and Sonder with hardly a serious complaint merited virtually any favor she asked. It was good to see her smiling again. "Okay, consider it booked."

Bess bent and kissed Frank, just a fraction wide of his lips. "Thank you," she whispered. She scooped up the bag with the costume and pirouetted out of the room.

Frank opened the lid/door of the sarcophagus within five minutes of stepping inside it. He was quite curious about looking at Manhattan as remembered by the ghosts who inhabited the island in Limbo. He carried a small, but powerful, flashlight as well as the lamp atop his pith helmet.

He knew the coffin cover had faced south on the Avery Fisher Hall stage. He moved straight forward, in case there was any relationship of his world's compass directions with those in the world of the unwilling dead. He thumbed on the flashlight and glided across the slick, heat-stealing surface of Limbo.

A few buildings rose in front of him. None was a modern skeleton of steel curtained in glass. The powerful flashlight beam did not show in the void, as its air apparently lacked the motes of dust as any normal cityscape would have. Frank had no idea of how far his throw of light reached. Within seconds, however, he got the notion that it went a long way. From what seemed a distance of miles, a ball of slowly expanding light moved toward him and the magic cabinet.

Damn! Frank thought. I shouldn't have left the box so quickly. Now I'm vulnerable for at least thirty-five minutes. He immediately snapped off the flashlight. The isolated ghost buildings close by that had begun to drift in his direction slowed in their progress but did not stop. The ball of light did not slow. It was as if it had taken a hard fix on Frank and would not be deterred, even without the beam of light.

When Frank glanced down at the flashlight in his hand and it brightened in his view, he realized he had not extinguished the pith helmet light. Fumbling, he found the ice-cold switch. Now the nearer buildings faltered in their advance and came to a halt. The ball of light continued its approach. Frank suddenly felt like Dorothy waiting in Munchkinland as Glinda's bubble of light settled in front of her. With that manner of luminescent apparition, he, too, might have waited patiently for revelation. Something about the intense, white ball coming toward him did not seem nearly so benign. It seemed to be moving not like every other Limbo building he had found but rather like an express train. It also did not glow but burned. Tongues of what looked like flame escaped from it. At the rate it moved, Frank knew that it would be upon him within another two or three minutes.

Frank turned toward what he believed was the interior of the island and began to walk with purpose. He counted the paces of his stride. Only when he had reached one hundred did he stop and switch on his flashlight. He pointed the beam at the ball of churning flame. It was near enough for him to realize that his efforts had been successful. It corrected its advance, coming straight at him. Frank set the light down on the invisible surface of Limbo, carefully made an about-face, and walked away exactly fifty paces.

Without producing any sound, the elongated cocoon of pulsing light came close enough to show a core. It held a three-and-a-half-story brick corner building, designed in the Federal style. It had a small, double-columned portico sheltering its front door. From the age and grime on the brickwork, it looked to be at least one-hundred-and-fifty years old. The intersection and parts of both streets that fronted the building had come along for the ride, as did a smaller, three-story brick structure behind it. In the blink of an eye, the flaming, transparent ball that encircled the vision vanished.

Frank looked up and down the street, expecting to find ghosts in Federal period costume. The pedestrians, however, looked contemporary. They emerged from darkness and returned to it. Although there were never fewer than a dozen in view, not one talked with another. He noticed a black, late-model Cadillac standing in a No Parking zone, with a driver sitting inside, as still as a mannequin.

The building came to a stop directly in front of the flashlight. None of the people passing along the pavement of the streets acknowledged Frank. They seemed as much props as the corner street lamp and the garbage bin. Frank was convinced that the mind that directed the elaborate scene was inside the larger building. Whoever that mind belonged to, it seemed to have expected the appearance in Limbo of a human and, further, that such a human would be brave enough to enter the apparition of his own volition. Other than the ball of fire that had delivered it, the place certainly looked to Frank no more dangerous than had the elementary school on his second visit to Limbo.

Moving cautiously nonetheless, Frank walked under the portico. He read the sign beside the door. It declared the place to be "The historic Fraunces Tavern." A brass plaque on the opposite wall further declared the building to have been erected "...on the site of George Washington's farewell address to his officers."

Frank opened the door and walked in. No one seemed to see him, as if he were the ghost. He moved through the foyer into the restaurant section. There, he saw tables and booths filled with patrons, mostly men in expensive three-piece suits. Frank looked down the length of the aisle.

A solitary man who did not seem to fit in with the others wiped his mouth with a linen napkin, took out his wallet, placed money on top of his check and rose from his table. He wore a rather rumpled two-piece suit. He grabbed a dark fedora from the tabletop as he left and covered his greasy, slicked-back, brown hair with the hat. Under his pencil-thin mustache, his mouth was open, as if needing extra air to fuel his rapid retreat from the room. Frank noted that one of his two central, upper incisors crossed prominently over the other. He altered his walk down the aisle as if he knew Frank was partially in his way, but his eyes did not acknowledge Frank's presence.

Once the man had passed by, Frank returned his inquiring gaze to the other patrons. Just behind the table the out-of-place man had quit, on either side of the aisle sat pairs of men. To Frank's left were a white-haired man wearing a grey suit and a man with horn-rim glasses and a red handkerchief peeking out of his lapel pocket. Across the aisle from them sat a bald-headed man facing away from Frank and the first person that Frank recognized. He had never met the man, but he had seen enough photographs to make no mistake who he was. For only a moment did Simon Magus lock eyes with Frank. Then he turned his torso and looked out the window beside his seat. His eyebrows knit with curiosity. He held up his hand to silence his dining partner. His head swiveled rapidly. He looked down, at something on the opposite side of the aisle. Frank followed his line of sight and saw a large, brown briefcase tucked under the table recently abandoned by the greasy-headed man.

Alarms sounded inside Frank's skull. He began backing down the aisle.

Simon Magus pushed himself up from his seat with great energy and glanced to the back of the room.

Frank had seen enough. He bolted toward the foyer. Three seconds later, the restaurant erupted with a deafening roar. The pressure of the blast threw Frank forward onto the floor. He felt the heat of the explosion on the back of his neck. He scrambled to his feet and ran through the front door.

The black Cadillac had pulled from the curb and was speeding away. In the front passenger seat was the greasy-headed man. He looked back over his shoulder at the tavern. Frank peered at the back of the car and its license plate. It read JE19, but two more figures were so blurred that he could not make them out. For a moment, Frank thought the blur was dirt, but as he stared at its retreating image, he realized it was like a permanently attached lump of smoke. The car vanished into total darkness.

Frank scooped up the flashlight and shone the beam on the face of his watch. He had only four minutes to get back inside the coffin on time. He pivoted to orient himself. Fiery adrenalin exploded into his veins as he realized he had lost the portal box in the limitless blackness. Not finding it in forty minutes would be a public embarrassment; not finding it in sixty almost surely spelled death. He looked to his right and saw the distant image of two women doing figure eights on skates. One wore red, and the other wore purple.

Bless you, Dexter! That must be east Frank reasoned. Then I should go away from them to reach the coffin.

Frank's shoes pounded along the invisible black base of Limbo. He felt the cold reaching in from everywhere to tear at him like a hungry beast. When he counted fifty strides, he thumbed his flashlight on. Although its dark mass was still invisible, he caught a few reflections off the angles of the coffin. He hurried toward it. When he reached the cold metal cabinet he chanced a last pass of the beam behind him. The figure of Simon Magus, in no way damaged by the explosion, walked with grim purpose toward him. Frank snapped off the beam and grabbed the pieces of his Egyptian costume. He snatched off his helmet and let it slip to the floor, put on the silk caftan and the mask, squeezed the crook and flail in his right hand, and slammed shut the door with his left. With only one hand free, he fumbled to find his key. Finally, he had it in the lock. He heard fingers scratching at the door, searching for the pivot ring. As quickly as he could, he turned the key and heard the tumblers engage.

214

"What a sea change!" Harlan Jessup praised. He stood outside Frank's dressing room, wearing an elegantly tailored double-breasted suit. His three-quarter-length wool coat was draped over his shoulders in a raffish manner. Frank wondered how the man had gotten backstage so quickly.

"Thanks," Frank replied.

"You're still very excited by all this?" Jessup asked.

Frank assumed he meant the new act. He also assumed that the observant Jessup was registering in Frank's expression the aftershocks of his harrowing experience minutes before in Limbo. "Shouldn't I be?" he countered, following his verbal parry with the thrust, "Aren't you overdressed for attending a magic show?"

Jessup looked down at himself. "Better over than under. I came here directly from a board of directors meeting. This is from H. Huntsman & Sons on Savile Row. The shoes are Gucci. You'll be able to afford such extravagance now. I'm hoping my investment in your show merits divulging the secret of King Karnak's Coffin."

"Not a chance," Frank was happy to say. He looked down the corridor and caught the figure of the Colonel. The bodyguard's suit was not expensive. Frank imagined that the ex-military man would be much more comfortable wearing fatigues featured on the cover of Soldier of Fortune magazine rather than GQ. He held a chauffeur's cap in his hands. Frank found it difficult to imagine why a man who had served in the military as long as this one had and who had earned the rank of colonel would be reduced to performing menial jobs for a civilian cutthroat like Jessup. He felt a distinct compassion.

"Please come in, Harlan." Frank crooked his finger at the chauffeur/bodyguard. "You, too, sir. How did you like the new show?"

"He didn't see it," Jessup replied on behalf of his factotum, even as he held up his hand to halt the man. "I have a car in the garage below. Why don't you bring it around now, Colonel?" The ex-military man left without having said a word. Jessup smiled broadly at Frank. "I've asked Elizabeth to dine with me tonight, and she's accepted."

Frank was surprised. Bess had said nothing about the date. He returned the smile. "Lucky man."

"I've talked your show up among my friends and business partners," Harlan let him know. "Doing my humble part to make you a smash hit in big spender circles."

"What do you think that holographic mirror trick would cost?" Frank asked.

Jessup folded his theater program. "Not cheap. Maybe eight thousand. Do you want me to extend another line of credit?"

Frank saw the image of himself as a hapless fish clamping down harder on the hook. "Not just yet."

"I've got a design concept. If you have a moment, I'll sketch it while I'm waiting for Elizabeth."

"Fine with me," Frank said. He was glad Jessup was not insisting on conversation, as his mind was still reeling from the images of Simon Magus and the destroyed restaurant.

By the time Frank had cleaned off his makeup, washed up, and changed out of his explorer outfit, Jessup had excellent sketches drawn on the back of a promotional flyer. He had noted as well the names of several optical firms and other technical companies.

"I'm ready, Harlan," Bess said from the hallway.

Harlan stepped back from the door. Bess wore a tight-fitting cocktail dress and held a matching clutch bag. Enormous articulated silver earrings sparkled in the room light. She had her golden hair swept back and held up with silver clasps. It was a look Frank had not seen. He realized he had never accompanied Elizabeth on a formal occasion. He registered the exquisite length of her neck and thought of Grace Kelly, the actress Bess was most often compared to. She had also recently lost the five to seven pounds he estimated she had gained during her years with him on the road and had returned to fashion model thinness.

"Whoa!" was all he could manage.

"Thanks." Bess grinned. "Don't wait up."

Frank nodded. Sharing his news about Simon Magus would have to wait.

"This is an apartment building," Bess realized as the elevator opened on the structure's penultimate floor.

"Absolutely," Jessup replied.

Bess hesitated at the mouth of the elevator. "But I thought…"

"What?"

"The lobby has a desk and is so fancy, and the building faces Central Park, so I assumed…"

"Let's just say it's a private hotel. Most of the space is apartments. Some of it lets out for a week at a time," Jessup explained, "but only to those well vetted and with wallets filled with cash." He stepped into the small hallway and put his hand out to keep the door from closing.

"So this is where you live," Bess said. "I feel kind of foolish dressed so formally."

"Don't. It's one of the most exclusive dining addresses in the city."

Bess stepped out. Jessup crossed to the door opposite, which gleamed in high-gloss red. He unlocked it and held it open. She realized that while the entrance and living room of the apartment were beautifully furnished in Deco, the combined space was not especially large. The building was very tall but narrow. With five long strides she could have paced from the front doorway to the long picture windows. The cut of her dress prevented such strides, so she glided gracefully across the living room and looked down upon the dark park whose Olmstead-designed curving drives and walkways were lit with pools of lamplight. In contrast, the upscale buildings that surrounded it as well as Central Park West, and Fifth Avenue glowed in golden auras, creating a gargantuan gilt frame. She picked out the zoo, the skating rink, the massive hulk of the Metropolitan Museum of Art in the distance.

"Beautiful," she admired.

"Not as beautiful as you are," Jessup responded.

Bess laughed. "I think it's difficult to compare a park with a woman."

Jessup moved up alongside her. "No. Beauty is beauty." He gestured to a long cart filled with silver covered dishes. "I had a cold meal set out. We can eat whenever you please."

"I'm not really that hungry," she said.

Jessup moved behind her and placed his hands lightly on her shoulders. He lowered his head so that he could inhale her delicate perfume and she could feel his exhalation on the nape of her neck. "I hope you mean that only regarding food."

"Not for what you're thinking either," Bess replied, although she did not move away.

Jessup's hands stole slowly along Bess's shoulders and down her arms. "I'm fascinated by your life. Why would an exquisite and intelligent woman choose to isolate herself from the greater world in a touring show?"

Bess stepped toward the food cart, letting her host's arms trail off her. "I'm a magician's assistant. It's a craft. I like what I do."

"But you're like a pearl of great price among swine," the millionaire argued.

Bess shook her head. "That's a harsh simile, Harlan, and quite inappropriate as well. The three men I travel with are all quality people."

Jessup laughed. "Nice people perhaps, but 'quality?' I want to expose you to people of class and accomplishment. Show you what the word 'quality' really means. I can't hope to make you understand this, Bess, but I'm sure it's my fate."

The woman turned with her eyebrow raised. "Who told you to call me Bess?"

Jessup's fingers seemed to tighten involuntarily. He pulled back and crossed the room. "Isn't that what Frank and the other two call you?" he asked as he switched on an amplifier that sat among a nest of expensive audio electronics on a recessed shelf.

Bess lifted a silver cover and found Beef Wellington surrounded by asparagus. "They're my workmates. I've known them for a long time." A covered tureen held vichyssoise. A gleaming porcelain plate contained a fresh fruit mold.

Jessup retraced his steps and came up close behind Bess again. "And that's why you're here tonight. I have to get to know you just as well. Accept that it's my mystic destiny. I certainly have." He kissed her lightly on the curve of her jaw, just under her ear.

"Mystic destiny or not, I'm uncomfortable being alone with you in your apartment, Harlan," Bess revealed.

"Abandon bourgeois morality," Jessup told her in a low, seductive voice. "I'm going to teach you the joys of rising above hidebound, Catholic behaviors." He placed his hand on her side and moved it upward, toward her left breast.

Bess ducked away and regarded him with narrowed, forbidding eyes. "I don't think so."

"Oh, come on!" Jessup said. "We're too old to play games."

"Who's playing a game?" Bess asked.

Jessup held his ground. He thrust his hands into his pockets. "You like me or you wouldn't be here. I like you more than you know. New moralities aside, you're no virgin and either am I. How many more years will we still have the confidence in our bodies to enjoy sex?"

"I was never a first, second, or even third date girl," Bess informed him. "I'm not about to change my ways just because time is against me. And it has nothing to do with being an old dog. I have to know and trust a man well before I can be intimate. It might never happen. Those are my rules, Harlan. If that's a game and you don't want to play it, I guess this mystic evening is over."

I small sound escaped from Jessup. He looked at her with his face lowered, through his eyebrows, then reached for the bottle of Dom Perignon that chilled in the ice bucket. When he elevated his chin again, he had affixed a warm smile. "I'm not ordinarily a patient man, but for you I will wait. I'm betting we have a future."

Bess said nothing.

"May I call you Bess…as a gesture of good faith?" Harlan asked as he worked at the wire confining the cork.

"All right," she relented.

"Good." Jessup worked the cork loose. It exploded across the room, and a small eruption of bubbling foam escaped the neck of the bottle. "That's a start."

FIFTEEN

DECEMBER 8, 1976

BESS RETURNED TO the Sheraton at ten minutes past three. She doffed her coat, hat, and shopping bag and dropped onto the bed the note she had been handed by the desk clerk. She had arisen earlier than normal and braved the holiday avenues of New York to complete her explorer's wardrobe for her first venture into Limbo that evening. On the way back to the hotel she had passed a movie theater and seen that it was offering a sneak preview of a remake of the classic A Star Is Born, with Barbra Streisand and Kris Kristofferson. Two of the things she loved best about New York were the cinemas that ran virtually around the clock and the next-to-final cuts of films presented to test audience reaction. She could not resist the temptation to purchase a ticket. She had been rather disappointed and had written the same on the questionnaire she was given.

Plopping herself onto the bed and kicking off her low heels, Bess was more than ready to catch two hours' sleep. She had an unfailing alarm clock inside her head and could set it within half an hour of when she wanted to wake, night or day. As she unzipped her skirt, she noticed that the light on the telephone was blinking. The first message was from her physician. His voice carried the usual doctor's mask of professionalism, but he said clearly that her blood and urine tests had shown abnormalities and that he wanted her to go to St.

Luke's Hospital on Friday morning, that he would have a battery of other tests scheduled for her.

Bess's lips compressed so tightly that they disappeared. Her eyes darted back and forth as she half-listened to the second message. It was from Harlan Jessup, asking her out after the show. She deleted both messages and sat quietly, thinking. She had known that her tests would show a problem. She had, in fact, informed Dr. Franz that she thought she had some form of anemia, as well as the reasons why. But there was always the possibility it was something far worse. She thought of her mother, who had been not much older than she when she received her news of terminal illness.

Bess left the telephone off the hook and lay down. She opened the note. It, too, was from Harlan Jessup. He apologized for having offended her the previous night and begged to be able to make up for it this evening.

"No chance," Bess muttered. She consulted her appointment and contact book and then dialed for an outside line.

Because it was the afternoon, Allan Salkin answered his own telephone. Bess identified herself and received an effusive greeting.

"Two things, Allan," Bess said. "The first is to ask you to keep Harlan Jessup at arm's length. I'll let you know the reasons later in detail, but for now just trust me." The agent, who was free with advice and always debating with Frank, knew better than to question the strong-willed assistant who he knew ran the troupe.

"I trust you implicitly, Lady," Salkin said, borrowing the term of respect he had heard Frank use for her.

"Second. None of us has been on a long vacation for years. This jam-packed holiday stint is going to kill us. Frank and I agree that we need fill-in talent which might become full-time as the act expands."

"I was thinking the same thing," the agent came back. "In fact, I've had two aggressive young women call me this morning, wondering if such openings exist. They must have seen the article I planted in Variety."

"Yes, terrific thinking," Bess said, understanding that the agent-to-the-second-rate badly needed his own kudos.

"I'll have them come in right away, and I'll send them to you if they can prove to me their resumes are for real."

"While you're at it, find the contact information for a magician named Patrick Keleher," Bess directed. "His stage name is Pat Kelly. He lives in the city. He's even better at sleight of hand and misdirection than Frank, but he's never gotten a break. He might want to back up Dexter and Alexander."

"Pat Kelly," Salkin echoed. "Yeah, Frank talked about him once. I'll do that. Anything else?"

"That's enough for now, if you get right on them."

"Consider it done."

"Oh, and if Frank hasn't called you already," she said, "we've solved the problem of doing King Karnak's Coffin more frequently."

"He did call, an hour ago. How do you feel about alternating with him?"

"I'm looking forward to it," she said truthfully.

"Great! Break a leg!"

"Thanks, Allan. Gotta go."

"Sure thing."

Bess felt drained. She hung up the telephone, curled into a ball on top of the bedspread, and was asleep within the minute.

Bess set her knitting down on the theater dressing table and answered the knock at her door.

Frank stood in the hallway, already made up and dressed. He said, "I can't get used to the luxury of separate dressing rooms. This knocking to talk with you stinks."

Bess wasn't buying his breezy delivery. She knew from his face that his words were masking something serious. "Okay, spill it."

Frank exhaled noisily. "I think we'd better skip doing King Karnak's Coffin tonight."

"What? Why?" Bess demanded, preparing herself for a cock-and-bull excuse to protect her.

Frank pulled out a café chair. "I had a very rough ride last night. I came face to face with the coffin's real owner." In detail, he told Bess about the incident.

"So that solves the mystery why he never picked up the trick. You think he's been waiting for the sarcophagus to arrive in New York?" she wondered.

"Maybe," Frank answered. "All I can tell you is that he and that tavern took off like a shot when I shone my flashlight beam in their direction. Do you know where the Fraunces Tavern is?"

"No."

"Down near Wall Street. That's a hell of a long way from Lincoln Center."

"You're right. So…"

Frank held up his hand. "Listen. There's more. Lots more. I spent the end of the morning and the beginning of the afternoon in the Periodicals Room of the 42nd Street Public Library. Dexter's successes with research inspired me."

"And?"

"The explosion happened in January. It killed four persons and injured fifty-three more. The one closest to the blast was so mutilated that they couldn't identify the pieces. What was left of his wallet had nothing but money in it."

"Simon Magus."

"I'm sure of it. This was one situation the escape artist couldn't beat. The guy he was sitting with was a big-time stock broker. My wild-ass guess is this rich boy was arranging to have Magus perform at a private surprise party. I called his office and spoke with his secretary, pretending to be a police detective checking on details. The guy had no record of the lunch, either on his business or his personal calendars."

"Who were the other two?" Bess asked.

"The first was a guy named Emilio Ramos. He was the one all the newspapers and the police assumed was the target. A group named the Armed Forces of the Puerto Rican National Liberation ostensibly claimed responsibility for the bombing. This Ramos was a high-level San Juan policeman, up in New York taking training on infiltrating dissident groups. The last victim was Elliott Saperstein. An assistant district attorney for the City."

"Working with Ramos."

"Exactly. Everyone accepted that Saperstein was an innocent casualty. I know better." Frank rubbed his eyes, as if he felt a headache coming on. Bess waited for him to continue.

Frank said, "There was this single sentence in one of the papers, meant as background. It said that Saperstein was 'at the time of his death also working on cleaning up Manhattan's 42nd Street district.' You know, all those sex-related enterprises across the street from the library and running down to Ninth Avenue are either run by the Mafia or pay protection to them. This assistant DA was evidently beginning to put a real crimp in their style."

"Couldn't the guy with the greasy hair and crooked teeth have been working for this Puerto Rican group?" Bess asked.

Frank shrugged. "I suppose. But if Hollywood was doing a Mafia film, Central Casting would have picked the guy in a heartbeat. That and the black Cadillac."

Bess leaned on the makeup table. "I suppose we'll never know."

Frank picked up her knitting and examined it. "Not necessarily."

"What did you do?"

"I wrote an anonymous tip letter to the NYPD, giving them a description of the man, the car and what I could see of the license plate. I believe the number was all Simon Magus could see from his seat. That's what the blurry numbers were about."

"He wants someone to solve his murder."

"I sure would."

Bess's shoulder shook. "Jeez. This is really creepy."

226

"But he may also want to escape back into this world," Frank said. "That's why I couldn't keep this secret from you."

"How could he return without a body?" Bess doubted.

A sarcastic noise escaped Frank's throat. "Hey, this is the guy who arranged to get the cabinet. He evidently hung around with people who have big-time supernormal abilities. Who's to say he couldn't grab my skin? Or yours?"

"Okay. I'm duly warned."

"And who's to say he didn't recognize me? In that case, he knows I'm a magician. Which means I was probably using his box to do a performance. Which means I am likely to be stepping out of the box in the same place tonight. He may not have moved an inch...or whatever length it is in Limbo."

Bess ordered her thoughts for a moment. "Say you're right. I step into the box. I turn the key and hold tight to the pivot ring. I look out the porthole. If I see the guy you described, I immediately turn the key again. Onstage, you wait three seconds before opening the cover. If I have to come right back, that's a risk we've taken. We let the audience know it's a work in progress and we tried. If I see nobody through the porthole, I hold onto the ring for thirty minutes and then risk moving outside. He'll probably be creating some halo of light, even if he hasn't dragged the tavern with him."

"It's just —"

Bess held up her hand. "Now it's your turn to listen. When I step outside, I will leave only the pith helmet lit. I will put it quickly on the floor of the box with myself between it and Limbo. I change like lightning. If I see Wall Street rumbling toward me, I leap inside and turn the key. But that will have given you at least thirty-two seconds. Just rush the display and spiel for me."

"Oh, man," Frank groaned.

"Right now, a giant auditorium is filling up with folks who spent beaucoup bucks to see this so-called trick," Bess argued. "If we fail to present it, we'll earn an instant reputation as welshers. That could haunt the team long after the coffin has stopped working for us."

"I don't know," Frank said.

Bess put her forefinger on his nose and pushed hard. "I'm the one who kept warning you, remember? I'm not going to do anything stupid. Trust me."

Frank threw up his hands, came up from his chair, and walked toward the dressing room door.

"Hold on, Spiegel," Bess called in her stern voice. "I still have new business before we can adjourn this meeting. You remember you were discussing the need to find competent substitutes for me, Dex, and Sonder so we can each go on a protracted vacation after this holiday grind?"

Frank's eyebrows furrowed as he struggled to remember a conversation that had never occurred. Bess tried not to use similar stratagems often, but the occasion demanded it. She had subtly gained control of the day-to-day operations of the troupe within three months of signing on. Frank had convinced himself that he was an excellent manager, but in fact he frequently forgot or neglected details. She found it best to inform him that he had made a decision even as she was acting on it.

"I said that?" he doubted.

"Yes. In Newark. At Hobby's Deli. You were worrying about how hard —"

"I believe you," Frank said, bamboozled by the quick barrage of her phony details.

"Just so we're not running around like chickens at the last minute, we should have Allan looking for good substitutes," she continued.

"Good thinking," Frank said. "I'll talk to him about it tomorrow."

Bess had picked up her hairbrush and ran it through her thick hair. "I'll do it. I have to tell him to avoid Harlan Jessup anyway."

"Really? Why?"

"I think he's crazy."

"Then why did you go out with him last night without telling us?"

"So that you wouldn't try to stop me. I figured I had the best chance of piercing his armor and getting his story, since he's obviously smitten with me."

"And?"

Bess rolled her eyes. "It's more like obsession. He not only wanted me to lie down and spread 'em on our first date, but he also gave me a lecture on abandoning all morality if I truly wanted to enjoy life."

"Whoa!"

"'Whoa' indeed. If he's not crazy, he's at least amoral." Thinking about the episode, Bess reflexively tightened the sash on her dressing gown. "When I informed him I'm an old-fashioned gal, his jaw went tight and his hands actually balled into fists. Then he realized what he looked like and stuck them into his pants pockets."

"So what you're telling me is that we have trouble inside the cabinet and outside it," Frank assessed.

"The live guy is more trouble," Bess decided. "He retraced his steps as quickly as he could and the rest of the evening was normal. But there was an edgy undercurrent. I didn't push him on any more of his philosophies. I had seen more than enough through that one open door. We need to discourage this spoiled boy from his strange interest in us in the strongest ways possible."

The warm sensation of having been right in his suspicions washed over Frank. "No problem here. I figure at the rate we're making money, we can retire his loan by June and be done with him forever."

Bess set down her hairbrush. "Amen." Her eyes went wide in a sudden remembrance. "Oh! Does Allan Salkin know I'm Roman Catholic?"

"He might. Why?"

"Because Harlan does. He made a passing reference to my Catholic upbringing. I certainly hope Allan was the one who clued him in. Otherwise…"

"Like I said," Frank supplied, "not good." He reached out and pulled Bess's face gently toward his. He pressed a kiss lightly on her forehead. "I worry because I love you. You know that."

"And I love you, too, Spiegel," Bess affirmed. She pushed him backward with not a little force. "Now get the hell out of my dressing room and let tonight's star finish her makeup!"

Bess allowed herself ten minutes inside the coffin to acclimate. Periodic peeks through the porthole revealed only a few old buildings. She remembered Dexter's theory that the dead in Limbo dragged their significant buildings around like crabs drag shells. It's more like vampires dragging their coffins, she thought. To her relief, there was no distant ball of fire rolling toward her and no close-up dead magician's face. She drew in a big, fortifying breath and opened the door.

The air was frigid beyond the open door, but not as cold as Bess had expected. In spite of Frank's coaching, she had trouble adjusting her eyes and feet to the invisible ground. Barely lifting her boots, she worked her way around to the back of the coffin. She saw nothing until she shone her flashlight into the dense blackness. She winced at the thought of having lied to Frank about staying inside the coffin, but she had much to do, to confirm, to learn before her appearance at the church near her girlhood home.

As if in response to her light, the trees, rocks and walkways of Central Park appeared under a leaden sky filled with snow clouds. Bess shut off her light. From a pocket, she took out the two-dozen dice that had not been used since they were in Texas. She moved toward the scene, dropping a die every ten steps. After dropping ten of the white cubes and noting that one dot always landed facing up, she discerned the Wollman Skating Rink. She saw not two but twenty skaters from a bygone era gliding, doing tricks and even falling with arms awhirl. All but two skaters, one dressed in red and one in purple, ignored her approach. Janet and Rosetta Van der Voort came up to the edge of the ice and waited.

Bess waved. The sisters waved back.

Bess wanted to shout out a hello but feared that the spirit of Simon Magus might hear her. She glanced around, to be sure nothing and no one was creeping up on her. The sisters stared at her but said nothing.

Bess came within ten feet of the young women. "Hello, Rosetta. Hello, Janet. I'm Elizabeth."

The one in red opened her mouth. Her hello was faint and sounded harsh and dry.

"You're dead, you know," Bess said, getting right to her objective.

Both women nodded slowly. The figures behind them continued to glide and twirl.

"You've tried to return to the world of living people, haven't you?"

Again, both women nodded. They consulted with each other in whispers. The one in purple tried to speak to Bess, but her voice was too faint to discern any words.

"I'm from the Bronx. Jonas Bronck's Farm, across the East River." Neither of the spirits acknowledged the reference. They regarded her as Bess might have greeted the sudden appearance of Moses. Bess pointed. "Are those real people?"

The purple-clad sister tried to speak again. Her voice sounded like a rusty hinge moving. She put a mitten to her throat and obviously tried to clear it. The one in red stepped off the ice and began to move clumsily toward Bess.

As Frank had trained her to do, Bess switched on her flashlight beam and pointed it directly in the bold sister's face. The spirit threw up her hands and averted her gaze. Bess lowered the beam. The determined creature resumed her advance. Again Bess attacked her with light. This time she sat on the ground and began to unlace her skates.

"The sky!" Bess called out. "You can make it bright if you wish.

It doesn't have to be like you remember. You can change your world. Try it! Think of a blue sky! See a blue sky in your mind!"

The red-coated sister continued to undo her skates, but the one in purple gazed upward with a quizzical look.

Bess shut off her light and backed carefully but quickly from the skating rink area. Only when she had counted forty paces did she pivot around and press her flashlight on. She found one of the dice almost directly under her. She sighed with relief when she took another forty steps and saw the back of the coffin. She extinguished her beam and minced forward the remainder of the way blindly.

Only when her gloved fingers rested against the sarcophagus did Bess take the time to look back for the sisters. She was surprised but overjoyed to see small flashes of blue appearing above the rink. And then a sudden shaft of glorious sunlight broke through the dark clouds, like a message from heaven. The involuntary grin on Bess's face slipped when she looked over her right shoulder and saw the ball of flame that Frank had described. It was barreling toward the ice skating rink.

Bess pulled the diaphanous caftan out from under her explorer jacket. She pulled open the coffin door. When she was inside, she swiftly set the helmet behind her and then produced the mask, crook, and flail. She risked turning on her flashlight one more time. Its beam fixed on the hourglass. More than half the sand lay in the bottom. Quivering from the cold, she consulted her wristwatch and confirmed that thirty-nine minutes had elapsed. The ball of conjured flame looked to be only five city blocks from the open coffin door. Bess closed the lid and pivoted the ring. She counted seconds. When she was by her reckoning within fifteen ticks of forty-one minutes, she peered through the porthole and saw that the old tavern loomed in front of the coffin. A man who could only be Simon Magus rushed out of the front door, through the bubble of glowing light. Bess turned the key in the lock.

"She's way better than you as the intrepid explorer, Frank!" Sonder joked as the three male members of the company fanned out within Bess's dressing room.

"Am not!" Bess returned.

"Let's call it a draw and Number Seven Hundred and Ninety Seven in the bag," said Frank diplomatically. He faced the other two men. "She is making it possible for us to fill all our commitments this year, so you just be ready to kiss her hand or whatever other part of her anatomy she dictates."

Sonder puckered up and bent low. "With pleasure."

Bess shoved him back hard against the door. "Too bad another of the green lights turned off. All of us together only get a total of twelve trips."

Dexter shrugged. "The guy who gave it to us said we had to accept the deal as one." A new, disturbing thought seemed to be coalescing in his brain from the look on his face, but Bess interrupted it.

"Hey!" she said to the group. "While I was standing around in Limbo with nothing to do, I thought of a tiny but...I think... excellent addition to the trick."

"What?" Dexter asked.

"Whichever of us goes inside will utter a new last phrase: "Either I shall return, or else the spirit of the evil Pharaoh Karnak will be released again upon the earth."

Sonder whistled with appreciation. "Now there's real tension."

"I like it," Frank decided. "When they see the figure in the mask, crook, and flail, they'll worry for a second that the trick went wrong."

Bess beamed at the group.

A resounding knock jiggled the dressing room door. Sonder stepped away from it as Bess gave permission for entry.

The Colonel held onto the knob and carefully swung the door back as he entered. He came only two steps into the room, registered the crowd, and stopped.

"I'm…here to…see if Miss Coleman is ready to be driven to her date," he said, in an uncharacteristically soft voice.

"I accepted no date," Bess declared. "Please call and tell your employer that my time is strictly spoken for over the next few days."

The Colonel seemed to mull over her words and finally replied, "I understand your feelings."

Something about the ambiguity in the man's response prompted Frank to a spur-of-the-moment decision. "What's your name, sir?"

"William Kirkbride," the Colonel said. "My friends called me Bill."

"Well, Mr. Kirkbride –"

"Bill," the powerful man invited.

Frank felt the collective tension in the room relax. He knew he was about to make the right decision. "Thank you. I wonder if you might like to catch some supper with us."

"I would like that very much," Kirkbride replied.

One aspect of a magic show that every member of the troupe appreciated was that an audience could be fully satisfied with two hours of entertainment. Hamlet might run for three-and-a-half hours; a Wagnerian opera might drone on for four; even a Broadway musical might last three hours. But Spiegel/Master of Magic offered so many delights and surprises in quick order that everyone seemed satisfied after one hundred and twenty minutes. If Frank found particularly interesting volunteers, he would sometimes stretch the performance as long as one hundred and twenty-five minutes. Since Bess knew that his free-form patter was a highly appreciated talent, she encouraged it and enthusiastically played his foil and straight man when needed. But the two-hour norm allowed them to beat virtually every other show in any big town out the stage door and therefore to the best showfolk eateries.

This evening their reservation had been made for Mamma Leones, in the heart of the theater district. It had once been an intimate Italian restaurant, but the sensational food had made the establishment a culinary hit. Now it occupied three adjacent buildings.

"Here's to spirits!" Sonic sang out, lifting his glass high. His double entendre was met with three sets of cocked and warning eyebrows. He was not cowed. Instead, he looked at Bill Kirkbride and said, "I don't know why they're glaring at me; I'm drinking a Coke. They've got the Chianti."

"You're a laugh riot," Dexter said, punching his companion hard enough on his left arm that Sonder was sure to censure his witticisms for the rest of the evening. Only the dessert remained to be ordered. Frank had just questioned the waiter about zabaglione when Kirkbride, who sat next to him, touched him lightly on the wrist.

"Excuse me. If I might." The military man smiled at the waiter. "I see you serve zuccotto. Do you know if you have a whole one uncut back there?"

The waiter's face brightened with the prospect of a much bigger tip. "I believe we do. Let me check."

"Has anyone tried it before?" Kirkbride asked. None had. "I think you'll be pleasantly surprised. But the main reason I ordered it is because it's like a cake. Actually, a cake in the shape of a dome. It's a Florentine specialty, and some people say it's made that way in honor of Brunelleschi's famous Duomo."

Four slightly stunned expressions revealed the troupe's collective amazement at the Colonel's unsuspected erudition.

"I was stationed in Germany for one tour," he revealed. "I used y free time to do a great deal of sightseeing. The reason I need a celebration cake is because today I inherited my uncle's estate." He quickly held up his hand. "Not that I wanted him to die, you understand. But he was eighty and lived a good life. Today I became a semi-wealthy man."

Genuine congratulations sprang up around the table.

Kirkbride leaned in and gathered each member of the group with his eyes before speaking. "You four are the only ones in this city who know."

"Harlan Jessup doesn't know?" Dexter wondered.

"That's right. And I want it to stay that way for a few more days."

No one dared to question the man further or speculate aloud why he had made the request of them.

The zuccotto, formed from pound cake, almonds, filberts, maraschino liqueur, semisweet chocolate drops, heavy whipping cream, confectioner's sugar and Cognac, was a tremendous hit at the table. The last of the wine flowed freely. When the check came, Bill Kirkbride insisted on paying.

As the group discussed whether to walk or take a cab back to the Sheraton, the Colonel leaned over toward Frank and said, "I'd appreciate it if you and I could take a walk together."

"I don't know," Sonder jumped in. "It's pretty dangerous this hour on the streets of New York. Are you sure you can defend yourself?"

Dexter punched him again and this time hoisted his companion up and bum's-rushed him toward the door. "Come on, Bess!" he called back.

Elizabeth picked up her purse, rose, and nodded at the two seated men.

"Thanks for dinner on behalf of me and the gremlins, Bill. Gentlemen, have a good conversation," she wished. And then she, too, moved toward the restaurant's main door.

Kirkbride said nothing of substance until they were out on the sidewalk. He established an unhurried pace, a tempo conducive to conversation.

"I'm the great-grandson of a civil war captain," he began without preamble. "On the side of the Confederacy. My father fought in World War I, as a lieutenant. I was born in 1924. I just turned fifty two a few weeks ago." When Frank declined to interrupt, he moved smoothly on. He described being sent to Virginia Military Institute as a teenager. He graduated on an accelerated schedule so that he could serve in World War II. His commission was as a second lieutenant and he was enlisted into the 4th Infantry. His first taste of battle was on Utah Beach, swiftly followed by the campaign to take Cherbourg. He claimed to have been one of the first American liberators to have entered Paris and to set foot on German soil. After the war, which he exited as a first lieutenant, he decided to make the military his career. He served in Korea and was promoted to captain. When John Kennedy decided to embroil the country in Vietnam, he did two tours early in the conflict. He moved into the Special Forces division, glamorized as the Green Berets. For leadership qualities and for meritorious valor, he was promoted to the rank of major. For his outspoken manner and disinclination toward Army politics, he never reached colonel.

"That's a little joke of Jessup's," Kirkbride revealed. "His way of telling me I'm a failure. He knows I refused to continue in Vietnam, that I openly contended I would no longer fight in a war the United States had no intention of winning."

"You gave him that information?" Frank asked, thinking that the man had asked to be mocked, considering Jessup's sarcastic and superior nature.

"When he pushed early on for personal details of my life, I point blank told him he shouldn't need any more than was on my resume or known by my references," Kirkbride replied. "He had me minutely investigated. He explained it as part of 'due diligence.'"

"I got that speech, too," Frank recalled.

"And that's something I need you to remember from what I tell you tonight," the gruff-voiced man said. "I stayed in the military for my required thirty years, so I could get a pension. But a thirty-year pension ain't enough to live well, so I advertised myself as a high-level bodyguard. Jessup realized, with my connections, that I could serve in even more valuable capacities."

"Spy work?" Frank hazarded.

"No. But I know a couple people who do it. I also know people who can rig accidents so no one ever knows they're accidents. Like the hole in the bottom of your old bus."

Frank slowed his pace, and his companion shortened his step as well.

"It was made by a very good mechanic with an old-fashioned beer bottle opener and a hammer. Then he stuck a wad of chewing gum in it. It worked even faster than he had promised. He also rigged the temperature sensor so it wouldn't register the rise."

"Why?"

"To make sure y'all would be in Jessup's debt. And to give him an excuse to stay near Miss Coleman."

"Bastard. What's the deal with his obsession?" Frank asked.

Kirkbride dug into his pocket and produced his wallet. From a secret compartment he pulled out a newspaper photograph of a blond-haired woman inside a plastic sleeve. She might for all the world have been Bess's twin sister. He gave Frank the photograph.

"Her name is Sunny Crabtree. It is now, anyway. When he first met her, it was Sunny Templeton. Her family settled in Texas even before the Alamo. They're as close to Texas blueblood as they get. He met her at a fundraising event when he was an up-and-coming banker and fell instantly in love with her looks, her personality, and her social status. He managed to get near her by various means. He even got her to like him. He swore to her that he would be very rich and important one day and begged her to wait for him."

"You got all this out of Jessup?" Frank said with astonishment.

"No. When I realized how thoroughly he'd investigated my life, I turned the tables on him. Anyway, he soon found that his only hope of rapid advancement was to marry the boss's daughter. Alberta DeHaviland was the only child of a man who controlled a group of Texas banks. She's a plain woman. I imagine he didn't have to work too hard to captivate her. Soon after they married he got himself put in charge of the bank's venture capital investments department. He's obviously good at what he does, because everything he touched turned to profits. But when he asked Sunny Crabtree to leave her husband of two years, she turned a deaf ear.

"She broke his heart, as they say," Kirkbride continued. "It may explain why he lacks one now, but I personally doubt he was born with it. His consolation was to substitute a succession of Sunny look-alikes as mistresses, until his wife got tired of the humiliation. But by that time, Jessup had his own financial empire going."

"So, he's endlessly chasing Sunny Templeton," Frank mused aloud.

"But he's never fallen for any substitute like he has for Miss Coleman," declared Kirkbride. "Then again, there's never been one who looked so much like her or one so independent."

"Crazy bastard," Frank said, amending his former pronouncement.

"You have no idea." They had reached the lobby of the Sheraton. Since the hour was late, little traffic came through the lobby. Kirkbride gestured to two chairs off in a corner. "Before I forget, I want to thank you for your kindnesses. Especially calling me 'sir' in front of Jessup last night."

Kirkbride had unbuttoned his coat. Before he could adjust his jacket, Frank caught sight of the base of a pistol's grip. "That was nothing," Frank said, averting his eyes.

"Not to me. In the military, we're taught to call every man 'sir.' You have manners and you're a kind person. And then tonight you asked my name. That's when I knew I'd open up all the way to you."

"I'm glad you have that confidence in me," Frank returned.

The ex-military man nodded curtly. Frank wondered if it was his imagination working that made it seem like Kirkbride was finally allowing his close-cropped hair to grow out. He noted also that the man had an old, ugly scar on the side of his neck, perhaps from a grazing bullet or a deflected bayonet.

"You need to know more," he said. "I understand why you want to keep Miss Coleman away from him. I'm glad she wasn't fooled."

"Can you help in any way?" Frank asked.

"Several. Let me tell you what Jessup's capable of. You know his financial empire is worldwide. Oil, precious metals. Money laundered overseas that needs to return to our shores. Now, he wouldn't dare operate this way inside the U.S, but in other countries he hasn't shied from harming his competitors."

"Physically?" Frank worried.

Kirkbride paused to consider how to frame his reply. "Let's just say I've been personally involved in killing on different ends of the world. Cruel killing. But at least it was face to face, where both sides were forewarned and held weapons. I've been a party to crueler and more senseless killing since I retired. I was his liaison for several operations I'm not proud of, even though the targets were invariably men as ruthless and amoral as he is. Inside the States, he confines himself to investigating the hell out of those he focuses on. Then he can either blackmail them or else leak damning facts to the press. He builds his empire by destroying others. As soon as he realizes he can't have Miss Coleman, he'll lash out at all of you to get even. It's his habitual modus operandi."

An icy cold similar to that of limbo penetrated Frank's chest. "But if he ruined us, he'd lose money on what he lent me."

Kirkbride laughed lightly. "He'd have the bus repossessed. And if he lost a couple of thousand on the deal, he'd write it off as a capital loss. Believe me: That would never stop him."

Frank mastered his panic and attempted a nonchalant smile. "But what could he possibly dig up to ruin us? We're not drugs lords or arms dealers. We're all as clean as fire engines."

Kirkbride shook his head slowly. "Not all. Dexter is clean. Aside from a bad habit of throwing himself on top of buddies in dangerous situations, he's much too intelligent to live carelessly." Frank knew the army man was speaking of the incident in which Dexter pushed a fellow Marine out of the way of an incoming hand grenade and was wounded by shrapnel. Before he could ask if Kirkbride had done the digging for Jessup, the man plowed on.

"Alexander is also small potatoes stuff. He was arrested a long time ago for grand theft auto. Ostensibly a prank done on a dare while he was drunk. There's also an outstanding warrant for him in Louisiana for breech of promise. The women take that seriously in bayou country."

Frank nodded, now understanding why Frank was so jumpy every time they entered that state.

"But Miss Coleman is another story," said Kirkbride.

Frank remembered with alarm Bess's words about Jessup knowing she was Catholic. He had indeed had her life investigated.

"Tell me," he said.

"She had a very serious teenage romance," Kirkbride disclosed. "She ended up pregnant, and even though the boy was also Catholic he refused to marry her. Before it showed she got an abortion. It was while her father was distracted with her mother's last days. She stayed with a girlfriend one long weekend. The friend knew a skilled abortionist, and the procedure was a success. But the friendship became strained, and the other woman must have talked to several people in later years."

"My God!" Frank exclaimed.

Kirkbride turned his chair so he could face the magician more fully on. "I'm telling you: he's incredibly thorough. The money he's spent on investigation has yielded high enough returns in the past to make his use of private detectives a habit. He also expressed great joy over the death of Miss Coleman's fiancée. Said he wouldn't have had – "

The unexpected words temporarily stunned Frank. Then he managed to interrupt. "Wait a second. What fiancée?"

"You didn't know she was to be married a little over three years ago?"

"No," Frank admitted. "I had no idea. It was before I'd met her."

"Brother. You guys act much closer than you actually are. You're a strange group." Kirkbride shrugged and moved on. "When she was thirty she met the man of her dreams. Rich Something. He was the number one representative for the Society of the Plastics Industry. Crisscrossed the country constantly to convince municipalities to change their codes so plastic plumbing and sewer piping could replace cast iron. Made *Time* magazine's list of the Top Ten Fastest Rising Executives in 1971. Anyway, he was not only always on the road but also busy extricating himself from an unhappy marriage. Finally he got divorced and, after a few months for the dust to settle, they set a date. He lived in a carriage house pad over in Brooklyn Heights. But the day of the wedding, the taxi cab he was riding in to the church was broadsided by a bus. Killed him and the driver. She pretty much went into shock for a couple of months. She was living with her father at the time, but after a couple weeks she moved into the carriage house.

"That's where she was when she first came to me," Frank told him. "Jesus."

"Does it explain a lot?" Kirkbride asked.

Frank scowled. "Volumes. And she must have lied to both her father and her priest about the man having been married before. They'd have given her a bad time of it otherwise. Did this happen in the fall of the year?"

"I think it was early October."

Frank nodded. "That explains her recurring blues. So, Jessup would come after me through her and the abortion information."

Kirkbride fixed his keen, assessing eyes on his audience of one. He seemed to be weighing if Frank could honestly be so ignorant. "He'd come after you through your father."

The icy panic returned. Frank could not find his voice.

Kirkbride made a noise in his throat. "I'm assuming you also didn't know that Helmut Spiegel led a former life as Helmut Seelig. He served the German cause on the Eastern Front during World War II in the SS. The unit he served in was responsible for what the Nazis euphemistically called 'pacification.' In brief, when they occupied a country to the east they eliminated organized resistance by systematically murdering the intelligentsia: the politicians, ministers and priests, doctors, lawyers, teachers."

"Was my father directly implicated in murder?" Frank managed to ask.

"He changed his name and came into Canada using false papers. Then he used those and his employment in Canada as a springboard to get into the United States. It doesn't really matter if he was guilty of murder or not, Frank. His association damns him," Kirkbride evaded. "I'm certain that Jessup has enough on him to get him deported."

"My father's a good man," Frank argued. "He would never kill anyone."

"He would, you would, I would if another man put a gun to our heads and told us it was us or them," lectured the ex-major. "Don't fixate on that. If you say he's led a good life since then, that's what's important."

"Goddamn the son of a bitch!" Frank hissed, wishing Harlan Jessup were standing in front of him. "What can I do?"

"You can do very little. However, Miss Coleman can keep Jessup in line for a long time. I hate to give you this advice, but it's best if you encourage her to keep seeing him. String him along, but don't allow him to get her completely alone."

"How long can we keep that up?" Frank lamented.

Kirkbride waited until a couple had walked by them before answering. "I was expecting you to ask me by now why I still served a monster like Jessup after what I've learned about him. The answer is that I need to atone for the sins he made me an accomplice to early in my employment. I've been carefully amassing information on him for more than a year. He's relying on me not exposing him, because if I did he would surely implicate me as well. I'm giving my two-week's notice on Monday, but I can't act before a couple months. Once I've liquidated all my uncle's resources and am out of the country with a cold trail, I'll turn over the proof I've gathered to highly motivated non-governmental persons and let them handle the situation as they see fit."

"Could he be murdered?" Frank asked.

"Ten times over," answered Kirkbride. "In the meantime, he'll have to let up on pestering Miss Coleman soon enough. On the 16th he begins an extended trip to Malaysia and the Philippines."

Frank sat for several moments, wondering how to break the news to the group, what to say without betraying individual secrets.

The man Franklin Spiegel had thought incapable of stringing five words together until this evening squeezed his shoulder solicitously. "Forewarned is forearmed. Let's stay in touch. I'll let you know where I am until this problem resolves itself."

Before Frank could think of a reply, Kirkbride was on his feet and heading toward the Sheraton's revolving door.

244

SIXTEEN

December 9, 1976

FRANK WONDERED JUST how much information Allan Salkin was releasing to the press. As he walked through the lobby of the Sheraton, he was accosted by two fans and their outthrust pens and programs. Never one to underestimate the value of loyal admirers, he took time to speak with them and answer their questions. When they at last seemed satisfied, he excused himself and went upstairs to Bess's room.

Bess wore no makeup, and Frank could see just how tired she truly looked. Even her legs, which he considered her best asset, looked too thin below the hem of her bathrobe.

"Have you gotten the results back from the doctor?"

"Not yet," she said, as she pulled the towel from her wet hair and moved into the bathroom. "So, who's giving me the excuse to avoid Jessup tonight?"

"I am. Unless you have other plans for dinner."

"I was going to order room service," Bess called out.

Frank moved aside Bess's knitting and picked up the Room Service menu. "Let's make it for two. There are autograph hounds in the lobby."

"That's a first!"

Frank sat. Bess emerged from the bathroom and regarded him with an expectant stare. Frank guided her gently onto the bed. He had rehearsed his words several times. He began by telling her of his conversation with William Kirkbride and the revelation of the amount of snooping Harlan Jessup did on the lives of those around him. Then he told her about the deliberate ruining of their bus. Next, he informed her of his father's war background and illegal entry into the United States. Finally, he shared what he knew of her abortion and of the tragic occurrence on her would-be wedding day. He had a wad of tissues ready in anticipation of the tears that flowed.

"The son of a bitch!" Bess said in a choked voice.

"Absolutely." Frank reached forward and gently took her hands in his. "Why didn't you want to share the story of your wedding?"

"Oh, I didn't want to face perpetual pity from you three. And then there's the fact that he was married before and a Catholic."

"He must have been some guy is all I can say," Frank offered.

"Yes, he was."

Frank cleared his throat nervously over the rest of the news he needed to deliver. "Listen, I didn't repeat all this just to ruin your night. The reason Kirkbride shared it was to help keep us safe. Jessup won't use any of it so long as he thinks he still has a chance with you."

"That's nuts!" Bess ejaculated.

"Oh, much more nuts than you think." As Frank took the photograph of Sunny Templeton from his wallet, he recalled ruefully the request for one photo of a loved one made of him by the Indian man who had sold them the magic sarcophagus. He handed over the photo.

"Holy Mary!" Bess uttered. "If it didn't have someone else's name under it, I'd swear it was me."

Frank told her as much as he knew about Harlan Jessup's obsession. As he spoke, Bess grew more and more agitated.

"If you think I'm playing Kim Novak to his Jimmy Stewart..."

"What?" Frank interrupted.

Bess exhaled with exasperation. "Come on! I know you've seen

Vertigo."

Frank rocked backward. "Oh, right. But before you draw some line in the sand, consider what's at stake here. Let me tell you about Jessup's upcoming travels and what the Colonel…excuse me…Mr. Kirkbride is about to do to end all of this crap."

The most important part of Frank's rehearsed speech had arrived. He knew that Elizabeth Coleman was a woman who believed in reason over emotionality, and he laid out the facts and what he considered their best option.

"I'm asking you to hold out just a shred of hope that he can cling to, to keep him in line. We can certainly use the success of the show and our expanding schedule to hold him at bay. Believe me, I won't allow anything bad to happen to you, Bess," he pledged.

Bess's tightly closed mouth worked left and right. "All right. But it will take every bit of my acting skills to disguise my revulsion. Have you told Dex and Sonder about all this?"

"No. Do you see any profit in that?" Frank returned.

"I guess not. They might kill the guy themselves. We're keeping secrets left and right from them. When do we tell them about Simon Magus?"

"I don't see the need," he replied. "We'll have exhausted the coffin's powers in only a few more performances."

Frank reached for the telephone and erected a passable imitation of his casual smile. "Let's try to pretend we don't know either secret for an hour and eat! Oh, tomorrow we meet with the two young ladies ever so anxious to back you up."

Bess studied the menu. "What time?"

"Noon. They both work in Midtown and are using their lunch hour."

Bess looked up. "Ouch. I promised my father I'd have lunch with him. I'll make it earlier, but if I'm a few minutes late you run them through their paces, get the history stuff, and so forth. I'll be at the theater by 12:30 at the latest."

248

Frank thought of his promised lunch with Jessup and wondered how he would get through it without leaping across the table and throttling the man. He was too busy keeping his thoughts to himself to consider Bess's last words with suspicion.

SEVENTEEN

DECEMBER 9, 1976

THE MESSAGE WAS transmitted to Frank by the maitre d' of the Palm Court. He consulted his reservation book before looking up.

"Yes, Mr. Spiegel. Mr. Jessup regrets that important business prevents him from keeping your luncheon engagement. Would you care to dine alone?"

Frank thanked the man and walked with relief out of the Plaza Hotel. The weather was crisply cold, but the sun shone brightly. He had begun to revel in the touch of its rays since entering the world of the unwilling dead. He strolled across the plaza to Fifth Avenue and turned downtown. Tiffany's, Scribners, and dozens of other smart establishments beckoned. He knew that, between the twin threats of the coffin and Jessup, his radically increased fame and fortune came with a dangerous price. He determined at least to make the most of the good times and to bring as much joy to as many others as he could before a disaster overtook him.

"Sandra was first," he declared in a soft voice. "She'll be first again." With established priorities, he redoubled his pace southward.

EIGHTEEN

DECEMBER 11, 1976

A CHORUS LINE had been running on Broadway for more than a year, but seats were still all but impossible to secure in less than six months' time. Nevertheless, when Sandra Greenfield called her old high school buddy and former musical partner, Sammy Williams, he snagged her four adjacent Saturday matinee tickets in the orchestra. To Frank's chagrin it became clear that Sammy, who had earned the Tony for Best Supporting Actor in a Musical, had kept up his friendship with Sandy better than he had.

Even Harlan Jessup was impressed by the seats and admitted as much. His contribution to the day was picking up the tab at Sardis after the show and then having "the Colonel" drive them over to Rockefeller Center. The foursome finished the night admiring the Christmas tree and the plaza skaters and then went up to the Rainbow Room to dine while listening to Mel Tormé sing about chestnuts roasting o'er an open fire.

When the planned portion of the night had ended, Sandy announced that she and Elizabeth would be taking the same train south out of Penn Station. Sandy would go home to Trenton, and Elizabeth would get off at Princeton Junction, to be picked up by her brother-in-law. Harlan stepped back from Bess and regarded her as if he could not believe her poor choice.

"My sister needs relief from the kids, for baking, wrapping

presents and so forth," Bess explained calmly. "This mini-break between shows is the only time before Christmas I have to give her."

"What a thoughtful sister you are," Jessup said in a cool voice.

Bess rubbed his upper arm as if with affection. "It's the giving time of year. Dexter's with his family this weekend. So is Alexander. But we had a quality day, didn't we?"

"Fantastic!" Sandy enthused, before Jessup could reply.

Frank piled into the taxi beside the women. When they turned south on Fifth Avenue, he looked through the rear window.

"I can't believe it. He's having Kirkbride shadow us."

"He really is a kook!" Sandy said. Frank had filled her in just enough to allow her to double-team the millionaire convincingly. "Does this mean I actually have to go home to my parents now?"

"No way," Frank said. "Not even if it means needing me to confront him."

Jessup's limousine trailed along a block behind them, until the taxi stopped at Penn Station. The three walked inside as if oblivious, but Frank lingered near the doors to be sure the long, black car moved away into traffic with no one having gotten out.

"We'll take you down to your train," he told Bess when he caught up with the women.

After the train pulled away, Frank and Sandy caught the subway south to Greenwich Village. Sandy had rented a furnished basement apartment on St Luke's Place. She stood back to allow Frank to have a look.

"I suppose I could afford something grander," she said, "but I want to be frugal until the big money starts coming in again."

As obliquely as he could manage throughout the day, Frank had let Sandy understand that he knew about her triumphs in Europe and her excellent upcoming contracts with the Met and Chicago Operas. She was patently pleased that he not only knew but also showed such pleasure in her successes.

Frank glanced at his watch. Midnight was still minutes away.

"Still early for me," he declared, hopefully.

"Me, too," his former lover said. She had looked at him and touched him throughout the day in ways that gave him real hope that what was lost might be reclaimed.

Sandy descended the steps and shrugged out of her coat. "I don't keep any liquor," she told him.

"I've had enough alcohol for one evening," he said, following her. He gathered her in his arms and brought his face close to hers. "But I could be talked into another kind of intoxication."

"What kind?" she asked softly.

Frank kissed her, first lightly and tenderly, then with increasing fervor and passion. While they embraced, he slipped his right hand into his jacket side pocket and pulled out a black velvet box.

"Happy Hanukkah," he breathed into her ear, raising the box to her eye level.

Sandy stared at it with increasing emotion. "What's this?"

"To make up for all the impoverished holidays we spent together."

The pendant was simple. A slender golden chain held a single, half-carat diamond. Frank knew that Sandra's taste in jewelry was understated. He was rewarded with a rush of tears and a reddening nose, immediately followed by her most generous smile. She held the box while he extracted the pendant and fitted it around her neck. A silent compact had been reaffirmed.

"I meant it when I said I'm doing very well," Frank said. He did not tell her that, between her pendant and other lavish gifts he had purchased the previous day, he would have only about two hundred dollars left in his checking account by the time the flood of money from his Lincoln Center engagement began clearing.

"Thank you," she said, in a tiny voice that gave no hint of the volumes of exquisite sound the soprano was capable of producing. Her fingers ran along the chain to the diamond. "I want to see what it looks like."

"Where's a long mirror?" he asked.

"In the bedroom."

Frank fitted his hand into hers. "How lucky. I'd also like to see what it looks like...without clothing detracting."

Within five minutes they were under the covers naked and fitting to each other, writing in the primitive rhythm. They made love furiously, eager to show their mutual need. Then they began again, slowly and expertly, laughing, teasing, remembering, whispering old endearments.

When they had recovered their breaths, Frank said there was something he needed to tell her. She excused herself first to get a glass of water. By the time she returned, he was fast asleep.

The digits in the bedside alarm clock rolled over to four o'clock. Sandy awoke, remembered the warmth and pressure of Frank behind her when she had fallen asleep, and missed both. She sat up with a start. The shadow of his pile of clothing on the dresser reassured her that he was still in the apartment. She threw on her bathrobe and padded out to the living/dining area. Frank sat on the next-to-bottom step of the stairs, wearing only his boxer shorts.

Sandy grabbed his coat from a dining chair and pulled it around Frank's shoulders. "You'll catch your death of cold," she scolded softly. "What are you doing out here?"

"I'm regretting the ten years I've wasted."

"Wasted? You're at the top of your profession," she argued.

"It shouldn't be my profession," he returned. "I've been fooling myself, lying and reinforcing the lie day after day."

Sandy's eyes grew enormous in disbelief. "What lie? I don't understand."

Frank stared at the ceiling, unblinking. "That kid's magic set I got from my cousin wasn't meant to show me my life's path; it was a means of escape. Practicing magic was something I could do for hours by myself. Greta got all the attention. There was no chance of me vying with her. And I certainly never got praise for behaving myself. It was expected." He sighed. "The first time I put on a magic show and everybody jumped to their feet applauding, it was like heaven had opened up to me. I told myself I had to keep doing it because I was so good at it. The truth was I had to do it to get something that seemed like genuine love. It's how I caught your attention."

"Nothing wrong with that," Sandy said. "But it's not how you held my attention."

"The point is I'm not especially good at magic."

"Are you crazy?"

"I mean no better than a hundred other guys. To be really good, you have to invent new illusions. The only illusions I've ever invented were about my own life."

Sandy put her arm over Frank's shoulder. "You're too hard on yourself."

"No. The person I was hard on was you. You're doing exactly what you should be doing, and I tried to inhibit you for my own selfish reasons."

"You must not have tried very hard, because I went off and succeeded anyway."

"Thank God. And what about Bess, Dexter, and Alexander? I've dragged them all over creation, telling myself I was keeping three lost souls together when the truth was they were keeping me together and feeding my delusions. I can never repay them."

"They're all adults. They do what they do because they enjoy it and they believe in you. And love you. Just like I do."

Sandy punctuated her last words with a kiss. That kiss led to another and another, until Frank had pulled her up from the stairs and backed her onto the bed. Amazingly, their second lovemaking session was more passionate than the first.

As the heat poured out of them and Frank felt the furious beating of Sandy's heart under her breast, he said, "The thing that made losing you worthwhile is that you got your dream."

"The thing that made finding you worthwhile is that I got my second dream," she replied.

NINETEEN

DECEMBER 13, 1976

ST. BENEDICT'S AUDITORIUM had never been so full. Word had passed along Tremont Avenue that one of their own, a girl who had grown up in the church and who had already made something of a name for herself in the greater world beyond New York City, was bringing the hottest magic show in the country right to their door. The price for admission the church council had set was twenty dollars, more than most of those in the North Bronx had ever paid for an evening of entertainment but without the hassle of trying to see it on Broadway. The priests and the ticket sellers made sure everyone knew that the majority of the money was going to feed hungry children in Catholic missions around the world.

Bess Coleman understood it would not matter that the troupe could not do their most complicated tricks on the jury-rigged stage of St. Benedict's. So long as they brought King Karnak's now-famous coffin off the impressive bus with sufficient ceremony and later stood it in the middle of the stage for the last trick, no one would complain. Frank filled in using old standards such as the Chinese linking rings, but no one seemed in the slightest critical. The guests invited to the stage were all known to Bess or her father, so that Frank had a wealth of "inside" material ready to spring upon them. His wit had rarely been so sharp or so appreciated.

When Frank, Bess, Dexter, and Sonder wheeled the dark box out onto the stage, the auditorium erupted with cheers and applause. Bess dashed offstage the moment it was off the dolly. Frank adjusted the mike that curved from his ear to his mouth, so that the wow from the many amplifiers distributed around the auditorium decreased.

"You may have read that I act as the intrepid explorer for the grand illusion we call King Karnak's Coffin," he told the throng. "That is true. However, tonight we have an even more famous explorer doing the honors. At least in this church Elizabeth Coleman is more famous."

The place went wild.

"While we're waiting for her to reappear, I require the assistance of four persons in the house. Ordinarily, we use four men because this heavy sarcophagus is hoisted into the air. This is to prove there is no trap door into a basement. However, you know there can't be a trap door under this stage. And, if you don't know that, then I am prepared to swear the same on a bible. Being a former altar boy, you know how much that means."

The auditorium erupted again. Frank lifted his hands for a modicum of silence.

"Since we're not lifting the box, I can choose women as well as men. I choose Father Joseph Driscoll, Sister Helen Valentine, Father James Galligan and Sister Marie Ward."

The hooting and calling became a din. It rose to riotous proportions as the members of the cloth took their places. Frank signaled for quiet. He lined the four long-time fixtures of St. Benedict's up and handed Father Driscoll a microphone.

"Now, I'm relying on you four to faithfully report what you see. Can I have some assurance that you'll be honest?"

"We'll try," said the priest, smiling.

"Cross your heart?" Frank asked.

"Don't push it, lad," Driscoll said with the last vestiges of an Irish accent. "And how long has it been since your last confession?"

"So long ago that by now it's a cardinal sin," Frank said in a stage whisper. "I understand you have a question for me." Frank had been prompted that the old priest was a purveyor of corny jokes.

"I do. Do you know the trick of making holy water?"

"No," Frank obliged. "How does one make holy water?"

"You boil the hell out of it!"

The audience was kind.

"I'll bet your homilies are a hoot, Father," Frank said, even as he stared into the makeshift wings. "But enough hilarity. Here comes our intrepid explorer right now!"

Bess entered wearing her safari outfit. She took bows for half a minute before stepping to the box with the vaguely human shape. Frank produced his golden key and opened the coffin. The priests and nuns were invited to poke their heads inside and encouraged to tap on the walls.

"Are you ready to journey back in time to the Land of the Pharaohs?" Frank asked his assistant.

"I am indeed!" she called out.

"Then please step inside."

Bess backed into the coffin and tilted the pith helmet higher on her head. "Either I shall return, or else the spirit of the evil Pharaoh Karnak will be released again upon the earth," she pronounced. A moment later, she closed the lid.

Bess did not tarry even to look out the door's porthole. The moment after Frank sealed her in, she inserted and turned her key, reopened the lid and stepped boldly out.

St. Benedict's lay only two blocks from Haskin Street, where Bess had grown up. She half-expected the block to appear as it did in her mind. She saw absolutely nothing. Because the Limbo world's portal coffin now sat in the northeast corner of the Bronx, she had no expectation that Simon Magus would be able to track her appearance. She switched on her helmet light. It found nothing. She took out the powerful flashlight she had slipped into her pocket, thumbed it on, and swung it slowly back and forth. Its strong beam reflected off nothing. She cupped her free, gloved hand to the side of her mouth.

"Richard! Richard!" she yelled. Her heart sank as she registered how effectively the dimension swallowed sound. "Richard Padovani!" she screamed with all her might.

A patch of light winked on to her right. It lingered for a moment and then flickered out. Bess hurried toward it.

"Richard Padovani!" she shouted again.

The light swelled. This time it remained. Bess dared another score of steps. She thrust her flashlight beam toward the phenomenon even as she glanced backward to be sure she could still discern the outline of the coffin. She had come as far as she dared.

Slowly, the phantom light began to move toward her and her light beams. Again and again she screamed out the name. The alien aura continued to close on her. Within another few minutes, as Bess stood hunched over and shivering, it showed the back of a tall and narrow dwelling. Bess recognized it as the rear of her house on Haskin Street.

"Oh, thank you, God!" she exhaled. "Thank you, thank you!" A single tear escaped her eye and froze into a sparkling jewel halfway down her cheek.

The house continued to expand in the flashlight beam. She saw that a man stood in the back yard. He held his hands up to shield his eyes from the beam. Bess quickly lowered it but kept it lit.

"It must be!" she said to herself aloud. "He did try to come back to me."

In another minute, the house was almost upon Bess.

"Richard!" she called out once more.

The man walked hesitantly toward her. He was as handsome as he had been the last time she saw him alive. He bore no traces of the horrific vehicular accident that had crushed his chest. He wore the tuxedo he had rented for the wedding.

"Bess?" His voice was clear but weak.

"Yes!"

"Are you dead?"

"No."

"Then how…?"

"It's a miracle. I've been allowed to visit you."

The shade of Richard Padovani came up close to his one-time fiancée. He reached out with infinite slowness and laid his fingertips against the skin of her cheek, plucking the tear away.

Bess flinched from the intense cold of his touch.

"I'm sorry," she apologized when he pulled back. "You're very cold."

"It's me who's sorry," he told her.

"But you don't have to be cold," she said eagerly. "You can control this place. You can make it do wonderful things if you concentrate."

"How do you know that?" he asked.

"We've spoken to others, in other parts of this dimension."

"We?"

"Never mind. I've come to tell you that this place can be like paradise if you set your mind and will to controlling it."

"I don't even know what happened to me."

"You were in a taxi cab. The driver ran through a red light, and the cab was hit by a bus."

Richard absorbed the news. "I had closed my eyes, thinking about how you would look at the altar. I never saw it."

"Good. So you never saw the taxi driver here?"

"I've seen almost no one. Those I have seen want nothing to do with me. It's very lonely. How long have I been dead?"

"More than three years."

"I…have no feeling for it. All I know is I wouldn't leave you behind. I tried to let you know I was all right…but was in another place."

Bess drew in an icy breath, willing herself not to fall apart. "I know. I saw you from my window."

"Good. I thought you had." Her beloved looked around. "I think I'm in purgatory for divorcing and living with you. It's not a good place."

"I understand. But you must believe it can be good. It doesn't have to be cold and dark."

"You're shivering," Richard noted, as if he had not heard her.

"Yes. I can't stay long."

Richard rubbed his thumb rapidly against his middle finger, as he had done when nervous in life. "I'm sorry. Can you visit me again?"

Bess glanced over her shoulder. "I will return to you. I don't know how long that will be, but I promise. Have faith. In the meantime, I want you to concentrate on making your surroundings warm and full of color. Think of the vacation we took to St. Croix. The Buccaneer Hotel."

"I have thought of it," he said.

"But this time say to yourself that it will become real around you. Christiansted, so colorful below the hill. The little harbor. The perfect beach. Buck Island off in the distance. Build the memories one at a time and then link them. Think of it as something in the present and not just the past. Please, Richard, try! Try to make that wonderful sky."

Richard looked up. For several moments nothing happened. Then, without warning, an arc above them burst into a mackerel sunset with streaks of dark-blue clouds running through it.

"That sunset we saw at the Brass Parrot!" she gasped.

"Yes." Richard stared wide-eyed at what he had accomplished. "I did that?"

"You did. It's beautiful. Keep at it, my love."

Richard looked down at her. The sunset vanished, and blackness swooped in.

Bess held up her flashlight to her watch. "I must go."

"All right." Richard leaned forward and puckered his lips.

Bess went up on tiptoe and pressed her lips to his. This time she was prepared for the icy touch. It was no different than the time she had kissed his marble gravestone in winter. She did not flinch.

When he pulled back, Bess said, "You must let me go."

"But now you know the way."

"Exactly. Please practice!" She turned and walked resolutely toward the coffin, realizing how little energy remained inside her. She held her head high and tried not to stumble as she moved. The coffin seemed very far away.

"The magic words that will bring her back are 'Open Sesame'," Frank called out after he, Dexter, the priests, and the nuns had labored to rotate the box one full circuit. Out of the corner of his eye, Frank saw that his watch's longer hand was coming up on thirty-nine seconds. "On the count of three, all together! One…"

He heard the click of the inner lock.

"Two! Three!"

The crowd screamed out the magic words.

Bess opened the coffin door. She stepped out wearing the colorful caftan and mask and carrying the crook and flail. She paused for a moment. The huge room gasped collectively at the image of the Egyptian king. With a flourish, she drew the mask from her face and broke into a dazzling smile.

Joyful pandemonium broke out. As one body, the audience leapt to its feet. The applause thundered on and on and soon became a rhythmic encouragement.

Frank led Bess forward. Then he swiftly retreated as she took her solo moments. He noted with concern that even though she had beamed and bowed gracefully, she walked heavy-footed across the raised stage. He took his bows and did his inevitable bit of finding an endless line of handkerchiefs in his pocket. He produced roses and threw them at the women in the front rows. He winked familiarly. But he could not vanish as usual, so he merely waved and waved as he followed Bess into the wings.

Father Galligan waited for him. "You know, using the Church was a favor to Mr. Coleman," he said, poking Frank hard in the chest. "Magic, whether real or not, is evil."

"We just raised twenty thousand dollars for charity, Father," Frank answered, fighting to absorb the unexpected attack with equanimity. "When Jesus borrowed the horse to ride into Jerusalem, I'm certain he didn't first look it in the mouth."

"It was an ass," the priest corrected.

"'A servant cannot serve two masters,'" Frank quoted, undeterred. "Therefore, we must be good. And speaking of serving two masters: Our group has donated our usual fee, but I understand St. Benedict's is holding back five thousand of what was taken in for expenses. Why don't you sacrifice and send all twenty thousand to the starving children?"

The priest's eyes narrowed. "If you aren't the Devil himself, I'd be surprised," he pronounced. "That trick is impossible."

"It can't be," Frank said. "It's a miracle, and we both know miracles happen every day." He put his hand on the old man's shoulder and pushed gently past. "Excuse me."

A church office served as Bess's dressing room. By the time Frank found her, she had changed. She sat droop-shouldered on a large wooden chair.

"Are you okay?" he worried.

She looked up and offered a faint smile. "I'm very okay. You know how much it takes out of you."

"Did you see anything in Limbo?"

"Nothing to speak of," she answered.

TWENTY

DECEMBER 14, 1976

ELIZABETH COLEMAN STARED at the telephone receiver for a long time before hanging it up. She rose from the bed, went to the hotel room window, and gazed down at the traffic and the crowds rushing by on the sidewalks. She noted the steam from vehicle exhausts, from people's breaths, from sewer openings. It represented the heat of life to her. She stood looking down for some time, barely breathing. Then she returned to the telephone and dialed for an outside line.

"This is Bess Coleman," she announced to the female voice. "Please tell Mr. Jessup that I'm on the line."

Within two minutes she heard the familiar baritone. "Bess! It's so good to hear from you."

"How busy is your schedule today, Harlan?"

"After two o'clock, it's pretty much empty. Why?"

"I want to see you before you fly off to Asia," she said brightly. "I have a present for you that you've been lusting after for some time."

"You're teasing me."

"I assure you I'm not."

"Really? Why don't you meet me at my apartment?"

"I'm talking about another present. You've been dying to learn how King Karnak's Coffin is done."

"Have I ever!"

"The whole show was delivered to the Neil Simon Theater this morning. The box should be on the stage right now. If you meet me there at, say, two-thirty, I'll show you the secrets of how it works."

"Do you have Frank's permission?" Jessup asked.

"You're a backer of the show, aren't you?"

"I am indeed."

"That should give you certain rights." Bess's hand trembled slightly as she spoke her rehearsed speech. She steadied the telephone mouthpiece with her other hand. "You said the mirror illusion would cost about eight thousand dollars to build?"

"Probably."

"I'll see that you become more intimately involved, in several ways. I want you to lend the money to me, Harlan."

Bess listened to the silence on the other end of the line.

"That's a chunk of change, Bess."

"It is, but not really for you. You've shown the vision that all of us have lacked. Part of that vision is that the show needs capital to reach the top. And I want to negotiate a bigger percentage of the take from Frank. He'd do it if I could finance the new trick."

"Well..."

"I'm also ready to supply the other present you've been lusting after," Bess dangled. "After I show you the coffin trick, we could go back to your place and I could show you some real magic tricks. Quality tricks."

"Are you on the level?" Jessup asked. She could almost hear the drool dripping off his lower lip.

"Absolutely. I'd prefer the money in hard cash, but a personal check is also okay," Bess said. "I believe I can trust you."

"Of course you can. I'll be there at two-thirty," he said with eagerness in his tone.

"Without the Colonel," Bess ordered. "I want nobody to know I've shown you the trick."

"The Colonel is no longer in my employ."

"Really? That happened suddenly."

"He was of diminishing use to me. I'll catch a cab and get off on Broadway. No one will see me."

"That's a good boy, Harlan," Bess said.

"I knew there was this side to you," the millionaire said.

"You're about to know a great deal more," Bess told him. "Bye." She hung up without waiting for a reply. Hand still trembling, she replaced the phone on its cradle. She lay back on the pillows and closed her eyes.

After making sure the stage of the Neil Simon Theater was empty, Bess took Jessup onto it. A single work light on a six-foot-high black stand burned at center stage, just enough illumination that someone passing across the expanse would not fall over a set or prop. In theater parlance, it was always called the "ghost light," because anyone who moved across the stage cast ghostly shadows.

Bess lowered the pipe holding the chains for King Karnak's Coffin. She approached the box holding the two sturdy locks.

"Can't we get more light on?" Jessup complained.

"No. Your eyes will adjust. I don't want anyone seeing you here." Bess moved to the opposite wing, where the large metal coffin rested on its gurney. "Help me move this to center stage."

They rolled the sarcophagus to center stage. Harlan swore under his breath as he wrestled the massive box toward the bottom of the cart. As its weight tipped the gurney downward, he anchored and held the opposite end down while Bess steadied the controlled fall to the stage.

"Damn! I hope I didn't pull a muscle. Why was it built so heavy?" Jessup asked her.

"Because it's the real thing."

"You mean it was once a real coffin?"

"I mean what I said," Bess said cryptically. She used her key to unlock the lid.

"Frank didn't devise this," he stated patently.

"What makes you so sure? Look at these four figures. Don't they have more than a passing resemblance to Frank, Dexter, Alexander, and me?"

"They do indeed," he granted. "But that only means whoever devised and built it for your troupe incorporated all of you. Maybe as his inside joke." As Harlan spoke, he pushed back the lid and minutely inspected the inside of the box. "The reason I'm so sure Frank didn't invent this is because everything else in the show is derivative. He really isn't that unique a magician, Bess. I don't have to tell you. He has two special things going for him. The first is you as his assistant. The second is his talent for gab. He likes talking to people, and it shows. He can instantly slip into speech patterns that conform to the people he interviews, putting them at ease. That's a gift. They willingly open up to him. And he has a quick but not mean-spirited wit, which is very entertaining. As far as I'm concerned, the tricks are an excuse to stare at you and to laugh at his patter."

"Very perceptive," Bess allowed.

"So then, who invented this trick?"

"I believe it was an Indian gentleman living in New Mexico. The Calcutta variety of Indian."

Harland laughed. "That's rich. A Calcutta Indian in New Mexico building a fake Egyptian sarcophagus. I can't find any escape door or even a release mechanism," he said.

Bess patted him lightly on the shoulder. "That's one of its beauties. Nobody without the secrets can. Patience. Help me secure these two chains to the handles." When they had finished, she said, "As you know, we hoist the coffin up so the four men around it can plainly see that there is no trap door."

"Right."

"You saw before we moved the box in place that there was no

trap in this spot, so let's forego that part."

"I'm betting the four men are in on the trick. Frank escapes straight out along a raised black plank at the back, concealed within a perfectly black cape," Jessup told her.

Bess smiled. "Could be. You have to climb inside to really appreciate the ingenuity."

Jessup held up his hand. "Wait a minute! What do I do when the door closes?"

Bess removed the key for the outer lock and held it up. "It's automatic. The only way to open the exit is with this key or the duplicate, which Frank has. When I close the front door, you push the key into its inner mechanism as far as it will go and turn it clockwise."

Jessup gave an elated nod. He held out his hand.

"You do have the money for me?"

"I have a personal check."

"Let me see it."

"I had no idea you could be so cold." Jessup reached into his suit jacket pocket and withdrew an envelope. He held it between the fingers of both hands.

Bess inspected the writing on the check. "You can be cold, too." When she went to grab it, Jessup pulled it back.

"Uh-uh! This envelope not only has the check but the completed design for the mirror illusion and the contact names for the people who can build it as well. Show me this trick first."

"Oh, Harlan!" Bess said, smirking so that her dimples showed. "You could rush right out and issue a stop payment if I held out on you."

"You're damned right, woman. I could still do it if you don't come through on the second part of your promise either. Remember: I pushed you into nothing."

"I know. And neither have I pushed you. Now give me your topcoat and step inside."

Jessup replaced the envelope containing the check inside his jacket pocket. He rubbed his palms together gleefully, like a child about to open his presents on Christmas and then snatched the key from Bess's fingers.

"This is very exciting," he shared. "You won't mind if I say the new words?"

"Not at all. Just do it softly, so nobody will come running."

Harlan Jessup stepped backward to the lip of the coffin. He cleared his throat. "Either I shall return, or else the spirit of the evil Pharaoh Karnak will be released again upon the earth." He glanced at Bess for approval.

"Perfect!" she praised. "Now step back."

When Jessup was motionless inside, she swung the door shut and leaned upon it. She put her eye to the dark porthole glass and listened for the telltale tumbling of the locking mechanism. The instant she heard it, she pivoted the latch ring and swung the door open. She held it wide as the second hand swung completely around her upheld wristwatch. She watched with emotionless expression as it completed another full turn.

Sighing deeply, Bess picked up Jessup's coat and walked off the stage.

Because it would be their home for two weeks, Frank arrived at the Neil Simon Theater early, to truly settle in. He carried in one hand his makeup case and a framed eight by ten professional photograph of Sandy, which he intended to prop up on the edge of his dressing table. He smiled at the thought that he also carried a small version of the same photo in his wallet. In his other hand he held a large Thermos filled with hot lemon tea. Over the crook of his arm hung his dry-cleaned formal tails.

Immediately after passing through the stage door, Frank pulled up short. He found himself staring at Helmut Spiegel.

"Hello, Franklin," he said.

"This guy says he's your father," the door guardian said. "He showed me his –"

"Yes, he's my father," Frank confirmed. The old man looked grim. "Is everything all right, Dad?"

"Yah. I came to see your show."

"What about Mom?"

Helmut shuffled a bit and shrugged. "Zey had only a few single tickets. Like you said, your show does very vell."

"Your dressing room is the first one on the left," the keeper of the door directed .

Frank nodded his thanks, lifted his hand to his father's shoulder, and guided him in that direction. "You never need to buy a ticket. You should have gotten in touch with me. We always have a couple of seats available until the last second, for needs like this."

"Vell, maybe next time," he replied. "She didn't vant to come into ze city anyway. She's afraid of ze crime."

Frank pushed open the door. "Sit down."

His father took the chair in the corner, waited quietly, and returned monosyllabic answers to Frank's inquiries about his mother's health and the status of the house and neighborhood while Frank distributed his belongings and shrugged out of his coat. Frank wondered if his father would ever voluntarily speak on his own. He stole a peek at his wristwatch. The last thing he wanted for his opening night in the prestigious New York theater was to take the stage in a frazzled condition, due to an argument with the thick-headed old German.

"I von't take much of your time, son," Helmut said, understanding. "I just sought I must come to you und say how happy I am zat you are doing vell as a magician."

Frank was so stunned by the unexpected words that he felt the need to sit. "Well…thanks a lot."

"You understand vy I vas not happy before zis?" Helmut asked.

"Because it's not easy to become a success in this line of work."

"Yah. I thought I vas protecting you. But also because I vanted you to be a person who had power."

"Power?" Frank said. He had never heard this thinking from his father.

"Yah. Ze power zat comes from money und politics. Ze people who make ze laws und see zat ze laws are fair. I grew up in a country vere nothing vas fair. My father vas a little guy. He had no power. I had no power. Ve did vat ve vere told. Othervise…"

"I think I understand, Dad," Frank said, reflecting on his defense of his father to Major Kirkbride, and on Kirkbride's assertion that the "little people" who failed to obey orders were themselves shot.

"They were tough times," Frank agreed.

Helmut cleared his throat. "I named you after Benjamin Franklin und Thomas Jefferson to honor zose great men. Also, because I hoped you vould become like zem. Zey vorked so hard to make zis country free for everyone in it. Even ze little guy can be great."

"Or can be free to fail," Frank added. "Fortunately, I made it."

Helmut jerked his head up and down several times.

"I really appreciate the visit and what you said," Frank told his father, rising and walking to the door. "You'll have a great time —"

"Wait, Franklin," his father interrupted. "I also must say I am sorry for being angry at you so much. It vas because of Greta, you know. She vas so rebellious. Und you vere alvays so good. Zen you came to us after ve had paid for four years of study in politics,und you said you vere throwing it avay. I could only zink of ze vay Greta acted mit us. You see?"

"I do, Dad," Frank said. He suddenly felt a great weight lifted from him. He wanted to rush over and hug the old man, but he suspected the formal Helmut Spiegel might become deeply embarrassed.

"In Germany, children did vat zeir parents told zem to do," Helmut said. The words came out as apology rather than argument.

"Apparently almost everyone did what they were told to do,"

Frank replied. "And look where it got them."

"Yah. Yah," the elder Spiegel agreed. At last he stood.

"I vill enjoy much vatching you tonight. Now I go."

Frank opened the door. "You know, I'd really like a photograph for my wallet of you and Mom. Do you have a little photo at home?" he found himself asking.

The question struck Helmut momentarily dumb. "Uh, yah. Ve have von of ze church directory photos. Zey made us little ones for ze wallet."

"Great! Next time I'm home, I'll get one," Frank said.

The words clearly touched the old man. He nodded several times. His mouth worked without talking. It clamped tightly shut for a moment.

"Your sister is dead," he suddenly blurted. "From drugs." Once his father had managed to deliver the news, the carefully constructed, ancient dike of his composure disintegrated. Tears sprang to his eyes. His shoulders slumped; his hand waved feebly and aimlessly in the air.

Frank rushed forward and placed his arms slowly around his father. "I'm sorry, Dad. I'm so sorry."

"Yah, yah. Danke. Ve tried so hard."

"I know you did."

"Everything ve could think of."

"I'm sure."

A plaintive sigh escaped his father's lungs. The old man allowed himself to be embraced for several seconds more. Then he pushed Frank back gently but firmly and reached into his pocket for his handkerchief. He blew his nose. "Und, of course, zis is also vy I haff been so hard mit you. I could do nothing mit her. All of our hopes came upon your shoulders." He then related how he and Frank's mother had gotten the news of Greta's death from a drug overdose. She had been working the streets of Detroit for several months when she died. Frank found the details harrowing, the sort of tale one read about others and never would suspect could come from one's own family.

"But it's finally over," Frank offered.

Helmut Spiegel stood. "Yah. Zat's vat I told your mother. She has been braver mit ze news zan haff I." And then he added words that chilled Frank as much as any visit into Limbo. "Vell, Greta is in a better place now." His wrinkled face pleaded with his son for confirmation.

"Yes, she is. I'll come home early on Saturday and see Mom," Frank said. "In the meantime, you go out front and enjoy the show. I'll make you proud."

Helmut patted his son's shoulder, stood as tall as his hard years allowed and exited the dressing room. Watching his father shuffle around the corner, Frank realized just how much sorrow the old man had carried throughout his life. He understood with sudden clarity how fortunate his existence had been. He returned to the dressing table, collapsed onto his chair and stared vacantly at his image. In spite of all his professional fortune, in spite of having Sandy back, he did not see a man at peace.

"Hey."

Bess appeared in the dressing room doorway.

Frank turned. "Hey yourself."

"The Big Time," she said softly.

"Absolutely."

"Is it is great as you fantasized?"

"Not yet."

"Not yet," Bess echoed softly.

Frank snapped open his makeup case and grabbed his hair brush. When he looked in the mirror, he saw Bess staring down at the top of his head.

"You know I took several courses at a cosmetology school," she said. "When I say your hair is falling out way too fast, I mean it. That damned magic box exacts an awful price."

"But it's only for four more times," he said.

"Three and a half, actually," Bess said.

Frank set down the brush. "What's that supposed to mean?"

"It means that I let Harlan Jessup go into Limbo, but I held the door open so he couldn't get back out."

Frank rocked back in his seat. "Jesus, Bess!"

"I say again: That damned magic box exacts an awful price. It was him or us, Frank."

"You did it this afternoon."

"Yes. That's why the coffin was standing center stage."

Frank looked at his beautiful assistant with wide eyes.

"In spite of the years we've spent together, you don't know me as well as you think," Bess said softly. "I'm finding I don't even know myself. It's easier the second time. After you've killed your own innocent, unborn child, how difficult is it to let a full-grown monster kill himself?" Bess shrugged. "You've substituted for my child, you know. I would do anything to protect you. I don't feel horrible, Frank. Maybe I'm an awful person. Maybe there is never a justification for killing, but…"

"Self-defense is a justification," he offered. "Protecting those you love is justification."

"Those are a stretch, but if you'll give me a hug, I'll accept them."

For the second time within ten minutes, Frank gathered a loved one into his arms. Unlike Helmut, Bess showed no inclination to push him away.

"I checked the zodiac," she said softly. "It still has four lights glowing. Returning to this world is definitely the thing that completes each cycle. When you go inside tonight, you'll have to find him to get my key. Also, there's a check made out to me in his jacket pocket. It served as the bait to bring him to the coffin. It will finance his magic mirror illusion. The plans are inside the same envelope."

"What if Simon Magus finds his body with the key?" Frank worried.

"I don't know how he would. We're blocks from where Magus discovered the box. And I gave Harlan no lights."

"Oh, God, Bess," Frank exhaled.

"I'll tell you, Frank," Bess said, "the Big Time is definitely not as great as I fantasized."

As Frank struggled to master the shocks of the deaths of his sister and Jessup so he could perform his show, Dexter appeared as a third visitor. He held his books on New York hauntings.

"New venue; new prep," Dex declared.

"Must we? We're only twelve blocks south of where we were," Frank complained.

"Hey, this is a crowded city, both in this world and the next." Dexter sat. "I'll be quick. The Belasco Theater on 44th is haunted. Some say by David Belasco himself. There's a place called Clinton Court on 46th Street with a potter's graveyard. A scurvy sailor named Old Moor was executed there, and he's been frightening people to death and taking them with him ever since. There's an advertising executive at DaVinci's Restaurant on 56th. He was a drunk and committed suicide. He now sips from patrons' drinks. There's a guy with one of those old advertising sandwich signs who walks up and down 50th after dark. On the corner of 44th and 9th is a basement apartment once owned by the actress June Havoc. The ghost is called Hungry Lucy, and she mostly moves things around the kitchen. And finally there are two spirits in the Medical Arts Building on 57th. Some socialite and her French lover who killed each other. They're supposed to be quite violent. They're the ones I'd watch out for."

"Bad neighborhood," Frank commented as Dexter snapped the second book shut, wondering what his prop man would think about Simon Magus and perhaps the spirit of Harlan Jessup haunting the same otherworldly neighborhood.

"And there must be many who haven't broken through to this world," Dexter concluded. "So you be careful!"

Frank ushered his concerned friend to the door. "Forewarned is forearmed...thanks to you."

Dexter grinned. "Yeah, you might actually need four arms."

Frank waited only five minutes before exiting the coffin into Limbo. He saw no ghostly figure of Harlan Jessup wandering around on the other side of the porthole. Nevertheless, his heart pounded like a trip hammer against the walls of his chest. To help restore some sense of security, he had tucked the Bowie-type knife they had purchased in Texas into the right outer pocket of his coat. He pivoted the ring and opened the door a crack.

The dark was too much for Frank to deal with. He switched on his flashlight but kept it pointed toward his feet. He attempted to open the door all the way but found that something prevented him. Bracing his back against the rear of the box, he lifted one leg and shoved hard. The door opened halfway.

Frank swung the flashlight around the opening.

Harlan Jessup's body lay on the invisible black surface of Limbo.

Frank shoved several more times, until he could wriggle into the killing cold. He went into a squat and shone the light on Jessup's face. The evidence of freeze drying was on him. He was covered with a fine frost, and his eyeballs appeared to have shrunk slightly. His lips were drawn back from his teeth in a rictus of agony.

Frank looked up from the body. "Harlan?" he called into the swallowing atmosphere without much expectation. He reassured himself that, at most, only thousands out of the billions of souls who had ever lived could have ended up in Limbo. If anybody was going straight to Hell, it would be Harlan Jessup. Frank laid the flashlight on the floor of the coffin, facing in so that nearby spirits would be less able to spot the light and move toward him. He dug into the dead man's suit jacket. He found the envelope but continued to pat other pockets in search of the large key. Even after turning every one out, he could not locate it.

Frank grabbed the flashlight from inside the coffin and swung it desperately in ever-expanding arcs. He caught no glint of gold. Cursing through the fog of his exhalations, he returned to the box. By kneeling, he found the intricately shaped piece of metal just under the bottom lip of the sarcophagus door. He tucked it deep into one of his trouser pockets.

When Frank stood and turned, he realized that two buildings had materialized and were sliding toward the box. The older one was colored in sepiatone, like a nineteenth-century photograph. The other glowed in garish neon purple. Frank extinguished his flashlight and worked solely by the faint glows of the two buildings.

Because Bess would be performing at least one more time inside the sarcophagus, Frank elected to hide Jessup's corpse by dragging it around to the back side. From repeated experience, he was not overwhelmed by the unnatural darkness. He simply closed his eyes and kept the coffin lightly against his right shoulder. The ground beneath him felt as solid, as cold and as smooth as a frozen lake, and the weight of the uncooperative body preoccupied him. When he let go, he could feel that it had become too stiff to collapse. He left it in the blackness, in a sitting-up position like a Rodin statue.

Frank worked his way quickly around to the front of the coffin. The buildings had all but faded into the blackness. A man and woman, dressed in outdated eveningwear, were about to enter the sepia-tone structure. Frank was fairly certain he watched the disappearing backs of the spirits of the socialite and her French lover. The man held a long, Deco statuette; the woman clutched a carving knife. Frank exhaled a visible sigh of relief. Moving purely by touch, he changed into his caftan, replaced his helmet with the mask and found the crook and flail. The moment he finished, he backed into the coffin and shut the door. He had earlier in the day purchased a watch with luminous dials. He saw that he still had fifteen minutes in Limbo. Keeping his eye close to the porthole, he waited.

TWENTY-ONE

DECEMBER 18, 1976

DEXTER BROWN ROLLED slowly up from the couch. Although the tiny house had three bedrooms, he could not bring himself to sleep in the one so recently occupied by his mother. As he stretched, he reminded himself that a perfectly good king-size bed at the Sheraton was going to waste in Manhattan. But he also knew he would not be fed or loved as well there.

Yesterday's local paper lay spread out in front of him on the coffee table. Out of habit, he reached for the Help Wanted section that advertised for part-time drivers. He thought about the promises he had made to Darnell to toss the football and, in the afternoon, to take him into Plainfield to the comic book and trading card store. A promise was a promise. Dexter let the paper slip to the floor, eased back down into a fetal position, closed his eyes and drew the blanket tightly around his chin.

Alexander Voloshin the Younger entered his parents' apartment like the Wabash Cannonball coming down a mountain. Under his arm he had the employment section of the local newspaper.

"Nine o'clock!" he sang out. "Anybody not up, rise and shine!" He steamed full-speed into the bedroom.

His father rolled over and regarded him with one swollen-lidded eye. He had obviously collapsed into bed the night before in his underwear. He swore a string of Russian expletives. "What is matter with you?"

"Me? Nothing is the matter with me. I have a great job and great friends. I'm clean and sober. Which is more than I can say for you."

"Go away, Mischa!" his mother cried out.

"Get up, Mom," Sonder said, undeterred. "You have dishes to wash, clothes to wash and a dog to walk. Now I can't get you good friends, but I can get you clean and sober. And today we look for a job for you, my dear Poppa."

"It's Saturday," Voloshin Senior complained.

"You know that? That's already more than I expected from you. Plenty of work is available for weekends. I've found three jobs that you can walk to from here."

"Oh, God!" his father groaned.

"It makes me happy to hear you calling on Him for help. But God helps those who help themselves," Sonder said. "While we're praying to God, let me help you into the shower."

The two performances at Avery Fisher Hall had produced residual magic. Offers were pouring in from around the country to book the show. Both Dick Cavett and Johnny Carson wanted Frank on their talk shows immediately after the New Year. A few inquiries for appearances had even come in from Japan and Europe. Requests for interviews were piling up. A couple of magazines wanted to do photo shoots. After years of struggling in near obscurity, the sudden torrent of attention astonished Frank. He was not awestruck enough, however, to be content to simply bask in the glory. He understood that Spiegel/Master of Magic was the event du jour, and soon enough other novelties would capture the same spotlight. All his spare time was occupied methodically mapping his immediate future with his agent. In what seemed gleeful tones, Salkin kept reinforcing Frank's knowledge, saying, "You never know how long this will last, kid. Make it while you can, even if you have to kill yourself."

In the little time remaining during the weekdays, Frank had been telephoning Huntsville, Alabama and finishing negotiations with the builders of the optical elements for the new mirror trick. He had spent the bulk of this Saturday in Edison, holding his mother's hand, getting closer to his father than he had since his teenage years, and trying to put the ghost of his sister behind all of them as rapidly as possible. Because Sandy was singing a Messiah that evening he would take a subway early the next morning and spend time with her until his two o'clock performance. His life had become like a man struggling to stay on a rolling river log just as the personal aspects had taken dramatically positive turns.

"That's eight hundred and three in the bag," Frank said to Bess as they walked off the stage. She merely nodded.

The pair slowed their stride as they caught sight of two men standing in the wings. Even though they dressed in plain clothes, their bearing betrayed them immediately as policemen.

"Mr. Spiegel, Miss Coleman," the taller of the two men greeted. He held out his hand and displayed a badge and license. "I'm Detective Westbrook. This is Detective Guzman."

"Who did you wish to see?" Bess asked before Frank could reply.

"Both of you, actually," Westbrook answered. He nodded to his partner and said to Bess, "Why don't you two go to your dressing room, and I'll speak with Mr. Spiegel."

On the way to the room, Frank kept telling himself the visit could only be about Harlan Jessup. He was mistaken. As soon as he was alone with Westbrook, the policeman pulled a sealed plastic sleeve from his pocket and held it up in front of Frank's eyes. Inside was the envelope he had mailed anonymously to the precinct closest to Lincoln Center. On a sheet of paper in block printing, he had detailed everything he had seen about the Fraunces Tavern explosion. He had then stuck the page inside a standard legal-size envelope and dropped it in the Neil Simon Theater's mail out basket. He saw with dismay that some diligent bureaucrat had stamped the address of the theater on the envelope's upper left corner.

"One of the ladies in the front office says that you were the one who put this into their outbound mail," Westbrook said.

Since he had no criminal record, Frank had not bothered to keep the envelope or letter free of his fingerprints. He realized denial was futile.

"Yes. I mailed it," he confirmed.

"May I sit?" Westbrook took a chair even as he asked. He beamed up at Frank. "Thanks to you, we're convinced it was members of New York organized crime eliminating Elliot Saperstein and not the work of Puerto Rican independence fighters. Based on what you caught of the license plate, it could only belong to one man. We've had corroborating descriptions of the bomber and the car, but without the plate, we were helpless. The City owes you a great debt of gratitude."

Frank waved the words away. "You owe me nothing."

"Then maybe you're interested in the reward upon conviction."

"Give it to Saperstein's family."

Westbrook returned the envelope to his inside pocket. His eyebrows furrowed. "But you've created as many questions as you've answered. We checked your itinerary on the day of the explosion. You were halfway across the country, performing."

"That's right. The answer is clairvoyance," Frank said.

Westbrook took a moment to absorb the explanation. He did not look happy. "Well, that sets us back a bit. You're not a real eyewitness."

"No, sir."

"You saw the murder like in a dream?"

"Very much like that." Frank offered a pleasant poker face. "Excuse me. I'm allergic to stage makeup and need to get it off as quickly as possible." He sat and put his back to the detective, grabbing a handful of tissues to wipe away not only the pancake makeup that darkened his complexion but also the sweat that had begun to burst out on his forehead. "I got the vision in the beginning of December, while performing at Lincoln Center."

"Do you show off your clairvoyant powers during your act?" the detective asked.

"As a matter of fact I do. I allow myself to be blindfolded on stage. Then Miss Coleman goes out into the house and asks for common items from the members of the audience. I see the image she has in her mind."

"That's also done as a trick, isn't it?" Westbrook said, not making it sound like a question. "I've heard of the assistant saying something like 'Precious time is wasting' when it's a gold watch."

Perspiration removed, Frank put down the box of tissues and presented his most sober stare. "Almost anything can be faked, Detective. I capitalize on a strange talent and do the trick the easy way. It's what got me interested in so-called magic in the first place."

"Have you solved other crimes?"

"Yes. But until now it was with total anonymity. I don't want to become famous for solving crimes," Frank dissembled. "If someone in the main office hadn't stamped a return address on what I sent you, my power would still be a secret. If word gets out that I have such power, my life will be badgered beyond endurance by every family with a missing member, by every police department with an unsolved mystery. Do you understand?"

"I'm trying to, but..."

Frank threw down the tissue box with some force. "No good deed goes unpunished. All I wanted to do was perform my civic duty and help you fix blame where it belongs. The other reason I chose to be anonymous was because sometimes I have visions that are dead wrong."

"Pardon the pun," Westbrook said.

"And that, frankly, is embarrassing. I'm a clairvoyant who can seldom find his keys," Frank barreled on. "Does that satisfy you?"

Westbrook shrugged. "I guess it has to. I suppose thanks are in order."

"Just keep my name out of the papers and donate the reward to charity if you can figure out how to nail the murderers. That's thanks enough. And if your partner has any problem getting corroboration from Miss Coleman, it's because I've never admitted even to her that I have this power. She does indeed use a complicated set of word signals when we play the mind reading game." Frank shrugged. "I just never wanted to freak her out."

"Detective Guzman is speaking with her about an entirely different matter," Westbrook revealed. "It seems that your mutual friend and admirer, Mr. Harlan Jessup, is missing."

Frank felt the professionally assessing eyes of the detective boring into his mind. By now, he had mastered his surprise and was not visibly rattled. "He's an acquaintance," Frank corrected. "A wealthy man who believed in our act so much he invested money in it…in exchange for a nice return. His being missing is news to me. He's supposed to be in Southeast Asia this week."

"He never arrived."

"Did you check with the airlines?"

"Of course. He never used his ticket. You know he was going to Southeast Asia because you're close to him."

"Not close at all. We only came to know him a few months ago. Why would Miss Coleman know anything special?"

"Because she was his last city appointment before he was to fly out."

"Was she? I know he delivered a check to her shortly before he was to leave."

"A banker's check."

"That's right."

"Has it been cashed?"

"I don't know. It's a personal loan."

"They were close?"

Frank realized the ground was becoming swampy under him. "I don't delve into my employees' personal affairs, and I certainly never discuss them with others. You'll have to ask her."

Westbrook stood and closed his note pad. "Believe me, we will."

.

TWENTY-TWO

THE TROUPE HAD just finished running Pat Kelly and Gabrielle Grant through the paces of the act. Both were accomplished members of the brother- and sisterhood of magic arts and needed little practice before they grasped the requirements of each segment of the show. The entire rehearsal had lasted less than three hours.

"What about the big illusion?" Gabrielle asked, standing her ground.

"What big illusion?" Dexter responded.

The young woman smirked. "King Karnak's Coffin. The trick the entire country seems to be talking about."

Together, Fran, Bess, Sonder and Dexter said, "Oh, that illusion."

"Like the news articles say," Frank answered, "it's a work in progress. We thought we had it perfected, but it's still dangerous. That's why we have the notice out front and at the box office saying that it's been temporarily removed from the show."

Kelly, who was seven years older than Frank and who had struggled in the business that much longer, had been too savvy to ask. He had retreated to the edge of the stage where he had left his coat and gloves.

"You both get a two-hundred-dollar retainer every week, even if you don't work," Frank told them. "Two hundred more for each night you work beyond the first."

Gabrielle looked manifestly pleased about the arrangement. She came out of her thrust-hip stance and turned toward the wings.

"One second, Gabby!" Frank said. He reached into a small leather bag he had placed on the apron of the stage. From it, he produced a 35-millimeter camera with a flash attachment. He turned it on.

"Do you know how to work one of these?" he asked the new assistant.

"Sure. I look through here, focus with this, turn this ring until the line comes into the circle and press this button."

"I knew you were the right woman to hire," said Frank, as he grabbed the original members of his company and pulled them together. "Take a half-dozen shots of us, will you?"

After much clowning from Sonder and protests from Bess that she did not look her best, images with the house seats as background were captured to Frank's satisfaction. He thanked Gabrielle, who sashayed off the stage.

"You know how to get me," she threw over her shoulder in ultra-feminine tones.

"But how can I get to you, baby?" Sonder asked under his voice.

"Ask her for the time of day, and she'll tell you the twelfth of never," Dexter told him.

As Frank tucked away the camera, he looked up at the two-level but shallow balcony of the theater. It truly was a perfect venue for the act. Although he was anxious for a break, he would regret leaving the place in another eleven days.

"Ten glossy copies pour moi," Sonder called out.

Frank threw up his hands. "Ten glossies for everyone, mes amis. Let's get some lunch. It's on me."

Out of the street, the group paused as Dexter bought a morning paper from a corner vendor. They had not traveled the length of another block when he came to a sudden halt.

"Holy shit!" he exclaimed. "I thought the police promised to keep your name out of this mob hit scandal."

Frank grabbed the newspaper. The article was on page three rather than the cover page, but it could not be missed. MASTER OF MAGIC SOLVES FRAUNCES TAVERN EXPLOSION it screamed in sixteen-point type. The story Frank had delivered was duplicated in four paragraphs. More dots had been connected since Saturday. Bruno Cavalieri had been proven to be the owner of the car and identified by eye witnesses and was now in custody. He was described as "a purported button man" for the five Mafia families who controlled organized crime in the boroughs of New York. The DeStefanos, a minor family within the syndicate, were singled out as the most prominent target of Elliot Saperstein's investigation of racketeering on 42nd Street. A mug shot of Cavalieri showed his greasy, dark hair and his overlapping upper incisor.

"Son of a bitch!" Frank wailed. "How many pieces of silver was this sold for?"

"Man, if not using the coffin has left any unsold seats, they'll be gone by noon now," Sonder speculated, peering over his shoulder.

"This is not a good thing," Bess said needlessly.

"Never mind about the Magician of the Year Award," Sonder continued. "Can I have the movie rights to our story? I'm gonna have Burt Reynolds play me."

"Posthumously?" Dexter asked.

Sonder looked up from the paper. "What do you mean?"

"I mean it is not cool to rat on the mob. You are about as oblivious as a brick and twice as callous."

"Whoa! I did nothing!" Sonder protested. "I'm just trying to lighten the mood, since we can't put the genie back in the bottle."

For a moment, the four stood on the sidewalk looking at each other. Frank knew each was thinking about the sarcophagus.

Frank said, "This is the down side of the box. It shows things we have no right to be tampering with."

"If you knew that, then why did you spill your guts?" Sonder asked.

"Could I allow those thugs to get away with murder?" He realized what he had said and glanced with apprehension at Bess. Dexter and Sonder had been told nothing about Harlan Jessup's death.

Bess reassuringly touched Frank's arm. "No, you couldn't. But we should stay off the street until the end of our run here."

"We should also talk with Major Kirkbride," Frank decided.

"He's retired," Dexter reminded everyone. "Nine chances out of ten he's far gone by now."

TWENTY-THREE

DECEMBER 23, 1976

THE RAPPING AT her hotel door was so soft that Bess thought for a time it must be a stranger knocking somewhere down the hallway. She looked at the alarm clock on the bedside table. It read 2:37. She grabbed her bathrobe and hurried to the door, putting her eye to the fisheye lens. William Kirkbride stood outside, against the far wall, so that she could plainly see him.

Bess opened the door. The ex-military man nodded gravely at her, then glanced up and down the empty hallway.

"Sorry to wake you. Can I come in?"

Bess stepped aside, and the large man entered. He flipped on the overhead light as he passed it and then began unbuttoning his coat. She noted that he wore casual slacks and a sport jacket with no tie.

"What brings you here at this hour, Mr. Kirkbride?" Bess worried.

"It's about the only time a hotel this big is quiet. I don't want anyone associating me with your group. Not the police and certainly not the Syndicate. About seven hours ago, Bruno Cavalieri supposedly committed suicide in his jail cell."

"The man who blew up the tavern."

"Correct. Cavalieri had his belt removed for his own protection. But somehow he managed to get it back."

"What does that mean?"

"It means that he was murdered to keep him from testifying. It also means that members of the police are in the pay of the Syndicate. If this investigation of 42nd Street corruption goes on long enough, I bet they'll find strings leading back to City Hall. Your boss really opened a can of worms."

Bess ran her hand self-consciously through her hair. "He couldn't ignore fixing something that was wrong."

Kirkbride pulled up a writing desk chair and sat. He took a quick glance at the large piles of wrapped Christmas presents sitting on the carpet beside skeins of ribbon, wrapping paper and unused bows. "And now we all have to live with that. Just exactly how did he find out about Cavalieri?"

"It's all in the papers," Bess evaded.

"No, I mean…The saying tells us to ignore half of what we read in the news," Kirkbride rejoined. "This is that half. Don't answer me yet on that subject. The second reason I'm here is because they still haven't found a trace of my former employer." He locked his eyes on Bess's. "You don't seem surprised."

"Why do you need to care now?" she asked.

"I care because people don't usually disappear that neatly unless they're trying to make themselves disappear. I need to know if he was feeling outside heat. If he was, it might come down on me as well. Or if he suspected I called the heat on him he may right now be ratting me out. I still have weeks of business to attend to in this country, Miss Coleman. It would be very difficult and costly for me to have to flee tonight."

"You don't have to leave the country," Bess assured him.

"How can you know that?"

"Because I was the last one to see Harlan Jessup."

"So I've learned. What do you know?"

Bess felt a wave of nausea sweep over her. She rose slowly.

"Are you all right?" Kirkbride asked.

Bess lifted her hand to hold him back. "Yes. I just need...a little time in the bathroom. Excuse me."

By immersing her face in a sink of cold water, Bess was able to quiet her stomach. She toweled off, took a minute to run a brush through her hair, and then returned to the bed. In the time she was gone, she had made several important decisions.

"Who alerted the authorities that Harlan was missing?" Bess asked as she sat.

"His secretary did here in New York, when he failed to contact her. And then his lawyer did from Texas at about the same time," Kirkbride revealed. "They're pretty much the only ones who care. He employs fewer than ten persons full-time. When your world is nothing but paper and electronic transactions, you can actually work that lean and mean."

"Do you know how his ex-wife and sons are reacting?"

"He's uniformly loathed. They'll be delighted to split up his fortune."

"What a sad epitaph."

"I'm sure his employees will mourn the end of their jobs if he's dead." Kirkbride's eyebrows elevated. "Is he dead, Miss Coleman?"

"He is absolutely dead."

"And how did that happen?"

"Let's just say he entered another world entirely of his own free will."

Kirkbride's smile broke slowly into a full-blown grin. He took a moment to crack his knuckles. "Merry Christmas!" He looked again at the piles of wrapped gifts.

"I went overboard this year," Bess admitted. "There's even a star ornament for you among them. For a Christmas tree. Do you have a holiday tree?"

"Not since I was a kid," the powerful man revealed. "But this year I would very much like to have one."

Bess found the gift and handed it over.

Kirkbride's ordinarily stern face softened. "This is very nice of you. It's actually the second present you've given me tonight. Did Jessup pay you eight thousand dollars for the privilege of entering this other world?"

"Something like that."

"He went into that magic box of yours, didn't he?"

"You're very perceptive, Mr. Kirkbride."

"Please, call me Bill. You've earned it."

"And you may call me Bess, since we're obviously moving into a more trusting relationship."

Bill raised a forefinger. "I want you to know that whatever you tell me never leaves this room, Bess. I need the truth only for my own welfare. I swear as an ex-officer and a Southern gentleman that I will maintain it for your welfare as well."

"Thank you. However, I'm not risking that much in what I tell you, Bill," she replied. "I shall be dead within the next two months."

"I'm sorry to hear that," Kirkbride said, shifting uncomfortably on his chair. "What's wrong with you?"

"Pancreatic cancer. It's not the most aggressive form, but it's swift enough. I had all the tests. My doctor's best prediction is that I have about five more good weeks. Then another two of increasing... I think the word he used was 'debilitation.' The last week will be hospice or hospital. The tubes, the needles, the indignities that finally make you relieved to be at an end."

"I am truly sad to hear that."

"Thanks. My mother died at about my age. It was cancer also, but she waited until the last days to seek attention. The cancer was everywhere by then. They had no idea where it started."

"I see."

Bess shrugged and affixed a stoic smile. "My prognosis has radically affected my outlook on things like morality and death, as you can imagine. But so has the 'magic box' you just referred to."

"It actually makes a person disappear, doesn't it?" he said.

"Yes. Into another dimension. A user can come back, however, as long as he or she doesn't stay too long. And as long as they have the key to reopen the box and the lid of its sister box in this world is closed."

"Jessup stepped inside without the key."

"No. I held the door open so he couldn't use it."

Kirkbride fixed his gaze on the cross that dangled from Bess's neck. "According to the law, you weren't merely an accessory."

"No. I might as well have pulled a trigger. What would the law say about Jessup's investigation of me and Frank, of all the times in the past he used the facts of his investigations to ruin or kill others?"

"How would it take into account the two Middle-eastern men he blackmailed over their secret homosexuality?" Kirkbride added. "What about the one he set up with a mistress and then blackmailed? What about the two he had murdered?" He raised his hands. "People often say, 'Let him be judged in the next world.' I suppose that's what happened. And the box has something to do with how Frank knew about Saperstein's murder as well?"

"That's right."

"That answers my first question. It's a very dangerous magic trick," Kirkbride decided.

"I've said that all along." Bess turned on her bedside light. "Are you above suspicion concerning Jessup's murder?"

"I am. I was willing for my job to be terminated on Monday morning when I tendered my resignation. But he asked that I stay on through Tuesday. His purpose was to have me drive a client from here to Philadelphia. The man could just as easily have taken a train, but I think Jessup wanted to make me play chauffeur once more. I was driving back on the New Jersey Turnpike when Jessup's flight left without him. I have the receipts to prove it."

"So that's your alibi," said Bess. "And now that you know he vanished on Tuesday afternoon, you have no more personal fears?"

"None." Kirkbride made no effort to move. "But that only half concludes my business with you."

"You began by speaking of the murdered hit man," Bess remembered.

"Correct. Frank is liable to meet the same fate."

"He can't do any more harm to them. Everyone believes he had a clairvoyant vision, so he can't testify."

"Their purpose won't be to silence him; it will be to make him an example to those in the tavern. The real in-person eyewitnesses."

Bess opened her night table drawer and took out a pint bottle of whiskey. "I use this as medicine to dull the pains I've started to have. Do you have any pains, Bill?"

"I have a passel of old wounds," he said, rising to accept the bottle. "If you mean the mental and spiritual kind, my pains are too numerous to mention." He went to the table and poured a finger's worth into a glass. "They won't make Frank's death look like an accident," he informed her. "It will be bloody. An unambiguous warning. They'll beat him to death if they can get him alone. If not, they'll ventilate him with a clip or two of bullets."

"The police asked Frank if he wanted protection."

"What did he say?"

"He didn't think it would do much good. He said, 'If they could get to Kennedy, they can get to me.'"

"He's actually better off without cops around him," Bill opined.

"Because of this phony hanging business," Bess understood.

"That's right. Anybody who thinks Frank Serpico and the Knapp Commission cleaned up the NYPD also believes in the Easter Bunny."

"Can anything be done to protect him?" Bess asked.

"He didn't come back to the hotel with you, Dexter and Sonder," Kirkbride stated.

"You've been watching us."

"Since I read about Cavalieri. Where does he stay?"

"With his girlfriend. She has an apartment in the Village, on St. Luke's Place."

Kirkbride drained the glass and laughed into it. He set it down carefully. "Give me the address. Jessup's lawyer hired me yesterday on a per diem basis, to see what I could dig up about his top client's disappearance. He gave me carte blanche to hire other investigators. Jessup's firm will pay to protect your boss. When I leave here, I'll put an excellent pair to work watching that apartment. I'll take the theater duty. Your job is to put the fear of God in him and keep him off the street. Once he's out of the city, he'll probably be safe."

Bess wrote down Sandra Greenfield's address on a piece of hotel notepaper. She handed it to Kirkbride. "I've been watching out for him for years. It will be good to have some help. Dear Lord, what will become of him when I'm gone?"

.

TWENTY-FOUR

DECEMBER 29, 1976

FRANK SPIEGEL COULD measure the increase in his fame from just the traffic at his dressing room door. Before they received the sarcophagus, he was lucky to get a visit from the members of his own troupe. More often than not, company was no more than Bess in a shared room. Now, even with added personnel watching the backstage entrances, all walks of people were getting through before and after the performances. He had taken to locking his door and calling through it for identification like a pioneer settler.

Not five minutes after Frank arrived at the Neil Simon, Sonder was knocking at the door.

"Is it important?" Frank asked before getting up.

"Incredibly important," Alexander Voloshin replied.

When Frank opened the door, he found himself staring at the cover of a bible. "Isn't the immortal soul everyone's most important concern?" Sonder asked. In the past, such a question would have invariably have been the set-up for a punch line. Frank knew that this time Sonder was in earnest. His shoulders sank.

"Have you joined the Jehovah's Witnesses?" he asked.

Sonder pushed past him. "Of course not. Don't belittle this, Frank. I've just gotten beyond the four gospels, into the letters. What a difference between the Old and New Testaments! Abraham's God is a god of wrath and demands. Jesus's God is like a loving mother. You don't have to earn forgiveness with his God. Because of His sacrifice, we're already forgiven. We simply have to live like we believe!"

"Have you shared this revelation with Bess and Dexter?" Frank asked.

"Yes. They both threw me out. Heathens."

Frank turned him around. "Wrong. We're all interested. There's simply a time and a place. You keep reading until you've finished the whole bible. Then order your thoughts and preach to us on the bus next year. You'll have a captive audience."

Sonder snapped the bible closed. "You can count on it. But I'm just anxious to tell you this part because of the parable of the seven foolish maidens. You never know when your time will come."

"I have three detectives watching over me, thank you," Frank replied, seeing through Sonder's concern. He held up his wristwatch. "You are now on company time. Go check the lights and sound, Billy Graham."

"Okay, okay."

Frank almost had the door closed when he felt it being pushed from the other side.

"Frank, do you have the pith helmet?" Bess asked.

"Yes." Frank pulled the door open. "I even dusted it off." For the first time since Frank had moved Harlan Jessup's frozen corpse, one of the troupe was returning to Limbo. Circumstances demanded the reappearance of King Karnak's Coffin.

"That's okay," she allowed. Frank was pleased to see that Bess wore the silk kerchief he had given her for Christmas. The night was cool and windy, a perfect occasion for a first use. He also noted the beautiful gold cross on a chain that Sonder had given her and insisted that she wear when she stepped into the coffin. As Frank handed over the helmet, he made his usual study of Bess's face, to judge the level of her fatigue.

Bess flashed a toothpaste advertisement smile and cocked her head coquettishly. "Do I pass inspection?"

"Almost," Frank said. "You could fool anybody but me."

"You made me promise not to harp on the box when you used it. Three more times and then it's history, whether we like it or not," Bess said. "I will survive." She circled her forefinger. "Okay, back to your preparations, Houdini."

Several hearty knocks vibrated the door.

"Fer cryin' out loud!" Frank exclaimed.

"Who is it?" Bess asked.

"It's Allan."

"Not by the hair of our chinny chin chins," she called back.

"Come on! Let me in!"

Bess pulled the door back. The agent had not even taken the time to unbutton his coat.

"What a zoo! Now I know we've really made it. Did you see the Catholic League of Decency out front picketing?"

"I tried to ignore it," Frank said.

"I'm sorry, boychick; it's my fault. I made sure the whole tri-state area knows that King Karnak's Coffin has returned." Salkin stared out the door, as if he could see the picketers on the sidewalk. "What ingrates! After you guys did that charity benefit in the Bronx! You think they'd give a Catholic boy a break."

"It's the lunatic fringe," Bess decided. She dug into her pocket and produced a flier that she handed to the agent. "This is what they're handing out. By doing stage magic, we are evidently encouraging black magic rituals, white witchery and the like."

"There is no such thing as bad publicity," Salkin declared. "You now have three tendered offers from Vegas and two from Reno. The total count of new places wanting to book you is up to one-hundred-and-seven."

"You know, performing the coffin trick tonight is like bait and switch," Frank said. "No place outside Manhattan is going to get

King Karnak's Coffin."

"No other place needs to," Salkin crowed. "It's the same thing as one great movie role making a star out of an unknown. The unknown has plenty of talent, but no one knows it until –"

"I get it."

"But you absolutely had to do the coffin trick tonight. I just got done feeding Dick's agent. He's sitting in D12 right now."

"I think you should have held out for Guy Lombardo," Bess said, winking at Frank from behind Salkin's back.

"I personally favor Lawrence Welk," Frank replied through a deadpan expression.

The agent's hands flew over his head. "Are you both crazy? *Dick Clark's New Year's Rockin' Eve* is the biggest thing on TV that night. From right here in the Big Apple." Salkin's words came out like machine gun fire. "We are so lucky that Rod Stewart has strep throat. *Tonight's the Night* was slated for the eleven-thirty slot. If you satisfy the scout, two nights from tonight, they will have cameras set up to catch King Karnak's Coffin live. You say you can't keep doing the trick? Fine. Do it tonight and then for twelve million viewers, and that will be enough to set you up forever. Have you figured out how to stretch your show for New Year's?"

"With a super-long intermission," Bess replied, "plus parlor tricks and lots more interviewing and chat from Frank."

Salkin patted his favorite client on the shoulder. "You're great at the chit-chat, and you know it."

Frank said, "It would have run until eleven anyway, but you can shell out the bucks to wine and dine the entire audience afterward."

"I shelled out for his scout, who eats like he's got a wooden leg. Dick Clark will pay on New Year's," the agent vowed. "He's the one over the barrel, having his butt saved by the hottest act in the country at the eleventh hour."

"Twelve million," Bess said. "That's a hell of a lot of people seeing us."

Frank nodded his understanding. He might never again be afforded such exposure.

"Seven minutes on New Year's Eve!" Salkin exulted.

Frank turned his agent and guided him toward the door. "Now leave me in peace, and don't call me until noon tomorrow."

"Your wish is my command, oh great genie of the box," Salkin said. "I gotta get back to the office anyway. Pick up all your messages."

Frank closed the door, leaned against it, winced and looked wearily at Bess. "Oh, for those long days on the road when it was just the four of us holding each other together. Plotting and planning about something great."

"And then all four us with our figures carved on a diabolical coffin. We should have known what came after the dreaming. Remember when you were a kid: Getting to Christmas morning was more fun than the day after," Bess agreed. "You've ripped open the presents. Now there are only more Christmases to contemplate."

"The important thing is having more Christmases with those you love," Frank said through a smile.

Bess nodded, turned quickly and exited the dressing room.

Bill Kirkbride was becoming weary of watching performances of Spiegel/Master of Magic. The army man had never been one for theater of any kind. Real life was where it was at for him. He longed to have his affairs neatly concluded and to retire to Virgin Gorda in the British Virgin Islands. Fishing, snorkeling, sailing, drinking and eating was the totality of his plan for the next six months. He had a schoolteacher friend who had shared her bed with him on and off for the past dozen years. She would retire in June, and then he would buy a sailboat in the 30-foot range, and they planned to sail slowly down the archipelago to Venezuela and back. He was finding it difficult to wait.

At least the guy he was guarding now deserved protection. The ex-major could not fault Frank Spiegel for turning witness against the mob, even if his method employed the supernatural. After this evening and two more, the troupe would finish their New York commitment. Kirkbride would have this self-appointed assignment done.

Kirkbride looked down on the orchestra seating in the Neil Simon Theater. He had the stage left box seating area all to himself. It provided a poor view of the stage, but it was perfect for looking at virtually all of the audience. Enough light spilled over the stage apron into the audience that he could see pronounced movements. He did not frankly expect an attack during a performance. Only a maniac like the actor John Wilkes Booth, who felt a need to make a public pronouncement as well as to assassinate, would risk shooting from a packed auditorium. Even if those around him were not the heroic type who might wrestle the contract killer into submission directly after his attempt, the ensuing panic of a gunshot would pack the aisles and severely hinder his escape. Kirkbride was convinced that the important part of his duties came before and after the performance, in the hallways backstage and between the alley and the different liveried car each night that whisked him and Franklin Spiegel away on a random route to Greenwich Village.

The lights had dimmed for the start of the second act. Spiegel had bounded out onto the stage to perform Desdemona and the Orange Tree. Kirkbride had long since figured out most of this trick, but he nonetheless acceded that it was spectacular. Bess appeared in her beguiling silks. Next came Dexter as Othello, wearing a white turban, sequined vest and white pantaloons and displaying his excellent physique where his arms, belly, and calves were exposed. The bodyguard suddenly realized that the box opposite from where he sat, which should have remained empty, was now occupied. The lone spectator wore a cleric's collar and a black outfit. After the noisy religious protest under the theater's marquee only a little more than an hour before, Kirkbride was more than a little surprised to see a priest watching the show.

Probably gathering ammunition and trying to stay inconspicuous Kirkbride speculated. I'll bet he writes a journal for some Roman Catholic publication. But why did he wait until the second act to appear?

As the last thought flashed through the bodyguard's mind, the priest's right hand came up. In his grip was a police special revolver fitted with a silencer.

"Watch out!" Kirkbride shouted to the stage, even as he kicked back his chair, dropped to one knee and wrapped his hand around the pistol inside his shoulder holster. A lifetime of training and experience told him that he would not be able to stop the assassin from firing his first bullet. He resisted the temptation to glance down at the stage.

Flame burst from the muzzle of the phony priest's gun. The crack of the supersonic projectile echoed from the auditorium walls. All around, people were screaming. Kirkbride shut out everything except his target. He swung his right hand from his jacket and, at the same time, reached up with his left to grasp the wrist and steady the shot. He pushed his pistol forward even as he thumbed off the safety and began to squeeze the trigger. In the last millisecond, he tightened the muscles around his lungs to further steady his aim.

The assassin stood. Having taken his intended shot, he swung his revolver in Kirkbride's direction, to rid himself of the only person preventing a second shot at Frank Spiegel.

Ex-major Kirkbride fired. Although he had aimed squarely at the assassin's chest, the man's moving hand and revolver happened in the way. Kirkbride recorded the spraying of blood as his bullet pierced the man's hand, registered the dropping of the gun over the lip of the box into the orchestra audience. He fired again, but the hit man had thrown himself backward and down, disappearing behind the balcony box's wall.

Hoping against hope that the wall was not too thick, Kirkbride fired two more bullets into the place where the would-be assassin should have lain. He did not wait to see if he had succeeded but spun out of the box seating area and flung his weight against the emergency fire exit door just beyond the curtain. He knew that if the hit man had survived, he would not try to escape through the hundreds of persons filling the balcony and orchestra aisles.

Kirkbride rattled down the metal stairs as quickly as he could and then raced directly across the fully lit stage. Out of the corner of his eye, he saw two men down on the ground and Elizabeth Coleman going onto her knees. He also caught a fleeting glimpse of the color of blood. He shut out the image and continued at a full run to the opposite side of the stage, where the stage door led into an alley. He heard a man cry out and, coming closer, heard someone hitting a wall hard. When he sprinted around the corner, he found the stage manager lying on the ground, shaking his head. Somewhere ahead, a heavy door banged open.

Bursting through the stage door, Kirkbride saw that the man in black had almost reached the alley door. Kirkbride steadied his pistol, lowered his aim and put a bullet into the man's knee.

The hit man screamed in pain, hurtled out the door on pure momentum and went flying onto the pavement. Kirkbride was on top of him a few seconds later.

"You're dead, asshole!" the hit man growled from under him.

Kirkbride grabbed the man by the hair and banged his forehead into the concrete. "Don't bet on it." The man lay still until a pair of policemen leapt from a squad car a half minute later.

"Call for two ambulances," Kirkbride told the officers. "Someone's hit inside on the stage."

"Go ahead and call it in," one of the cops told his partner. To Kirkbride, he said, "One's already on the way."

The ex-military man rolled off his captive and hurried back into the theater. His mind ran through the most likely possibility of what had happened. A pair of plainclothesmen in the lobby had been randomly checking patrons for firearms as they filed in for the show. Once the intermission happened, however, the police were long gone. Those who wanted to smoke were allowed to spill out of the foyer onto the pavement. No one checked to see that only ticket holders re-entered. Someone had tipped off those who wanted to kill Franklin Spiegel that the stage right box was unoccupied for every performance. He swore at himself for not having anticipated the move and forcing the management to lock the other box.

Kirkbride found a large circle of onlookers ringing the limits of the stage. He pushed his way through roughly. Virtually the same tableau he had passed a few minutes before confronted him. Now, however, a large first aid kit lay open on the stage. He saw that the red he had glimpsed came from Dexter Brown's turban, which someone had removed. Frank was gently cradling Dexter's head in his lap as he applied pressure with a soaked gauze bandage.

"He pushed Frank out of the way," Bess told Kirkbride.

The burly bodyguard knelt close to the two men. He saw that Dexter Brown's eyes were open and unblinking. He also saw that the hero's pupils were enormous.

TWENTY-FIVE

DECEMBER 31, 1976

BESS COLEMAN HAD never felt so tired. All around her were doctors and nurses and drugs that could have made her feel considerably better. But she was not at New York Presbyterian Hospital for herself. Dexter Brown lay in a room on the other side of double doors that led to the hospital's Intensive Care Unit. Bess consulted her watch. The hour was approaching one in the afternoon. They had received the bad news forty-five minutes earlier.

For more than a day, Dexter had been holding his own with the severe wound to his head. Surgeons had been able to remove both fragments of bullet that had come through the thick wrappings of the turban when Dex had launched himself sideways and shoved Frank out of the way of the killer's aim. He had not regained consciousness, but the operating surgeon had held out hope that he might not only survive but with little effect to his brain functions. And then, at ten minutes past twelve, all hopes were shattered. The machines kept his heart beating and his lungs exchanging air, but his brain wave patterns had gone almost totally flat.

Dexter's sister, Sharlene, had spent the entire previous day and night in vigil. With a message that survival past twenty-four hours boded well, the attending physician had suggested that she go home and catch some sleep. Frank had stepped in and offered his hotel room. She had been called back at around twenty minutes past noon. Bess expected her to arrive at any moment.

Frank and Alexander stood at a window, staring out at the winter-cold city and saying nothing. Bess crossed to them.

"Listen, guys, the cafeteria isn't open forever. Why don't you two run down and get something? I'll stand guard, and then I'll take my break."

"I'm not hungry," Sonder muttered.

"You have to eat," Bess insisted. "We have the biggest show of our lives to put on in a few hours. If there ever was a 'The show must go on' moment for the three of us, it's tonight."

"She's right as usual. Let's go, Alex," Frank said.

The rare use of his given name startled Sonder. He nodded meekly and followed Frank toward the elevator.

Bess watched the metal door slide shut. Only then did she allow herself to collapse onto the couch behind her. She closed her eyes and drew in several long, fortifying breaths. Not two minutes later the second elevator door opened, and Sharlene Brown stepped out. Her face was still puffy from non-stop crying. She registered Bess's presence and came to a halt. Bess stood.

"He's still the same," she reported.

Sharlene's shoulders slumped. "My son just lost his grandma. How will he survive this?"

"Listen to me, please! Listen very carefully," Bess said. "No matter what the doctors say to you, do not let them take him off life support today. You must make it crystal clear that his body is to be kept alive at least until tomorrow."

"Of course," Sharlene said. "If there's any chance…"

Bess said, "There is definitely a chance Dexter can come back to you and your son."

"Isn't that sort of magic a little beyond you?" Sharlene asked with a touch of bitterness.

Bess softly touched her shoulder. "Not necessarily."

"What exactly can you do?" Vera asked.

Bess pressed the elevator button. "Nothing, unless you make sure Dexter's body stays alive." She nodded toward the double doors and watched as the sister went through them.

Bess pressed the elevator button impatiently. It was most important for her to find Frank and Sonder and prevent them from returning to their vigil.

When Frank, Sonder and Bess stepped out of the cab at the curb in front of the Neil Simon Theater, they saw that the protestors had finally given up their picketing.

"Even the lunatic fringe takes off for New Year's, I suppose," Sonder surmised.

"Or they're embarrassed that somebody in a priest outfit shot a member of the cast," Bess countered.

The chaos of that evening had not ended when Bill Kirkbride brought the would-be killer down. The two ostensible policemen who arrived in such record time had been inside a stolen patrol car, had not waited for an ambulance to arrive but rather loaded the hit man into the back of the car, and had never called for a back-up ambulance. New York's organized crime syndicate had neatly arranged to dispose of the assassin so that the trail back to them would be erased.

"I can't wait to get out of this town," Frank said as he handed a five-dollar bill to the taxi driver. He consulted his watch. The time was six-thirty, a full half-hour earlier than they usually arrived for a performance. When he looked up, he saw Pat Kelly and Gabrielle Grant walking up the street at a brisk clip.

"What's Gabby doing with Pat?" Bess asked Frank, with a defensive look.

"I've already paid her for one performance." Frank said, "This is our last one in the City, so I figured she could relieve you on half the illusions."

Bess grabbed Frank's wrist hard. "Not Desdemona or Lady Lakshmi. And don't you try to relieve me inside the coffin. I didn't get to do it two nights ago, so it's still my fucking turn. Live TV or not, I go to Limbo tonight!"

"Yow, take it easy, Bess!" Sonder exclaimed. "I never heard that word from you before."

"Be quiet, Sonder," she snapped, "unless you want to hear it again."

Frank had never seen Bess so adamant or emotional. He guided her off the pavement and into the alley. "Fine. You're the explorer, and I do the spiel. Relax. I just want you to be able to lie down every few minutes, because of your anemia. You want to look good in front of those television cameras, don't you?"

"Yes," Bess said quietly, having gotten what she wanted.

Frank kept his arm around her shoulders. "When you get inside, take a good, hard look in the mirror, Bess. You're totally worn out."

"I'm sorry."

"Don't be. This tragedy with Dexter has pushed us all over the edge. If there was any way I could cancel tonight, I would."

"Dexter would never forgive you," Bess argued. "Not after all the driving and work he put in to get us here. Twelve-million viewers. You could play live to filled houses until you were sixty and never reach that many people."

"I know."

"If praying can do anything, then a miracle will happen," Sonder proclaimed. He held tightly to his Bible as Frank rapped on the stage door and they were let inside.

"You keep praying," Bess told him. "It's important, Alex."

"Ah, Jeez!" Frank exclaimed under his breath.

Bess and Sonder followed his focus. At the end of the hall stood Allan Salkin, fedora in hand. He half-raised his hand and gave a little, apologetic wave.

The group advanced on the agent.

Salkin offered the support magician and Bess's assistant perfunctory smiles and then turned his back on them. "Dick's people can't get anything else to fill in for our slot," he said in a small voice.

"Gee, what a surprise," Frank returned bitterly.

"It's New Year's Eve! They swear that everyone else is contractually committed or the places they're playing at refuse to allow cameras inside." Salkin put on his exasperated face and flapped his hat. "I can only tell you what they told me."

"They want us for the shock value," Frank decided. "The shock value and people's morbid curiosity. By now, everybody in the country must have heard about the shooting and the cursed coffin trick." He pointed a finger at his agent. "I don't want one single word said on camera about the incident or Dexter's condition. No phony crocodile tears and wishes for speedy recoveries. Dick introduces us, the theater and the trick – and that's it. Understood?"

"Of course, of course."

Frank nodded at Sonder. "Sonic will be wearing a headset. If he hears one sensationalistic word he's gonna signal me, and I then refuse to go on."

Salkin held up his hands in a pleading attitude. "All right, all right! Don't you threaten me, too. My New Year's resolution is not to have a nervous breakdown."

"Naturally not. It would cost something. Instead of making empty promises you personally can't keep, why don't you find a phone and make absolutely certain that others keep them, huh?" Frank said with a hostile edge. He unlocked the door to his dressing room but blocked the way. "Just Bess," he told the group.

Bess switched on the overhead lighting as she entered the room. Frank locked them inside.

"I'm pretty much ready to implode," he admitted.

Elizabeth shook her head slowly back and forth. "Take ten deep breaths. A new year is coming, and it will all work out for the best. Bess guarantees it."

"I was thinking of flying the three of us and Sandy down to the Bahamas," Frank revealed.

Bess stopped shrugging out of her coat. "Why spend all that money? Let's use the coffin's last trip and visit Emily in Newark for a good tan." Before Frank could reply, she leaned forward and kissed him. For the first time in their relationship the kiss was not just off-center but planted firmly on his lips. She keep her mouth pressed to his longer than any mere friendly kiss, and he was so astonished that he stood there with no reaction.

"That Sandy is a lucky girl," Bess pronounced as she pulled suddenly away and grabbed the door to the hallway.

Frank ran his fingers across his lips, and then turned and stared at himself in the long mirror.

The New York New Year's audience had even the Halloween audiences beat. The costumes were "dress-up" rather than "scary" or "funny." Enforced hilarity was the order of the evening, and since the ultra-hot tickets to Spiegel/Master of Magic had sold for an astronomical fifty dollars apiece, the audience was determined to get their money's worth. The addition of Gabrielle Grant was definitely succeeding with the men, since she was almost as beautiful as Bess, fifteen years younger, and had a more voluptuous figure. Moreover, her fiery red hair was like a moving flame on the stage. She wore reds and oranges in contrast to Bess's blues and golds. Sonder had added the Lovin' Spoonful song "Do You Believe in Magic" to the end of the intermission, and most of the crowd was singing along with it. Against the request of the management, champagne flutes had been carried into the auditorium, and bubbly liquid was sloshing onto expensive tuxedoes and gowns.

The show had started ten minutes late on purpose, giving it the expectant air of a rock concert. Frank had seen to it that the first act ran twenty minutes longer than usual. With a stretched intermission as well, he needed only to extend the second act twenty minutes to begin King Karnak's Coffin precisely at eleven thirty. The audience was happy to cooperate, and no one seemed ready to end the evening before midnight. One after the next, Desdemona, Gold Fishing, the Glass Balls, Lifting Lady Lakshmi, the Disc of Death, Pffft and the Horn of Plenty were met with tumultuous applause. The audience had been assured by the media that the show was dynamite, and they were not about to make fools of themselves by questioning professional opinions. Frank suspected that the wealthy who could afford the price of the tickets were not the ordinary magic-show-going group and were only present because the show was the talk of the town. It was all new to them, and they could not have been critical if they wanted to be.

Because it was easy to perform and allowed limitless patter, Frank had inserted the Vanishing Vase as the illusion that would bring them up to King Karnak's Coffin. He needed no help other than a willing member of the audience. His choice was a vapid-looking young woman dressed to the nines in the fourth row. She had been clacking gum throughout the entire show, and after every trick she turned to her boyfriend and pestered him to explain what was clearly beyond his ability to divine. As each illusion reached its conclusion, she invariably stopped chewing and her mouth hung open in the same astonished, bovine pose. Her platinum-blond hair was the final factor that compelled Frank to invite her up for a little fun. Her sequin-bespangled skirt and bodice combination with bare midriff was so tight it appeared to have been spray-painted onto her excellent figure, and she had trouble climbing the stairs onto the stage.

"And your name is…?" Frank began.

The young woman gazed at him with expectation.

"Could you tell me your name?" he rephrased.

"Oh!" she exclaimed and then let out an infectious giggle. "I thought you were going to guess it."

"No, that part of the show is over."

"Doreen."

"Doreen. I love that name. It's my middle name, in fact."

"Really?"

"Yes, but I spell it backward. That's quite a stunning outfit you're wearing."

"Thank you."

"I once asked a young woman how one got into a skirt like that, and she said 'You might start by buying me a drink.'"

Half the audience laughed; the rest groaned.

"You want a better show, come to the normal two-hour version," Frank quipped affably.

"Is that a radio?" Doreen asked, pointing to the headset Frank had put on just before the trick, to be able to hear his introduction from the New Year's Rockin' Eve show.

"Absolutely. I've seen this magic show so many times that I get bored. They're counting down the hit tunes of 1976 on WABC and we're on number seven. Want to hear?"

"Sure."

"I'm just teasing you, Doreen. I'm deaf, and it's a hearing aid."

"I'm sorry."

"Speak up."

"I said I'm sorry," Doreen half-shouted.

"No need to apologize. It wasn't your fault. Now, I want you to confirm for the rest of the audience that this sheet of glass is solid. Rap on it."

Doreen gave the glass a timid tap.

"No, really knock on it," Frank invited. "It's plate glass and won't shatter."

"Okay, but I've been scared of hitting things ever since I walked through a screen door."

"I see. Did you strain yourself?"

The audience apprehended the pun at various speeds, extending the laughs and groans.

"I don't get it," said Doreen.

Frank smiled. "Has anyone ever called you a dumb blonde?"

"In high school they did."

He peered with narrowed eyes at her scalp line. "Well, you got the last laugh on them, didn't you?"

Doreen's eyes brightened. "That's right! I'm not a real blonde! So there!"

"Good for you. Okay, before you confuse me: Is the glass solid?"

"It sure is," she affirmed.

"Then let's put the vase on top of it and cover it with this tube. You push the tube down."

"This way?" Doreen asked.

"If you can push it down toward the ceiling, that's okay too," Frank replied.

Doreen did her part.

"Now say the magic words," Frank directed.

Doreen shook her platinum hair. "What magic words?"

Frank leaned in and whispered in her ear.

Doreen giggled loudly. "I can't say those."

"Then say 'Presto, vase go through the glass/When I shake my sequined bottom.'"

More than a minute later, after several prompts, Doreen was able to repeat the lines properly and wiggle her posterior. Frank whisked away the top tube, showing that the vase had disappeared. After the applause he lifted up the sheet of glass.

"Now remove the bottom, Doreen," he directed.

"The bottom tube?"

"Either that or the bottom of your outfit. You pick."

"The tube."

"Good choice."

Doreen lifted the tube, to reveal the vase. "Golly!" she exclaimed.

"Golly indeed!" Frank called out. "Let's hear it for Doreen, who is not blonde!"

While the audience exploded with delight, Frank glanced into the stage right wing. Bess waited in her explorer outfit. She pointed to her watch and then to her nose, signaling that Frank had timed the vase illusion perfectly.

Frank pulled a single red rose from inside his jacket and offered it to his volunteer. "Thank you, Doreen. You can find your way back to your seat…I hope." He looked out to the back of the orchestra seats where a red light had just winked on at the top of the television camera. A second camera had been positioned in the box where Bill Kirkbride had sat on the night Dexter was shot. In spite of pressure from Dick Clark's production staff, Frank had adamantly refused to allow a third camera behind the line of the proscenium. In his ear, he heard Dick Clark say, "And now, live from the stage of the Neil Simon Theater in New York, Frank Spiegel/Master of Magic!"

"Good evening, America," Frank said. "The birth of a new year causes us to think about all the years past. Not just those of our own youth, but those of ancient ancestors. Come with us now to the opening of a recently discovered artifact of great antiquity. We have pre-selected four men from our theater audience to aid in this journey. They are waiting just offstage with…King Karnak's Cursed Coffin."

Sonic potted up the nasal Oriental woodwind music as the four men rolled the black metal coffin onto the stage, directed by Pat Kelly in a considerably smaller Moorish costume than Dexter wore. His "Texas Dirt" make-up was also merely swarthy so that no one could accuse the troupe of doing blackface. As always, the coffin rested horizontally upon the funeral home collapsible gurney that so many associated with death. Precisely because it was not gaudily painted as most magicians' illusions were, the box looked genuine and frightening. Like every group who had witnessed the sarcophagus, this audience murmured in awe.

As the coffin came onstage and was tipped carefully off the cart and upended, Frank recited, "This authentic and magical sarcophagus was recently discovered in the Valley of Kings along the Nile Valley.

It was intended to be buried for eternity, but, alas, that was not to be. Foreseeing that possibility, the hated despot King Karnak had a terrible curse inscribed on the lid of his coffin." Frank looked up at the camera located in the stage left box. As they had rehearsed that afternoon, it zoomed in on the hieroglyphs rising in bas relief on the lid. "I quote: 'Whoever opens this sacred sarcophagus will be drawn into the afterworld where I now reign.'" Frank turned from the cover and faced the camera directly. He affixed his most somber look and raised one eyebrow. "Clearly, only the most intrepid of explorers dare to enter this box. Having narrowly escaped with my life several times, I am no longer eager. There is but one among us still brave enough: Professor Elizabeth Coleman!"

Bess had been perched on a stool in the wings all during the Vanishing Vase, but she had barely registered the lighthearted interview or the execution of that trick. Her mind was busy fortifying her for the deed she was about to commit. She dredged her memory for the first time she met Richard Padovani, when he was an executive for the organization that represented the plastic pipe industry and she had been hired as the spokesmodel. According to the advertising agency, her hips, knees and elbows perfectly demonstrated the flexible benefits of plastic. She and Richard had caught each others' eye immediately. In spite of her strict Catholic upbringing, she swiftly found herself dating and then going to bed with a married man. Her love had given him the resolve to leave a failed marriage, in spite of his faith. His carriage house apartment on the Brooklyn Heights had been like a separate world to her. They rarely left the district but rather reveled in their intimacy and mutual interests. Most favorite for her was lying in bed after they had made love and staring at downtown Manhattan across the dark East River, the skyscrapers defined by thousands of tiny lights. The image was indelible, as was every item in the apartment, and she looked forward eagerly to recreating it.

Bess strode onto the stage with perfect posture. The pith helmet, safari jacket and jodhpurs could not conceal her riveting presence or enormous smile. Frank saw out of the corner of his eye the unusual fact that she held something in her left hand. He had no time to focus hard on it. He turned upstage to the four large men, each of whom had also been selected because of the attractive tuxedoes they wore.

"Gentlemen, please place your hands on the coffin. Assure yourselves that there are no false walls. Make certain that it is solid and very heavy."

As they did, the pair of thick chains descended from the stage fly space.

"Now, work with me to thread these chains around the coffin handles, so that we may lift the coffin and prove that no escape is possible out the bottom."

The work was swiftly done, and two massive padlocks were snapped through the looped ends of the chains. Consulting his watch, Frank instructed the four men to take up places at four angles around the box. The Moor placed the spindly, two-step steel ladder in front of the coffin, and the coffin was elevated two feet off the stage floor.

Frank called out, "One of you gentlemen, if you please: Kneel and make sure the floor has no trap door."

"It's solid," the youngest-appearing of the men declared as he came up brushing off his hands.

Frank had used the moment to extract his golden key. He put his foot on the first step and turned his key counterclockwise in the lock. He drew open the coffin door and stepped down, careful to keep his wrist high so he could observe the sweep second hand of his wristwatch.

Bess, who had been adjusting her helmet and now had the light turned on, crossed the stage. She climbed onto the second step and faced the audience. As she cleared her throat, she seemed for a moment to lose her balance slightly. Frank automatically reached out to steady her. In that instant, she pressed a small slip of paper into his hand.

"Either I shall return," she said in a loud and clear voice, "or else the spirit of the evil Pharaoh Karnak will be released again upon the earth."

Even as she recited her speech, Frank had surreptitiously opened the paper with the fingers of one hand and had begun to read the message. As his eyes swept over the final word, the lid of the coffin slammed closed.

Bess immediately turned her key within the inner lock and left it there. She listened for the shifting of the sand in the hourglass. By putting her eye to the porthole, she assured herself that the theater had vanished. After buttoning her safari jacket to the neck, dropping the flaps on the helmet and slipping on her gloves, she turned the pivot ring in the door and opened it into utter blackness. The sight did not cause her to hesitate. First, she turned and withdrew from a jacket pocket a carefully folded sheet of paper with a key taped inside it. She laid the items on the sarcophagus floor. Then she stepped into the void and thumbed on the small but powerful flashlight she held. She paced off exactly one hundred measured steps and set it down on the surface of Limbo, facing what she believed to be east. Her previous experiences helped her overcome the shock of the void, and she moved with purpose. Her plan was predicated on the possibility that Dexter had not passed over to some other plane but was unwilling to leave the world of the living and had come instead into Limbo when his physical brain went all but dead. Presbyterian Hospital lay about one mile from the theater, in the world of the living. If Bess walked briskly all the way and shone her light in that direction, the hospital and Dexter might come partway to her. She needed to find and communicate with him in fewer than sixty minutes, when she was certain she would die of the void's terrible cold. He needed to get to the coffin in less than ten minutes after that.

Bess aligned herself with the flashlight beam and continued with striding steps, clutching a second, smaller flashlight inside a trouser pocket. To her astonishment, she had been in Limbo only eight minutes when she heard Dexter's voice.

"Bess! Here!"

She swung her flashlight frantically back and forth until she could make out her friend's figure. He was dressed in his Moorish outfit, and there was no blood on his turban.

The pair hugged. Bess realized that Dexter's mass was like her fiancé Richard's had been, a phantom sensation of weight.

"God, it's good to touch something warm!" Dexter exclaimed.

Bess noted that his face possessed a suggestion of warmth as well. "How did you know how to get here?"

Dexter grinned. "I'm the walking encyclopedia, remember? Because I wanted to give you and Frank a warning about all the spirits in mid-town Manhattan, I got to know where they are. Over the past…I guess …hours, I've been watching them and trying to speak with them. I went from one to the other until I knew I was close to Fifty-second and Broadway."

"You clever man."

"It's been so strange, Bess. I felt this awful pain in my head, and then nothing. Suddenly, it was like I woke up. But I was out of my body and floating above it. And I looked down, and nurses were running around and trying to bring me back. And there was that bright light people with near-death experiences talk about."

"Really?"

"Far off. I don't know if it was a tunnel or not. I certainly didn't see anybody I knew who had died waiting to greet me."

"You didn't want to head toward the light?"

"No."

"Because you knew about Limbo. Do you think that's right?"

"I suppose so." Dexter's reflective expression suddenly turned somber. "While I was wandering here, I had a big surprise. I stumbled on Harlan Jessup."

"Not his spirit," Bess worried.

"No. Just the body. He didn't have any marks on him, but I suspect you managed to bring him here."

Bess looked Dex boldly in the eye. "In the Deep South they have a saying: 'He needed killin' bad.' I could never shoot or stab even the worst person, but letting him kill himself is another matter. He kept bugging me about how the coffin works; I showed him how to explore it." She expected the usual lecture on morality from Dexter, but he merely nodded. "I know; I'm guilty," she continued. "But I've done worse before that, Dex. I took a life when I aborted a baby years ago. If this is indeed purgatory, then I belong here twice over."

"You have to let a power greater than you decide that," he said.

"I think that power already did, when we were offered the coffin," she replied. "This is part of a complex master plan. I was even more convinced when I learned I'm dying." The warm plume of her exhalation hung and froze in the darkness.

"Dying? Of what?" Dexter asked. His voice had almost all the power it possessed in life. He reached out for Bess with his massive hand. She could barely feel his grip through the glove.

She said, "Everyone around me suspected I was sick. I know you did. I told Frank it's a form of anemia, but it's really pancreatic cancer. I would only have a few more weeks if I returned."

Dexter let go of her hand. "What are you talking about?"

"You and I are about to trade places." Bess watched Dexter's reaction. "Yes, dare to hope, Dex! They've stabilized your body; it's healing. Just before I closed myself in, I handed Frank a note. It said, 'I'm dying. You guessed right. Stretch to sixty seconds. If you don't hear my key, use your key exactly at seventy.'"

"You shouldn't rush from the world, Lady. Can't we fit in the box together? I'm not exactly real flesh."

The natural fear of death made Bess hesitate. Almost as quickly, she regained her resolve. "No. The man I love is in this world. You're making the trip alone."

Dexter walked silently beside Bess as she followed the flashlight beam back toward the coffin, with buildings and a few ghostly figures cautiously advancing behind them.

As the dark sarcophagus emerged from the blackness, Dexter looked to his left. "What's that?"

A large ball of glowing light seemed to be hurtling toward them from far away.

"Hell! That must be Simon Magus," Bess replied. "I have no idea of his powers. He might be able to steal your body."

"What do we do?"

The sepia-tone and neon-blue buildings from past visits appeared.

Bess shone the second flashlight on her watch. "Damn! Frank isn't going to open the box for another forty-eight minutes."

"Why does he have to?"

"Because you have no mass to turn a real key."

Dexter looked toward the expanding ball. "How long until it gets here?"

Bess hugged her arms close to her chest, conserving heat. "A lot sooner than forty-eight minutes. Maybe ten?"

"Think! It's two against one."

"But this isn't my realm yet," Bess reminded him.

"It's not completely mine either," Dex revealed. "I've tried to do the kinds of things you said Emily could do, and I can barely get a glow around myself. If I make a hot campfire appear and then try to make a tree, the fire disappears."

"Can you conjure up a rope?" Bess asked.

"Let's see." Dexter held out his hand. Coil by coil, a large bundle of clothesline rope materialized. "I don't know if I can keep it in one piece, though."

"Yes, you can," Bess encouraged. She ran to the flashlight she had left behind. "I set this down away from the coffin so nothing would run into it, but we're still too close. I want you to hold onto one end of this rope right here. Don't move."

"Okay."

"I'll move out to its far end."

"What about when that thing gets close?" Dex worried.

"You'll see." Bess took the coil of rope into her gloved hand. It was solid enough to work with. She smiled at Dexter and then walked back in the direction from where he had appeared and away from the coffin. She counted off seconds and knew that she had walked for more than five minutes, far longer than the rope should have stretched. Dexter's conjured miracle hardly seemed to have lost any coils in her hand.

The bubble of pulsing light had come so close to her that she could make out a large building inside it. Bess set down the flashlight, turned off her helmet light and began to follow the rope back toward Dexter, pulling the excess behind her. The bubble passed between the sepia-tone and neon-blue buildings, which seemed to be drawn forward by its aura.

Within another two minutes, the glowing sphere was upon the flashlight. Bess saw from over her shoulder the figure of a man dashing through the circle of light toward the dimming battery-charged beam. She redoubled her efforts to distance herself from the group. She heard through the darkness of Limbo an anguished scream.

On and on she moved through nothingness, depending on the rope. A few minutes later, she collided with an invisible mass and yelped in surprise.

"It's me, Dex!" Dexter assured her.

"Thank God. We have to stand perfectly still now."

"For how long?"

"Maybe thirty minutes. I wish I had Frank's luminescent watch."

They stood stock still for several minutes.

"The ball of light is fading," Dexter reported. "That's got to be good."

"Does it?" Bess worried. "What if he wants us to think he's gone?"

"Let him play his game. Right now I'm thinking of heat coming up from a noonday street in August. Can you feel it?" Dexter stretched out his hands, palms up, toward the base of Limbo.

Bess had despaired of being able to survive the invading cold for sixty minutes in her weakened condition. Although Dexter's effort was far from realistic, nevertheless, she felt a welcome degree of warmth rising from below. "Yes! Bless you!" she whispered. "Look, we both have a good sense of time from the act. Let's set our mental watches for twenty minutes. While we wait, there are things I need to tell you, so you can bring them back to Frank and Sonder."

"Okay."

"But first, you tell me what you read about the spirits of New York City, including the Bronx, and how I get myself through this blackness to the church we performed at."

After Dexter finished his report, Bess talked of her illness and the assurance of imminent death. "I am doing now what I should do. The soul I'm destined to spend eternity with is trapped in this place. I found that out when we did that charity show near where I lived." She spoke at length about Richard Padovani, their relationship, wedding plans and his untimely and terrible death. "After he died, I told myself over and over that giving love was enough for me."

Dex understood. "That's why your figure was surrounded by three little boys on the lid of the sarcophagus."

"Yes. That's why traveling with the three of you was so important. But when I came back to New York and realized Richard was one of the spirits stuck on the other side of that coffin lid, I knew that I needed love as well. Only saints can go their entire existences satisfied with the love of God. I want to be in this plane because Richard is here."

"So that was your illusion," Dexter said.

"What?"

"The Indian man in the magic shop said all four of us had to sacrifice an illusion."

"Sly bastard!"

"Mine was that money, power and social position will guarantee happiness," he shared. He squeezed Bess's hand. "You really think you can get the other kind of love here?"

"It's my only choice now. I've run out of time in the world of the living. As long as this world can be controlled, Richard and I can make it into our own paradise."

"But for how long?" Dexter worried.

Bess shook her head. "Does that matter? If, in two hundred years, we wink out like candles, what's the problem? Our joy will be at an end, but we also won't know pain. Were you unhappy before you were born?"

"I don't know. I can't remember," Dexter said.

The emotional conversation had caused Dex to forget about creating warmth, and Bess began to freeze once more. She was convinced, however, that the revitalizing minutes had been enough to sustain her to the end, and she did not press him to divide his attention in conjuring.

"If you can't remember, then it must have been fine. If we go back to nothingness, what's wrong with that? If we're meant to pass on to another plane of existence, then that will be fine, too. But I have to grab what was taken from me, Dex. I was given this opportunity for a reason – and I won't pass it up."

"I understand," Dexter said. "You really believe I'll be able to pass back into my body by using the box?"

"It's worth a try," Bess answered. "You of all people are not ready to leave that life."

"That's true." Dexter's eyes shifted left and right, attempting to scan the blackness. "All right."

"Don't tell anyone about Harlan Jessup," Bess admonished. "I want to be remembered well."

"Of course. But even if I did, no one would ever think anything but the best of you, Lady. Because you are the best." He reached out again to touch his friend and found her gloved hand quivering. "Oh, sorry. I forgot the cold."

Suddenly, a burst of heat traveled upward. At its base was a small campfire.

"No, Dex!" Bess warned.

"Oh, shit!" he cried out, having forgotten the necessity of hiding in total darkness.

In the moment it took for Dexter to extinguish the fire in his mind, Bess checked her watch. Five minutes remained until the sixty minute mark.

Bess swung around and spotted a narrow pillar of light with a man marching in it from where they had last spotted Simon Magus. He strode resolutely in their direction.

"Retreat to the box!" Bess ordered.

"I'll hold him off," Dexter said.

"You can't. You have to get inside."

"I still have almost fifteen minutes until Frank uses his key."

Bess tugged at the icy figure of her friend. "I think he's after me. He can't get into the other world without a living body. In five minutes, there won't be one. I doubt he knows you're here. Hide on the far side of the coffin!" Bess shifted her weight in the direction of the box, to give Dexter a bearing.

"And then what?"

"Be ready to grab him when I come around it." Bess shut off the helmet light.

"Okay."

Bess listened to the soft sounds of Dexter's retreat. She ran blindly on a vector that she calculated would put her on the lid side of the coffin.

Out of the blackness emerged the figures of the dead socialite and her French boyfriend victim. Before she could defend herself, Bess felt the pressure of the woman's carving knife go through her left shoulder. Outraged by the added adversity, she punched the spirit in the face and was rewarded with the sight of the woman's features collapsing in. With a face as distorted as that of a Picasso figure, the socialite uttered a muffled scream and fell to the ground. The boyfriend advanced on Bess with his artfully-elongated metal statuette.

Simon Magus had been traveling in a narrow, upward-shining beacon of blue light. He paused, apparently confused. He thrust out his right arm and the beacon swung down, knifing horizontal to the surface of Limbo. Like a lighthouse lamp, it rotated in a slow circle until it caught Bess.

Bess registered Magus's beam and backed swiftly toward it, drawing the spirit of the Frenchman with her. She was certain that the dead magician would do everything in his power to protect her living body.

As she had expected, Simon fairly flew at the man brandishing the statuette. From his extended fingers, jagged lines of bright blue electricity shot toward the man and danced around the metal figurine he held. Bathed in sparkling light, the Frenchman dropped his weapon and threw himself at the magician.

Not waiting to see the outcome of the otherworldly struggle, Bess ran on a new vector to where she knew the coffin must be. Her wounded shoulder ached, and she felt the heat and trickle of her own blood. When she had gone several dozen paces, she dared to look back. Magus followed alone, much more quickly than her near-frozen legs would move. When he had closed to less than a hundred feet from her, she switched on her helmet and headed directly for the coffin. Although her fingers felt like wood inside her fur-lined gloves, she shook the gloves off and ripped open the clasps that held her two thigh pockets closed. She thrust her hands as far as she could into the pockets, spun around and contented herself with backing the remainder of the way to the sarcophagus.

"Stay back, Simon!" she called out.

The sound of his name caused a hitch in the man's step. He intensified the light shining directly on her, so that it captured as well the dark sarcophagus. The spill of the same light showed the evidence of the magician's battle with the Frenchman; long scars crisscrossed his face.

"That's my box!" Simon pronounced, in a raspy, low voice.

"Haven't you heard 'You can't take it with you'?" Bess replied. "The only way a coffin is yours is if you're buried in it."

"There wasn't enough left of me to bury," he replied.

"So there's no way you can return from here."

"Yes, there is." Simon Magus resumed his advance. "In you."

Bess tried one more verbal riposte, but the words caught in her throat. She was surprised that the dead magician had been able to decipher her last sentences through the chattering of her teeth. She continued her retreat on legs she could barely feel.

Magus broke into a loping run.

Bess turned and followed his light to the coffin. She was acutely aware that she had almost no strength left. She stepped around the sarcophagus lid to the far side of the box, out of Magus' view. Dexter put up his arms to halt her progress. Realizing she was collapsing, he held her up. Her ungloved hands came out of her pockets.

As she had suspected he would do, Simon rushed around the opposite side to surprise her. Before he could stop himself, he fell over the frozen corpse of Harlan Jessup.

Mustering the last of her strength, Bess collapsed upon Simon's back. Reaching around his face, she drove the solid aluminum knitting needles frozen to her palms and fingers through his eyeballs and deeply into his brain.

The magician shrieked.

Bess pitched forward on top of the two forms, exhaling her last breath.

An inferno of flame leapt up around the furious Simon Magus.

Dexter's foot lashed out and caught Magus fully in the face. The dead magician's sightless and badly-disfigured head jerked up in shock.

"Who are you?" he demanded.

"I've come from hell to drag you there," Dexter answered.

A new coil materialized in Dexter's hand. As Magus struggled to free his arms from the mass of the two earthly bodies, Dexter encircled him with loop after loop of not rope but steel wire. When he was done, he consulted the watch on Bess's limp wrist and saw that only ninety seconds remained until the seventy-minute deadline. For almost a minute, he pummeled Simon Magus's form with his massive arms and strong legs, preventing the man from concentrating on freeing himself. When he could raise his arms and legs no longer, he backed away and circled the coffin. He pushed himself through the half-opened lid.

Dexter found to his shock that his fingers could not make the inner pivot ring respond. The door remained partway open. He knew that fewer than twenty seconds remained until Frank would open his manifestation of the coffin, effectively blocking Dexter from escape. His fingers clawed at the ring again and again without success.

Roaring, Simon Magus threw back the door. The knitting needles had disappeared, and his reconstituted eyes were wide with rage. He lifted his hands, and crackling tendrils of lightning swirled around his fingers. Before he could unleash his shocking power, he suddenly flew backward onto the floor of Limbo. His hard landing so astonished him that his hands lost their blue-white auras. Before Dexter could register more, the door slammed shut from the outside. Dexter put his eye to the porthole. He saw Bess's spirit standing just on the other side, her right arm raised in benediction.

Frank's mind whirred in a near-panic state. He was acutely aware that twelve million pairs of eyes were fixed on him. He also knew that the note he had shoved in his pocket bore the worst news he had ever received. While he mechanically recited the directions to the four men around him and simultaneously stole peeks at his watch, he struggled to understand the meaning behind Bess's message. It seemed to him that she had not yet made up her mind what to do. She might unlock the box from the inside within the time predictated by the hourglass. And then the trick would finish as always. But why would she want him to wait another ten seconds if she failed to use her key? What would take seventy minutes in the world of limbo? By then she would be dead. Bess would never leave him with an empty coffin on such an important night. But who else could possibly emerge to finish the trick if not she?

And then, at the fifty-second mark, he understood. It had something to do with Dexter. The coffin had been shown empty. The four men had taken their time in examining the box. It had been allowed to spin back and forth and settle atop the short ladder with its closed lid facing the audience and the cameras. Frank had said his speech completely; the trick had been timed to take forty-five seconds at its longest. He had to act.

Frank knew well that an unprepared twenty-five seconds on stage feels like eternity. In spite of more than eight hundred performances "in the bag" and countless free-form interviews with members of his audiences, he felt tongue-tied after his last rehearsed word. He looked out at the hushed and expectant audience. He exhaled loudly.

"Ladies and gentleman, as you may have heard or read, this trick has proven extremely dangerous to perform. It does indeed touch upon true magic, and this genuine ancient Egyptian coffin is indeed cursed. I have the gravest feeling about this. Is a powerful spirit from the past about to invade our world?"

Frank had his hand raised dramatically. He pivoted it slightly and saw the sweep hand passing over the sixty-second mark. He placed his ear against the cold coffin and listened in vain for the telltale inner sound of the lock turning. In the sold-out audience, not a sound interrupted the expectant silence.

With his hand shaking noticeably, Frank yanked at the golden key around his neck. The chain snapped, snaked to the floor and made a faint but discernible hiss when its length found the stage. He looked out at the audience with genuinely anguished eyes. "Prepare yourselves for the worst," he told them, even as he did the same. He inserted the key. At precisely the seventy-second mark, he turned it and yanked back the heavy coffin lid.

From out of the box emerged the ethereal figure of Dexter in his Moorish costume. His form was like captive smoke, not completely translucent but certainly not solid. Its color was white tinged with blue.

Simultaneously, a dozen members of the audience shrieked in terror. Within seconds, the entire house was in an uproar.

Dexter stepped forward with his hands lifting and then extending like Karloff's Mummy. The screaming became louder.

Dexter gave out a low moan, glided to the apron of the stage and took yet one more incorporeal step. Instead of falling, his figure seemed to walk on air. He continued above the middle aisle, heading toward the back of the house.

The audience shrank from the ghostly figure like the waters of the Red Sea parting for Moses. Bodies pressed against bodies as those toward the center of the house struggled frantically to put as much distance as possible between 'King Karnak' and themselves.

"People, please!" Frank shouted over the screaming. "It is only an illusion. It isn't real. Please stay in your seats!" His words had no effect. The four men behind him rushed forward for a better look.

Only one brave soul rushed out of a center-aisle seat in Row G and attempted to intercept the hazy figure. Dexter spied the man and stepped to the right to avoid him. The man countered the move. Affixing a sudden, impatient scowl, Dexter bulled directly through him. The man's eyes went wide and then rolled up into his head. He collapsed backward like a felled tree. The screaming ratcheted up another notch.

In his ear, Frank heard the calm voice of Dick Clark saying, "Well, now I know what all the excitement is about over Spiegel/ Master of Magic. That is the most incredibly real illusion I have ever seen. I wish I was in the theater instead of up here above Times Square. On second thought, maybe it's safer up here. That's worse pandemonium than under the ball at midnight!"

Frank turned and stared into the coffin case. There was no sign, no vestige of Elizabeth Coleman.

The curtain fell on the third of the audience who had not yet escaped. The rest had stampeded from every exit out onto 52nd Street.

"What the hell happened?" Pat Kelly demanded as he marched onstage from the wings.

"I'll explain later. You and Gabby guard the door. No one gets onto this stage for the next five minutes. Nobody, understand?"

"I guess."

"No guessing. Make it happen!"

Frank watched the deeply-confused assistant rush off to do his bidding. A moment later, Frank bent to check the zodiac. One of the twelve green lights remained lit. He retrieved the second key from the inside of the lock. Where the pith helmet usually lay, he spied a tightly-folded sheet of paper. Lifting it, he felt the added weight concealed in its center. He carried Bess's second message of the evening into the empty stage's ghost light.

The paper read:

Dearest Frank,

I used the coffin as it intended I use it. If I was completely successful, you will find Dexter recovered at the hospital. You knew I was seriously ill. The details of my sickness are contained in an envelope marked with your name inside my dressing room. You should also now have both keys to this magic place. Taped to this note is the key to my father's apartment on Haskin Street. Your envelope also has the story of my love affair with Richard Padovani, its unfortunate ending in your world and the possibility of a second chance in Limbo. If you must know that I was able to remain in Limbo with him, bring the box to my father's place. According to the zodiac lights, there will be one trip remaining. My father is moving down to Florida in stages and will be away at the end of January. You can set the box up in his apartment and use the key then. I intend to be in that part of Limbo with Richard, teaching him what Emily tried to teach you. You will also find in my dressing room detailed letters to my father and sister. Please deliver them personally. I have attempted to explain my disappearance in a way their minds can accept, in spite of what they may have watched on the television tonight.

I am sorry to have to leave you, but I know that you will be fine. Everyone, even Harlan Jessup, knew that your greatest asset is your ability to interview people and to encourage them to open up. If one day you grow tired of traveling, perhaps you will figure out how to use your best talent in another fashion. Know also that whatever has happened to me, I am content. Enjoy the rest of your life, and be prepared for the next to come.

Your loving Bess

TWENTY-SIX

"WHAT WOULD IT hurt you, Pop?" Sonder had circled Alexander Voloshin the Elder's easy chair four times while making his arguments. Each time he passed in front of the television, his father rocked left and right, to miss as little of the quiz show as he could. "Hey, I'm still talking with you!"

"Church is not for men," the elder Alexander answered. "If anybody should go to church, it's your mother."

"If church isn't for men, then who's the Patriarch? Who's the Pope? Who were the Pharisees and Sadducees?"

"Chicken shits." Alexander laughed at his own joke.

Sonder grabbed the remote control and stabbed off the picture.

"Hey, you punk!" his father yelled.

Sonder tossed the control onto the floor, grabbed the arms of the easy chair and leaned down close to his father's face. "Hey, you drunk! Aren't you afraid for your immortal soul?"

"I have no soul," answered the elder Voloshin, pushing his son away. "The Communists are wrong about almost everything but not about religion. It's opium of masses. If a god made me, he don't care any more about me than I do about last crap I made."

"That's blasphemy," Sonder managed.

"Otherwise, why would he allow Hitler and Stalin? Why would he leave me here?"

"He gave the rest of us the minds and arms to reject Hitler and Stalin. Those monsters were our fault, not His." Sonder pushed back from the chair, making it rock wildly several times. "Just like it's your own fault you put yourself here."

"Then leave me here alone," his father said.

"Come on, Sonder," his brother said from the apartment's front door. "The dog is ready for her walk."

Out in the hallway, waiting for the elevator, Mischa asked, "Why do you keep banging your head up against the wall? Neither of them wants to go to church."

Sonder elevated one eyebrow. "Maybe they would if we both set a good example."

"This is the wrong time of year to bug me," Mischa replied. "I'm killing myself from Monday to Saturday night with my two jobs. When tax season is over I'll go with you."

"God should come first, even at tax time," Sonder said. "And you should bring Rebecca along. She should know what the Orthodox Church is about."

"Jesus!" Mischa exclaimed.

Sonder stepped out of the elevator. "Exactly."

"Faith is one thing; fanaticism is another," Mischa commented under his breath.

Sonder refrained from the answer he could have given. Since first learning what lay beyond the lid of the magic coffin, he had been turned toward faith. Next, the words of *The Bible* had informed and solidified that faith. Then Dexter had literally returned like Lazarus from the dead.

Finally, when he, Dexter and Frank had entered George Coleman's apartment using Bess's key at the end of January, he had another personal proof that a soul lived on after death. Just as Dexter's will power kept him in Limbo, Bess had refused to pass on to any other place. By the time Frank was able to use the coffin's last trip to visit her and Richard, Bess had mastered many tricks of that plane and showed him her version of Yosemite Park, the Grand Canyon and the Great Smokey Mountains. She took great pains to impress upon Frank her gratitude that without having been a part of Frank's touring company she would never have experienced such beautiful places firsthand. She had passed to a world without sickness, hunger, thirst or aging. Moreover, with her beloved Richard at her side, she had lost every vestige of the melancholy that had always lain beneath the surface of her sunny disposition. When Frank stepped from the coffin for the last time and delivered Bess's message, Alexander Voloshin had his final proof that there was a master plan beyond human life. For the rest of his life, he intended to do his grateful best to satisfy the teachings of Jesus and his apostles.

Milyinka set off with spirit on her habitual path toward the Hudson River. Mischa tugged back at her leash.

"I'm leaving the troupe," Sonder announced as he and his brother fell into a common stride.

"You're kidding."

"Not at all. It's time."

"For years you were doing poorly, and I couldn't convince you to try something else," Mischa reminded him. "Now that you're on top you're disbanding?"

"That's the best time. Actually, it's pretty much falling apart on its own. Most venues don't want us without the coffin. We do our last contracted engagement in May. I start the new job the first week of August. I applied for a technical position at the Papermill Playhouse."

"That's a major theater. You didn't need a degree for the job?" Mischa asked.

"I was more surprised than you are. Experience is enough." As he spoke, Sonder wondered privately if all the theaters he had worked in and all the generous technicians who had showed him how to employ every tool of the stage were not due to the benevolent guidance of a greater power.

"That's terrific," Mischa said, although without the matching enthusiasm in his tone.

"And I've met a really nice woman at church. Her name is Anya. I think I could get serious about her"

"Will wonders never cease?"

"Here, give me the leash," said Sonder. "The dog has no respect for you." They walked the rest of the block in silence. Then Sonder remarked, "Based on what I've just said, I'm sure you think things will go on as they have with Mom and Pop for the past three months."

"You mean with us both watching over them?" Mischa asked.

"I mean with me now not only paying fifty percent of their costs but also stopping in and playing servant twice a week."

Mischa looked both ways at the corner. "That was our agreement." Without waiting for reply, he dashed through the traffic to the park that bordered the cliffs of the Palisades and overlooked Manhattan.

Sonder caught up with his brother, who had set his elbows on the metal fence that prevented accidents on the cliffs. He hooked the dog's collar over one of the rails. "We had no agreement, Mischa."

"Oh, yes we did."

"No. You called me out as a self-centered shit and informed me that I was capable of much more than I gave. You told me you had done your best for years, and you challenged me to find out what my best is."

"And you obviously agreed with me and started pulling your fair share of the load."

As his younger brother had done almost three months earlier, Sonder's hand swung out. It caught Mischa in the side of the head, but the cuffing was much harder than Sonder had received. Anger suffused Mischa's face. His fists balled up. Sonder delivered another blow. When Mischa charged at him, he stepped calmly aside and then grabbed the back of his brother's collar and swung him into the fence. He leaned his full weight hard against him.

Sonder put his lips up close to Mischa's ear and spoke in a calm voice. "First of all, you had no call to hit me when you did. It doesn't feel good, does it?"

"Get off me!" Mischa yelled.

"Shut up and listen, and you won't be embarrassed for nearly as long, little brother. You're no match for Marine training – and you know it."

"Are you finished?"

"Not nearly. Would you rather stand here like a cornered criminal or sit like a rational human being?"

"Sit. Jesus!"

Sonder boxed his ear lightly. "Don't use the Lord's name like that." He swung Mischa around and deposited him rather roughly on one of the concrete benches behind them. He remained with his back to the iron fence.

"First of all, I paid for your college education – and I don't want to hear how you would have done it without me. You took the money, so you ought to be grateful. If not for the money, then for the years I saved you. Nowhere in the law does it say a brother has to pay for his little brother's college. Right?"

Mischa scowled, "Right."

"I was glad to do it. Proud to do it. You're a good man. Now, as far as being selfish concerning Mom and Pop, you were wrong there as well."

Mischa cocked his eyebrow at his brother. "Are you telling me you thought you were a good son for the past six years?"

"Absolutely. Nowhere in the law does it say a son has to pay for his parents' keeping. Parents must care for children, but children are not obligated to care for parents. The money I've given them alone makes me a good son."

"They have a sickness!" Mischa argued.

"What? Like cancer? Like diabetes? The two of them chose to

give in to alcoholism before I was born. Nobody pours it down their throats. Never once did either of them seek help. Up until she got that mental condition…which, for all I know, is caused by drinking… the two of them had good minds and strong backs. You haven't demanded that they act like human beings, Mischa; you've helped them sink lower than beasts. You've done worse than nothing for them. And you want me to act guilty?"

Mischa slapped the stone table. "And if they can't or won't change? Should we walk away from them?"

"We should at least lay down laws that will make them less of a burden and give them self-respect. That's what honoring our father and mother requires. We should also demand that we have the time for our own lives first, so we don't end up hating them. I've made enough extra money in the past three months to take care of their basic needs for a couple years. You challenged me last time we sat here? Now it's my turn. You either go back to that apartment and lay down some rules with me, or I hand over the money and walk away. If we both insist on change, it may happen. This includes their sitting in church at least every other Sunday. I will take care of that. I don't give a damn if they both sleep through it. What do you say, Mischa?"

His brother stood and lifted the leash from the fence rail. "Okay. You've made your points."

"Good points, wouldn't you say?" Sonder pressed.

"Yes."

"One last thing: I have not been self-centered and good to myself. If I was someone else, I wouldn't have me for a friend. For example, just because I could stop drinking when I worked doesn't mean I was in charge of it. I couldn't even hold myself together unless someone laid down rules for me. Working for Frank Spiegel was the only thing that gave me focus and purpose. The truth is I haven't liked my life or who I am, and I was constantly running. But, you know, everywhere I ran there I was. The last few months have forced me to drop the self-lies and really make changes. I'm working on it. And that has nothing to do with you, Mom, or Pop."

"Fair enough," Mischa said, looking at his older brother with new eyes.

"Okay, let's start laying down those good rules for Mom and Pop right now."

Mischa stood and grabbed the leash from the fence. "Come on, you damned mutt!"

Sonder smiled as he rose slowly from the freezing bench. He followed along after his brother and the dog. "And don't listen to what the vodka-besotted old man says; there is definitely a god who cares. I know first-hand."

Frank paced slowly back and forth along the hallway outside Allan Salkin's office. His pacing was purely for exercise. He felt no nervousness or anxiety. Over the past three months, he had come to wear his new, expensive clothes without self-consciousness. The terrors of December had dulled considerably, especially when the troupe left New York. Harlan Jessup was in a place where he would never again threaten members of his group. The show's notorious reputation, both from Dexter's shooting and from "King Karnak's" miraculous appearance on New Year's Eve, had caused a spike in the demand for appearances. Because the sarcophagus no longer functioned, there was no choice but to declare that it had been too dangerous to continue. By mid-February, when they were sure it would not be resurrected, many large theater producers lost interest in bookings. King Karnak's Cursed Coffin, however, had mantled the troupe in a lingering glory. Dexter had recovered from his gunshot wound with almost superhuman speed. Most importantly, Bess was where she wanted to be. And this day, it seemed, Frank might actually be headed toward where his real talents lay.

Allan Salkin slowed his rush from the elevator the instant he entered the hall. "Impatient, aren't you?" he asked, without disguising his annoyance.

"You have no idea." Frank pushed through the door the moment Salkin had it open. He unbuttoned his coat and threw it on top of the secretary's desk.

"How was Boston and New Haven?"

"Everyone expects us to be the best, so we are," Frank replied.

"Exactly. The best," the agent blurted. "The new mirror illusion is working out?"

"Working to perfection and keeping our reputation four star."

"Good. And when are you going to tell me how you used a holographic recording of Dexter on New Year's Eve?"

"Never."

"Amazing. I could swear Dex was looking at real people in the audience. I –"

"Never," Frank repeated.

Salkin stalked heavy-footed into his office and threw himself into his upholstered chair. "Fine. With sold-out houses and Spiegel's Mirror, how can you want to walk away from more adulation and money?"

"Because I've already stood on the highest mountain peak, Allan," said Frank. "The view isn't changing. How many times do I have to tell you?"

"Even without the coffin, I can still get you twice the bookings at twice the money…and you toss it aside."

"I'm not tossing anything aside. I'm moving on."

"Don't you think 'moving on' will kill votes for Magician of the Year and Las Vegas Entertainer of the Year?"

"Frankly, Allan, I don't give a damn," Frank replied.

"Man, you have changed!" Salkin's forefinger thrust out. "I can't tell you how annoyed I am that ethics forced me to pass along this offer. Just don't tell me you're backing out on any of the dates we signed up through the end of May."

"What day haven't you signed us up for through the end of May?" Frank asked sarcastically. When his agent refused to dignify the dig, he said, "I wouldn't dream of backing out. After all...these may be my swansong."

Salkin grunted his modified satisfaction and ran his finger down a sheet of paper in the center of his desk. "That's eighteen bookings and ninety-two more performances."

Frank finally sat, seeing that he would have his way with the agent. "Slave driver. I have them engraved inside my head. Now, tell me about this television deal."

Salkin allowed a sly smile. "Aside from five afternoons and five thousand a week, what more should you have to know? Chicago is wide open and waiting for you. This is a major network affiliate looking to syndicate you if you do well in their market. A talk show host who specializes in the supernatural has never been tried. We book any and all horror and occult movie promotion. You bring in any magic acts you want, as well as performing your own stuff. You travel six weeks a year and investigate famous hauntings. You work with psychics who think they can beat your vision of the Saperstein murder. You talk with the near-death folk and the UFO crazies and the Loch Ness and Big Foot investigators. Most of all, you get celebrities to talk about anything strange that has happened in their lives. Bess was right; your ability to put people at ease and to talk their language is your strongest suit. I think we'll do pretty well." He held up his finger again. "Not as well as running your magic act around the major cities, but well."

"You couldn't have landed this deal before I bought the house in Metuchen?" Frank teased.

"Rent it out. You never know if you'll be cancelled after the first thirteen weeks."

"You're such an optimist," Frank said. "What's the next step?"

"We fly to the Windy City in a few days, hammer out the details and you put your John Hancock to a contract." Salkin rested his chin on the back of his fist and gave Franklin a hard look. "I think they're gonna insist on you wearing a hair piece. Now that I'm convinced you're giving up the road shows, I have to admit that it's probably for the best. You seem to have aged a couple of years in the past few months."

"I have," Frank replied. "When you start playing tough-guy on my behalf, tell the TV execs that one thing is non-negotiable."

Salkin rolled his eyes. "Now what?"

"I can't start until after the Fourth of July. I'll be desperate for a vacation by the end of May. If I'm lucky it might be a honeymoon." He paused, as if considering whether or not to add his next words. "And there's something else I have to do. Something very important."

"Would you mind sharing it with the man who cares about you like a father?" Salkin asked.

Frank pushed up out of his chair. "Sorry, Allan. I don't intend to share it with my real father, if you must know."

TWENTY-SEVEN

MAY 31, 1977

DEXTER CONSULTED THE detailed, accordion-pleated map of New Mexico he had purchased weeks before at the Rand-McNally store in New York City. Coming off Highway 40, he worked the pedals of the huge touring bus and slipped the shift into second gear. He could see the town of Santa Rosa immediately ahead and knew that within another ten miles they should reach Puerto de Luna.

When their two-week stint in the main room of The Sands in Las Vegas was finished, they put Pat Kelly and Gabrielle Grant on a plane back to New York. The core of the troupe and Sandy Greenfield continued with the bus. For their penultimate engagement, they had elected not to kill themselves but to drive to Austin at a leisurely pace. There, they would sell the bus back to the same dealership that had brokered it the previous fall. They had spent the night in Albuquerque, mainly because none of them had ever "done the tourist thing" there. In the morning they set out again. As midday approached, they were about to retrace the short-cut that had brought them to the unmarked town of Puerta de Siempre.

"I'm now on Highway 84," Dexter announced to the group, figuring that nothing more needed to be said. He looked over his shoulder. Sonder had his cowboy boots up on one of the tables and his ten-gallon hat tipped over his eyes. Frank made notes on a pad.

Sandy worked on her Danish thread count. Similar images had greeted him across the past four months. He had almost gotten used to not seeing Bess. Memories of their days together in the old converted school bus were the fondest, but even ones such as this he would sorely miss.

"Okay, I've finally got my plan down pat," Dexter announced brightly.

Sonder groaned. "What? Version six hundred sixty seven? This is worse than when Frank used to drone on and on about needing one spectacular illusion."

"Hear me out," Dexter said. "For old time's sake."

"Not for that," Sonder countered. "I'll hear you out only because I won't have to much longer."

"Your loss," Dexter replied. His voice was soft. When he glanced in the mirror at Alexander Voloshin, he saw a face made somber by the sound man's expectations of their imminent dissolution.

"Go on, Dex," Frank invited.

"I finished putting aside enough for college prep tutors for Darnell to last right through to his senior year at Montclair State. That way, Sharlene and Darnell can stay exactly where they are. By the time we do our last performance, I also have enough put aside to add a little study room out the back. The yard hasn't been used for anything, and it will only improve the value of the place. I put a second bathroom with a shower next to it and run the water and sewer pipes from the kitchen. No big deal; I'll do it myself. Then I have my own corner of the house on the weekends I'm there."

"And what about your Chicago digs?" Sonder asked.

"Rent to purchase. Otherwise, it's money down the drain. I find a good co-op and buy in, once we get through that initial thirteen-week period. Since I'm only working thirty hours a week for Frank, I go part-time for my teaching degree in History."

After the talk-show deal had been completed with the Chicago television station, Dexter had decided to join Frank as his technical assistant and the planner of the road trips that would seek out genuine hauntings.

"That is indeed a plan," Sonder agreed.

Dexter's eyes stole right, envisioning the sarcophagus resting in one of the tour bus bays under the seats. The nearer they came to their destination, the more it dominated his thinking. "Man, I hope we get some answers about that box...even though we can't tell anybody else."

Frank looked up from his note pad and waited until Dexter's eyes found his in the rearview mirror. "Never. Not even in a private diary."

"I hear you, I hear you. You know, we never even learned who was shouting at you from the back of the auditorium the first few times we did the coffin trick."

Frank shrugged. "Life does not neatly provide us all the answers."

Sandy looked up from her needlepoint. "What does it matter if you get no other answers? The magic served its purpose." She glanced at Frank.

"'Served' is the right word. It was a faithful servant to every one of us," Frank reminded the others. "We don't need to know its history."

Because Sandra Greenfield's spring singing schedule was sparse, she had volunteered to learn the female assistant role and help with several performances far from the New York area. Frank had let her know the truth shortly after the New Year's Eve spectacle. A believer in the occult and supernatural since long before she had known Frank, Sandy was delighted with the news. Her oft-stated regret was having had no personal experience in Limbo.

"I wonder if Bess and Richard have found Newark and that beautiful spirit, Emily Lord," Sandy said.

"It was a top priority," Frank answered.

"Just as long they steer clear of the south side of Manhattan," Dexter added. Bess and Richard had seen nothing of Simon Magus as of one month after Bess's death, but they had vowed to Frank that they would give the malevolent spirit a perpetual wide berth.

Everyone in the bus seemed to return to private reveries for several minutes. In truth, they were all concentrating on what lay literally around the bend.

At approximately ten miles beyond Santa Rosa, another small town loomed ahead on the highway. It looked equally like Puerto de Luna and Puerta de Siempre. As they reached its limits, no identifying signage greeted them.

A familiar gas station appeared on the western side of the street. The moment it came into view, everyone moved to the left side of the bus and stared out the windows.

"My God! It's here!" Sandy said for them all.

The one-story building with the false front and the words 'GAMES' and 'MAGIC' on the window stood as if it had been rooted there for many years. The sand-blasted, silver-gray wood looked exactly as Frank had remembered it.

"You guessed right," Sonder said softly to Frank.

"It was more than a guess," Frank responded.

Dexter pulled the bus into the gas station parking area and turned off the engine.

The three men approached the luggage hold in silence. Dexter opened the bay door. Together, they stared at the forbidding box.

"At least it has handles this time," Sonder said. "Ready? One, two, heave!"

"We...should take the handles...off before we return it," Frank said, between grunts. The man-sized coffin slid into the bright daylight. The three stepped back.

Frank mopped the sweat from his forehead with the back of his hand. He did not finish the motion. What he saw on the surface of the lid had stopped him.

"The four figures: they're gone."

"Son of a bitch!" Sonic said.

"It's severed its relationship with us," Dexter declared.

Frank smiled. "It did its work. We each sacrificed our most treasured illusions. Can you and Alexander get it up on the gurney without my help?" Frank asked.

"Sure. You go ahead."

Frank gestured for Sandy to exit the bus. When they were both on the asphalt, he took her hand and led her across the street to the magic shop. Frank pushed open the door. A bell tinkled above them, and Frank knew for certain that this was the same store.

"Hello?" he called out.

"Welcome." The voice from the other side of the shelves was female.

"Where is the gentleman who owns this shop?" Frank asked.

A young woman appeared from around the shelving. She had dark skin and black hair, and the unmistakable narrow but hooked nose and full lips of a person of Indian subcontinent lineage. She wore a traditional sari.

"You are mistaken. I own the shop."

"For how long?" Frank asked, peering into the dim light.

"Forever. You have traveled a great distance," she said.

Frank heard in his mind's ear an echo of similar words from the lips of the old Indian man.

"That's correct." Frank reached into his back pocket and took out his wallet. "I have something to show you." He stood his ground, compelling the young woman to advance.

She came into the light that spilled directly through the display window. Frank noted without surprise that she had green eyes, and that each eye had a dash of copper color, close to the bridge of her nose.

"We do not take credit cards," she said placidly. She reached out with her left hand to move a game back from the edge of its display shelf.

"I'm not here to buy anything. I wish to show you several

photographs of people I love."

The woman stepped closer and tilted her head toward the upraised wallet.

"This one," Frank said, "is my fiancée, Sandra."

The woman smiled in recognition at Sandy. Sandy, in turn, held up her left hand and displayed her engagement ring.

"These are my mother and father. And here are the members of my troupe. You know what I do?"

"You do magic," replied the woman.

"Yes. Exactly."

"And illusions?"

"Some of what people call illusions," Frank answered. "We all used to have other illusions, but something made us give them up."

"How fortunate for you. How may I help you?" asked the woman.

"We have a sarcophagus that we no longer have need of. It does magic, but we've used up our share. We wish to trade it for something less…exotic."

The woman cocked one hawkish eyebrow. "It might be of interest to me. May I see it?"

As if on cue, the front door opened, and Sonder and Dexter rolled the dark metal mass into the shop.

"Where's the old man?" Sonder asked.

"Later," said Frank. He turned back to the woman. "You will take this, I'm sure."

The woman glided forward and ran her hand lightly over the intricate bas relief carvings. "And what do you ask for it?"

"Surely you have something more appropriate for me in your shop. I think it's best if you decide."

"Have you need of a full-length mirror?" she asked.

Sonder snapped his finger and pointed through the front window at the bus. "I broke your practice mirror that day. Right out there."

Frank bowed slightly to the owner of the shop. "I believe I could use a mirror. Does it do magic?"

"Under certain circumstances," the woman said.

"Under what circumstances?" Frank asked.

"That remains to be seen."

Frank's head bobbed slightly at hearing the woman use his favorite phrase. She stepped back and gestured for the men to bring the borrowed black case into the shop. After much maneuvering, it was returned to the dark corner whence it had rested the previous year. Beside it stood a long object covered by a white sheet. The sheet was tied in place it by four pieces of heavy hemp twine.

"That is the mirror," the shop owner said.

Without waiting for instruction, Dexter and Sonder lifted the mirror onto the gurney and carted it out of the shop. Sandy followed them.

Frank looked into the shop owner's smiling eyes and asked, "Since you have so readily accepted this sarcophagus that does magic, do you know how it works?"

She smiled. "Where is the fun if one is not allowed to learn such things by oneself?"

"We certainly had...I don't know if it was all fun, but it was all interesting. I was hoping –"

"Yes?" the Indian woman asked.

"Never mind."

The proprietress held out her hand. "The keys, if you please."

Frank dug into his pocket and produced the pair of ornate, golden keys. "Sorry."

"Quite all right. I wish you a most excellent day, sir."

Frank backed slowly out of the shop, attempting to memorize every detail. When he passed through the door and the little bell rang, the noonday sun came hard into his eyes. He squinted. When he opened them again, he found that he was standing in front of a store whose window signs read 'GUNS' and 'ROD & REEL.' The wood of the store was well cared for. He shook his head in wonderment and hurried to the bus.

When he came around the big road machine, Frank found Dexter and Sonder cutting the twine that held the sheet in place.

"Just making sure you get what she promised," Dexter said.

Sonder whisked the sheet off the free-standing, full-length mirror. The reflective backing behind the glass was slightly hazed. The frame of what looked to be teakwood, however, seemed almost new, in spite of ancient Celtic interlaced scrollwork. Sonder and Dexter stood it up on its feet. Sonder put himself directly in front of it, stared, and then preened a bit. Then Dexter pushed him out of the way and took his turn.

"Looks like a regular old mirror," he decided.

"Yeah, what was that crap about it doing magic?" Sonder asked. "And we already have Spiegel's Mirror. We oughta go back –"

"There is no going back," Frank said. He touched Sonder on the shoulder and turned him toward the transformed store. "It's fine. I would have been happy with nothing. I should say with nothing more."

Sonder looked at the Coke machine located under the shadow of the gas station's awning. He dug into his pants pocket and jingled his change. "Who's thirsty? I'm buying."

Sandy and Dexter gave enthusiastic replies. They followed Sonder into the shade.

Frank stood in front of the mirror, staring. Everything in its world was backward, as it should be. Everything except his head.

About the Author

Brent Monahan has spent his life fascinated with and passionate about questioning the world – and arriving at unique, thoughtful, insightful and, quite often, spear-tip pointedly amusing answers that find their expression in his many novels. Whether he is offering a rational explanation to an historical haunting, as in *The Bell Witch: An American Haunting*, or delving into the psyches and machinations of such icons of financial and political power as J.P. Morgan in *The Jekyl Island Club*, Mr. Monahan does so with an unparalleled depth of research and smart, witty writing that has engaged decades of readers and garnered him considerable critical recognition from both reviewers and his peers.

Mr. Monahan has authored twelve novels, two of which have been made into movies – including *An American Haunting*, starring Donald Sutherland and Sissy Spacek. He has taught writing at Rutgers University and Westminster Choir College of Rider University, even though his terminal degree was in musical arts from Indiana University, Bloomington. He lives in Yardley, Pennsylvania.

Made in the USA
Charleston, SC
06 January 2015